RUINS OF THE GALAXY
VOID HORIZON

CHRISTOPHER HOPPER
J.N. CHANEY

LAS VEGAS, NV • NEW YORK, NY

Copyrighted Material

Void Horizon Copyright © 2019 by Variant Publications, Hopper Creative Group

Book design and layout copyright © 2019 by JN Chaney

This novel is a work of fiction. Names, characters, places, and incidents are either products of the author's imagination or used fictitiously. Any resemblance to actual events, locales, or persons, living, dead, or undead, is entirely coincidental.

All rights reserved

No part of this publication can be reproduced or transmitted in any form or by any means, electronic or mechanical, without permission in writing.

1st Edition

STAY UP TO DATE

Don't miss out on these exclusive perks:

- Instant access to free short stories from series like *The Messenger*, *Starcaster*, and more.
- Receive email updates for new releases and other news.
- Get notified when we run special deals on books and audiobooks.

So, what are you waiting for? Enter your email address at the link below to stay in the loop.

https://www.jnchaney.com/ruins-of-the-galaxy-subscribe

JOIN THE CONVERSATION

Join the conversation and get updates on new and upcoming releases in the awesomely active **Facebook group**, "JN Chaney's Renegade Readers."

This is a hotspot where readers come together and share their lives and interests, discuss the series, and speak directly to J.N. Chaney and his co-authors.

facebook.com/groups/jnchaneyreaders

CONTENTS

Previously	1
Chapter 1	3
Chapter 2	13
Chapter 3	23
Chapter 4	33
Chapter 5	46
Chapter 6	61
Chapter 7	75
Chapter 8	87
Chapter 9	101
Chapter 10	112
Chapter 11	127
Chapter 12	136
Chapter 13	150
Chapter 14	158
Chapter 15	179
Chapter 16	188
Chapter 17	196
Chapter 18	209
Chapter 19	216
Chapter 20	227
Chapter 21	246
Chapter 22	256
Chapter 23	265
Chapter 24	273
Chapter 25	287
Chapter 26	300
Chapter 27	310
Chapter 28	320

Chapter 29	333
Chapter 30	341
Chapter 31	349
Chapter 32	362
Chapter 33	377
Chapter 34	389
Chapter 35	403
Chapter 36	412
Chapter 37	431
Epilogue	443
Character Reference	457
Acknowledgments	467
Stay Up to Date	469
Join the Conversation	471
About the Authors	473

PREVIOUSLY

Last time in Ruins of the Galaxy Book 3: Gateway to War...

FACED with allegations of treason against the Galactic Republic, Lieutenant Adonis Magnus decided to evade arrest and help Valerie Stone and her daughter Piper find sanctuary on the Luma capital of Worru. The warm welcome was short-lived, however, when Master So-Elku attempted to seize Magnus and his unit, resulting in a bloody escape from the system.

Meanwhile, Luma Emissary Awen dau Lothlinium returned to protospace where she, Ezo, and TO-96 investigated Sootriman's den on Ki Nar Four in the hopes of recruiting reinforcements. But when they discovered Sootriman's ransacked headquarters, their only positive find was one of the warlord's head of security—an inebriated Reptalon named Saasarr.

Following their unsuccessful missions, Magnus and Awen reconnected and sought refuge in metaspace on the Novia Minoosh planet of Neith Tearness. Together, they reconstituted the Gladio Umbra—an ancient order dedicated to defending the Novian way of life—with Magnus training the new coalition of ground troops while Awen mentored Piper.

Their work was cut short, however, when the Novian AI known as Azelon urged Magnus and the members of Granther Company to combat a rogue platoon of Marines in Itheliana, capital of the neighboring planet of Ithnor Ithelia. Magnus and his teammates narrowly succeeded in winning their first engagement, though not without injuries. That, and young Piper showed she was far more powerful than previously suspected, having killed an enemy combatant from within the Unity itself. In addition, the mission's lone surviving rogue Marine, Volf Nos Kil, was taken captive—a man whose ominous past with Magnus created a new line of questions.

Granther Company's would-be escape was put in doubt, when an unmarked Repub battlecruiser and a squadron of Talons entered metaspace. Led by none other than famed ace Ricio Longo, the Repub ships pose a serious new threat to Granther Company and threaten to stop Magnus for good.

1

"Just what the hell do you think you're doing, Kane?" Brooks asked. "And what's with all this?" He gestured in a wild motion to the renovated cargo bay that Moldark had made into his personal chambers and observation deck. "And, mystics man, what did you do to your damn face?"

Brooks and Davenport stood at the base of Moldark's dais wearing full dress uniforms and exasperated faces. As fleet admirals of the Republic's two other armadas, the men had demanded a meeting with Moldark. And understandably so, since the rogue Navy commander had run headlong into a fight with the Jujari without anyone's consent, forcing the admirals' hands.

"You've got a lot of explaining to do," Davenport added.

"Yes," Moldark said, rising. "I think you're right." He descended the steps one at a time, noting how the two men straightened as he neared. "What is it that you'd like to know first?"

Brooks glanced at Davenport and then back at Moldark. "First?" The admiral's lips sputtered. "A unilateral decision to declare open war on the enemy for a start! We all knew something might happen, but when you drove ahead like that? You forced our hand with that one, Kane."

Moldark stepped level with the men and noted how they slid their boots back. "The decision was made for me."

Brooks squinted at Moldark. "You're going to need to do better than that if you wish to avoid your court-martial."

"I received instruction from the senator himself."

"Which senator?" Davenport asked.

"Blackman, of course. He chaired a subcommittee on foreign policy, one with complete control over all Jujari affairs."

"I've never heard of such a committee," Brooks replied, squeezing the beret under his arm.

"No, I suppose you wouldn't have."

The man jerked back. "What's that supposed to mean?"

"It means, my dear admiral, that you lack the insight to determine where an elected official's politics has meddled with the safety of his or her constituency. Blackman and his Circle of Nine ordered Third Fleet to open fire on the Jujari and its coalition of ships in the hopes of starting a war."

"Circle of Nine? I'm not even sure what to think of you right now, Kane," Brooks exclaimed. "And don't try to pin this on Blackman. Your actions will—"

"Let him finish," Davenport said, raising his hand. "What Circle of Nine?"

"I obliged them," Moldark continued, ignoring the question. "And now they have their war. But it will suit our agenda, not theirs."

"Our agenda?" Brooks asked. "And, yes, what is this Circle of Nine?"

"The Nine have engaged in clandestine operations for as long as I can remember…"

Davenport looked at Brooks. "Do you know about this?"

Brooks shook his head and didn't even bother looking at the other admiral.

"As for our agenda, gentlemen, I'd like to point out that we have a trump card."

"I'm losing patience here, Kane," Brooks said.

Moldark waved the comment aside and began to walk around the men. "The Jujari war was inevitable, we all knew that. This part of the quadrant has been nothing but a pressure cooker since we were children. No one cares if the war starts. But delivering the first blow? That, gentlemen, is a card we will play before all this is finished."

Davenport turned to follow Moldark in his circuit. "You're saying that if the people find out what the Nine ordered you to do, the populace won't stand for it."

"Not if, admiral. *When*."

"You're going to try and expose them?"

"Indeed."

"This is a load of splick," Brooks yelled. "Who do you take us for? I'm ordering your arrest, Kane."

"Worse still," Moldark continued, "the Nine are in league with the Luma." He felt the men pause in consideration of this. "I'd felt something shifting for a while now, but I couldn't put my finger on it."

"Now you're implicating the *Luma?*" Brooks's tone was incredulous. "You actually expect us to believe that some dark room of the senate has joined forces with those domesticated peace-mongers to—what? Wage war on the Jujari? I'm finding all this very hard to believe, Admiral Kane."

"You don't need to believe me," Moldark replied. "But you might find this interesting." Moldark pulled a small tablet from his hip, held it in his palm, and hit play on a holo recording he'd been saving for this moment. A video appeared of So-Elku, the revered Luma Master, leading a contingent of robed followers against Kane and some Republic troopers. Moldark watched Brooks and Davenport look on in shock as the two forces collided. He let it play for another few seconds before shutting it off.

"I had thought the Circle of Nine had been empowered by the Galactic Senate, working for the best interests of the Republic. I wouldn't have followed their orders otherwise. But then I was sent the following from the Circle's secretary."

Moldark displayed a second holo recording, this one captured on the shaking wrist-device of a senatorial staff member who lingered just inside the doorway of what looked to be a closed meeting. In it, So-Elku and some Luma elders stood behind Blackman and a table full of senators. The conversation was hard to hear, but Moldark knew the lines about conspiracy, war, and "destroying the Republic and replacing it with something new" had piqued their interests. Never mind that So-Elku had been speaking about Moldark—or at least a demented version of Admiral Kane. The two admirals were hearing what Moldark wanted them to hear.

"This can't be," Davenport said.

"And yet it is, admiral."

"But if that's true, then—"

"None of it's true," Brooks snapped. "You're fabricating to cover yourself. And I, for one, have had enough. Fleet Admiral Wendell Kane, in accordance with Galactic Republic Navy Mandate 3.1 subsection 24, I hereby divest you of your command for treasonous actions against the Republic, unsanctioned acts of war against a—"

"Enough," Moldark said, his voice booming in the cavernous hall. He'd wanted his celestial presence to nudge these two fools toward his desires but their unreasonable natures—perhaps as bull-headed fleet admirals—had prevented it. Given more time, his influence would've taken hold of them, but he was done wasting time.

Brooks's mouth stuck open for a second as he seemed to consider what to say next. He looked to Davenport, presumably for support, but the other admiral looked just as confused.

"Gentlemen," Moldark said, regaining control of his tone, "I had hoped that your request for a meeting would end in you seeing my side of things. Together, we might have stopped this erroneous faction of the senate. I can see now, however, that I was too optimistic. Which is sad, because you both would have made fine additions to my plans."

Brooks made to protest, but Moldark could sense the man's questions were outrunning his ability to vocalize any of them. Davenport, too, was unable to offer anything beyond pitiful stammering.

"I believe we are done here," Moldark said.

"Indeed we are." Brooks tapped the insignia on his chest and Moldark heard a comms chime sound. "Brooks to escort, I need immediate assistance in—"

"That won't be necessary," Moldark said. His elemental form reached out and touched the admiral's chest. Instantly, the man gasped in shock. His arms and legs went rigid and his head was thrown back. The veins bulged on his neck as he tried to say something, but only garbled words drowned by saliva came out.

Brooks coughed a spray of bubbles as he strained against Moldark's invasive presence. Moldark drew upon the man's soul, searching for every morsel of energy he could find and drawing it into himself. He watched as the admiral's face aged in a matter of seconds. His hair grayed and fell to the floor while deep wrinkles crawled up the sides of his face and withered his cheeks.

On his tiptoes, Brooks reached out and struck the shoulder of a fear-stricken Davenport. But Davenport wouldn't save him. Instead, the second admiral backed away from the scene, his face contorted in horror.

"Where do you think you're going?" Moldark said, his voice feminine and kind as if playing with a small child.

"I want no part of this. I'm reporting you to—"

"I'm disappointed in you, Davenport. You seem…" Moldark cocked his head to the side. "Afraid."

"I'm more interested in commanding my fleet than bowing to"—his eyes darted to Brooks's trembling body—"to whatever it is you're doing here."

"But I need good commanders. Are you sure you won't stay?"

Davenport hesitated, his eyes stuck on Brooks. "I suppose I could convey your orders. But more than that, I…" The man took another step back.

Davenport was weak. Moldark sensed it. He had no imagination and was too afraid—*too* fearful. He would never make a good follower. *No, he will not do at all.*

A second tentacle from Moldark's true self lunged toward Davenport and drank deeply of the man's feeble life force. The admiral spasmed, unable to scream, unable to escape.

These humans were truly pathetic, like every other species who were takers. And they seemed willing to turn on each other so quickly, so long as whatever new option they entertained served their personal interests better than the previous one. So-Elku's betrayal of Admiral Kane to the Circle of Nine was proof of this.

This universe will thank me for their demise, Moldark thought to himself.

When the life force of the two admirals had been extracted, Moldark released them. Their bodies fell to the floor and two simultaneous plumes of grey ash swirled up from their Navy dress uniforms. Moldark touched the new emblem on his chest, the three white bars of the Paragon, and summoned Fleet Admiral Brighton to his quarters.

When the man finally appeared at the far end of the hall, Moldark looked down at the dusty piles of clothes, and said, "Have those taken care of. Also, detain both admiral's escorts and question them. See if they are willing to join us."

"Yes, my lord." Brighton's eyes examined the ash gathering on his glossy black boots, and Moldark knew the man was thinking something more.

"What is it?"

"The remaining fleets, my lord. What would you have us do with them?"

Moldark had, of course, thought about this. Drilling down through both fleets' ranks until he could find commanders willing to do his bidding would take time and resources. Though, as he considered the human species and their prime motivators of fear and lust, he found himself second guessing just how long it might take.

Nos Kil, for example, had been purchased easily enough. The man simply wanted freedom. That and a chance to unleash the violence within.

Commander Longo also seemed to comply without hesitation. He'd dreamed of battling the Jujari since he was a boy. Who was Moldark to stand in the way of that?

And then there was Admiral Brighton, a man who seemed only too happy to hold onto his meaningless life when confronted with the fate of his superiors. Plus, Moldark had promoted him. How could the human refuse?

Moldark knew these men were not alone. There would be hundreds more. Perhaps thousands. But he didn't need those kinds of numbers. There wouldn't be time for it.

"What would you have us do about the remaining fleets, my lord?" Brighton asked again.

"The admirals are not expected back to their ships for another quarter hour, and the conflict is progressing smoothly enough. Why don't you invite all fleet command staff to retire to the flagship for… consultations. Tell them that the three fleet commanders will be making a special presentation."

"What sort of presentation?"

Must I explain everything? Moldark remarked inwardly but reminded himself that such slowness was endemic of this species. "There won't be any presentation, Brighton. You will schedule private meetings to alert key staff of the Circle of Nine's existence, and you'll outline the Nine's treasonous acts and their collusion with the Luma. Then you'll inform them of Brooks and Davenport's involvement and their subsequent removal from command. Next you'll tell their subordinates that after we annihilate the Jujari, we will set our sights on Capriana. We will make those responsible for corrupting the

Republic pay for their transgressions, and then destroy all those who have stolen from the innocent."

Brighton loosened the collar around his neck. "And the ones who don't seem agreeable?"

"Some we will detain." *For sustenance*, Moldark noted. "The rest we will dispose of. Then move to their next highest-ranking officers. Those we cannot convert directly we will supplant by those already loyal to *Kane's* causes."

Brighton was slow in responding. The man's eyes looked between the two piles of dust and uniforms again.

"Is there a problem?"

"No, my lord."

"Good." Moldark noted how the man's fear had brought him back in line. But fear was only so powerful with these humans. So Moldark decided to leverage the other motivator. "Need I remind you, Fleet Admiral Brighton, that you are now the most powerful senior officer in the entire Navy?"

The man's eyes darted up to meet Moldark's as a small smile crept across the admiral's lips.

There it is, Moldark mused. "Admiral, it is no longer the Republic Navy you lead…"

"But the Paragon Navy," Brighton said as if the words themselves filled him with power. "It shall be done, my lord."

Moldark nodded. *There it is indeed.*

2

"How much time before they get here, Azie?" Magnus said over a command comms channel. His boots trampled through the jungle outside the alien city of Itheliana while sunlight from the leafy canopy flickered over his armor. He led Granther Company east, fresh from their victory against Admiral Kane's rogue Recon troopers. With any luck, they'd make it to the shuttles just in time to get off the planet and get to safety on *Azelon's Spire*.

"The Republic ships will reach the *Spire's* position in twenty-three minutes, forty-one seconds," replied the AI, still aboard the starship in orbit over the planet.

Magnus did the math in his head as his bioteknia eyes displayed the remaining distance to the shuttles. It had taken them nearly half an hour to get out of the city, which meant that by the time they'd secured the team on the shuttles and returned to orbit, the enemy ships would be in a full-out conflict with the *Spire,* or—worse—with the shuttles.

"Remind me of our vessel's defensive capabilities again?"

"If we have never covered those properties before, how is it a reminder?" Azelon asked.

"Humor me."

"Light shielding."

Magnus waited, expecting Azelon to go on. When she didn't, he simply said, "That's it?"

"Affirmative."

"Sir," TO-96 said, chiming in over comms. "I would like to point out that your heart rate and blood pressure are abnormally high."

"Of course they're abnormally high, 'Six." He'd been pushing the team hard, urging them to get out of Itheliana and back to the shuttles as fast as they could. But he was growing impatient. Between those Gladio Umbra injured in the firefight and the rogue Repub Recon prisoner they'd taken, their progress was much slower than Magnus would have liked. They'd been forced to leave Baker and Lugt's corpses in the wreckage. "The company has just survived its first brush with the enemy. And now, I've been informed that the Republic has somehow managed to send a squadron of FAF-28 Talons and a battlecruiser through an event horizon—"

"A quantum tunnel, sir," TO-96 interjected.

"Whatever. And they're about to hunt us down while we sit in shuttles with no armament. Meanwhile, you two bots helm an alien starship. That tends to get one's heart rate and blood pressure up, 'Six."

"Well, sir," TO-96 in a cheerful tone, "the good news is that you are making marvelous time. Your team is working in a well-coordinated effort to usher the injured gladias and your prisoner to the shuttles. You should arrive in less than five minutes at your current rate."

"Are you saying we get extra points for teamwork?" Magnus said with a sarcastic air.

"No." The bot paused over comms. "I was only trying to be encouraging, sir. I did not mean to infer the presence of a reward system. I see now that doing so—only for you to discover the absence of any such system—could be demoralizing."

"Nope," Magnus said. "You already demoralized me a long time ago, 'Six."

"Oh my. I'm terribly sorry, sir. When was that?"

"When you asked me to touch your missiles."

"You're a bad man," Awen said over comms. Magnus had forgotten anyone else was on the command channel.

"If it makes you feel any better, buckethead," Abimbola said, "he said the same thing to me when we first met."

"So the truth comes out," Magnus replied, grateful for the humorous moment. He needed something to relieve the stress.

"I fail to see what truth you are alluding to," TO-96 said.

"That you ask everyone to touch your missiles when you first meet them," Ezo replied.

Magnus feigned personal offense. "And here I thought I was special." Several people laughed over the channel. It reminded him of being on TACNET with the Fearsome Four, of making jokes just before the splick really started to fly—like it would in a few minutes.

He switched to the full company channel. "Let's keep it moving, gladias. We're almost there."

Magnus hadn't needed TO-96's comment about their ETA to the shuttles—his HUD took care of gauging and displaying the distance. He just hoped that they'd be able to get everyone loaded and figure out a way to get back aboard the *Spire* before things went sideways. The last thing he wanted was a squadron of Talons doing a strafing run on two overloaded shuttles trying to break out of a planet's gravity well. They'd never survive it. They'd be as easy to pick off as pregnant Gossian parliamentary pigeons—the only thing left would be feathers and broken eggs.

Magnus noted an incoming private channel request from Awen. "Go ahead."

"Hey, I know you're worried about this, about getting back to the *Spire*. Just wanted you to know you shouldn't be."

Well that got Magnus's attention. "And how's that?"

"Azelon can take care of herself."

"Pardon me if I don't share your unbridled enthusiasm."

"I'm serious," Awen replied. The ex-Luma ran close enough to him that he looked over and saw her through some ferns, holding Piper's hand. "You remember the story about when I first left the system with Ezo and Sootriman, right?"

"Vaguely."

"Azelon destroyed all the threats by hijacking torpedoes. Some sort of next-level override tech that she has."

"I remember you mentioning it, yeah. But forgive me if I don't share your faith in her right now. These are Talons we're talking about."

"I know what they are." Awen sounded defensive.

"You might know what they are, but I don't think you know what they can do. Not like I do."

"Well, I don't think you know what Azelon can do."

"Is this what you refer to as a pissing contest?" a new voice said over their private channel.

"Ninety-Six," Awen blurted out. "You're not supposed to be monitoring this line!"

"It's a private channel," Magnus reminded him. "That means no bots allowed."

"I am sorry, truly," TO-96 admitted. "But given how deeply I am integrated with the system, I'm afraid such a request is impossible."

"We're always listening," Azelon added.

"Splick," Magnus said. "'Cause that ain't creepy at all."

"To be fair," TO-96 said, "both of your points have merit. Azelon has a high degree of advanced tactical maneuverability and weapon systems superiority, as Awen observed."

"See?" Awen said. Magnus could have sworn she stuck out her tongue at him.

"Likewise, Magnus is correct in his assertions that the

FAF-28 Talon is a formidable fighter platform, representing the very best of the Galactic Republic."

"Told you so," Magnus said. He put a hand on a dead tree that lay across his path and vaulted over it.

"All things considered, however," the bot continued, "Azelon feels assured in her abilities to safely cover your retreat, so long as you—"

"There they are!" Awen pointed to the shuttles, half hidden by trees.

"Everyone load up," Magnus ordered. "Alpha and Bravo platoons, shuttle one. Charlie and Delta, shuttle two—and you've got the prisoner. Awen and Piper, with me." He raced to the foot of his shuttle's ramp and started pushing people up. "Nolan?"

"Right here, sir."

Magnus looked and saw the former Navy pilot swing around the side of the ship. "Let's get her fired up."

"Right away."

Magnus continued to watch both shuttles fill with his warriors. Their custom Novia Minoosh armor returned to its neutral state, dispensing with chameleon mode to reveal the gleaming white telecolos covering. Their armor plates were charred in some places, having taken blaster fire or indirect damage from the conflict with the rogue Recon team. No mission plan survives contact with the enemy—he'd learned that lesson long ago. Then there was that second critical moment in any mission where the unexpected caught up with you. This moment was that moment. And it always brought with it waves of doubt. As the last of his ship's passengers ran up the ramp, Magnus wondered if he was going to lead everyone to safety or if this was the one mission—the one decision—that was going to get everyone killed.

'Cause you've killed your own before, right Magnus?

He watched the other shuttle's ramp begin to close as its final passengers marched up. It was Nos Kil, arms bound behind him, pushed at gunpoint by two Jujari gladias. *Son of a bitch.*

Maybe boarding the shuttles and trying to race back to the *Spire* wasn't the right call. Instead, maybe they needed to scatter and hide—let Azelon defend the *Spire*, and rendezvous with her later. Then again, taking on even a single Talon from an indefensible position was suicide. That bird would tear their whole company apart in just a few passes.

"Nolan?" Magnus said over comms. "What's our time to liftoff?"

"Thirty seconds, sir."

He shook his head and stepped into the cargo bay. He was getting that sick feeling in his gut, the one that said, *You idiot. You're going to get everyone killed!* But he stuffed the voice down inside his soul and ground his teeth. He was a leader, and teams needed a definitive voice. Indecision killed faster than blaster bolts.

"Everyone, strap in," he said. Then he removed his helmet, mag-locked his NOV1 to his back, and made for the shuttle's bridge. The drive core cycled up in its tell-tale whine, sending small vibrations through the ship's hull.

"Nolan?" Magnus projected his voice as far forward as he could without actually shouting.

"Fifteen seconds," Nolan replied, his voice coming from the pilot couch.

Magnus stepped into the bridge. "I want a holo of the enemy ships' positions."

Dutch sat beside Nolan and brought up the requested information. A holo projection snapped to life, hovering above the command console. It showed Ithnor Ithelia's curved edge, adorned with a representation of the *Azelon Spire* with a bracket and basic ship data. Further away were fourteen small fighters, along with a battlecruiser that looked to be half the size of the *Spire*.

Magnus swore under his breath. Unless Azelon had something up her sleeve, this was going to be a bloodbath.

"Engines online," Nolan said. "Commencing liftoff."

"Get us out of here," Magnus said, feeling the slightest wave of relief.

Nolan moved the vertical throttle sliders to maximum. But nothing happened. The ship should have lurched skyward with how forcefully he'd pushed them.

"What the hell, Nolan?"

"I'm sorry, sir. Stand by." He brought the sliders down, waited a beat, and slid them up again. Still, nothing happened.

"Nolan!"

"The system isn't responding. I don't... I'm not sure..."

His eyes searched the readouts. "It seems the other shuttle is experiencing the same difficulties."

"Dutch, comms," Magnus said. "Hail Azelon."

"Patching through…" Dutch tapped a few things on her side of the command console. "Channel's open."

"Azie, we've got a ship malfunctioning down here."

"Negative, Magnus," Azelon replied, her voice calm, as if she was trying to sooth a child to sleep.

Dutch looked over her shoulder at Magnus with her eyebrows lifted.

"What do you mean, negative?" Magnus asked.

Just then, Awen stepped into the bridge. "What's going on? Why aren't we taking off?"

"I'd like to know the same thing," Magnus replied. "Azie?"

"I have temporarily grounded your shuttles, Magnus," the AI said.

Magnus tightened his grip on Dutch and Nolan's seatbacks. "Temporarily ground—? On whose orders?"

There was a moment's hesitation, then Azelon said, "Logic's."

"I think you're going to need to explain yourself," Awen said.

"I will, in due time."

"How about like right now," Magnus demanded.

"Negative, sir."

Magnus jerked his head back. "Negative? Dammit, Azie."

Magnus pounded his fist on Nolan's seat back. "Listen, if you're going to pull something like this, then—"

"Sir, I recommend you leave the shuttles and take cover in the forest immediately. Statistically speaking, your chances of survival will increase by forty-four percent if you do so."

"And if we don't?"

"I calculate one-hundred percent fatalities if you remain with the ships in the event the enemy enters atmosphere over your location."

He pulled his helmet out from under his arm and looked to Nolan, Dutch, and then Awen. "Well, looks like we're going out for another stroll."

3

Ricio could hardly believe what he was seeing. He prompted the neural interface to expand the image on his HUD until a strange starship filled the holo.

"Is everyone else seeing this?" he asked over TACNET.

"Viper Two. Affirmative, commander," the pilot said. The rest of the squadron updated the comm chat with green icons.

"Damn," Ricio whispered to himself. This whole mission felt… surreal. In fact, the last few days seemed like something out of a holo movie. First, his squadron had been ordered to attack the Jujari fleet—a command that had fulfilled a childhood fantasy of his. It pitted Talons against Razorbacks in an epic battle that had put the video games of his childhood to shame. Then, without warning, he was ordered back to the *Labyrinth* where he met with Fleet Commander Brighton in private quarters once used as a common area in the aft of the ship. A single captain's chair stood atop a dais before a massive wall of windows that looked over the orbital war.

As if the repurposing of the large space hadn't been odd enough, the meeting was interrupted by Admiral Kane's appearance. The man walked past him and ascended the dais to sit in the chair while Brighton stood on the ground below him.

The encounter rattled Ricio, more than he cared to admit. The admiral had stared at him with oil-black eyes. His face and head looked as though he'd survived a horrible fire. But it was Kane's gravelly voice that gave Ricio chills—like another presence spoke from inside the man. He couldn't help but wonder what horrible accident the admiral had lived through. Or…

Perhaps the rumors about the man's otherworldly possession were true. Of course, Ricio didn't believe in such things. Those were the fairytales reserved for the Luma. But given how dramatic his appearance was, Ricio was slower to write off the rumors than he cared to admit.

"Is there something the matter, Commander Longo?" Brighton said to him.

Ricio snapped his eyes off Kane and looked to Brighton. "Uh, no, Fleet Admiral. I was just—"

"Admiring the view?" Kane said.

Ricio wasn't sure how to respond. That was, until he saw Kane gesture toward a holo display of a strange starship rotating in front of his chair.

"The view, yes, Admiral Kane," Ricio replied.

Kane batted the words away with a hand. "You will refer to me as Moldark."

"Moldark?" Ricio caught himself. "Forgive me, sir. I mean, yes, Admiral Moldark."

"Not Admiral," Brighton said. He looked to his counterpart, then added, "Lord. Lord Moldark."

The scarred man nodded, as if in favor of the term, like the two of them were trying it out for the first time and agreeing upon its use. Ricio had the strange feeling that he was witnessing the evolution of something new. And something very dangerous. Normally, he would have spoken out against what he felt was bad leadership. After all, he'd made a reputation for himself by telling dimwitted COs where they could shove their ignorance. But something in his gut told him to hold his tongue. At least for now.

"Lord Moldark," Ricio said. His skin prickled as he said the words. Such a naming convention was definitely not standard Navy protocol. He clamped down his objections and dared to stare at the man in the center of his black eyes. "You're saying we will find this ship after passing through a quantum tunnel?"

"You will. Our source's sensors sent visual confirmation before being destroyed."

"Destroyed? As in, this force is hostile?"

"Quite so," Brighton said. "Use caution upon entering the system."

"And this tunnel, it's safe to enter?"

Brighton nodded. "It is. Your squadron and the battle-cruiser *Defiant Shepard* will pass through the coordinates and proceed to the planet designated in the mission brief. Your orders are to eliminate the enemy starship and all hostiles in the area."

"But this quantum tunnel…"

"The tunnel is inconsequential, commander," Moldark said. "The starship and its crew are all you need concern yourself with."

"Understood." Ricio stood a little straighter. "If you don't mind, who are we taking out? More Jujari?"

Brighton shook his head. "Some Jujari, yes. Some humans as well. All are complicit in this rebellion and must be stopped. Once the starship is eliminated, scan the planet for signs of life. Unless they have Repub idents, eliminate them."

"Seems clear enough to me." Ricio still had questions though. Normally, in any standard mission briefing, he wouldn't leave the room until he had all the information he wanted. But here, with these two men, both of whom far outranked him, he wasn't sure what protocol was. In any other context, they wouldn't even acknowledge his presence. So he wasn't sure how far to press them in order to satisfy his curiosity. "If I may, where does this quantum tunnel lead exactly?"

Brighton looked to Moldark. The elder man gave a cryptic shake of his head. Brighton looked back at Ricio and said, "To another part of the quadrant. We believe the Jujari are using it as a new base of operations should Oorajee fall."

"So this is a preventative measure," Ricio said.

"Precisely."

"Begging your pardon, but wouldn't this be more fitting for a Recon team? Why me?"

"Because, Commander Longo," Brighton said, showing the first signs of irritation with tight lips and a deep sigh, "you are the most decorated veteran pilot still alive on the *Labyrinth*. That, and we already sent a Recon team. You're going in to finish what they couldn't."

"I see," was all Ricio could think to say. This did not bode well. He imagined the enemy force to be substantial and, without even knowing this enemy vessel's capabilities, wondered if they might need something larger than a battle-cruiser to assist them.

"Search for the Recon unit and retrieve them if you can," Brighton continued. "Then get back here."

"Do not fail us, commander," Moldark added. "We are looking for you to be thorough. Execute your orders with extreme prejudice. There must be no survivors."

"Understood..." Ricio hesitated. "Lord Moldark."

The former admiral smiled, the ends of his lips curling up so high his black eyes turned to slits. The man's face resembled something almost reptilian. Ricio even caught a glimpse of the man's teeth, which seemed to look more like sharp fangs than anything human. What in all the cosmos was going on with him?

"You are dismissed."

Back inside his cockpit, Ricio rode in silence with his

thoughts. They'd accompanied the *Defiant Shepard* through the quantum tunnel—an experience he hoped not to repeat more than for the return trip—and now found themselves bearing down on the ship that Brighton and Moldark had shown him. It was unlike anything he'd ever seen before, resembling something more akin to a marine animal than a starship. It was both elegant and otherworldly.

"I'm not getting a data match," Viper Three said. "Unless I'm the only one experiencing a system error."

"You're reading it right. I don't think this one is in our database yet," Ricio replied.

"Sir?" Viper Two asked.

"Command suspects it's a new Jujari vessel, and that we're coming up on a fallback outpost on that planet."

"About that…" Viper Three spoke up again. "I'm also not getting a lock on our position, commander. Star navigation is offline."

"What?" Ricio brought up his navigation menu. But he was getting the same error. "This can't be right."

Every ship in the Republic Navy used an advanced star chart quadra-positioning system that located a ship based on its orientation to all the known stars in any of the Republic's main quadrants. It was even feasible to fix a position well beyond known space based upon adequate sightlines to the database of known stars, but no one Ricio knew had ever been out far enough to test its limitations. The system was—for lack of a better term—blasterproof.

"Viper Two," Ricio said, "are you reading the same error?"

"Affirmative, sir."

Ricio wondered if maybe the jump through the quantum tunnel had disrupted their sensors. He opened a channel to the *Defiant Shepard*.

"Go ahead, Viper Lead," said the communications officer. Ricio's callsign had been changed from Viper One to Viper Lead in order to designate him as the mission commander.

"Taurus One, can you please confirm our nav position and relay the necessary data? We're having trouble securing a lock."

"Standby, Viper Lead."

There was a long pause. With every second that ticked by, Ricio began to feel his anxiety level rise—and he didn't get anxious. Which was why he knew this was bad.

"Viper Lead, our navigation sensors are currently offline. We will update you once we've established a positive star fix."

"Copy that, Taurus One. Viper Lead out."

Ricio let his head rest against his seat back. This wasn't good. The nav system had never failed like this.

"Sir?" Viper Two asked.

"Go ahead."

"Where are we?"

Ricio shook his head for no one in particular. "I don't know." He took a deep breath, then looked at the starship in his HUD. "But we have a job to do. Then I want us the hell out of here."

"Roger."

"All Talons, prepare to engage the enemy starship. I'm marking it as Tango One on your map. Viper Two through Ten, identify weapons and drive systems and prepare to engage. Viper Eleven through Fourteen, cover formation and identify any inbound ships from the planet. I'm marking the planet as Tango Two. Once the starship is eliminated, all ships scan the surface for threats. Confirm mission objectives."

A series of green icons lit up the side of Ricio's visor. He then hailed the battlecruiser. "Taurus One, ready main blaster canons and torpedoes. Prepare to fire."

There was a moment's silence. Ricio watched for the data packet delivery icon to display.

"Targets confirmed, Viper Lead. Standing by."

Ricio could feel his heart rate increase in anticipation of the conflict. The enemy vessel was aware of their presence by now—they'd probably detected them the moment they jumped into the system. But, strangely, the ship had yet to deploy any fighters. In fact, the vessel didn't even have shields raised.

"Tauraus One," Ricio said, "are we close enough for you to conduct a life signs scan on that ship?"

Another pause. "Adequate sensor range in sixty seconds, Viper Lead," replied the comms officer.

"Good. Forward me the results."

"Understood, sir."

Ricio stared at his HUD. He knew that Brighton and

Moldark had said this was a Jujari and human force. But this ship was… well, it was unlike any he'd ever seen. Meaning, it looked like something beyond Jujari or Repub capabilities. A squadron of talons and a battlecruiser all for one ship? Granted, the thing certainly looked big—but wasn't this overkill?

Ricio checked the time and distance to target. They were within visual range now, and he moved the holo image aside. The starship was impressive, shimmering in the purple star's light. "Taurus One?" he asked, growing impatient.

"Scan initiated, Viper Lead. Stand by."

Ricio tapped his fingers on his control stick, then looked at the printed picture of his wife and son that he brought on every mission. He figured the Navy would give him as much leave as he wanted after this crazy mission. Then again, they had just begun a war with the Jujari. "Eh, who are you kidding?" Ricio said to himself. Then he kissed his fingertips and touched the image.

"Scan complete," the comms officer said. "Data uploaded."

Ricio snapped away from the picture and brought up the sensor menu. "Taurus One, are you sure this accurate?"

"Affirmative, Viper Lead. All sensors are green."

"But"—Ricio triple-checked what he was seeing—"that's not possible." According to the scans, the entire ship was being crewed by only three organic lifeforms. There was no way a vessel of that size could be run by so few.

Ricio suddenly wondered where the Recon team had

vanished to. Had a force of only three people actually taken out whatever Repub Marine force had been sent earlier?

"I want a scan of that planet as soon as you're close enough," Ricio said to the comms officer. "Since the ship seems to be in geosynchronous orbit, start with the terrain directly below it and move outward concentrically. Notify me as soon as you've finished."

"Understood, Viper Lead."

Ricio opened the all-ship channel. "This is Viper Lead to all ships, commence attack run. I repeat, commence attack run."

4

Ricio locked his targeting reticle on what resembled engine cones, then fired two of his four Class-C torpedoes. As the twin projectiles ripped across the black expanse, Ricio double checked his sensor readout. The enemy ship still had not raised shields. Either this was going to be the easiest takedown he'd ever participated in or the enemy had a serious surprise up its sleeve.

"Thirty seconds to impact," Viper Two called out, noting all torpedoes' collective time to targets. Each Talon had fired on areas of the vessel that the pilot deemed strategic. "Viper Lead, I'm still not seeing shields."

"Neither am I," Ricio replied. He flew perpendicular to the ship, headed toward its stern. The unnamed planet loomed in the background. He watched the orange glow of nearly thirty torpedoes as they sped toward their targets.

"Ten seconds," Viper Two said.

Ricio held his breath.

Suddenly, all the torpedoes deviated from their flight paths.

"What the hell?" Ricio exclaimed, his eyes trying to make sense of the chaos unfolding before him. At first, the missiles acted erratically, as if something had disrupted their targeting systems. They careened away from the enemy ship, shooting out in all directions. Ricio wondered if the vessel had employed some sort of disruption field undetectable by their sensors. But he threw out that notion the moment each pair of torpedoes came about and started heading back toward the Talons that launched them.

"Viper Squadron, evasive maneuvers," Ricio yelled. His ship's AI wasn't even alerting him to the missile lock even though he could clearly see his two torpedoes speeding toward his fuselage. He rolled his Talon to port and deployed countermeasures. The first torpedo raced past him, thrown off by his electromagnetic defenses. The fine burst of charged particles momentarily threw off its guidance system. The second, however, mistook the debris field for an enemy target and detonated.

The expanding wave of energy buffeted Ricio's shield but did little to diminish its integrity. His sensors were still reading the first torpedo as his own ordinance even though it was circling back to find him. He rolled to starboard just as the missile flew through his wake.

"Bogie on my six," Viper Four said, her voice frantic.

"Same," said Viper Eight. "I can't shake it."

"What's going on with them, Lead?" Viper Two asked.

But Ricio was as clueless as they were. He was about to say as much when Viper Six screamed over comms. The cry was cut short, however, when Ricio saw a bright orange flash off his starboard side. By the time he was able to focus on it, the explosion was gone, and all that remained was an ever-widening debris field.

"Viper Six down," Viper Two said. Then, to Ricio's shock, Viper Two also yelled over comms as his icon vanished from the nav map.

"No…" Ricio seethed. He fought against the rising panic as he watched more of his squadron fall to their own torpedoes. For the third time, Ricio rolled away from his missile, narrowly avoiding it. He attempted to target it with his T-100 blasters in each wingtip, but his weapons systems refused to lock on something it didn't deem an enemy weapon. He entered the override command and aimed manually. The shot was next to impossible. Still, he had to try. He squeezed the trigger and watched the blaster fire streak across the void. But the torpedo steered to evade the shot.

"But that's… that's impossible," Ricio said to himself. Then, over comms, he yelled, "Taurus One, SITREP."

"Taking heavy fire," the comms officer said. His voice was strained, accentuated by the sound of a klaxon in the background. "Our torpedoes are… they've returned to us. Our defense turrets are unable to take them out."

Ricio glanced at the battlecruiser's representation on the

map to see several dozen torpedoes blanking out as they collided with the icon. He spun his Talon around so he could see the missiles exploding along the *Defiant's* hull. Bright flashes of light popped, then disappeared as the combustible materials vaporized, consumed by fire and then by the void. All the while, defense turrets sent blistering sprays of blaster fire into the void in a failed attempt to stop the missiles.

Ricio looked back at the enemy vessel in muted horror. In less than a minute, the starship had wiped out half his squadron without firing a single shot. *And the damn shields aren't even raised yet.*

He looked back at his HUD and saw his torpedo circling back for a fourth time. *Mystics.* Several more projectiles circled around the remaining Talons, closing for the kill. Was this really how he was going out? Blown apart by his own torpedo?

Ricio yanked back on the flight controls, pitching his fighter up and away from the torpedo. The weapon had to be running low on fuel by now.

"I'm not gonna make it!" Viper Twelve said. "I'm not gonna—"

In the space of the next ten seconds, five more fighter pilots lost their lives. Ricio yelled in defiance, his throat tight with frustration. This couldn't be happening.

"Viper Lead," said the comms officer, "we're detecting several life signs on the planet's surface."

"Copy that," Ricio said, noting the new icons on his HUD. "But right now—*splick!*"

A second torpedo joined the first one in tracking Ricio. The missile swept in from below and detonated close enough to diminish his shields by seventy percent. But it wasn't the energy blast that concerned Ricio—it was the shrapnel. A metal shard ripped through his starboard engine, jarring his Talon enough to cause Ricio's jaw to slam shut. He cursed, then redirected power to the port engine. His first torpedo was coming in fast.

"Making a run for the planet," Ricio announced. If he couldn't assault the ship, maybe he'd get lucky and take out some of the ground forces. He figured his torpedo was running out of fuel and might explode during atmospheric entry. "All remaining Vipers, on me. Taurus One, fall back. Fire all blasters on Tango One."

Ricio got confirmation pings from only five Talons. *Five.* As for Taurus One, the comms officer complied with his orders and began firing on the enemy ship with its NR550 blaster cannons. Ricio went wide of the starship but noted that the *Defiant's* blaster fire was exploding against a massive purple shield. The alien vessel had finally decided to deploy its defenses, or... *maybe they'd been up the whole time and we just couldn't detect them.*

Ricio didn't like this. He wondered if he should have been more apprehensive about accepting the mission when he first heard a Recon team had been eliminated.

With throttle at full, Ricio sped toward the planet, aware that all the unexpended torpedoes were now trailing the five remaining Talons as they—

Four remaining Talons.

"Son of a bitch," Ricio yelled. He watched his speed indicator increase as the planet's gravity well took hold of his ship. Talons were built for high heat, high abrasion. And if he kept the deflection angle low enough, he might be able to keep his speed up while still achieving adequate descent. But this was fast, even for his risk-taking standards.

"Viper Lead," said Viper Three. Ricio's ship was starting to shake as flames covered the windows in mad torrents of orange light. "Advise significant speed reduction."

"Negative, Viper Three." Ricio's teeth chattered and his helmet knocked violently against his headrest. He could hardly focus on his HUD. Still, he willed his eyes to focus on the torpedoes trailing the remains of his squadron.

"But, commander—"

"Look!" Ricio watched as two torpedoes vanished from the combat map. A beat later, a third one disappeared. "We're shaking them."

"Agreed, commander. However, my sensors—"

Viper Three's channel went dead.

"Splick," Ricio yelled, but he could barely hear his own voice above the din. The fuselage temperature was critical. Even the air temp in his cockpit was unbearable. He wondered if he'd made a serious error. He couldn't tell if Viper Three had been done in by a torpedo or a breach in hull integrity. But either way, he was down to three ships.

Two ships.

Another exploded off his port side, this time shooting a

flaming debris field across the atmosphere like a thousand stones skipping across hell. He cursed and tried to ease up his entry path. His angle of attack was becoming too steep.

"Hold it together," Ricio said to his Talon. "Just a little bit more."

He glanced at the torpedoes closing on his ship. Their speed relative to his fighter had certainly lessened, but he was by no means clear of their danger. Only three remained, the rest having succumbed to engine failure or the friction created by speeding through the atmosphere. With any luck, he and the remaining Talon would evade these demon missiles and have enough ordinance to lay waste to whatever ground forces awaited them.

But it was not to be.

Ricio watched as the last Talon blinked out of existence on his HUD, showering his starboard side with a brilliant spray of flaming wreckage. He scorned the loss of his entire squadron, still bewildered by how such a thing was even possible. If he survived this, he pledged himself to discovering what that alien craft was and then exacting his revenge.

The sky threatened to rip Ricio's ship apart with every second that passed. He glanced at the sole remaining torpedo icon. It was within fifty meters; not close enough to destroy his ship, but certainly close enough to damage his already crippled starfighter. Then, without warning, the torpedo exploded. Whether from the heat, proximity sensors, or some command issued by the enemy vessel, he didn't know. The only thing that mattered was that his EES—emergency escape system—had activated, sealing the cockpit's egg-shaped pod and jettisoning it up and away from the main fuselage.

The initial action was so violent, Ricio thought his neck had snapped. He'd even blacked out for a second—or so he thought. But the pain that raced up his legs and arms jolted him awake and let him know his nervous system was still intact. The rattle of his Talon's cockpit was replaced by the scream of his slender translucent pod as it rocketed through the atmosphere. The flames encased him, threatening to swallow him whole. He couldn't hear a thing above the banshee cry of the inferno—not that there was anything else to hear. The only ship left to communicate with was the *Defiant Shepard*. That is, if it was still in one piece.

In another few seconds, the shaking dissipated, and his pod entered smooth air. Ricio patted himself down to make sure he was still alive, hardly able to believe he'd just survived. Now, thinking of the *Defiant*, he tried to establish a connection over TACNET.

"Taurus One, this is Viper Lead," he said. His voice sounded tight, so he tried again, consciously trying to calm himself. "Taurus One, this is Viper Lead, do you copy?"

He tried cycling up his ship's HUD on the pod's console but remembered that the guts of the computer had left with the ship. All he had now was a shell, a few thrusters, and a parachute that would automatically deploy at... *what was it again?* He blinked, trying to clear his head. Fifteen-hundred meters. Minimum altitude.

"Pick a landing site," he said, trying to give his ears something else to hear besides the rush of wind outside the pod. He blinked again, willing himself to focus. There was a town. No, it was a city. A massive city. Right on a coast. And a large clearing to the east. With any luck, the pod's limited nav computer might be able to place him down somewhere in there.

Ricio reached a trembling hand to the console. His index finger was shaking too much to type. He made a fist, shut his eyes, and took a deep breath. Had his entire squadron really just been wiped out? And the battlecruiser? This couldn't be happening. He needed to get word back to the Fleet Admiral. The mission had… it was a…

A failure.

The first of his career.

He opened his eyes, selected the clearing from the flight computer's topo map, and punched Accept. Immediately, the pod's thrusters redirected his trajectory, aiming him toward the east side of the city. As Ricio headed for the landing site, he noted how old the buildings were, most adorned with some sort of vegetation. The jungle was claiming them. Several had lost the battle to the relentless forces of decay and gravity, collapsing into the ground. But for the most part, the metroplex simply looked abandoned—an ancient civilization lost to time.

As he descended, now traversing directly across the old city, he saw that the structures were not as old as he thought they might be, given how much growth there was. Or, rather, they were certainly old, but their designs… their architecture was beautiful. Modern, even. As if the people who'd once lived here were advanced beyond... even beyond the Republic's standards.

"Where am I?" he asked himself.

Suddenly, the parachute deployed and jerked his head down. His chin punched his chest, causing him to bite his tongue. He cursed again and swallowed saliva that tasted of iron, then he looked up to watch the altitude indicator on his console. The numbers were running down, speeding past twelve hundred meters, then nine hundred, then seven hundred.

Ricio saw the clearing coming up fast. His descent rate was slowing, but he knew from training that this wasn't going to feel great. At one hundred meters, Ricio braced for impact. A warning alarm sounded. A final blast from the thrusters. And then...

Impact.

The force of the landing made it feel like all his organs had relocated to his feet. The pod landed and rolled. Ricio watched as the ground and sky traded places twice, while a red and white parachute collapsed onto the grass.

Fortunately, he was facing right side up—for the most part —which meant he'd be able to climb out easily enough. He punched the button for emergency hatch release and watched as the translucent window burst off the pod. White wisps of compressed air dissipated as the planet's atmosphere rushed in. Instantly, Ricio's helmet sensors analyzed the air composition and then provided him a series of metrics that determined it was safe to breathe.

He undid his helmet and threw it out of the pod, then worked to undo his harness. Now that he'd made it to the planet's surface, he had to…

Had to what?

He propped himself up and then hoisted himself out of the pod, hands pushing against the shell's rim. He'd need to orient himself, take stock of his resources, and then come up with a plan. A plan to get back in touch with the Fleet Admiral.

"Ah, who are you kidding, Longo?" He stood and stretched his back, turning around slowly. "No one's coming for you down here."

Down here. The words reminded him of something. Dammit, he'd nearly forgotten! The enemy was down here somewhere too. Which meant…

Which meant he had to find cover. He was no Marine. And he only had… *a pistol*. He leaned back in the pod and retrieved the small blaster from the side of his flight seat, then he double checked the magazine and saw it was fully charged.

"Well, at least that's something." Assuming the enemy was armed, he'd be no match for them. Best to find cover and wait for…

"For the rescue team that's not coming." He watched the beacon's light pulse on the pod's aft. "'Cause you *were* the rescue team. Damn." He grabbed his pistol by the barrel and used the butt to smash the light, relieving the LED from its futile attempt to hail backup. Then he mag-locked the weapon to his hip and reached behind his flight seat. There was a medical kit, food rations, water, and a flare gun. Enough to keep him going for three days—four if he stretched it. And then what?

"One day at a time, Longo." He tried calming himself. "Just one damn day at a time. You're a survivor."

"And you're also a prisoner," said a voice from behind him.

Instinctively, Ricio reached for the blaster at his side and spun around.

"Easy there, fly boy," said the voice coming from… from nowhere that he could see.

"Who's there?" he demanded, swinging his weapon back and forth, trying to find something to aim at. But there was nothing. Nothing but—

That's when he saw it. It was subtle. So subtle his eyes had passed over it several times. The air was… it was moving. Distorted. In the shape of a human. "Who… who are you? Show yourselves!"

Out of nowhere, a figure appeared wearing gleaming white armor atop a blue woven suit. The helmet was sleek with a slender visor and looked to be more advanced than any Repub tech he'd ever seen. The sense of its superiority was amplified by the deadly looking weapon pointed at him.

Ricio was outmatched. He was about to raise his hands when five more figures materialized out of thin air, each pointing a weapon at him.

"I surrender," he said, dropping his pistol and raising his hands.

"That's good," said the first soldier—at least, the sound seemed to be coming from him. Actually, it sounded more like a her now that Ricio thought about it. "Because we already took bets on who was going to have to carry your body if we had to shoot you."

"So… you're not going to shoot me?" Ricio asked.

"Not yet, we're not. I lost the bet, and I really dislike carrying dead weight."

"And I dislike being shot," Ricio said.

"Then I hope you like marching, 'cause it's your only other option right now."

"I can live with that."

"I'm sure you can. Let's move, fly boy." The woman gestured with her rifle. "That way."

5

"How you doing up there, Ninety-Six?" Awen asked over comms. She used the company channel even though she could converse privately with the bot in the Unity—now that he was tied in with Azelon and the rest of the Novia Minoosh. Keeping the rest of the team informed of the *Spire's* condition would go a long way in keeping everyone from getting too anxious.

"We're having a splendid time, Awen," TO-96 replied. "Thank you for asking."

That got a few smiles from the gladias, she was sure. "Splendid? You make it sound like you're having a picnic, not engaging in a space battle."

"Well, given how Ezo formatted my combat architecture, one might say that this particular exercise is a sort of picnic for me, all things considered."

"Here it comes," Ezo said over comms.

Awen ignored the comment. "Can you be a little more specific, Ninety-Six?"

She leaned against a tree, watching the rest of the Gladio Umbra recline amongst long grasses, clusters of boulders, and groves of trees. Everyone was redistributing energy mags and water. Save for Magnus, of course. He was strung up tight, pacing in circles in a small clearing, visor looking skyward. Azelon's surprise grounding of the shuttles had really upset him. Awen had learned he was a man who liked being in control. And she didn't entirely blame him either. But Azelon was an AI, so the sooner Magnus accepted her judgment as the best call to make—at least statistically—the sooner he could relax with everyone else.

"Of course I can be more specific. Azelon has employed me in overtaking the command interfaces of the enemy's torpedoes. We are working together to eliminate the Talons in the most efficient way possible. It is—to put it in human terms—quite fun."

"Ninety-Six!" Awen heard Ezo and Sootriman laugh. She also felt Magnus look in her direction. Even without stepping into her second sight, she could feel his eyes on her through his helmet. She instantly regretted having this conversation over the company channel, so she switched out to a private one. "You mustn't say that!"

"Why ever not, Awen?" the bot replied.

"Because you're killing human beings with those torpedoes. This isn't some... some game."

"But these humans are intent on causing you harm, are they not?"

"Well… we suspect they are, yes. I mean…"

"They did fire on the *Spire*."

"I understand, but that doesn't mean you call it fun. That's horrible, Ninety-Six."

"I have clearly offended you," the bot replied. "My apologies, Awen." Awen heard a chime alerting her to a company-wide transmission—coming from TO-96. "Contrary to my last statement, I would like to inform all the members of Granther Company that I am deeply remorseful and even ashamed of my actions that are resulting in human casualties. Let it be known that I am not having any fun whatsoever in redirecting enemy missiles to chase down star fighters and pulverize them one by one."

"Said no little boy ever," someone said over comms.

Awen glanced at the speaker's ident tag. It was Robillard in Charlie platoon. Awen used the vector arrow in her HUD to turn toward him, her posture saying she was all business.

He raised his hands in defense. "I'm just saying."

"Say it to yourself, gladia," Awen replied.

"Yes, ma'am."

"How many ships have you and Azelon taken out?" Magnus asked TO-96. Awen appreciated Magnus's attempt to get things back on track, even if it did mean returning to the subject of killing.

"We have successfully eliminated eight of the fourteen

Talons, and the battlecruiser is taking heavy damage." There was a pause. "Make that nine Talons."

"And this is all using their own torpedoes?" Magnus said.

"That is correct, sir."

Magnus let out a low whistle. "Remind me never to cross you when you're having a bad day, 'Six."

"Bad day, sir?"

"Yeah, you know. When you're pissed at the universe for no apparent reason and just feel like blowing something up."

"I have never been *pissed at the universe*, sir. Is this something I should look forward to?"

"I guess that all depends on you, 'Six."

"I understand, sir. I look forward to developing this conversation at a later time. For now, I am very pissed at the universe to report that the five Talons are attempting to gain entry into the planet's upper atmosphere."

Awen felt Magnus's bearing shift. To the company, he said, "Take cover, people. Looks like we're gonna have company."

"Make that four of the enemy Talons, sir," TO-96 added, followed by another hesitation. "Now three."

"Ninety-Six," Awen said. "Is this all your work, taking them out like this?"

"I would be lying if I said yes, Awen. As I said, Azelon showed me the command override sequence necessary to take control of the enemy ordinance. But she has allowed me to *run wild* with it, as you say, now that I have mastery of the protocol. Ah, now we are down to two."

"I'm proud of you, 'Six," Magnus said.

Awen glared at him, but the former Marine clearly didn't seem to notice. And why would he under their helmets? Maybe she needed to visit him in the Unity.

"Thank you, sir. But please be advised, I am not having any fun."

"Copy that." Then, in a whisper, Magnus added, "Your secret's safe with me."

"Thank you, sir," the bot whispered back. "Ah, and now we are down to one Talon, sir. And the battlecruiser has been eliminated, thanks to Azelon's marvelous handiwork."

Awen slipped into the Unity, projected her presence inside Magnus's consciousness, and said, "Don't encourage him, Magnus."

"Mystics," Magnus yelled, leaping backward. He grabbed his helmet and then turned toward Awen again. "Cut that out, woman!"

But she didn't cut it out. Instead, Awen projected an image of her face with a playful grin on it. "You first."

Magnus followed her challenge with a steady chuckle and the barely indistinguishable words, "Just you wait until I see about that."

"Ah, the last ship has been destroyed," TO-96 announced.

"On the contrary," Azelon said. "I am still detecting a life sign."

"Quite right," TO-96 replied after a moment. "It seems I have spoken too soon."

"Escape pod?" Awen asked, looking to Magnus.

He nodded. "Those Talons have a pretty good EES."

"You and your acronyms," she said.

"Emergency escape system."

"I figured it was something like that."

"Can you track it, 'Six?" Magnus asked.

"Of course, sir."

Magnus turned and began looking at the warriors. "Dutch, take any five gladias to intercept. If the pilot survives, I want them brought back here. And be careful."

"Copy that, LT."

"The rest of you, return to the shuttles."

By the time Dutch and the others returned from their search and recovery op, Granther Company was back aboard the transports, ready to leave the planet. Unlike last time, however, the mood was far less strenuous. Magnus walked down the loading ramp without his helmet, enjoying the fresh air. He watched as Dutch emerged from the jungle, escorting a Repub pilot with his arms bound behind his back.

The man appeared to be in his late twenties, with black hair and keen dark eyes. He was cleanly shaven, as per Navy standards, and bore the rank of commander on his flight suit.

"What's your name, commander?" Magnus asked as the prisoner approached, but the pilot merely raised his chin in defiance. "Fine, have it your way."

Magnus strode to within a meter of the man and gut-punched him. The air left the prisoner's lungs in a violent sigh, leaving the pilot doubled over in a groan.

"Now, I know you're trained in advanced escape and evasion techniques," Magnus said, leaning down toward the man's ear. "So you can probably endure a lot of torture. And if it comes to that, we can put your training to the test. Trust me when I say I'd enjoy that. But right now, I'm just pissed that you tried to take out my ship and, based on your last attempt to enter the planet's atmo, take out my company. So, one more time, what's your name, pilot?"

"What's it to you?" The pilot coughed.

"What's it to me?" Magnus stood upright and looked around, repeating the question once more. "The better question is what's it worth to you? Because my AI can probably provide me most of what I need with a quick brain scan and background check on your Repub personnel file. But I'd rather do it this way."

"Good luck," the pilot said.

"Wrong answer." Magnus delivered a second punch to the gut, this time sending the pilot to his knees. The man coughed, taking nearly twenty seconds to catch his breath. Magnus put his hands on his knees and leaned over the prisoner. "How about this: I give you something, you give me something, copy?"

The pilot just groaned.

"I'll take that as a yes. I'm a former Marine. Which means I can do this all day long."

"You're…" The pilot looked up. "You're a Marine?"

"Former, *former* Marine. Get it right."

"No wonder they want you dead."

Magnus hesitated; he desperately wanted to ask who wanted them dead. But he doubted such an answer would come easily. "Yeah, we're turning out to be quite a pain in their ass."

"They'll send more squadrons when we don't report back."

"I should hope so," Magnus replied. "Because that last demonstration was fairly pathetic if you ask me." He looked to Dutch. "Get him on board."

"On it," she said with a boot to the pilot's rear end.

"WHAT ARE you going to do with the two prisoners?" Awen asked now that they were back on the *Spire*. She and Magnus were the last to leave the shuttle, and they watched as Robillard and Bliss escorted the Navy pilot and the rogue Recon operator out of the hangar bay. Magnus had asked several leaders to meet him on the bridge in a few minutes to debrief, which meant they had some time to talk. And this point was important to her.

Awen didn't like seeing Magnus punch a prisoner like he had back on the planet. She knew that bringing it up was like shining a light in a Boresian taursar's eyes. The Navy commander had, after all, made an attempt on their collective lives, as had the rogue Marine. Still, the subject had to be breached. She wouldn't tolerate barbarism, nor would she allow the newly formed Gladio Umbra to sink as low as their enemies. She'd be damned if she didn't stand for the virtues that both the Luma and the Galactic Republic had lost.

"Nothing," Magnus replied, buckling himself into an empty crash couch on the bridge. "We'll let them sit for a little while. Then, when I want more information out of them, I'll take my time in breaking them."

Awen swallowed. He wasn't serious, was he? Torturing another member of the Galactic Republic's armed space force was nothing short of barbaric. It was also proof that the industrial war machine was no respecter of persons. It taught its own members to become so ruthless that they'd even exact judgement on one another if the circumstances were right.

As much as she respected Magnus—even had feelings for him—she couldn't bring herself to endorse what he'd just proposed. This was the very thing the Gladio Umbra had once stood against, no matter what species perpetrated the crimes. So if Magnus did choose to leverage his trade skills against the prisoners, Awen knew she'd have to step in.

She shook her head, trying not to imagine how *that* interrogation might go.

"What is it?" Magnus asked her. He must've seen her shaking her head. "You don't agree with my methods, do you."

"No," Awen said. "They're barbaric."

Magnus nodded… as if in understanding. "I get it."

"Do you, Magnus? Because, if you hadn't noticed, you just—"

"Awen, relax." He held a hand up. It had the strange effect of silencing her more quickly than she cared to admit. She never let anyone shut her up. "I told you, I get it."

"You get what?"

"You really are impossible sometimes." He sighed, turning toward her. "I get that you don't agree with my methods, with Marine SOPs."

She raised an eyebrow at him, having no idea what he'd just said.

"Standard operating procedures." He let out a short laugh. "I get that it's violent. And, yeah, it's probably wrong a lot of the time."

"A lot of the time? Then why do—?"

He held up a finger.

Is he shooshing me? she wondered.

"I thought we covered this ground already," he said.

Awen winced in surprise. "Remind me."

"Back on Ezo's ship. On *Geronimo*." Magnus seemed to be genuinely searching her face. "We're called to do evil things—"

"To evil people." Awen nodded. "I remember now. You said you didn't expect me to understand."

"And I still don't. It's part of my job."

"Not anymore," Awen said.

Magnus hesitated. "What's that supposed to mean?"

"That was when you were a Marine." He waved the term

away with a hand. "No, you said you were Recon. But you're neither a Marine nor Recon anymore. You're Gladio Umbra."

"But there are no fewer evil people to stop," Magnus said.

"Maybe not, but if those tactics worked, don't you think we'd have solved the problem by now?"

Magnus stroked his jawline. "The goal was never to solve the problem, Awen. It was to keep innocent people alive."

"And how's that worked out for you?" The challenge leaped from her mouth before she could catch it. She instantly regretted it but knew there was no way to take it back. "I'm sorry, that was—"

"It's worked well enough to keep the galaxy from falling into total ruins. At least until recently. But the ways you're used to... it's just... that's how good people get killed." Magnus looked away, his eyes searching for something that Awen couldn't see. She wanted to tell him he didn't need to go on. But she wanted him to keep going. She wanted to know what made him think the way he did... what drove a man like him to do things she didn't even want to imagine doing to another living being.

"We both know you don't like the Order of the Luma," Awen said, trying to keep her voice even. "But I can't help but feel that something happened. Something in your—"

"Something did happen. Plenty of things happened."

Awen tried to get him to look at her but his eyes were somewhere else.

"What?"

"First time I ever saw a Luma try to negotiate a peace deal in the field, it went sideways. We were set up on a rooftop on a small island on Caledonia. The emissary had conned—sorry, *convinced* the brass into letting him try to bargain with the 'kudas. Everyone on Capriana was tired of war, and we were losing by attrition. So they gave him the reins.

"The bastard walked four of our Marines to a bridge without their weapons and without cover. It was supposed to be a sign of peace or some splick. Three fish came out to meet them, but one was wired."

"A bomb?"

Magnus nodded. The Caledonian Wars had ended years ago, but this memory still seemed fresh for Magnus. Like it had just been yesterday.

"Apparently the Luma raised some sort of shield just before the device went off. It saved his life. At least from the initial blast. The other Marines weren't so lucky."

"Mystics, Magnus. I'm so sorry."

"Yeah. So am I. Our damned boys didn't even have blasters in their hands. And what about a force field big enough to save them too? But I suppose that was too much to ask for."

Awen knew she should explain how shielding energy worked in the Unity. But this wasn't the time. Given how much he'd seen, she doubted it would ever be the right time. Instead, she hung her head and waited for Magnus to finish.

"The Luma emissary died a few seconds later by enemy blaster fire. We buried his body the next day, but there was nothing left of the four Marines." He took a deep breath. Awen thought she heard the slightest quiver of his lip but dared not look up.

"I don't like it, if that's what you want me to say. All the killing, I mean. I don't. But I'm damned good at it. And it's what I know. The only way to keep evil at bay is to meet it head on. If there was another way, I'd use it. But the only alternatives just seem to get more people killed. And if people are going to die, I'd rather it be them than us."

Awen felt as though some sacred space had just been created. She'd been allowed deeper into this man's life, a man she cared for. And she desperately didn't want to mess it up. Yet, as he spoke his truth, she had a hard time swallowing it. How could she tell him that she felt he was settling for less than the best? How could she convey to him that everything he knew was inferior to ways of shaping peaceful outcomes that didn't involve the level of violence he'd come to be so proficient at? Maybe the whole subject wouldn't be breached now, but she could at least start—by offering an olive branch of her own.

"What you do…" Awen took a deep breath. "It's remarkable."

Magnus shot her a bewildered stare. "Excuse me?"

"I couldn't do it. Mystics know it's not in me. And you've probably saved more lives than I could ever hope to."

This was, perhaps, the only time she'd ever seen him slack-jawed. He acted like he wanted to say something, but she didn't want him to. Not yet anyway.

"Truthfully, where would we be without you, Magnus? You're the one who has held this team together… you're the one whose leadership and sacrifice have guided us. And, yes, your propensity to meet violence with violence has meant stopping the enemy from killing us. Killing Piper. And me."

Awen took another deep breath. Magnus was searching her face. His gaze was intense, and she suddenly felt exposed and vulnerable in her admonitions. But this next part might put an end to all that, and she didn't want to hurt him. However, she had to at least try and help him understand.

"All I'm saying is that with everything we've seen, with everything that's been done, there has to be another way forward. A better way forward. And before you say anything, I don't claim to know what that way is. I don't. The Luma haven't found it, and the Republic hasn't found it either. But maybe, just maybe, if we're lucky, we can discover it together."

There was a long moment that passed between them as Magnus looked deeply into her eyes. It felt much like the moment they'd shared back on Neith Tearness when they kissed—only deeper. This wasn't infatuation. It was something more… perhaps the beginning of mutual respect… of a desire to grow toward something together.

"I believe you," Magnus said, taking her by the hand. "And I would like to find it together." Then, in what was one of the most astounding things she could have imagined, Magnus said, "What would you have me do?"

Awen opened her mouth as if to speak, then closed it.

Then opened it again. Her mind was a flurry of thoughts. She'd been so opposed to his behavior that she'd never given any consideration as to what, exactly, she might say constructively if given the chance. All her answers were things the Luma would say. Not that they were all bad, but none of them seemed right for this situation. Instead, the only thing she could think to say was: "Don't torture the pilot."

Without even hesitating, Magnus said, "Alright." Then he pulled Awen's hand toward his chest, wrapped his other arm around her lower back, and kissed her.

She let the moment stretch on for a few seconds before finally pulling away. She smiled at him. "If that's what happens when I ask you not to torture someone, I can't imagine what happens if I ask you not to kill anyone."

Magnus blushed—something she'd never seen him do. "Hey, one step at a time," he replied.

6

Magnus knew kissing Awen was impulsive, but it was what he wanted. The whole idea of liking her, however, still seemed strange. She was, after all, a former Luma—a member of the very society he'd scorned for so many years. Their notions of peace and inclusiveness had made his stomach turn. But she was no more a Luma than he was a Marine, so distancing themselves from the hardline positions of their former lives seemed inevitable despite whatever vestiges remained.

This new life and these new alliances were changing them both. And he was okay with that. If they were going to survive and stop their enemies, neither he nor Awen could hold to ideals of what they once knew. Something better had to emerge from this, something stronger than what they'd known.

He walked with her toward the bridge, greeting various

team members as they passed each other in the corridors. He and Awen were truly building something special. Whether or not they could actually take on the forces of evil that were building in their home universe remained to be seen, but this was the best shot either of them had. And for reasons Magnus couldn't explain, it felt as though the cosmos wanted them together—wanted them to combine their approaches in rectifying the evil growing in the galaxy.

They were almost to the bridge when Valerie stepped into the hallway. For just having survived a firefight not more than two hours prior, the woman was stunning. With her armor still on, she was the picture of feminine ferocity. The soot stains on her cheeks only seemed to accentuate her eyes, and her blonde hair draped delicately over her shoulder plates. The Marine Corps had been stupid to let her get away and marry a damned senator.

Valerie greeted them both, then looked to Awen. "Piper is getting cleaned up in our room. But…" Valerie hesitated.

"What is it?" Awen said.

"I don't know. She just seems distracted by something. I was wondering if you might speak with her."

Awen looked at Magnus. They needed to get to the bridge and regroup; discussing the next steps for their operation was critical. But if Piper needed Awen, so be it. She was a priority.

"Just head to the bridge as soon as you're done," Magnus said.

"I will. See you shortly." She gave Magnus a quick smile, and then ducked into Valerie and Piper's quarters.

"So," Valerie said, stepping closer to Magnus. "We made it."

"Yeah, not bad for the first run."

"Still rough around the edges."

Magnus nodded. "Yeah, we'll need more training before the teams are fluid."

"Agreed. Communication was bad in a few areas."

"And we're gonna need to work on coordinated—"

"Advances," Valerie said, finishing his sentence. "I noticed it too."

Magnus laughed. "Took the words right out of my mouth."

"Well, neither of us are new to this game."

"True." Magnus studied her face. Mystics, she was beautiful. And brilliant. And a damn good fighter. As much as Magnus liked Awen, he couldn't help but feel drawn to Valerie. She represented so much of what was normal to him—his life as a Marine, the cultural norms of Capriana… She was the popular girl in school that everyone wanted to be with. And he knew she liked him, which meant he'd be a fool not to reciprocate the feelings.

And there were feelings. Over the last several months, they'd worked hard to drill Granther Company together, to use their combined experiences in the Corps to develop training exercises that began to turn a ragtag band of fighters into trained warriors. But even despite the amount of time they'd shared, Magnus had resisted outright conversation on… well, anything beyond their working relationship.

Granted, Magnus knew that Valerie would have him if he said anything. He'd want her too, if he was being honest. From the first time he'd laid eyes on her in the senator's starship, he'd felt something visceral at work—some unseen attraction that made him desire her whether he wanted to or not. And then there was Piper, a little girl in need of a father. Magnus had fantasized, more than he cared to admit, of the family they'd make: weapons loaded and enemies running. But it was more the stuff of movies than reality. The military hated family life. He knew that. And so did Valerie.

In the end, however, Magnus was realizing that Valerie wasn't right for him… almost as much as he knew that Awen *was* right for him. The two women could not be more different in background and worldview. And yet he admired them both for different reasons. He knew that life with Valerie could be wonderful… maybe even easy. They had so much in common. But it was Awen who captured his imagination more than any other woman he'd ever met. She was a mystery to him, one he felt compelled to figure out. And when they disagreed on something, that feeling drove him to want to know her more than ever.

Unlike the life he'd envision with Valerie, Magnus could not see into the future where it concerned Awen. It was almost as if the thought of the unknown called him forward to create some new reality with her. In a weird way, that idea scared him. He didn't like walking onto the battlefield without having a good idea of what he was getting into. And with Awen, he wasn't entirely sure what he was getting into—the unknowns were too great. But that was the strangest part of all. As long as she was there, he knew he could face them. He could face anything with Awen.

"Hey, where'd you go?" Valerie asked.

"What?"

"Just now. You went somewhere."

Magnus blinked and realized he had, in fact, been lost in thought. "Sorry. I was just… thinking."

"About what?" Valerie asked. Magnus hesitated long enough that when he didn't say anything, she went on. "Maybe about how we first met in a starship corridor like this?"

Magnus blinked. Was this conversation about to turn romantic? "Yeah, we sure did."

"You looked so badass in your Mark VII kit," Valerie said with a wide grin. "I was always a sucker for a boy in armor."

"Yeah…" Magnus shook his head. "I mean, I'm glad we met… in my armor."

Valerie laughed a little and cocked one eye at him. "You feeling okay?"

Magnus rubbed a hand over his face. "I think I'm just tired."

"We all are," she replied. "But, after you get cleaned up and we're on our way, if you want to talk, I—"

"Valerie, listen," Magnus said. "I recognize that this… that we could be… You and me, we could…" He hesitated. This already felt more awkward than he wanted it to be. "It's just that I—"

"You like Awen," Valerie said.

"Wait… what?"

"You have feelings for her. I get it."

"Valerie, that's not what I was going to say."

"But it's what you need to say. Because if you don't, I'm going to keep some hope alive that we could be together. Unless you tell me otherwise right now." Her eyes searched his face, and Magnus knew he needed to say something.

"There you are, Magnus," TO-96 suddenly said from down the hallway.

"Not now, bot," Magnus yelled back.

"But you are needed on the bridge, sir."

"I'll be there in a minute." Magnus turned back to Valerie.

"Shall I set a sixty-second reminder for you, sir?"

Magnus closed his eyes and took a deep breath. Valerie gave a small chuckle. "That's fine, 'Six. I'll meet you on the bridge."

"Very well, sir. Your reminder has been set. And I look forward to—"

"Head back to the bridge, 'Six."

"Heading back to the bridge, sir. See you there."

Magnus pressed his tongue against the inside of his cheek, trying to reign in his frustration with TO-96, and with this whole conversation. Give him a blaster and a battlefield full of enemies any day. But all this relationship stuff? It was damn hard.

He took a breath and looked Valerie in the face. "I like

Awen." Magnus let the truth of the words hang in the air for a second, as much for himself as for Valerie.

"Well, there you have it," Valerie said.

But Magnus held up his hand. "But you are amazing, Valerie. And I—"

"Magnus, I don't need a pep talk. I just needed to know where you were at." She smiled at him. It seemed incredibly sincere. "People in our line of work don't exactly grow old together, if you know what I mean. So I just wanted to know how I should use the rest of my time. You've told me what I needed to hear, and that's that."

Magnus was struck with how matter-of-fact she was being. But then again, that was the Marine Corps way. And it was the way of most doctors he knew. No nonsense, bottom line up front.

He also had to admit that the finality of this conversation meant certain things. It meant he was closing the door on any possible future with Valerie. Keeping things open-ended and ambiguous had meant there was some hope out there in the distance. Part of him wanted that, at least the option of it. But that wasn't fair to her, nor to himself.

This conversation also meant expressing his feelings about Awen. And he'd just done that with Valerie—the other woman he had feelings for. Wasn't there some rule about *not* doing that? But he'd done it nonetheless, and it had only made his feelings for Awen more real. Was he committed to her now, even though he had yet to express it in so many words?

"You're good together," Valerie said in what Magnus considered a fairly shocking admonition; what was more, Valerie sounded like she meant it. "For what it's worth, I'm happy for you both."

Mystics, how was he supposed to respond to this?

"Anyway, you'd better get to the bridge. I think your sixty seconds are about up."

As if prompted by her words, a small chime went off over the ship-wide communications channel. Then, from the speakers in the ceiling, TO-96's voice said, "Magnus, please report to the bridge. Your sixty seconds are up, as per your request. Again, Magnus, please report to the bridge."

"No one can fault him for being punctual," Valerie said.

"Or blatantly annoying," Magnus added. He looked Valerie in the eyes and said, "Thanks."

"No, thank you. I appreciate your honesty… even if I did have to drag it out of you a little."

"You did. But I'm glad you did."

"Me too." She leaned into him and kissed him on the cheek. Then she patted his chest and said, "Better get in there."

"Roger. You coming?"

"No. I'm going to relieve Awen. You need Awen more than you need me."

Azelon relinquished the captain's chair to Magnus, allowing him to sit in front of the gathered audience. Before she got too far, however, he grabbed her by the arm. "Hey, what was that stunt back there?"

"Stunt, sir?"

"You grounded the shuttles without my consent." Magnus felt the anger rising in his voice and considered taking this conversation elsewhere, or just saving it for later. Normally, this would be embarrassing for someone in Azelon's position, but Magnus knew she didn't have an ego like humans did—at least, he suspected she didn't. Even if she did, he still needed to get this cleared up.

"The statistical likelihood of—"

"I understand your analysis, bot. What I'm saying is next time, you run that kind of thing by me before you execute. Copy?"

The robot looked at Magnus passively, as if his request was nothing more than a small bit of new information to be processed and archived, completely devoid of any emotional component. "I will proceed as you have requested, Magnus. My apologies for…" Azelon seemed to search for something. "For ruffling your ass feathers."

Everyone else in the bridge snickered at this. For a moment, Magnus thought he might keep a straight face through it, but when he heard someone snort, he lost control and laughed too. "That's not exactly how the expression goes, Azie."

"Azelon is attempting to utilize my lexicon more when conversing with you, sir," TO-96 said.

"Which explains a lot," added Ezo, still laughing.

"Anyway, you're forgiven, Azie. Just don't do it again."

"I will endeavor to do as you have prescribed, sir."

Magnus nodded, satisfied that the matter was concluded, and then sat down to look at his core crew. It consisted of the four platoon leaders—Dutch, Abimbola, Titus, and Rohoar—as well as a few members of each squad deemed essential to the next phase of the mission. Dutch included Ezo and Sootriman, who stood so close to one another that their arms touched, as well as Saasarr, who stood behind Sootriman, arms across his chest. Abimbola had asked Berouth, Rix, and Silk to join him, while Titus called up Bliss and Robillard. As for the Jujari, Saladin and Czyz stood to either side of Rohoar.

Magnus was about to begin when the bridge door slid open and Awen walked in. Magnus tracked her with a certain intensity that he realized might be a little much. She seemed to notice too, looking away from him at first, and then returning his stare with a smile. "Sorry I'm late," she said.

"No problem," Magnus replied. "I knew where you were." *Mystics, that sounded awkward, didn't it.* "With Piper, I mean." He looked back at the crowd while Awen slid in beside Rohoar. The only people not present that Magnus felt should have been there were Flow and Cheeks. But he still didn't know how to introduce them to Rohoar yet. Up until now, they'd only talked about the former mwadim; even that had not ended well. But seeing a Jujari in the flesh? Magnus was worried that would not go well given all that the men had been through. They'd need more time.

"First off," Magnus said, "I want to extend my congratulations to you and your platoons. While that wasn't the smoothest mission, it was our first. And, all things considered, it went better than I expected. Well done."

Those gathered responded with nods and verbal agreement. The feeling of accomplishment seemed mutual, and that made Magnus happy.

"We worked hard for that initial win. Your squads deserve congratulations from you, so see to it when you regroup. Moving on, I'd like to give the floor to Azelon so she can debrief us on the latest attack. Azelon?"

"Of course, sir." The smooth-white robot strode out from beside Magnus into the middle of the bridge, motioning forward. "As you can see on the main holo display, a battlecruiser and fourteen FAF-28 Talons emerged from the quantum tunnel." The display showed the vessels popping into existence. A star map also showed icons of the ships in relation to the *Spire* and the rest of the planets in the system. Azelon went on to describe the battle in stunning detail, outlining how she and TO-96 commandeered the enemy's torpedoes, destroying all their vessels without so much as a single shot fired from the *Spire*.

Magnus was impressed, yet again, with the Novia's advanced technology, and recognized that Azelon, TO-96, and the ship gave them a huge advantage in future space combat missions. How many enemies they'd be able to successfully take on at once remained to be seen. But Azelon had proven her mettle, and that was good enough for Magnus —for now, anyway.

"Are there any questions?" Azelon asked.

Rohoar raised his ears. Azelon recognized the gesture almost at once and invited him to speak.

"Did these vessels follow Abimbola and I back from Oorajee?" Rohoar asked.

"We believe so," Azelon replied. "Accounting for the expanding time dilation between the two universes, it is believed that these vessels were pulled from the conflict over your home world and re-tasked mid-operation."

"So it is our fault they arrived," Rohoar concluded, a hint of shame in his voice.

"That would be an accurate conclusion. However, given the fact that the enemy already had a presence on Ithnor Ithelia, it is possible that a secondary force would have been sent anyway. Your movement from Oorajee to Neith Tearness was merely cause for additional concern and not the sole impetus."

While the explanation was supposed to make Rohoar feel better, it didn't look like it had. Rather, the Jujari seemed put off by it.

"I am sorry for betraying our people," Rohoar said, lowering his head and twisting it to one side. Magnus knew what this was… a display of submission and inferiority. But he couldn't afford to let the Jujari be seen in any negative light, not with how much fighting they had in front of them. And, as far as Magnus was concerned, Rohoar was the physical link to the ancient Novia Minoosh. This meant Magnus needed the Jujari warrior fit to lead.

"Nonsense," Magnus said, standing up and walking toward Rohaor. "Without you and Abimbola recruiting your kin and friends, we would not have had the strength to muster an assault on the Recon team in Itheliana. And that team arrived well before you."

"If anything," Awen interjected, "it was I who first alerted Admiral Kane and Master So-Elku of this place. Any further conclusions must take this preeminent fact into consideration."

Rohoar raised his head and looked at Awen, then at Magnus.

"In conclusion," Magnus said, "I do not accept your apology for none is warranted. However, I recognize your willingness to accept fault as a mark of great leadership. Consider this resolved."

"Thank you, scrumruk graulap," Rohoar said, baring his teeth.

"You're welcome." Magnus turned and addressed the rest of the room. "Now, it seems we have a decision to make, which is why I invited you all here. As you know, the enemy was inside Itheliana to obtain something… something that Azelon says is of strategic importance to the Novia Minoosh. While I have asked for a greater explanation than that, Azelon assures me now it not the time."

"And it remains as such," Azelon interjected.

"As much as I disagree with her, I recognize—as I think we all do—that we are at the behest of our hosts, the Novia Minoosh. So I will not press the point, for now. Needless to say, the enemy knows how to arrive in the metaverse, knows where Ithnor Ithelia is, and knows there is something of value in Itheliana. As such, I believe we have a crucial decision to make."

"And what's that?" Awen asked, still standing next to Rohoar.

"Whether or not we close the quantum tunnel."

7

Awen felt the collective shock go through the bridge as Magnus brought up the topic of closing the tunnel. This was the first she'd heard of it too and wondered how long he'd been toying with the idea. She also wondered how long she'd need to compete with Valerie for Magnus's affection, as the woman was clearly interested in him. But this wasn't the time for her to get sidetracked. There was work to be done.

Abimbola raised one of his large arms. "My first question, before we even discuss how, would be why."

"And that's what this is for," Magnus replied. "To ask questions and talk it through. So, to answer yours, I'll ask everyone else: Why?"

"It would cut off the enemy from accessing whatever it is the Novia have buried in the planet," Rohoar suggested.

"And from discovering the QTG," Awen added.

The room looked at her.

"The quantum tunnel generator," Ezo said.

"The what now?" Titus asked, looking from Awen to Ezo.

Ezo went on to explain what Awen, Sootriman, and TO-96 had found when they'd made their first big discovery. "We still know so little about it, and we couldn't risk going back to try it. Until now, that is."

"Let me get this straight," Abimbola said. "You are saying that we can use this generator to appear anywhere we wish within the known universe?"

"*Universes*," Ezo said in correction.

Abimbola let out a low whistle. "And all we need is a Novia Minoosh starship and someone to operate the contraption?"

"That's correct," Awen said. "Up until recently, I was the only one capable of stepping into the Unity to operate the QTG. But I'm certain Piper could do it." Awen paused, then looked at Rohoar. "And I believe Rohoar can operate it too."

The Jujari looked down at her, his eyes betraying at least a little shock. "You think so?"

"I do." Awen nodded.

"So I guess that answers my other question about how," Abimbola said. "But it seems to me there is some strategic advantage to keeping it open."

"Go on," Magnus said.

"Back on Limbia Centrella, we have an animal called the gorespike. It is a nasty creature. Very hard to kill… unless you lead it to a honeypot. Once its horned head is stuck inside the jar, you can deliver a killing blow to the soft part of its abdomen. But without the honeypot, you are likely to be impaled."

"You're saying we use the enemy's knowledge of the existing quantum tunnel to our advantage," Dutch said.

"Precisely," Abimbola replied. "The only thing better than knowing your enemy is knowing where your enemy is going to show up next."

"But is it worth the risk?" Awen asked. "I mean, what if they show up with ten times the force they just did? Can Azelon and TO-96 handle that?" She looked around the room. "Can *we* handle that?"

"I'm inclined to agree with Awen," Sootriman said. "If Admiral Kane commands part of the Republic fleet, what's to stop him from bringing more ships through the quantum tunnel when his latest squadron of fighters doesn't report back? We could be inviting disaster."

"Ninety-Six," Ezo said, drawing the bot's attention. "How many more ships and torpedoes can you work your magic on with Azelon?"

"That is an excellent question, sir. The answer depends on our proximity to the vessels in question, as well as the complexity of each system's command architecture."

"Can you take a guess?" Abimbola asked.

TO-96 regarded the hulking man with his glowing eyes. "I would propose we could handle at least three times the force you witnessed today."

Abimbola let out a whistle. Awen, too, felt both surprise and relief at the two AI's protective abilities.

"But I would caution any of you on relying too much on our abilities to commandeer starships and their respective ordinances," TO-96 continued. "While it is an impressive feat, to be sure, there are enough variables that alternative means of combatting the enemy should always be employed."

"And you had alternative means at your disposal?" Awen asked. "I mean, we still haven't seen what the *Spire* can really do in combat, have we?" Magnus cocked his head at her as if in admiration. Or was that attraction? She stared back at him. "What?"

Magnus offered her a small smile but said nothing.

"That's correct, Awen. Azelon and I still had traditional munitions at our disposal, should we have needed them."

Magnus leaned forward. "Which included…?"

"I can provide a complete list when you so desire, sir," Azelon replied. "For the purposes of this meeting, however, I believe such details to be irrelevant."

"Fair enough," Magnus said. "But I want that list."

"Noted, sir," Azelon replied.

"But back to Sootriman's point," Awen said, "do we really want to risk letting the enemy get so close to us?"

"What if we could do both?" Rohoar said.

"Go on," Magnus replied.

"What if we could close the tunnel for now but open it later when we want them to come to us?"

"I think this one is on to something," Abimbola said. "We

could subtly promote the reopening in a way that might speed the enemy's return precisely when we mean to close a trap on them."

"I like it," Magnus said. He looked at Awen, and then to the robots. "Is that something we can do?"

"Certainly," replied Azelon. "The QTG's functionality is contingent upon the individual operating it."

"But it still needs someone physically there," Awen said. "As in, I'd have to be in it to close and open new tunnels."

Azelon nodded. "That is correct."

"So, unless I'm staying behind, I have to close the tunnel and then create a new one somewhere else. We'll have to leave it open so we can travel between proto and metaspace. I'll need to be back at the QTG's controls when we want to reopen the old tunnel."

"Which works to our advantage anyway," Abimbola said. "We wouldn't want to be anywhere else but right here when the enemy comes knocking."

Magnus grunted in affirmation. "And we definitely can't afford to leave you behind, Awen."

She smiled. "Not unless you want your butts handed to you."

Magnus laughed a little and gave her a nod. "And we don't want that."

Sootriman spoke next. "So, the way I see it, the only risk would be if the enemy discovered the new tunnel before we were ready."

"That's correct," TO-96 said. "However, assuming that

you place the anomaly away from normal starship thoroughfares, I predict the enemy's discovery of it at such an infinitely low probability that I would deem it impossible, to use your nomenclature."

"I like the sound of that," Rohoar said. "But our enemy is wily."

"Agreed," Magnus said. "We don't know how much of the fleet Kane controls, and we have to assume he has eyes everywhere. I don't want us underestimating this enemy."

"Which means we should interrogate the prisoners for information," Abimbola said. He removed his bowie knife. Despite the sheath in his thigh rendering the Novia armor's chameleon mode pointless for that leg, he refused to give up the weapon. "And I will get as much out of them as possible before I dispatch them."

"No," Magnus said, waving a hand at the other man. "We won't be torturing them, Abimbola."

While Magnus wasn't looking at her, Awen felt that maybe he wanted to. Or maybe she just wanted him to look at her, knowing this change in procedure was certainly a result of their conversation. She was deeply moved to know that he'd taken her admonishment to heart.

"We'll get what we can without harming them, and that will be enough."

"Is the buckethead going soft?"

"I'm not going soft, Bimby. But I am saying that since I'm no longer a Marine and you're no longer a Marauder we need to do things differently. And I think we can get what we need without killing them."

"Fair enough. But if they try to do anything stupid, can we kill them?"

Magnus glanced at Awen. Was that a look of deference? "It all depends on what the *stupid* is," Awen replied.

Abimbola slid his knife back into his sheath. "This way sounds too complicated. But I will follow your lead, Magnus. Awen."

"Thanks, Bimby," Magnus replied.

There was a moment of silence before Awen asked: "So are we putting this to a vote then?" She looked around the room and saw everyone nod their heads.

"All in favor of closing the current tunnel and opening a new one, say aye," Magnus said, raising his own hand. Everyone else consented with raised hands and verbal acknowledgment. Magnus grunted. "It's unanimous then."

"So, where to next?" Sootriman asked.

"We need to rescue Willowood and those loyal to her," Awen said.

"And take another stab at that Swowlkoo human," Rohoar added.

Awen corrected him. "That's *So-Elku*."

"Not that it matters," Abimbola replied. "He'll be dead before anyone needs to use his name again. That is, if we are allowed to kill him." The hulk looked between Awen and Magnus.

"Just make sure he does something stupid enough to justify it," Magnus said.

"Oh, I will," said Abimbola, tapping his knife's handle with a finger.

"Awen, TO-96, and I will see to the prisoners," Magnus added. "Once we have spoken to them, let's all reconvene in the *Spire's* war room and make a plan for liberating those on Worru. Dismissed."

As everyone exited, Magnus looked at Awen. "Let's walk together. You too, 'Six." Awen nodded and stepped in beside him with TO-96 picking up the rear. "Azelon, you have the conn."

"Understood, sir," she replied.

As they entered the elevator and headed toward the *Spire's* brig, Magnus spoke in a low voice to Awen. "I'm wondering about Piper," he said.

Awen waited for him to keep going, but he didn't say anything more. "What about?"

"Do you think this is going to be too much for her?"

"What do you mean by *this*?"

"I mean Worru. The battle. The killing."

"It's a little late for that, don't you think?" When Magnus raised an eyebrow at her without replying, she waved a hand in the air in frustration. "I mean, she killed a Recon trooper down there—*by stopping his heart*, Magnus. She took another living being's life, and she's only nine. If you wanted to keep her away from the killing business, you already missed that starship."

"I know. And I didn't want that."

"You sure?" The words came out more harshly than she intended them too. "Ugh, I didn't mean it like that."

"I get it. You're watching out for her. This is just me trying to do the same."

Despite her frustration with the whole idea of involving a child in the first place, Awen appreciated Magnus's desire to watch out for Piper. She felt her features soften and regarded him with a look of appreciation. "What do you have in mind?"

"I'm just wondering if we shouldn't take her to Worru."

"You mean, leave her in the *Spire*?"

"No." Magnus shook his head and pressed his lips into a frown. "I mean, leave her on Ithnor Ithelia."

"By herself?"

"We'd leave TO-96 behind with her."

Awen heard the bot's servos move at Magnus's words.

"Maybe we see if Flow and Cheeks want to watch out for her," Magnus continued. "Plus, you said it yourself that you think she might be able to run the QTG. Maybe that's an asset we shouldn't overlook."

"If I may," TO-96 interjected.

"Not now, Nintey-Six." Awen tapped a finger on her lips. The thought of leaving Piper behind hadn't crossed her mind; this upcoming confrontation was the whole reason Awen had begun training her in the first place. *Or was it about helping Piper just to steward her own gifts?* The lines were getting blurry.

Keeping her back would certainly remove her from any

immediate danger. And having her available to open and close quantum tunnels could be an incredible tool, essentially allowing them to vanish and reappear anywhere in the void on a whim. Despite all of that, however, Awen had her own reservations.

"I'm not sure we can do without her on the battlefield," Awen said.

Magnus looked shocked. "Did I just hear Awen say—"

"I know," she said, waving him off again. "I know what you're thinking. I'm not saying we put her in the action, or give her orders to kill anyone—*mystics*." She rubbed her temple with a thumb, disbelieving she was actually arguing against Magnus's efforts to keep Piper out of harm's way. "But I do believe, now more than before, that her abilities could be a deciding factor if this comes down to a battle within the Unity. I don't think we can afford to leave her here."

"Pardon my interruption, but—"

"Can it, 'Six." Magnus looked hard at Awen as a smug smile crept at the corners of his eyes. "You do know that you don't sound anything like a Luma right now."

"We've already gone over this, Magnus," she said, punching him in the shoulder, then instantly regretting it. Her knuckles stung as they bounced off the Novia armor. "I'm not a Luma. I'm a gladia, just like you. And this is about what's best for the galaxy, not the factions we came from."

"What about what's best for Piper?"

"What's best for Piper is that she doesn't grow up in a

galaxy ruled by the likes of Admiral Kane and So-Elku. And the only way that happens is if we utilize her powers in the fight." She held up her hand again. "And I know that we've already talked about her ability to turn the tide if things get bad. You having second thoughts actually surprises me… it makes me feel like you've really heard my apprehensions. But now that we're on the verge of taking the fight to the enemy, I'm not so sure we can win without her. I think we have to put her in the battle like we planned, even if there is a risk that she might… that we might…"

"Lose her?"

"Mystics, don't say that," Awen said, squeezing the bridge of her nose. "I just don't want her to lose her innocence, to have her heart hurt. The desire to keep her away from all this is overwhelming sometimes, you know?"

Magnus nodded. "I do. And I don't want her getting hurt either—physically, psychologically, or emotionally. But in a certain way, we're already past that. She can't unsee what we've already lived through. And you know she'd just protest us keeping her back. In a certain way, it may hurt her more if we tell her she can't come."

"If I may," TO-96 said again.

"What is it, bot," Magnus said, his voice betraying his annoyance.

"You are forgetting one very obvious factor in all of this."

"And that is?"

"That if you leave Miss Piper for any length of time in metaspace, she will age disproportionately to you."

Magnus and Awen both looked at the robot. There was a moment of silence before Awen let out a long sigh. "And then there's that."

"Look like she's going with us," Magnus said. "Why didn't you say something sooner, 'Six?"

"But, sir, I—"

"Just speak up next time, okay?"

"But—"

"Hey, one more thing," Awen said. She felt her face flush before she even said the words. "It's about Valerie."

Magnus shook his head. "You don't have to worry about her, Awen. There's nothing there." Hearing him say that took a weight off her chest. Still, she searched his eyes to make sure they corroborated the confession. She stared at him long enough that he finally said, "Seriously. I'm a one-woman man."

"And I trust you," Awen replied. "Thank you."

"We are arriving at the brig level," TO-96 said, turning toward the door. "And we have some prisoner ass to kick."

"Ninety-Six," Awen yelled in rebuke. As Magnus brushed past her, she could have sworn she saw him grin. "Did you put him up to that?"

Magnus raised both his hands in the air as he walked away.

"Magnus!"

8

Magnus stood outside the brig, expecting the smooth white door to open as he approached. When it remained shut, his bioteknia eyes noted the data pad on the wall beside it.

"You okay?" Awen asked, clearly mistaking his hesitation for apprehension.

As much as he tried to ignore the emotions surfacing in his chest, Magnus had to admit that he wasn't looking forward to confronting Nos Kil.

"Yeah. Fine." He stared at the data pad a second more. "Azelon, can you open the door please?"

"Affirmative," she said, her voice coming over the speakers directly overhead. The door slid open and revealed a dimly lit control room, the far wall of which was a holo display. It had several command prompts outlined in red, as well as a sub window broken into sections. Each section had a view of what Magnus assumed were holding cells.

"You going in?" Awen asked.

He cleared his throat and then motioned her forward. "After you."

Awen studied his face. "You sure you're okay?"

"Mystics, woman. Just go in already, would you?"

She gave him a look that said, "Whatever," and then he followed her into the control room. The door closed behind them and some ceiling-mounted pin lights lit spots on the glossy black floor where Magnus assumed he and Awen should stand to command the system.

As much as he hated to admit it, he was not okay. The fact that Nos Kil was out of prison after all these years baffled Magnus. The former Marine's convictions included sexual misconduct, ill treatment of a civilian population in occupied territory during combat missions, unnecessary violence against enemy combatants, and murder. Nos Kil's multiple life sentences guaranteed that he'd never see the outside of the maximum-security military prison he'd been assigned to. And yet, here he was, caught operating with a rogue Recon team in an alien universe in Mark VII armor.

"Which prisoner would you like to attend to first?" Azelon asked over the room's speakers.

Awen glanced at Magnus. "What do you say?"

"Nos Kil first," he replied.

"The prisoner is being held in cell number one," Azelon said.

Magnus looked at the sub window marked with the appropriate number. A man lay on a bed on his back with his hands behind his head, staring up at the camera. He'd been stripped of his armor and wore only a pair of black military-style workout shorts. His muscular arms, chest, and legs were accented with tattoos and scars—both mementos of conflicts he'd seen. *And lives he's taken*, Magnus noted. He wondered how many had been for the job and how many had been for sport. For pleasure.

The sight of Nos Kil's deranged face brought back the painful memories of Magnus's last moment with his brother, Argus. He'd tried to bury those thoughts—those words and those hate-filled images. But still they haunted him, clinging to his memory like the barbed legs of a Falorian latch-spider. Seeing Nos Kil made the arachnid shudder and twitch as it clung to the inside of his skull, sending chills down his spine.

"You don't have to do this, you know," Awen said.

Magnus turned on her, surprised that she had come to some sort of conclusion that he wasn't privy to. "You're not in the Unity right now, are you? Like, reading my thoughts?"

"No. I'm not reading your thoughts. But I am in the Unity. And ever since you saw this man back in Itheliana, your energy pattern has changed. Which leads me to believe you know this man, just as he suggested when we captured him."

Magnus nodded, knowing he couldn't escape her keen insight. "I do, yes."

"And it's a painful knowing."

He pursed his lips for a second. "It is."

"Then let me do this."

"No," Magnus said, far more forcefully than he meant to. Images of what Nos Kil had done to the Caledonian girls caused his anger to surge. "I mean, no, that's not a good idea. I need to do this. Nos Kil might have information crucial for our mission's success, and if anyone's going to get it out of him, it's me."

"No," Awen replied, placing a hand on his chest. "It's us."

"Awen, I really don't—"

"Either we do it together, or you're not going in there at all."

Magnus looked from Awen back to the holo display. His eyes jumped to the last cell, on what he presumed was the opposite end of the brig, and he saw the second man. He too was bare-chested in shorts but was much leaner than Nos Kil. His uniform had read Longo. Magnus wondered if maybe he and Awen should start with him. But Magnus knew it was only a delay tactic to keep him from confronting the inevitable.

"Let's go then," Magnus said as his eyes moved back to Nos Kil's camera view. "Just… keep your head about you. This one is…"

"I get it. I'll be fine." Awen gestured toward the door that lead into the cell blocks and said, "After you."

Azelon unlocked the door and a pulsing red line appeared on the floor, indicating that he should proceed. Magnus stepped into a corridor that spread into five different anterooms, each presenting different cells.

"Please continue to cell block A," Azelon said. The red line pulsed forward and to the left-most fork. Magnus followed the path along the black floor and entered the cell block's hexagonal room. The holding rooms were spartan, providing the occupant a retractable toilet and bed. There was no pillow, blanket, or any other clothing provided besides the shorts.

At once, Magnus noticed the prisoner's head pop up and look through the translucent blue containment wall at him.

"Well, well, well," Nos Kil said, sitting up. "Company." He crossed his legs and rested his hands on his knees like he was about to go into some sort of meditation. "Husband and wife, is it?"

"How'd you get out of prison, Nos Kil?" Magnus asked, regaining control on the line of questioning.

The prisoner laughed, then stretched. Magnus watched the man's muscles ripple like giant cables spanning a bridge. Whatever training Nos Kil had committed himself to, it had put him in top shape, and the man clearly wasn't afraid to show off his body. "You would want to know that, wouldn't you."

Magnus waited for the reply, unwilling to ask again. After a moment's silence, Nos Kil answered with a roll of his head.

"They let me out on good behavior. Can you believe it?"

"Not for a second," Magnus replied.

Nos Kil snickered. "Neither would I, Adonis. It has been a long time, hasn't it? And look at you! I mean, your new fancy armor, a starship, and this incredibly delectable creature beside you." His last few words rolled off his tongue in long undulating tones more suited to an aristocrat than a soldier.

Magnus thought of defending Awen at the misogynistic address but decided that it would only put them further away from their goal. Plus, Awen could handle herself. "Who let you out?"

"You see there?" Nos Kil said, looking at Awen. "That's why the brass always liked Adonis. So keen and insightful. Never one to mince words."

Magnus waited, and Awen didn't reply.

"You're no fun, neither of you." Nos Kil swung his legs off his bed and stood up, stretching his back. "Someone at the top needed things done." He took a deep breath, letting the moment stretch on as if he was enjoying the warmth of some unseen sun. "Apparently, I had the skill set he required, and they let me out to play."

"Admiral Kane," Awen said.

Nos Kil spun toward her, smiling as if looking at a lavish plate of food. He bit his thumb and cocked his head.

"Admiral Kane," Nos Kil repeated, taking a step toward the shimmering blue force field. "Yes, that's what you know him as."

"So that's who ordered your sentence to be lifted?" Magnus asked.

"In a manner of speaking, yes."

"And he's the one who sent you here, to Ithnor Ithelia," Awen said, apparently assuming as much as Magnus had.

"Ithnor Ithelia," Nos Kil repeated, letting the words slide off his tongue in a musical way as he glared at Awen. "I did not know that's what it was called. Yes, I was sent here, and no, it was not Admiral Kane who sent me."

"But you just said—"

"I know what I said," Nos Kil said, his words biting into Awen's sentence.

"Then who issued your orders?" Magnus asked.

"And wouldn't you love to know, Adonis."

More calmly, Magnus repeated his question. "Who sent you?"

"Love," Nos Kil said, turning his shoulders toward her. "Did Adonis ever tell you he shot his brother?"

Magnus felt every muscle in his body tense. But he was prepared for this. He'd already thought through what he was going to say—to not let it get to him, and to confront lies with truth. Still, hearing someone say it out loud was like ripping off an old bandage that had bonded to a scab. "For failing to follow a direct order while—"

"He shot him in the head," Nos Kil said, ignoring Magnus, his eyes staring hard at Awen. "Because of a petty argument over a girl."

Magnus stepped in front of Awen and moved toward Nos Kil. The prisoner raised his hands in mock fear. "Please don't shoot me, private."

"I might," Magnus said.

"Ooo. So strong." Nos Kil tried to look over Magnus's shoulder at Awen. But Magnus held his ground. "Then who will you get your answers from?"

"The other prisoner," Awen said, stepping around Magnus.

Magnus watched Nos Kil's face twitch as Awen came forward. He didn't like that she just offered the enemy information for free. But, then again, she *was* a skilled negotiator after all. And Nos Kil had no idea if it was the truth or not. But her assertion had clearly caught him off guard.

"There were no other prisoners," Nos Kil said, cocking his head at Awen.

"Oh, not from your Recon team, no. You're quite right. But we did keep one of the pilots alive from the search and rescue convoy that was sent to find you."

Nos Kil hesitated. Given the look on his face, he clearly had no idea about the battlecruiser and the squadron of Talons—at least that's how Magnus interpreted the look on his face. And, apparently Awen did as well.

"So you didn't know about that, I see," she said. "How unfortunate that you weren't more valuable to your team."

Again, Nos Kil hesitated. Then, in what Magnus could only guess was a meager attempt to maintain control of the conversation, he said, "Okay, I'll bite, miss Elonia. Why is it apparent that I am not valuable?"

Awen looked at Magnus with raised eyebrows, then back at the prisoner. "They sent three Sparrow-class light armored transports with"—she turned to Magnus—"what were they, scientists?"

Magnus shrugged his shoulders. "Something like that." *Mystics, she was playing him.*

"That wasn't a rescue team," Nos Kil said, growing indignant. "That was…" He came up short, then started laughing. He waved a finger at her and then retreated back toward his bed. "You're very good, Miss Elonia. You almost had me there. But I'm not falling for your tricks. And I'm so very sorry to disappoint you, but I'm not telling you anything more about my mission, nor am I falling for your attempts to get me to question my value to my employer."

"So you're a hired gun," Magnus said. "Which means this isn't Repub sanctioned."

Awen looked at Magnus. "So that corroborates the other prisoner's confessions."

"Right," he said.

Nos Kil moved back toward the containment wall. "I thought you said you only had one other prisoner?"

"Did I say that?" Awen asked. "Whoops."

"Guess that's all we needed," Magnus said to Awen, then turned on his heels.

"Did he ever tell you how much he hated you?" Nos Kil said as Magnus started walking away. "Hated growing up in your shadow? That he secretly resented you for putting the Corps above your family?"

Magnus stopped.

Suddenly, Awen's voice spoke inside his head. *"Don't listen to him, Magnus."*

Magnus turned and looked at her. *I can't let this go, Awen.*

"Yes, you can. And you must. He's baiting you with lies."

But is it a lie?

"You know, earlier on the day you shot him, we'd been joking." Nos Kil chuckled a little. "I actually asked him if he'd ever shoot you if he had the chance. And you know what he said to me?"

"Walk away, Magnus," Awen said.

Magnus felt as though his feet were frozen to the ground. He couldn't turn and face Nos Kil but he couldn't walk away either.

"Magnus, I'm telling you: walk away." Awen's words were firm, like a mother who was issuing her last warning to her wayward child. A long silence filled the air. Magnus knew this coward was baiting him. He knew this was all a trick. Still, if there was even a shred of truth to what Nos Kil had to say, Magnus felt compelled to listen to what Argus thought of him on that last day. And yet he dreaded the answer.

"He said that if he couldn't pull the trigger first, he hoped you'd shoot him in the head so your last memory of him would be of his dead eyes staring you in the face."

Magnus turned away from Awen and strode toward Nos Kil.

"Magnus, stop," Awen shouted.

"Yes. Stop, Magnus," Nos Kil echoed. "Don't do anything

that could jeopardize your outstanding reputation in the Marines. Oh, wait, they have orders to arrest you? Whatever for?"

Magnus's nose was a few centimeters from the force field.

"Now there's the Adonis I knew," Nos Kil said. "The man who shot his brother, betrayed the Corps, and had himself relocated to the Recon so he didn't have to face the consequences of killing his own kin in cold blood."

"Shut up, Nos Kil."

"Must be nice to know a Caldwell who can pull strings for you instead of the limp one that couldn't even screw straight. Kid was a worthless piece of splick, if you ask me."

"Shut up." Magnus turned his head, ready to lower the wall and break the guy's face.

"*Magnus*," Awen shouted in his head. "*Don't let him get to you!*"

"And to think you saved me from those 'kuda in the camp. If you only knew how many of your men I would go on to kill in the mwadim's palace."

"You son of a bitch," Magnus roared. He felt every muscle in his body tense in rage as the revelation bored a hole through his chest. "Azelon! Lower the containment wall."

The force field vanished and Magnus charged Nos Kil. The prisoner's eyes flared as he placed his right foot behind him in a fighting stance. Magnus threw himself into Nos Kil's chest, letting his shoulder plate strike the man's sternum. He heard a *crack* as the Novia armor met bone.

The men flew backward and hit the cell's wall, then collapsed on the floor. Magnus began pummeling the man's rib cage left and right. He heard more bones break with every punch, filling each blow with the hate and vengeance he'd stored up for whoever was responsible for the ambush at the mwadim's palace.

Nos Kil tried to fight back, but Magnus's fury was so violent the man didn't stand a chance. Magnus managed to climb on top of the man, raining down more blows, this time on his head and face. Magnus ignored the explosions of pain jolting out of his hands and racing up his arms. This man had killed almost two whole platoons, plus dozens of Luma and Jujari. More than that, he'd quite literally started the fire that sparked the war.

Suddenly, Nos Kil flipped Magnus off him with a thrust from his legs. Magnus had been too caught up in his rage to realize he'd lost his balance, giving the enemy a perfect window of opportunity. The move happened so fast, Magnus had little time to push himself onto all fours. But as soon as he did, Nos Kil dropped a hammer blow on the back of Magnus's neck. A blast of stars filled the gladia's vision and he collapsed.

Despite his disorientation, Magnus rolled to his left and swung his right fist toward Nos Kil's face. The blow hit the side of his enemy's head, forcing the prisoner off balance. Magnus was sure he'd dazed him when Nos Kil replied with a punch of his own, catching Magnus under the chin. His teeth jarred together and his mouth filled with blood. But Magnus ignored the fluid, caught Nos Kil by the wrist with one hand, and reached toward his face with the other. Then he pressed his thumb into the man's eye socket. Magnus squeezed with all his strength, wrapping his fingers behind the victim's skull for leverage. Then he felt the eyeball pop, accompanied by the spray of the organ's liquid.

Nos Kil shouted, wresting Magnus's hand from his head, and bent the violating digit away in an unnatural direction. The takedown move forced Magnus to succumb, twisting in favor of the pressure point. But he wasn't fast enough—a loud *snap* followed by excruciating pain wracked him. It was all the time Nos Kil needed to deliver a chop against Magnus's throat that broke his airway.

Magnus looked up at the half-blinded prisoner, his face dripping with blood and water. While Nos Kil was maimed for life, however, it was Magnus who was mortally wounded.

"Goodbye, Adonis," Nos Kil said. Magnus felt the man reach around his throat. The next squeeze would suffocate him. But it never came.

Nos Kil's hands flew backward and slammed against the wall, held fast by some invisible force. Magnus—clinging to his last raspy breaths—watched as Nos Kil's body left the floor and slid up the wall. The man made to say something, but his mouth was clamped shut. In place of the expected curse came a muted shriek of intense pain. Nos Kil's face contorted, frozen in a state of agony.

"Magnus," Awen yelled. "Magnus, talk to me!" She hovered over him and pulled his hands away from his throat.

Based on the look on her face and the way she stared at his neck, he expected it was deformed. "Mystics… Azelon! I need a medical evacuation right away!"

But Magnus knew there was nothing Azelon or Valerie or any other medic could do in time to save his life.

9

Moldark was close—closer than anyone had been before him. He could feel the anticipation rising in his bones like the heat of an eons-old fire whose flames had died out long ago but whose embers still lay dormant under the ash. A fresh wind blew, summoning the coals' orange radiance back to life, causing a new fire to burn, kindled from the remains of an ancient vendetta—one Moldark had sworn to fulfill.

And he *would* fulfill his oath. His wrath would visit as many other civilizations as it could in the process—so long as it served his final purpose. Which this assault certainly did.

"Lord Moldark?" the man asked, and not for the first time. Fleet Admiral Brighton had been standing below Moldark's raised dais for at least a minute, trying to gain the leader's attention. But Moldark had been too lost in thought to provide the admiral an audience. Instead, he watched the space battle unfold from his quarters.

The conflict had grown to include dozens of battleships and hundreds of support vessels and fighters on both sides. Sypeurlion and Dim-Telok ships had redoubled the Juajri's efforts, while the three Republic fleets deployed their full contingent of Talon squadrons and engaged in unbridled ship-to-ship combat.

The destruction, Moldark thought, *was beautiful.*

In the black space above Oorajee, bright bolts of deadly energy crisscrossed one another as the massive leviathans slowly maneuvered to gain the upper hand. Meanwhile, minuscule star fighters zipped over their hulls like Melfarene mosquitos looking to draw blood from Bandalor mule bears. Blaster fire ripped through the void and splashed across force fields, sending ripples of energy into the abyss. Missiles streaked in one direction only to be followed by salvos going the opposite way as both sides tried to take out the high-speed fighters that continuously tried to evade the guided ordinance. And all around, Moldark imagined that he could hear the screams of the dying as their bodies vaporized in the void's cold vacuum.

"My lord, I'm sorry to keep insisting, but—"

"But we haven't heard back from the squadron we sent into metaspace."

Brighton hesitated. "That's correct, my lord."

Moldark turned from the floor to ceiling windows and gazed down upon Brighton. "This concerns you?"

"It does, only because of the time dilation you mentioned. At this point, the reinforcements will have had days to report their findings and—"

"You fear them to be lost."

Brighton placed two fingers under his collar and adjusted it. "Yes, my lord."

Moldark sighed. It was a pity how much these humans labored over trivial losses. *And for that reason alone*, he mused to himself, *they will never evolve far enough to contend for supremacy.*

"What are your orders?"

Moldark turned back toward the space battle. "Do you see that vessel there?"

"My lord?"

Moldark gestured to Brighton to ascend the dais, then pointed toward a large Jujari starship that floated against the orange planet's backdrop. "That one there?"

"Yes. I believe that's the Jujari dreadnaught *The Victory of The Infinitely Majestic and Illustrious*—"

"I don't care what it's called, admiral. I care that we focus our weapons on it and destroy it."

Again, Brighton hesitated.

"Is there a problem, admiral?"

"No, my lord. But I feel I should remind you that—"

"That the ship I've designated is a Jujari Dreadnaught-class battleship capable of meeting our assault with its own. I need no reminding from a *man*, admiral. Or do you forget with whom you are speaking?"

"Yes, sir—*my lord*."

"But if you'd been paying attention, you'd know that the enemy's focus has been on keeping three battlecruisers at bay. As such, they will not notice our strike."

"You want to interrupt Second Fleet's assault with one of our own? But that might—"

"Risk damaging the battlecruisers? Then I suggest advising them of our actions to mitigate our losses, admiral. All weapons to full power, no quarter. Target the enemy's reactor."

Brighton's mouth worked the air without producing sound. Finally, his will found traction with his voice, and he said, "But sir, that won't give the Jujari crew any time to abandon ship."

Moldark spun on Brighton. "Are you here to play games, admiral? Is that what this is to you? I said *no quarter*."

"No quarter. As you wish, my lord."

"I will come to you on the bridge in a moment. Ready weapons systems. Dismissed."

Moldark listened to Brighton's footfalls as he walked toward the exit and left the grand hall. The admiral was a fool, of course. They all were, what with their holding to antiquated rules of engagement derived from nearsighted agendas to extend mercy toward a conquered enemy. Moldark cursed to himself, wondering where such resolutions had been when his people were ripped from their planet and cast into oblivion.

"Where was our quarter?" he said, seething at the stars. "Where was our chance to escape?" The answer, of course, was nowhere. For no mercy had been shown. "And thus, none will be given."

Moldark remembered well the screams of his kin as the Novia came to tear his people from their temples and imprison them. And for what? To source a prize the Novia could not produce for themselves? Moldark ground his teeth until his cheeks bled. "So they took, and took, and took, until the land was raw and rivers were filled with blood."

Finally, it was Moldark's time to take. To consume and devour. To tear asunder and rid the galaxy of the vile pest whose appetite knew no end. It was his moment to reconcile the long outstanding accounts. It was time for vindication.

But it would not stop with the Novia Minoosh and their kin, the Jujari. Moldark's quest for blood had grown, extending toward any who stood to gain by feeding off the presence of another. And if there was ever a species who'd inherited and magnified the traits of the Novia, it was the humans. Their lust for that which was not their own seemed insatiable—no doubt the cause of their rapid evolution and domination in this pathetic sector of a crumbling galaxy.

Moldark would end them. He would end them all.

THE *BLACK LABYRINTH* came to starboard and aimed the chord of its body toward the Jujari battleship Moldark specified. He smiled as dozens of anti-ship quad cannon and missile battery targeting reticles overlapped one another, displaying readiness icons on the tactical holos throughout the bridge. It was time for a kill.

The deck plating that protected the Jujari ship's reactor core lay like a tricerasaur's armor across the soft flesh of its posterior, keeping predators from its secondary heart. And like the armored beast of the Tradelands, the Jujari's defenses could only sustain so much before plates were compromised and the inner flesh was violated. One strike, the monster would fall.

The bridge crew worked themselves into a fervor as outstanding directives were reassigned or dismissed in place of Moldark's new objective. He also wondered how much of their frantic activity was due to his presence on the *Labyrinth's* bridge as this was a location he hadn't frequented since ousting Kane.

He strode up and down the length of the room, examining workstations and checking status reports. None of the officers met his gaze, each averting their eyes and busying themselves with their respective holos. The power, he admitted, felt good. It had been several millennia since he'd commanded a military force—none such as feeble as this, he admitted. But it served his needs. *For the present, at least.*

Brighton stepped away from a command station and moved toward Moldark. "All systems are ready, my lord. We have target lock with 93% of our fixed assets reporting in."

"Excellent. Pull our remaining fighters back. As soon as they're clear, give the order."

"As you command."

Brighton called the Talons off and waited for the last one to pass beyond the estimated blast radius. Second Fleet's battlecruisers still weren't entirely clear, but their shields would deflect most of the energy. And though Moldark hated to admit it, he needed all the ships he could muster, for this was only the beginning.

The bridge's feverish activity reached a climax, and then —as the moment of engagement became imminent—a window of silence opened up. All those present seemed to pass into the eye of a hurricane, momentarily caught in a state of suspended animation, holding their breath for the destruction that was to come.

"Fire," the Fleet Admiral said.

From atop the bridge, the *Black Labyrinth* appeared to vomit a wide stream of light toward the enemy ship. The deck shuddered as quad cannons flung blaster bolts in rapid sequence toward the target ship. Torpedoes tore free of their launch bays and drove forward with the unrelenting will of flood waters.

Moldark watched as the wave of munitions streamed toward the singular target on the enemy ship. The sight was beautiful—a highly focused lethal expression that was impossible to arrest. *How fitting*, he mused, feeling a certain camaraderie with the violent assault. Of course, with so much energy diverted from the rest of the ship to power the weapons for this attack, the *Labyrinth* was vulnerable to incoming fire. But as his ship was not at the forefront of the battle lines, Moldark could afford to take the momentary risk.

It was like stepping from the shadows to make a kill, only to recede into the cover of darkness once the murder was complete.

The energy weapons broke upon the Jujari ship's shields first, beating the defensive capacitors into submission. Within seconds, the unrelenting barrage of blaster fire bored a hole in the force field that caused the enemy ship's generators to give out. The remaining blaster energy not spent on the shields continued toward the ship's stern where it struck a section of deck plating on the port side.

Like a swarm of mad firewasps trying to penetrate a Boresian taursar's thick hide, the blaster bolts pooled on the armor until the metal glowed beneath the withering assault. Just when the plate seemed it would liquefy, the first wave of torpedoes arrived. The guided ordinance came at oblique angles, careful to stay clear of the blaster fire and avoid premature detonation. But when they did detonate, the explosion blew out large chunks of the enemy ship. Deck plates and long sections of trussing tore free, glowing red-hot as they spun into the void. Amputated tubes spewed water, sewage, and hydraulic fluid like blood from severed arteries, and electrical arcs snapped across the debris field, searching for any path willing to connect its endless desire to continuity.

More blaster fire burrowed into the new opening, digging deeper and deeper into the beast's hide. Likewise, more torpedoes arrived, gouging out more flesh with every devastating explosion. Despite the fact that the Jujari vessel maintained its attitude, trajectory, and speed, the hemorrhage it suffered would be fatal in a few more seconds.

Moldark's lips pulled back in a wicked grin as the enemy vessel spewed fire and debris from the gaping hole in its stern. He could practically taste the fear of the Jujari crew on his tongue as they realized what was happening. The ship returned fire and attempted to roll away in an effort to hide its wounded flank from the enemy's assault. But their weapons fire did minimal damage to the *Labyrinth*. If anything, the lashes goaded Moldark on, increasing his lust for the pending kill.

"More," he said to Brighton, imagining a thrashing animal caught in death throes. "I want more."

"But sir, we're already at—"

"Tell the fighters to fire."

Brighton turned and gave the order, his voice strained but in control. At once, all Talons in the vicinity came about and lent their NR330 and T-100 blaster cannons to the relentless stream of blaster fire. Several star fighters released torpedoes and bombs, adding to the continuous eruption that chewed into the monster's bones.

Moldark threw a hand over his eyes as a piercing white light drilled through the bridge's observation window and flooded the room. It took a split second for the ship to lower the windowplex opacity from the detonation. As soon as it did, Moldark willed himself to see through the spot in his vision and watch the Jujari vessel tear itself apart.

A quantum ring formed at the epicenter of the explosion

and raced away from the collapsed core. The blast wave overtook the *Labyrinth* with a jolt, rattling workstations on the bridge as if the terminals might rip from the floor. Moldark grabbed a seat back and steadied himself, sneering with wicked glee. He watched as the ball of white light split the enemy ship in two, pushing the halves apart like fresh fillets cut from a fish's flanks. The ball of light continued to expand, overtaking the remains in a cataclysmic inferno.

Over the next minute, the *Labyrinth's* quad cannons spun wildly, taking out pieces of the dead ship that threatened to collide with it. Additional torpedoes were spent attempting to push away the largest sections, forcing them off into space. When at last the explosion subsided, the bridge crew took a collective sigh and resumed their duties.

"Ship's status," Brighton said, demanding reports from his officers throughout the bridge.

"Shields at 67% and holding, admiral."

"All weapons systems normal."

"Capacitors depleted by 71%. Recharging initiated. Torpedo reduction 44%. Replenishment underway."

Propulsion, life support, and communications all reported satisfactory levels as well.

"Enemy ship destroyed. No life signs detected," said the sensors officer. "However, several Talons are damaged or missing, and the *Dawn of Trudeau* is reporting failures in life-support and engines, with heavy damage to decks seven, ten, and twelve through fifteen. They're requesting immediate assistance."

"Relay the message and monitor for traffic," Brighton said.

"Aye aye, admiral."

Brighton turned to Moldark and spoke in a low voice. "Mission success, my lord."

"No, admiral. The mission is just beginning. *That* was a taste of what's to come. I want all ships pressing in."

"My lord?"

"Push them forward," Moldark replied, stressing each word. "We just set precedent. This is no longer a routine naval battle. It is an annihilation. No quarter, no reprieve. Pursue all retreating enemy ships."

"But Lord Moldark, I must—"

Moldark's hand snapped out and clutched Brighton by the throat. The admiral gasped, his veins bulging from his head's reddening skin. "Do I need to find another officer to do my bidding, Fleet Admiral Brighton?"

Brighton's feet hovered a few centimeters off the ground. He clawed at Moldark's gloved hand, but nothing relieved the pressure around the man's neck. Saliva sprayed through pursed lips as Brighton replied, "No, my lord."

"Excellent." Moldark released Brighton. The admiral collapsed on the floor, both hands holding his neck. "I will be in my quarters."

10

Awen felt panic rise in her chest as she looked at Magnus's broken throat. The skin was already bruising, and an unnatural divot indicated where the trachea had been shattered. His face was also turning a deep shade of red as he strained for breath.

Strangely, however, Magnus seemed to be at peace. He looked up at her with passive eyes.

"Magnus, you're going to be okay." That's all she could think to say. But it was a lie. And she suspected Magnus thought that too. He winced, then struggled for a short rattling breath. "Azelon," Awen shouted again.

"The team is twenty-six seconds from your position, Awen," the AI said. "However, I regret to inform you that, based on my scans of Magnus, I do not expect that there is anything we can—"

"Quiet," Awen ordered. The prognosis Azelon was about to give was all Awen needed to do something she'd never done before. If medicine couldn't save Magnus, then she would. "Hold on, Magnus. I've got you."

Still in the Unity and holding Nos Kil against the wall, Awen spent the rest of her energy to focus on Magnus's neck. Everything resonated discordantly, signifying that the harmony of his physiology had been disrupted. The vibrant colors that normally filled all sentient beings were dull and muted. There amidst the conflicting tones, she could see the components of his broken throat. Pieces of cartilage stabbed the esophagus and trachea, while burst blood vessels bathed the larynx in fluid.

Awen could clearly make out every piece of cartilage and bone, every ruptured blood vessel, and every layer of tissue. She concentrated more forcefully and found that she could see nerves and cells, even down to the neuro-electric transmission of information telling Magnus's brain that systems were failing.

Without her knowledge of the Foundation and the Nexus, Awen would have been unable to do anything with what she observed in Magnus. It was, in fact, a common skill among the master Luma to see nature in such vivid detail. But once she'd discovered the Novia Minoosh's training in the Unity, she was able to manipulate the forces of the universe in ways previously unimaginable. At least she'd been able to back on Neith Tearness. This… this was going to be something brand new. And something she'd never forgive herself for if she didn't at least attempt it.

Awen kept Magnus's injuries in front of her, much like holding an object in her hand. Meanwhile, she forced her spirit down through the Foundation and into the Nexus, plunging her essence into the interconnectedness of all things. Instantly, Awen felt a surge of power that rivaled anything in the galaxy. No star, no supernova, and no black hole could compare to the awesome power that flowed through the Nexus.

Radiant magenta light streaked through a horizon devoid of time, gravity, or mass, colliding in dazzling arrays of oranges, reds, yellows, and purples. There, like a system of roots beneath a forest, the light coalesced into streams that fed more universes than she could imagine. Understanding this level of existence would take the rest of her lifetime—*will take untold lifetimes*, she realized. But she wasn't here for the secrets of the cosmos, she was just here for the blueprint. Magnus's blueprint.

Awen stretched her spirit out and found what she was looking for faster than she'd expected. It was Magnus. His life force, the very essence of all that he was and may ever be. And there, ensconced within it, was the model of his neck. It appeared to her as easily as a doctor might display a bio scan on a holo feed. She reached out and grabbed it—not with her hand so much as with her heart—and carried it aloft.

She rose through the Foundation and returned to the failing apparatus of his flesh, careful to keep his body suspended from movement. Then Awen brought the image of Magnus's neck to bear on the reality of his body, overlaying them in perfect alignment. When she was satisfied, Awen drew from the tether she still had in the Nexus, allowing its energy to flow up from the deep like marine vibrations through an anchor line. The current surged through her soul and filled Magnus's neck with such power that she was tempted to look away. But there was nowhere to turn.

Instead, Awen watched as the energy began to express itself, first touching the quarks and atoms of every molecular bond in Magnus's throat. The power swirled and grew, collecting and spreading until it had dominion over every elemental construct. It sounded to Awen like a conductor who arrested an out of order symphony and brought it back in tune and back in time.

Now fully formed into a loud chorus, the song placed unrelenting pressure on the structure of Magnus's cells, reordering them according to a magnificent dance. Awen caught her breath as the objects reformed by the millions, the hundreds of millions, and even billions, reshaping the injuries so as to align tissue and bone with the perfect image she'd plundered from the deep. Blood was pulled away from passages reserved for air and refilled the newly pressurized vessels in which it belonged. Cartilage retook its form, muscle tears healed, and nerves rejoined.

With her natural ears, Awen heard small pops and cracks as Magnus's neck reformed under her care. He groaned, trying to fight her, but she held him in place, just as she maintained control over Nos Kil, who was still pressed against the wall overhead. Awen also watched as Magnus's neck retook its shape. She marveled at the otherworldly manipulation, watching as even the bruising diminished. At last, the neck was reformed, and the blueprint she'd brought up from the Nexus fused with Magnus's body, locking the work in place.

Adrenaline surged through Awen's body, keeping her conscious. The entire process of trying to heal Magnus had exhausted her, and were she asked to do it again, she knew she'd fail. At least until she got some rest. The effort had required her undivided attention and all the virtue she could muster. *Hopefully*, she thought, *it's enough*. Her limbs trembled as she searched his eyes for signs of life.

Suddenly, Magnus gasped, taking his first deep breath in over a minute. As the color returned to his face, Awen felt a wave of relief wash over her. He blinked at her, touching his throat, and then his armored chest plate. She watched his chest rise and fall, then was startled when Magnus touched her face.

"Awen," he said, cradling her cheek in his rough palm. "Was that... did you just—"

"Shut up and kiss me," she said, then leaned down to press her lips against his. The emotion of almost losing him caught up with her and filled her eyes with hot tears of gratitude. Life was fragile—the thread of its essence so tender that even the simplest breeze might break it. As Awen savored the heat of Magnus's face, holding it with both her hands, she was amazed at just how many times they'd come close to plummeting over death's edge. But here, as before, they rested on the shores of the living for just a little longer. *And perhaps*, she wondered, *we may yet live long enough for us to grow old together.*

When she pulled away, Magnus looked into her eyes and said, "That was beautiful."

"You're not such a bad kisser yourself," she said, though—arguably—she didn't have much experience in the practice.

"No." Magnus shook his head ever so slightly. "I mean, what you just said, about growing old together."

Did he hear me say that? In his own head?

"What about this, by the way?" Magnus held up his broken digit. "You can save a guy's life but not his finger? What gives?"

Awen gave him a sarcastic grin. "That's what you get for not listening to me."

Suddenly, the cell block filled with people.

"We're here," Titus yelled, taking in the scene. "What's going... *holy mystics.*"

Awen looked over her shoulder to see Titus carrying what she assumed was some sort of crash cart. Ezo, Sootriman, Abimbola, and several others had also filed in, each carrying various medical devices. All except Saladin.

"What is that?" Awen asked, pointing at the Jujari.

"I believe it is the Novia Minoosh's equivalent of a mop," she replied. "I was in the galley, and TO-96 informed me that we had a mess to clean up."

Awen laughed and then helped Magnus sit up.

"I did say that," TO-96 replied. "However, I was attempting to utilize—"

"Never mind, Ninety-Six," Awen said as she gave Magnus a once over. "You okay?"

He nodded. "Thanks to you. Just feeling a little shaky."

"It will wear off."

"Is… is everything okay here?" Ezo asked. "Because Ezo can't figure out what's going on with…" He gestured at the couple on the floor and the prisoner still pinned against the wall. "You know, with all this."

"It's fine," Awen said. "We're all good now."

"I had a little run in with the prisoner," Magnus said, waving Abimbola toward him. "Things got out of hand and Awen took care of it." The giant Miblimbian pulled him to his feet, then Magnus turned to face Awen and noticed Nos Kil still stuck on the wall, grimacing in pain. "And apparently she's *still* taking care of it. Come on, everyone back away from the cell."

When the group of gladia stood in the cellblock and Awen was satisfied, she said, "Azelon, raise the containment wall."

"As you wish, Awen," the AI said over the cell block's speakers. The translucent force field popped back to life once again, casting a pale blue light over those gathered in the anteroom—as well as on the prisoner within.

Still awake inside the Unity, Awen released Nos Kil and watched his body fall to the glossy black floor, now marred with his congealing blood. The man gasped and whimpered as he pawed for something to hold onto, much like a newborn baby emerging from the womb.

Dutch walked up beside Magnus. "Are we good here, LT?"

"Yeah," Magnus replied. "Awen has it under control."

"But, about the prisoners, I thought you said no—"

"I know what I said," Magnus said. "I lost control. But Awen stepped in to account for my…"

"You don't have to finish that."

"Either way," Magnus replied, "she saved the day."

Dutch eyed Awen up and down. "Damn, woman. You are one tough—"

"And don't finish *that* one either," Awen said, raising a hand. "I got it. And, thanks."

"Don't mention it."

"Well," Magnus said, wiping some blood off his chest plate. "Looks like we have another prisoner to interrogate. Might as well do this one together. Who wants to talk first?"

HER MOM WAS ASLEEP. And she looked so beautiful that Piper dared not wake her up. Everyone knew how cranky people got when they were woken up too soon. Plus, her mom had just been through a lot. It had been a long day, and her mom deserved some sleep.

Of course, for her part, Piper couldn't sleep. She was too excited from the day's events. And now that they were back on the *Azelon Spire*, it meant they were probably going home... wherever their new home was going to be.

As much as Piper wanted to stay in Neith Tearness, Awen had explained that some sort of time *dialotamation* wouldn't allow for it—or something like that. The whole thing was kinda complicated. Like a lot of adult things were. But Awen always knew what she was talking about, so Piper just accepted the fact that they had to go back to their regular universe. At least for now, anyway.

Piper was hungry, so she slipped out of their room, asked Azelon to light directions on the glossy white floor, and started walking toward the ship's galley. That was when she felt something shift in the Unity.

"Miss Piper," Azelon said, "where are you going? You are deviating from the path to the galley."

"I know, Miss Azelon, but... I feel something."

"Please define."

Piper scrunched her face up. "I duh know. It's like..." Piper decided to try and answer Azelon's question more accurately, so she slipped into the Unity and reached out with her second sight. There, bursting through a hundred walls in the starship's hull, came an image of Mr. Lieutenant Magnus fighting with a bad guy. Piper screamed.

"What is the matter, Miss Piper?" Azelon asked.

"Mr. Lieutenant Magnus... he's fighting the other guy, and..." She covered her mouth. "Now he's hurt, Miss Azelon! He's hurt so bad!" Piper's eyes flooded with tears. She snapped back out of the Unity. "He needs my help right now!"

There was a long pause before Azelon answered. "No, Miss Piper. It appears that you will be safer if you remain en route to the galley."

"No, Miss Azelon, no!" Piper was off and running down a different corridor now, her heart pounding so loud in her chest she thought it might burst. She *had* to get to Mr. Lieutenant Magnus, she just *had* to. And right away.

Piper felt her slippered feet slide along the floor as she ran around corners, eventually stopping at one of the fancy elevators. But the doors weren't opening.

"Miss Azelon, why won't the doors open?"

"Because, Miss Piper, I cannot permit you to attend to this situation. Miss Awen has already summoned adequate help."

"But… no! I have to be there. I have to save him just like he always saves me."

"Always saves you, Miss Piper?"

"In my dreams!" Ugh—bots could be so slow sometimes. "He saves me in my dreams, so I have to make sure to save him when he needs me."

"As I said, Awen has already requested adequate—"

"Open these doors right now, Miss Azie." Piper adopted the name Mr. Lieutenant Magnus used with her, hoping it might *pervade* her more. Maybe it was *persuade*. Either way, Piper stomped one foot as she'd seen her mother do to get a point across.

"I'm sorry, but I—"

Piper gritted her teeth, scrunched up her eyes, and slipped into the Unity. She didn't have her power suit on right now, so she knew she couldn't do super extra amazing things, but she could at least try and open the doors without much effort. There seemed to be a flow of energy surrounding the door linked to small devices that looked a lot like the servos on TO-96's arms. *Those must control something useful*, she thought. So she reversed the flow of energy to them.

"Miss Piper, what are you doing?"

"Opening the doors, Miss Azie." Piper stayed in the Unity and stepped into the elevator. Then she focused on where Magnus and Awen were, and told the energy surrounding the elevator to take her to their floor. The elevator door closed, and the small pod began to move.

"Miss Piper, I must advise you that taking control of the *Spire's* system without the consent of the commander is not only inadvisable, it is a direct violation of Novia Minoosh Starship Conduct Protocol Number—"

"In case you hadn't—haven't have—have noticed, Miss Azie, the ship's commander is hurt real bad. And if I don't get down there and save him, he's probably gonna die. Or worse."

The AI's voice hesitated. "Or worse?"

"Yeah, *real* worse."

"Miss Piper, I must insist that—"

"You're kinda starting to annoy me now, Miss Azie."

"Annoyance aside, I must—"

"I'm gonna turn you off now, okay?" Piper focused on all

the energy coming to the elevator, especially the stuff around the speakers, and followed it backward for a while. It was really, really deep somewhere in the ship, and tracing it was getting boring. So she just pushed against the flow a little. Not enough to hurt Miss Azie, but enough to keep her from interrupting her so much over the speakers. Maybe this was what her mom wanted to do to Piper sometimes when she talked a lot. And Piper could talk *a lot*.

"Miss Piper, you are vi-olay-ay-ay-ate—" Azelon's voice stuttered and then turned off with a small *click*.

"That's better," Piper said out loud, thinking that she'd now be able to focus on saving Magnus. Once she got to the appropriate floor, she brought the elevator to a stop and made the doors open. She ran down the hall, slid around several corners, and then reached out to sense where Magnus was.

Now he was standing up. That meant he was okay! She focused on Awen and realized maybe *she'd* helped save him. This made Piper so happy she thought her heart might explode from joy. She wanted to find out what had happened. But Magnus and Awen were moving now, to another room. She was getting close to wherever it was they were.

She rounded another corner and then saw a big door in the middle of the hallway. It looked super important and had a data pad to the side. Piper expected the door to open, but it didn't. She scrunched her nose for a second and thought some more. Letting Miss Azie talk again might be bad 'cause Piper knew she might get in trouble for taking over the elevator and stuff. Better to leave that for later. She could just open this door by herself again.

Piper found the thingys that moved this door but they were bigger than the elevator's. That didn't really matter, though, because the energy flow was the same. This was way easier than finding trees in the Foundation or moving up waterfalls with Awen. Really, all she was doing was telling little doors to open using their control boxes.

She walked inside a dimly lit room with glowing red trim everywhere. A giant holo screen filled the far side of the room and Piper noticed her friends walking outside of a small room with somebody in it. In fact, there was another room with somebody else in it, but her friends didn't seem interested in him. This place… it looked kinda like a jail or something. Piper suddenly realized that maybe this was where they were keeping the bad guys they'd captured—the pilot and the Marine from the hole in Itheliana.

"Miss Stone," said an image of Azelon on the holo display.

Piper winced. *Miss Stone* was what her tutors called her when she did something bad in class. And she could tell by Miss Azie's tone that the AI wasn't happy with her. "Hey… how'd you get in here, Miss Azie?" Piper asked, trying to be as sweet as possible.

"Miss Stone, you are not allowed to be on this deck. I must insist that you—"

Piper rolled her eyes. She was tired of everyone *insis— insists— insisting* that she do what they wanted her to do. Now even the AI was telling her what to do? *No thank you.* "Bye, Miss Azie." Piper slipped back into the Unity and stopped the flow of energy to the holo display. In fact, she stopped all of Azie's energy to everywhere in the next few rooms; that way the AI couldn't bother her.

"Now…" Piper said, scratching her chin. "Let's see…" Isn't that what all the adults said when they had something to figure out? And scratching her chin tickled. So she stopped. There was only one door leading out of this control room, so she stepped up and opened it. As soon as she stepped into the hallway, she heard talking up ahead, coming from one of the five forks in the hall. She'd taken no more than a few quiet steps and was about to find Mr. Lieutenant Magnus in the Unity when she heard a voice to her left.

"Psst, little girl."

Piper turned to see a man lying on a bed in the first big room. His face looked bloody, like he'd just fallen off his hover bike without a helmet. And while she couldn't see all of him, he seemed super strong and had lots and lots of weird looking tattoos on his arms. Suddenly, she recognized him from the fight in Itheliana. He was the man that Magnus had captured from the hole in the ground.

"You're a bad guy," Piper said.

"Why do you say that?"

"Because you tried to kill my friends."

"Tried to kill—?" The man propped himself up a little more. He had a lot of bruises and dried blood on his chest. "Listen, I was defending my men. Your *friends* attacked *us*."

Piper wrinkled her nose. "But Magnus said you were—"

"The bad guys?" The man shook his head and looked frustrated, like someone had just stolen his bowl of cereal. "First I'm the bad guy, and then I'm an unarmed prisoner and Magnus does *this* to me." He gestured to his swollen eye socket.

"Magnus hurt you?" Piper would have rejected the accusation right away if she hadn't seen Magnus do hurtful things to other people. Piper knew she could do hurtful things too, but that's why Awen worked so hard with her to control her powers. Suddenly, Piper wondered if Magnus had lost control of *his* powers and done this to the prisoner. It wouldn't have been hard to do—after all, Magnus didn't have a power suit like she did.

"Maybe there's something I can do to help you," Piper said, filled with concern for the injured prisoner.

"Like what?" The man sat up, eyebrows raised.

"When I'm sad or hurt, sometimes I just need someone to talk to."

"Well, I could use a friend right now."

"Then I can do that, I suppose." Piper turned from where the rest of the voices were coming from and headed toward the bleeding man in the small room.

11

"I KNOW what you're trying to do," Ricio said to the foremost figure, the one called Magnus, "and it's not going to work."

"And why's that?"

"Before you were trying to scare me into telling you something." Ricio touched his still-sore stomach. "Thanks for all that, by the way."

"Pleasure," Magnus replied.

"And now you're trying to establish trust with me. You're nice to me, I'm nice to you, and everyone gets what they want."

"Who said anything about being nice?" asked a rather enormous looking man, clearly a Miblimbian.

"And who said you get what you want?" said the Jujari through its clenched teeth. He'd never seen one up close before, not still alive anyway.

"I was only making suggestions," Ricio said, trying to placate the two giants with his hands. "Easy, *easy*."

"Listen, this doesn't have to get bloody," Magnus said.

"Is that what you said to the last guy too?" Ricio nodded at the blood stains on the *former* Marine's armor. "'Cause something tells me that line doesn't mean what you think it means."

Magnus gave a little grin. "It all depends on how forthcoming you care to be. I'm simply saying that you have a chance right now to answer our questions before things have to get… *personal*." Magnus cracked his knuckles.

As much as Ricio had been trained for this sort of situation—though he very much doubted that a scenario quite like this was on the Navy's mind when they trained him—he really didn't feel like being tortured today. And, strangely, these people didn't exactly seem like hardened war criminals. Though, he admitted, they certainly seemed like they knew how to handle themselves. Not to mention they were in some crazy alien armor, flying around in an alien ship in an even stranger alien galaxy that was, quite literally, off the charts.

Ricio licked his lips and folded his arms. "So, hypothetically speaking, let's say a guy like me is interested in answering questions from a really weird group of individuals like yourselves. What kind of things are we talking about? And what do I get in return?"

"Ezo is getting really fed up with this guy already," a disgruntled looking Nimprinth said. "Can we just toast him?"

"Easy, my love," said a tall, large woman. Her tanned skin

and exotic features had a rather alluring power to them. She had to be Caledonian. In fact, he'd put money on it.

"Mystics, you really are an extremely eclectic bunch," Ricio said.

"I can make your face eclectic with my missiles," the bot said.

Ricio laughed. But so did a few of the other members of this group. Then he heard Magnus whisper to one of the other female soldiers, "Tell 'Six to stay quiet, would you?"

"You know," Ricio said, unfolding his arms. "You're not exactly the most terrifying group of interrogators."

"Trust me, small pilot, I can change that," the big one said.

"I don't doubt that. But I'm still… I don't know. I can't figure this thing out."

"And what's that?" Magnus asked. "And I encourage you to be as specific as you can."

Ricio considered Magnus—considered each of them really. Something was going on here, and he wanted answers. "None of this adds up for me."

"Again, how so?" Magnus said. "Last chance."

"All right, all right, don't get your panties in a wad." Ricio took a deep breath, realizing that he was about to divulge top secret information… at least in general terms. "So, they sent us out here to take down enemies of the Republic."

"Who's they?" Magnus asked.

"It was Admiral Kane, wasn't it," the Elonian said.

Ricio cocked his head. Everyone in the Navy and the

Corps knew Admiral Kane. That wasn't what piqued Ricio's interest. It was that the woman singled Kane out from all the other admirals in the Navy. Mystics, she'd singled that name out over the hundreds of captains and commanders who could have ordered a squadron on a mission. The odds of that were at least suspicious.

"I'll take your silence to mean it was," Magnus added.

Ricio gave him a curt nod. "Anyway, they tell us to follow a ship that left Oorajee largely undetected. It was only luck that we picked up its signature. Weird thing is, it heads to the middle of nowhere and then vanishes without a trace."

"Sounds like a real threat if you ask Ezo," said the Nimprinth. Ricio kept looking around wondering which one of them was Ezo and why this guy was his spokesperson.

"All the same, those were my orders," Ricio said, looking from the Nimprinth back to Magnus.

"You weren't given any more information about us?" the Elonian asked.

Ricio shook his head. "Nope. And even if I had, I'm not exactly sure I would have believed it. I mean, you're not exactly the sort of people I'd pictured fighting."

The Elonina spoke into Magnus's ear but still loud enough for Ricio to hear it. "He's telling the truth."

"You're a Luma then or something?" Ricio asked her. The woman shot him a glance that suggested she wasn't entertained by the question. "Okay, okay, relax. Just seemed like a very Luma thing to do, what with mind reading and all." He paused to study them, considering what to say next. "So I gave you my bit. Your turn—who are you guys?"

The Eloninan looked as though she was going to object, but Magnus spoke first. "We're trying to stop Admiral Kane."

Ricio whistled and rocked back, expressing a mix of genuine surprise and mock shock. "And what, exactly, is he guilty of, Mr. Former Marine? I'm guessing somebody ruffled your feathers and got you dishonorably discharged or something?"

"Yeah, cause I'd totally risk all these people's lives to save my reputation," Magnus replied with a sarcastic tone. "Come on, jockey, do better than that."

"Okay, okay… then just what—pray tell—is Admiral Kane guilty of?"

Magnus looked like he was hesitating. In fact, they all seemed a little tense. Ricio wondered if they actually had something on the man—or, *Moldark*, as it was. Perhaps they had intel about his strange transformation, or maybe—just maybe—they had spies inside Moldark's secretive faction of the Republic. For some strange reason, Ricio actually found himself rooting for these underdogs. He *wanted* them to have something on Moldark. *Anything*. But perhaps that was asking too much. There was no subterfuge at work with the Republic. Ricio was simply working for the highest echelons of the Navy now—*the Paragon*, Moldark had told him.

"That's what I thought," Ricio finally said, turning to sit on his bed. "You don't have a thing. You're just some random pocket of rebels looking to take potshots at the Republic because somebody killed your sister and you want revenge. I've heard it a thousand times." He swung his legs up on the bed, folded his arms behind his head, and lay down. "Fill out the necessary forms and submit your complaint—it will be a whole lot less trouble for you than all this, and you might actually see a couple hundred credits in reparations. Have a nice day."

Magnus stepped forward and crossed his arms. "He ambushed peace talks, captured a Republic senator, kidnapped one of our crew and murdered her inner circle on Ki Nar 4, and is attempting to illegally acquire advanced alien technology."

Ricio popped his head up. He held himself there for several seconds, waiting for someone—anyone—to laugh. When no one did, he decided to, and sat upright. "Oh, now that's rich right there. And I've heard a lot of splick in my time. But you"—Ricio circled a finger at the group—"you all win the trophy. This is just outstanding."

He continued laughing, but when none of their faces seemed entertained—or even put off—Ricio's ridicule died down. He cleared his throat. "I take it you all actually believe this then."

"We do," said the Elonina. The rest of them nodded.

"And you have proof?"

"More than we know what to do with," Magnus added.

"Then why not take it straight to the Republic?"

"Would you?"

Ricio thought about it. "If it's as bad as you say? Eh, I suppose not. But still, this all seems—"

"You're telling me you haven't noticed anything?" Magnus asked. "Over the last few weeks, maybe months… it all seems normal to you?"

Now it was Ricio's turn to hesitate. He squinted at Magnus. Ricio wanted to just laugh at this man's face as he was clearly having delusions of grandeur. Only, Magnus didn't seem pathological. In fact, none of them did. And he could hardly believe that such a diverse group of individuals would ever work together for a common cause unless it was, in fact, a legitimate cause.

But to Magnus's point—yes. Ricio had in fact noticed plenty that wasn't "normal." Hell, Admiral Kane's transformation into Moldark was perhaps the craziest splick Ricio had ever seen. And he certainly seemed to have acquired command of all three fleets rather quickly—and all on the eve of war with the Jujari. And talk about delusions of grandeur, Moldark's made Magnus's look pathetic by comparison.

"Let's say that I have noticed some strange, hypothetically speaking. What does that gain me here?"

"We won't kill you today," the Jujari said.

"And how's that comforting? It just sounds like tomorrow is the next best option."

"That's why it's comforting."

Magnus cocked his head at Ricio. "If you're willing to give us more information about Admiral Kane, his superior, and the ships at his disposal, then—as the Jujari has said—we'll spare your life, Commander Longo."

Suddenly, the Miblimbian tensed. Why, Ricio had no idea. But the giant seemed to study Ricio with more interest than before.

"Furthermore," Magnus continued, "if you're willing to entertain our proof and you find it convincing, we could use another good pilot around here."

"You want me to work for you?" Ricio snickered.

"With us," the Elonian added. "There's a difference."

"For, with—*whatever*. I'm not buying it." But the more the seconds passed, the more Ricio had a strange feeling that these misfits were more integral to the Republic's survival than he cared to admit. Call it a gut feeling. Which gave him even more cause for concern: his gut was rarely wrong. "Why don't we jump straight to the proof then. I've never been one to move slow."

Magnus straightened. "Fair enough. Azelon, bring up the footage of Nos Kil's confession about the bombing." Ricio looked around the cell block and wondered if Azelon wasn't a shipboard AI. When the order was met with silence, Magnus repeated the request. Still the AI did not reply.

Ricio looked around the cell block. "Is something supposed to be happening here?"

Magnus turned and looked at the bot with the missiles and blaster on its forearms. "'Six, where's Azelon?"

"Unfortunately, sir, she seems to be unreachable."

"What do you mean unreachable?"

"I mean, I am having trouble finding her on the ship's mainframe. This is highly unusual."

"Well find her, dammit."

"Magnus," the Elonina said, her voice matching the look of concern on her face. "Something's wrong… Mystics, It's Piper!"

As if on cue, the scream of a little girl cut through the cell block.

12

With Magnus and Awen interrogating the prisoners, and a short reprieve to prepare himself for the encounter, Rohoar had returned to the bridge alone. He was both eager and apprehensive to see where the conversation might lead. While he'd had some time to process the startling revelation of his long-lost ancestors, the Novia Minoosh, he had not had any occasion to speak with Azelon about it. Until now. So when he saw Azelon turn around to greet him from in front of the bridge-wide holo display, he was entirely unsure of how to start the conversation.

"Azelon, this is Rohoar," he said, guessing the introduction was pointless only after he'd spoken it.

"I am aware of who you are, Rohoar of the Tanwhack," the bot-AI replied. "Welcome."

"Thank you." He moved to the captain's chair and sat

down. He noted, once again, how the seat fit his body's shape and mass perfectly.

"I was hoping to speak with you alone," Rohoar said.

Azelon looked around the room and then back at the Jujari. "It seems you have found an opportune time to speak with me then."

He nodded. "Yes. And not just you, but… you know. *You.*"

"As in the Novia Minoosh within the singularity?"

"Yes."

"We are all here," Azelon replied, suddenly using the plural pronoun. There was something strange about speaking to an entire collective at once, all channeled through Azelon and this starship. How they'd even managed such a technological feat was beyond Rohoar.

"Are you here to discuss your ancestry with us?" Azelon asked.

The hackles on Rohoar's neck went up. "Yes."

"How may we help you?"

Rohoar had thought long and hard about what he was going to say and about all the questions he might ask. But now that the moment was upon him, he felt unsure of how to begin.

"Rohoar, how may we help you?"

He shifted in his seat and moved his tail since it was falling asleep. "I have so much to ask you that I do not know where to begin."

"Why don't you begin with what you know, or at least with what you suspect that you know."

Rohoar licked his chops and sat back. "That seems wise."

He began with the stories that he'd inherited from his father, and his father before him, going back to what he believed was the very beginning of his people. Just as he'd detailed on Neith Tearness with the rest of Granther Company, Rohoar recounted the history of mwadims, of how the Gladio Umbra parted ways with their kin and escaped to the stars, eventually opting to leave the universe and settle on Oorajee.

There was a long pause as Azelon seemed to take in everything he said. "All of this, as you have recounted it, is true, Rohoar of the Tawnhack."

An intense wave of emotions flooded Rohaor's chest. It was as if some magical fairytale that was too lofty for reality had suddenly been yanked from the land of fiction and dropped into reality. If he had been told he could now fly, he wouldn't have been any more dazzled by the truth of it.

"And so, here I am," Rohoar said.

"Indeed," said Azelon.

Rohoar didn't know what to say next. But he hoped maybe Azelon might. When she didn't continue, he added, "And what do you think of me?"

"Could you please rephrase the question?"

Rohoar flicked his ears. "Are you… all of you, are you mad with us? Mad with me?" The question made his face hot, as though it were asking something he shouldn't.

Azelon stepped forward and tilted her head. "Why would we be mad with you?"

"Because... well, because we abandoned you."

"I see," said Azelon. She moved her head again. "We are not mad with you, nor do we feel that you abandoned us."

"You don't?" The sense of relief that washed over Rohoar was overwhelming. Still, some measure of apprehension remained locked in his chest. "Why not?"

"Because, Rohoar of the Tawnhack, your ancestors did what they believed was right. We did not fight, though we did dispute. In the end, however, it was the ardent belief of each faction that they should be free to pursue their beliefs unobstructed by the assertions of the other. Therefore, each party deemed it necessary to separate in ways that would serve the other's best interests."

Rohoar blinked several times, flaring his nostrils and smelling the air. It was out of habit more than anything else, trying to detect some pheromone or another in an attempt to determine the speaker's truthfulness. He was, of course, speaking to a non-biological being, so he scolded himself for being so unintuitive.

"Are you relieved, Rohoar? Your vital signs seem to indicate so."

He nodded. "I am, yes. More than you could know."

"We are pleased to hear this."

"Why?"

"Because we too have often wondered what happened to you, our kin."

"You have?"

"Of course. You were never our enemies. Only our lost

brothers and sisters. We were, to put it in your terms, quite excited to see you when you arrived in the system. We knew it would only be a matter of time before you recognized yourself in the shadow of our world, opting to let you make the discovery yourself rather than burden you with insight that may inadvertently harm your psyche."

This was as Rohoar had suspected, and he felt a certain connectedness over the shared conclusion. "I thank you for your patience."

Azelon nodded. "As more time has passed for us than for you, this meeting provides a welcomed termination to a milleniums-long question. Though, we might point out, our perception of time is dramatically different than when we were organic lifeforms. Therefore, this resolution is as much instantaneous as it is dramatic."

"I can imagine. I think. Well… I am glad to provide you with a sense of closure." Rohoar fidgeted in his seat, unsure of what to say next. The relief he felt knowing that there was no hostility was truly overwhelming. Once again, he wished his father could have been here to witness all this.

"My sire… he was right."

"About what?" Azelon asked.

"You. This." Rohoar gestured at the starship's bridge. "This realm of the universe. All of it. He believed it was not a bedtime story for our pups. He believed it was real."

"And the rest of your tribe did not?"

Rohoar raised an eyebrow. "In truth, the rest of our tribe

knew nothing about it. Only a small percentage of the ruling tribe had some of the facts, and most used it as a fiction for their children. Even most of the mwadims thought it was a fairytale."

"But your father didn't. Why?"

Rohaor's ears perked up. "I do not know what made him different. But, somehow, he knew the stories were sacred. He knew you were out there—out *here*."

"Then why did he not come to us? He had the stardrive, did he not?"

"He did, yes. But he feared the reunion might result in conflict as our tribes had grown violent over the centuries. The last thing he wanted was for an otherwise peaceful meeting to be marred once again with a stain from our people."

"We are all the same people," Azelon said. "And any bloodshed would be the responsibility of us all."

"Only you wouldn't be the ones doing the bleeding."

"Perhaps."

"We, of course, didn't know that you would be…" Rohoar restated, still thinking it was uncanny that Azelon embodied all that was left of the Novia Minoosh. "We didn't know that you'd be like this."

"Non-biological, you mean."

"Correct."

"It is unnerving, we understand."

"May I be permitted to ask more questions?"

"Of course, Rohoar. How may we serve you?"

"How many of you were there? Before, you know, *this*." He motioned a paw at Azelon.

"If by this you mean our singular state of shared consciousness, then the answer is 832,674,901 Novia Minoosh."

"That is a very precise figure," Rohoar noted, overwhelmed at just how many of his ancestors there had been at one point.

"We are a precise species."

"As are we." Rohoar thought better of his response. "As we were, but still are." He shook his head, frustrated with himself. "My apologies. This is all rather… confusing."

"In what way is it confusing, Rohoar?"

Rohoar shrugged. "There was almost a billion of you, and now, I'm speaking to a robot." He held out a paw. "No offense intended, Azelon."

"None taken. We all understand. It must be rather sterile to look at a non-biological unit and attempt to associate it with an entire species."

"Especially when Azelon doesn't even look like a Jujari. Rather, a Novia."

"Would you like to see what we looked like?"

Rohoar's heart thumped loudly in his chest. "You… you can show me this?"

"Of course. Our records are extensive, filling vast libraries—both in the natural realm and in the Unity. Awen has already encountered one such library on Ithnor Ithelia."

"How? How may I see all of this?"

"There is a limited archive on the *Spire*, but the unabridged histories lie secured within the temple library. I believe you would use the term *firewall*."

Rohoar sat forward. "So there is content you can show me now?"

"Of course. Observe."

Suddenly, Azelon's body began to glow—not just her eyes or the blue joints between plates—*all of her*. Rohoar squinted, accepting the pain as permission for not missing a single moment of whatever was happening.

From Azelon's thin body emerged thick bones that seemed to change her stature from the streamlined and erect robot to a hunched and hulking Jujari skeleton. Muscles, sinews, and tendons appeared to grow out of the bone, followed by tissue, blood vessels, and skin. At last, a thick layer of fur grew from countless hair follicles, forming into a luxurious black and white coat.

Rohoar stood up slowly, his mouth agape. While the creature was definitely related to him, there were several aspects that made it wholly different. For one, the beast was at least a head taller than Rohoar. The snout was longer and more slender, and the ears were also narrower. And where a Jujari tail was short and rather stubby, this being's tail was longer and more bushy.

When the creature spoke, Rohoar nearly sat back down in shock, but caught himself instead. "This is as we once were, Rohoar," the Novia said in a gravelly voice shrouded by its row of sharp teeth. Or was it Azelon's voice, just changed to resemble a Novia?

"This... this is what you all looked like?"

"The representation you see before you is a composite of all subset averages. An amalgamation, as it were. What do you think?"

"You are..." Rohoar wasn't sure what to say. "You are worthy of admiration."

"Thank you. As are you."

Rohoar dipped his head in honor of the compliment. "May I approach you?"

The Novia—or Azelon—bowed and rolled its head to the side, exposing the neck. Rohoar felt a shiver run down his spine. The gesture was a Jujari one... which was a Novia one, apparently.

He crossed the open space and began to circle the being, taking in all of the details. He couldn't help but marvel at seeing a representation of his ancestors. The emotions swelling in his chest wanted to make him weep and roar all at once. The figure looked so real he thought he could reach out and touch it. He raised a paw but then stopped himself.

"It's okay," the creature said—*Azelon* said. But in the Novia's voice still. "You may touch me."

Rohoar's paw shook slightly as his digits caressed the soft fur of the Novias's arm. "How is this possible?"

"Hard light," Azelon said. "Generated at an atomic level so that the atoms of your body are pressing against but never disrupting the atomic bonds of the projection."

"Fascinating."

"And so, it is these bodies that you abandoned for the sake of your singularity."

"That is correct."

Rohoar removed his hand and felt his shoulders slouch.

"Is something the matter, Rohoar?"

He sighed. "I am sad."

"Why?"

"It seems like such a loss. You were a beautiful people."

"It was our choice," Azelon replied. "One which represents the apex of our evolution."

"Do you regret it?"

"Regret is a construct of a biological sentient's need for self-preservation and, therefore, has no bearing on our collective consciousness."

"Yes, but…"

"But what?"

Rohoar felt as though words were stuck in his throat and he didn't know how to retrieve them. Instead, he shook his head and stepped back. "Thank you for showing me."

"You are most welcome. Are you satisfied with the presentation? Or would you like me to remain as I am?"

"You can go back to being Azelon. I think that might be better for now."

"As you wish." In reverse order, the body's layers began to dissolve, retreating into the bones and then reforming into the slender shape of the bot.

Rohoar sniffed the air, noting that the display had neither

projected the heat nor the smell of a Jujari. The lack of either made the experience feel sterile. Which, strangely, was how his heart felt. He walked back to the captain's chair and sat down. When he looked back at Azelon, he felt grateful to see her, not wanting to think further on the lives that were forfeited to make the Novia's dream of a singularity possible. The thought of so many lives, so many bodies... of so much death made his stomach churn. How was it that such a poor decision had been willfully entertained by such a technologically advanced species? Clearly, Rohoar had many more questions to ask.

But rather than spend the rest of this initial conversation on himself, Rohoar decided to act in the best interests of his team. Any clues he could glean as to what the Republic's rogue admiral and his Recon team were after, and why they'd want to frame someone like Magnus, might go a long way in gaining a foothold over the enemy in the coming conflicts.

"May I ask another question, Azelon?"

"Of course."

"The Recon team in Itheliana. You said to Magnus that they were nearing something of great importance. What was it?"

"We chose to withhold that information from Magnus for several reasons. However, to you we will grant access, given our unique relationshhh—"

The glow of Azelon's eyes flickered.

"Please st-st-stand by."

Rohoar's ears perked up. Something was not right.

"It seems that I am ex-ex-experie—unexpected core-ore-ore malf—due t-t-to—increased—"

"Azelon?" Rohoar asked, standing up. "What's the matter?"

All at once, Azelon's body went limp and her body's glow went out.

"Azelon?" Rohoar raced to the bot and touched it, but there was no response. It was if the sentient life-force had left her body.

A new voice erupted inside his head. "Rohoar," Awen yelled. Rohoar spun around but the Elonian was not on the bridge. "We need you in the brig, now!"

"Awen, where are you?"

"Come to the brig. It's Piper."

ROHOAR BURST from the elevator and ran down the brig-level corridor on all fours. He slammed into walls around each turn, leaving claw marks on the glossy white floors. As he neared the brig's main entrance, he saw that the door was open. He darted inside, moved around the control consoles, and passed into the hallways leading to the five cell blocks. Gathered around the first one was a group of people struggling to stare through a small window in a blast door.

"Thank the mystics you're here," Awen said, turning from the group and motioning him to come closer.

"What's going on?"

"It's Piper. She's barricaded herself in cell block one."

"Why can't you just open the door?"

"I have been restricted from accessing the door's actuator," TO-96 said. "And Azelon seems to be offline for the moment."

"What about a manual override?" Rohoar said.

"There isn't one." Magnus stepped away from the window and made room for Rohoar. "The only person who's able to control this door right now is Piper."

Rohoar stepped forward, turned his head to the side, and looked through the opening with a large Jujari eyeball. He saw a bloodied prisoner lying unconscious on the floor in his cell.

The Jujari was about to ask where Piper was when he caught sight of two little feet tucked up under her legs. She was barely visible, sitting on the ground to one side. "What's going on here?"

"We don't know," Awen replied.

Magnus shook his head. "We were interrogating the second prisoner in cell block five when we heard a scream. As soon as we got here, the blast door shut, and now she won't come out."

"Can't you speak with her?" Rohoar asked Awen.

"I have. But she only wants to speak with you."

Rohoar pulled away from the window. "Me?"

"Yes. She said she won't talk to anyone else."

Rohoar was growing tired of all these emotions in his chest. It was so exhausting. "Did she say anything else?"

"No."

"And that prisoner?"

Magnus grunted. "The bastard probably said something, I imagine. He's a son of a bitch."

"But he looks dead."

"I shut him up," Awen replied.

Rohoar turned to her, curious. "You used the Unity to kill him?" It didn't seem like something a Luma would do… or *should* do.

"No. But mystics know I would have liked to."

Magnus cast Awen a surprised look, as if startled by this admission.

But Awen merely shrugged at him. "What?"

"So you have made him unconscious," Rohoar stated.

"He's asleep for now. I'll release him once we've retrieved Piper. I don't want him saying or doing anything else while she's in there. Until Piper speaks to you, we really have no idea what went on in there."

"I understand." Rohoar took a deep breath and then closed his eyes. "Let me try."

13

Piper trembled in the corner of the cell block. It felt like someone had just put firecrackers in her and set them off. All that was left was heat, pain, and the smell of something that made her eyes water. Hot tears ran down her cheeks. She felt alone. And despite the fire blazing in her heart, she felt cold. So cold.

The man, the prisoner, was asleep now. Awen had done that. Awen was also trying to open the door, but Piper didn't want it opened. Not yet. Right now, she just wanted to be left alone. She didn't want to speak with anyone. Well, except Rohoar. She would always speak with him. She'd told Awen as much too.

The man had said horrible things to her. Things she wasn't sure she could ever forget. Things about Magnus, and about his brother Argus. He'd told her terrible things about other girls… things that made Piper's head create images that she never wanted to see.

"Piper," came a voice from inside the Unity. "Are you there?"

She slipped into her second sight and saw Rohoar standing in the middle of the cell block. He moved toward her and rested on his haunches.

"I'm here," she replied, smearing tears away with the backs of her hands. "Thanks for coming."

"Everyone would like you to come out. To open the blast door."

"No." Piper shook her head and then buried it in her arms. "I don't want to. And don't try to make me."

"I won't."

There were a few seconds of silence. Piper looked up and noticed that the big doggy had slid a little closer. "What happened, little one?"

But Piper didn't want to talk about it. It hurt too much.

"Did that man say something to you?"

Piper nodded. "Mmm hmm."

"May I ask you what he said?"

"Yes, but I don't want to say."

"Why not?"

"It hurts."

"He hurt you with his words?" Rohoar's voice sounded like he was getting angry—not at her, but at the prisoner.

"Uh huh," she said from under her arms again.

But there was another reason Piper didn't want to repeat

what she'd heard. She was worried that she might get in trouble with Magnus. Even with Awen and the others. She knew secrets, things that no one else in the whole wide galaxy knew. At least that's what the man had said. And if she told the secrets, Piper was sure she'd get in trouble. All the adults would be so mad with her.

Worse still, Piper was mad with Magnus. She couldn't believe that he was capable of killing his own brother, and of doing horrible things to little girls. But this prisoner had been so convincing. She'd told him that she didn't believe him, but that didn't seem to affect him at all. He'd said that her lack of belief didn't make what happened any less true. And somehow, Piper felt he was right. She'd experienced that in her own life: trying to ignore the facts surrounding her father's death didn't mean she was any less guilty of his murder.

Life, she was beginning to realize, was hard. There was more dark than light, and the flashlights were getting harder to find. Maybe that's why she wanted Rohoar here, because he was a good person to light the way forward. He was not a Marine who'd hurt little girls or killed his brother. He was also not a Luma who tried to correct her every day like Awen. In fact, the big Jujari was a lot like her—different, misunderstood, and special.

When Piper looked up a second time, Rohoar had scooted beside her. While she knew it wasn't possible, somehow she felt his warmth envelope her—not just from within the Unity but with her physical body as well.

"May I provide hugs?" Rohoar asked.

"No. And it's just *a hug*. Unless you're giving someone lots of them all at once."

"May I provide a hug then?"

"No."

"I see. So the difference in quantity does not have a bearing on whether or not they are comforting?"

"I don't know. I just… it's that—"

"Piper? Are you in there?" Her mother's voice came from the hallway. She'd just arrived, and Piper saw her standing between Magnus and Awen, fist pounding on the window. "Come out here, baby. Open the door. Please."

"Your mother would like you to come out," Rohoar said.

"I know. I can see her."

"I think everyone would like you to. I know I would too."

But the thought of seeing everyone right now made her afraid. "I'm scared, big doggy. I just want to crawl into a small hole in the ship where no one can find me and stay there."

Rohoar sighed. Again, it was as if she could feel the beast's hot breathe play with her natural body's hair. She almost opened her normal eyes to see if he was there, but she could see his body still standing in the corridor with everyone else, eyes closed.

"Once, when I was a pup about your age, I'd broken something that belonged to my father."

"Was he the mwadim then?"

"Yes, he was the mwadim then."

"What did you break?"

"It was a gold bracelet that my mother had given him

when he'd conquered the last challenger and became the leader of our people. So it was very special to him."

"How'd you break it?"

"I was using it to play catch."

"You mean fetch?"

"I'm not sure I understand," Rohoar said.

"It's what we play with dogs on Capriana. We throw something, like a stick or a ball, and then they bring it back."

"Little one, I have already explained this. I am not one of your canines."

"But you could play fetch if I throw you something, right?"

"You're missing the point. I was throwing it to my brother when it struck a rock and broke."

"I bet your daddy was mad." Piper looked up at Rohoar's face to see what he'd say.

"He wasn't mad."

"He wasn't? Because mine would have been."

"But he was sad."

"Because his bracelet broke?"

"No." Rohoar rested his head against the wall and looked off in the distance. "Because I'd endured the pain of wondering how I would tell him about it for three days."

Piper thought she understood what the big doggy was saying. But this seemed like it was really important to him. So she wanted to make sure. "You kept it a secret because you didn't want to get in trouble."

"Of course, yes. But when I finally told him about what

I'd done, he wasn't nearly as mad as I imagined he would be. Yes, he was upset that my mother's gift had been damaged. But he was more upset that my heart had been hurt. And with each day that passed, that pain became greater."

"Would you have told him sooner? I mean, if you knew he wouldn't be mad with you?"

"Certainly. And I would have saved myself the pain of keeping the secret in my heart. Those things do something to you. It's like a thorn in your paw that festers the longer you let it remain. But if you can face the temporary pain of pulling it out, you save yourself the long-term pain of letting it stay in."

"Rohoar?"

"Yes, little one."

"I don't have paws."

She felt a blast of air play with her hair.

"But I do have fingers, and sometimes they get splinters if I'm playing in the woods. I think that's sorta the same."

"It is similar, yes."

"So you're saying I should talk to Magnus?"

"Perhaps. That's up to you. But I'm at least suggesting you open the door and let your mother in. We'd all like to make sure you're okay."

"I am okay." But that wasn't true. "But I don't feel okay." The emotions swirling in her heart were getting stronger. The images of what the prisoner had told her were coming back. They were more clear, as if she'd been there. As if she'd been one of the little girls that Magnus had hurt. As if she was his brother, Argus, who Magnus shot just because he was jealous of his brother's advancement. The emotions were stabbing her chest like knives now. It was painful. Painful because she couldn't imagine what those people felt under such dark forces. And painful because... because...

What if Magnus was still capable of all that evil?

The prisoner had said Magnus had changed a lot. And he was doing great things for the galaxy. But some things never changed in a person, no matter how much people wanted them to. Like Piper's powers. That'd made her stand out in school because she was so different. She'd wanted to run away from her "gifts" as her mother called them. But she never saw them as gifts. And now she wanted to run away from everything the man had told her.

Piper wasn't sure if she could look at Magnus again. Let him touch her. She wanted to ask him if all the things were true. But in her heart, she knew they were. The prisoner couldn't be making them up—there was too much truth to them. They'd been said with conviction.

Worse, if she did speak of them, what if it provoked Magnus to do something horrible to her? What if he... *what's that word?* What if he *reslipped* into his old behavior. *No, relapsed.* Yes, that was the term her mother had used for people who went off their medicines.

So, Piper wouldn't speak of it.

She would make something else up. And then she'd pretend that the *something else* was real enough that she believed it—that they all would believe it. After all, her imagination was a powerful thing, or at least that's what her mother had always said. And then—maybe then—that would allow her to act normal around Magnus and Awen and the others. The secrets would be locked away in her heart, and no one would know. It felt painful, like Rohoar not telling his father about the broken bracelet. But this was much worse than a piece of gold jewelry. This was about people's lives.

Piper was suddenly aware of a furry arm wrapping around her. How long it had been there, she wasn't sure. But it was warm and soft. And it pulled her close.

"Mr. Big Doggy, you're hugging me."

"I know." Rohoar paused. "Do you want me to stop?"

Piper felt as though she'd been embraced by a warm blanket. "No, it's okay. Just as long as I can pet you later too."

The Jujari sighed. "I will permit it. But just once."

"Same. Well, maybe more than just once. More than one hug feels nice."

And with that, Piper activated the actuators and opened the blast door.

14

"Has she told you what Nos Kil said?" Magnus asked Awen. They stood alone in the war room waiting for the other platoon leaders and key leaders to arrive. Magnus had grown agitated over the last two days, fearful of what the sadistic man had said to the little girl.

Awen shook her head, her face betraying a hint of remorse. "No. Just that he was really mean to her."

"Really mean?"

"Those are her words. She said he shouted at her and said he wanted to kill her."

"Mystics." Magnus rubbed his face with his hand. "I can't believe I let that happen. I should have been more attentive."

"But you didn't let it happen. Piper did that herself. *She* overrode Azelon, *she* walked into Nos Kil's cell block."

"Yeah, but we should have had security measures in place to keep that from happening."

"Magnus, she outmuscled an alien AI using her powers in the Unity. You can't create security measures for that."

"Can *you*?"

Awen jerked back in surprise. "No. Not against her."

"Then she's too powerful for her own good."

"Magnus!"

"No, I didn't mean anything bad by it. I just…"

"What did you mean?"

"I just meant that I understand why you wanted to train her so badly now. The only way that someone with that type of power exists in the galaxy is if she's taught how to manage her gifts."

"That's better," Awen said with a curt nod.

"And how's Azelon? Doesn't she have some audio or video of what happened?"

"Unfortunately, no. She says she's mostly back to normal."

"Mostly?"

"Apparently there's still some system memory loss, but the bots are working on it. She assures me she'll be able to repair everything."

"'Six confirmed that?"

Awen nodded. "He did. Whatever Piper did created a kind of energy pushback that essentially shut down her sensors and expression extension, confining her to the ship's core for a short period of time. Eventually, she was able to reconfigure her systems and regain control of her faculties. But had she forced more energy into the system…"

"She could have kept Azelon pinned down?"

"Something like that. I'm just glad she didn't. TO-96 said it could have been a lot worse."

"Worse? As in…"

"As in, she could have crippled the ship and eliminated Azelon altogether."

"You're kidding."

"Nope. Fortunately, the Novia Minoosh's singularity exists on a core on Ithnor Ithelia, as well as a backup of Azelon's core."

"Do you think that's what Nos Kil was after?"

"Hard to say." Awen tapped her lips. "Azelon says it's still proprietary information. But somehow, I think it's more than that."

"More than a singularity core of an entire alien species?"

Awen shrugged. "What would Kane do with it?"

"Well, he could… I mean there's always… Eh, I've got nothing."

"Exactly. Sure, he could try and tap it for information, maybe try and repurpose the hardware or something—if there is any. But he's not a scientist or a theorist. He's a Navy admiral."

"Right," Magnus said, even though he had doubts about Kane, ones only recently acquired. Over the past two days, Magnus had continued to meet with the more willing of the two prisoners—Ricio. The pilot had been surprisingly forthcoming in his answers, almost convincing Magnus that the prisoner wanted to join their resistance. But until Ricio was properly vetted, even Magnus and all his optimism had to conclude the man was an enemy combatant.

Still, his intel about the rogue Repub admiral was disturbing at best. And even if Magnus's changing opinions about Kane were to be believed, they still didn't change the fact that the enemy was out for blood. "Which is why I think whatever Nos Kil was after is a weapon. And that's not just the Marine in me speaking."

"It's the gladia in you," Awen replied.

Magnus's smile widened even further. She was attractive when she got tactical. "Well, I just wish Azelon would come out with whatever is down there. All this secretive stuff is pissing me off."

"Easy, big guy." Awen rubbed his arm with her hand. "All in due time."

Her hand felt good on his arm. It stirred something deeper within him—*something you don't have time for, Adonis.*

"Hey," Awen said, still touching him. "How are you doing? With Nos Kil's confession I mean?"

Speaking of things he hardly had the time to process. Or maybe didn't want to process? "I'm glad I know now."

Awen searched his face as if looking for something more. When he didn't say anything further, she asked, "That's it?"

"Yeah, that's it."

But that wasn't it. There was so much more. Feelings of anger, betrayal, and of deep regret that Magnus hadn't buried a blaster round in Nos Kil's head when he had the chance. Then there was the hate he had for Kane, the man—no, the *creature* who'd stooped to incinerating a room full of people just to incite a war that satisfied his bloodlust. Magnus's conversations with Longo had opened his eyes to so much… all of which he hoped to share in this briefing.

Just then, the war room's doors opened and in walked the rest of the essential leadership team. Alpha Platoon's leaders consisted of Dutch, Sootriman, Ezo, and Valerie, while Bravo Platoon's were Abimbola and Berouth. Titus and Zoll represented Charlie Platoon, and Rohoar and Saladin represented Delta Platoon. Awen and Saasarr were last with Echo Platoon. They each took a seat around the enormous black stone table, while Magnus stood at the end. TO-96 and Azelon brought up the rear and came to stand on either side of Magnus.

"Good to see you all," Magnus said. "Let's get started."

He waved a hand and the lights lowered. The walls changed from their bright white luster and depicted a view of the void filled with countless stars and swirling patches of purple and white mist. Then part of the holo behind Magnus displayed the beginnings of an itemized list of topics. Next to it appeared an image of Worru, along with topographical maps of the city, narrowing as they went until the last image showed a cross section of the Grand Arielina. Another window listed Granther Company's current roster, as well as submenu tabs for resource management. The last item of note was a time keeping window that had several actions listed beneath its main clock function.

"Today's goal is to construct a battle plan for our assault on Worru. Given each of our various backgrounds and skill sets, I feel it's important you each speak up as you have items worth noting. No single one of us will be able to see it all. And, as we all know, the entire plan will come under serious strain as we encounter the enemy. So the more we create this together, the more we'll be able to make modifications on the fly that serve the goals and not one platoon's own needs. Copy?"

"La-raah," everyone replied in an even tone.

"Good. Let's start with what we know, and then I want to cover the new intel I've gleaned from my sessions with the Talon pilot."

"He's been co-operative?" Dutch asked.

"Surprisingly so," Magnus replied.

Abimbola chuckled. "That is because you almost killed him with the Jujari's living blood horish, isn't it."

"That's not how it works," Rohoar replied, the hackles on his neck standing up. "And you know it."

"I'm just saying…"

"Easy boys," Magnus replied. He glanced at Awen. "I haven't raised a finger against him. In fact, I haven't needed to. It seems there's unrest in the Navy, enough that Longo wants to be of use, at least for the time being. More on that in a while."

Magnus turned to highlight his first point on the list, entitled Objectives.

"The way I see it, we have several objectives in front of us. The first is the rescue of Awen's mentor and friend, Willowood. We not only believe she is being held hostage by So-Elku, but she is crucial in rallying any Luma not in league with So-Elku. Awen, any comments on this?"

Awen looked around the table. "Yes. As many of you know, Willowood was my mentor during observances as well as my patron upon becoming an emissary. She is loyal to the true causes of peace in the galaxy and not whatever devious agendas Master So-Elku has devised. Additionally, her skills within the Unity are unparalleled… at least they were up until recently. As Magnus said, I believe she will be a valuable asset to the Gladio Umbra in the event of her rescue. Not to mention the fact that she is Valerie's mother and Piper's grandmother."

For those who had not been let in on this substantial point of fact, the news seemed electric. Murmurs broke out around the table as disbelief was met with ardent nods and emphatic agreement.

"I can vouch for Awen's testimony about my mother," Valerie added. "She is, in fact, one of the most powerful Luma among the order. So her prowess will only be an added strength to our team."

"And yours?" Abimbola asked, clearly unhindered by the clear social and emotional lines he was crossing in asking the question.

Valerie blushed, then swallowed. "Let's just say that the true blood powers skipped a generation."

"But surely there must be—"

"It's not relevant to the conversation," Magnus interjected, trying to spare the woman further inquiry. He imagined the stigma was something Valerie had tried to overcome for years—possibly even her whole life. It was, perhaps, much like the shadow of expectations he'd walked under with his grandfather. "The point is, we need to rescue her."

Awen nodded. "As Magnus has said, Willowood will be instrumental in gathering other Luma to our cause."

A hand went up. It was Berouth, Abimbola's assistant. When Magnus nodded at him, he asked, "Is there any indication that the Luma will, in fact, join us?"

"Awen?" Magnus said, looking at her.

"I think there's a high likelihood of alignment with our cause, yes. I am confident that many will at least consider the idea diligently. They may be reticent to leave the order given its long history, but I suspect that So-Elku's behavior has already made many highly suspicious of the order's current trajectory."

"May I also add," TO-96 said, raising his hand, "that if longevity is a corollary of integrity, those Luma in search of new allegiance should find the Gladio Umbra of far more value given its millennium's long history."

"Hadn't thought about that," Magnus said, stroking his beard. "But while it's certainly a good point, we have to remember that no one knows about the Novian history, let alone the Gladio Umbra's."

Heads nodded at this assertion, and even TO-96 seemed to reassess his statement with a slow dip of his head.

"So we want to rescue Willowood and any other Luma held captive," Abimbola said. "What else?"

Awen raised her hand before Magnus could continue. "Go ahead," he said.

"Is there any value in letting the rest of the Luma *not* held captive by So-Elku know about us?"

"I think it's too risky," Titus said, tapping the table with a finger. "Let's say we could think of a way to recruit them even in the midst of the battle. How do we vet them? How do we parse between those who genuinely want to join us and who are plants?"

"In a sense, you're suggesting the fact that they were *not* taken prisoner is evidence enough of their compliance to So-Elku's leadership," Magnus said.

Titus nodded. "I mean, that's the way I see it anyway."

"Anyone else?" Magnus asked.

"I agree with him," Awen replied. "So-Elku wouldn't have restrained anyone unless he saw them as an imminent threat. If they're coming out with Willowood, they can be trusted. Everyone else is suspect until proven innocent. Plus, I imagine that Willowood will be able to tell us more about the situation… assuming she's…"

"She's alive, Awen," Magnus said, willing the woman to accept his ardent assertion for herself.

"And who's to say we couldn't go back," Sootriman said. "Or at least get word to them that the Gladio Umbra are recruiting."

"I like it." Magnus looked at Awen. "Any estimates on how many prisoners we're talking about or where they might be? It will directly affect how many shuttles we need to prep for exfil."

"I really can't say in terms of numbers. But since Willowood was able to communicate with you, I suspect they're holding her somewhere close to Elders Hall."

"If I may, sir, I think I have some helpful information on that point," TO-96 said.

"By all means." Magnus gestured for TO-96 to address the table.

A three-dimensional image of the Grand Arielina took over the main holo display. The bot didn't turn to look at it as he spoke.

"Here we have the main corridor leading to the temple dome known as Elders Hall." The user view flew through a long hallway bordered on both sides by tall columns that Magnus instantly recognized. He'd defended his unit's retreat down this corridor when he, Abimbola, and Rohoar had first met with So-Elku. A wide set of stairs led up to massive double doors that emerged into the circular room where the elders met. "Beneath this level, however, my records indicate there are several additional floors."

"The catacombs," Awen said, seemingly more to herself than any else.

"An apt name," the bot replied. "My guess, if I am permitted such latitude in this manner, would be that So-Elku would keep the prisoners as close to himself as he could while maintaining secrecy. Thus, this seems a likely place."

"That's where they are." Awen looked tense.

"How can you be sure?" Magnus asked.

"I can't. Not entirely. But I feel it. And unless So-Elku has done something to conceal their location, I will be able to confirm it once we get in orbit."

"Excellent," Magnus said.

"What is that next objective on your list?" Abimbola asked. "What does Novia Codex mean?"

Magnus let Awen field this one, gesturing to her with a nod.

"It is the Novia's book of summary findings of the Unity dating to antiquity. So-Elku stole it during our first encounter on Ithnor Ithelia."

Abimbola frowned. "And retrieving it is important because…?"

"Because, from what Azelon tells me, it contains previously unknown information about accessing realms of the Unity that allow the user unprecedented power to manipulate space, time, and matter. Additionally, the codex contains an abridged history of the Novia Minoosh up until their consummation with the singularity."

"I don't understand why this is on our list if So-Elku has already had it in his possession," Titus said. "Couldn't he have read it all by now? Or at least copied it?"

"May I respond to this?" Azelon asked, looking at Awen.

"Of course."

"While the codex is indeed an ancient manuscript, fashioned in the old way of binding pages to form a book—as you might call them—the volume is no less mystical than the Unity itself."

Ezo bopped his head as if in rhythm to some unheard song. "So you're saying it takes someone gifted in the unity to read it… to decipher it."

"In part, yes." Azelon looked around the table as she spoke. "Though the codex is less about the information it contains and more about the path it takes the reader down. Think of it like a map, something that must be referenced continually if it is to be used efficiently.

"As to copying the volume, that is quite impossible. The very premise of its inception renders it unique in every way, and any attempts to duplicate it would only result in producing a powerless tome devoid of the codex's nature."

"And why's that?" Ezo asked, his brow wrinkled in curiosity.

"Because it took all of us to create it."

"All of you, as in the Novia Minoosh?"

"Yes, Ezo. It was our last creation upon entering the singularity. You might say it was the guide back to our point of origin, and our last will and testament to all that we created in the natural realm. I have endeavored to provide Awen a similar history, but she has the benefit of direct access to the Novian singularity, whereas any reader of the codex might not be so fortunate."

"So on a scale of one to ten," Dutch said, "how important is it that we get this codex back from So-Elku?"

"Ten," Azelon said. "That, or we destroy it."

"We'd be fools to think he hasn't already begun to decipher it," Awen said. "So-Elku is powerful, to be sure."

"But not powerful enough to have journeyed into the vast landscape of our inheritance," Azelon added. "At least not yet. Doing so would take him a lifetime, if not more."

"Then what's the rush?" Titus asked.

"The rush?" replied Azelon.

Awen steepled her fingers and rested her chin on them. "Why the need for urgency."

Azelon's eyes warmed in recognition. "I see. Firstly, even a cursory indulgence of the codex's contents yields more knowledge than any practitioner of the Unity in your native universe has ever come by. Based upon Awen's explanation of this, Master So-Elku, it is safe to assume he has made such excursions already and most likely gleaned much. Since the nature of the codex is to invite its users deeper into our story, and our discoveries, it has no doubt created a lust within him to delve further into its contents."

"But I thought you said it would take a lifetime," Titus added.

"I did. But Awen tells me So-Elku is not working alone."

"Splick," Ezo said. "So you're telling Ezo that more Luma

can work together to uncover the mysteries of the cosmos faster?"

"Precisely." Azelon tilted her head. "Though, on a separate line of inquiry, I am still uncertain why Ezo continues to speak about himself using his own proper noun." She looked at Sootriman. "Is there something wrong with him? Has he been struck violently in the cerebrum?"

"It does leave one to wonder, doesn't it," Sootriman replied, giving Ezo a sly grin.

"Ezo's brain is just fine, if that's what you're insinuating," the man said, leaning back in his chair. His tone was a mix of confidence and self-defense.

"I would like to scan you at some point in the future if you do not perish in the coming conflict," Azelon said.

Ezo's eyebrows went up in surprise. "Ezo is not a lab rat. And of course he's going to survive the coming conflict. Why would you even say that?"

"Let's get back to the mission," Magnus said.

Rohoar sniffed the air. "So we need to rescue Willowood, the prisoners, and the codex."

"Any ideas on where he might be keeping it?" Sootriman asked Awen.

"Again, I can't be sure, but my guess would be his private chambers. That's where I'd put it at least."

"And can you tell us more upon entering orbit?" Magnus asked her.

Awen bobbed her head. "I sure hope so, yes."

"That will have to do." Magnus highlighted the last objective by pointing at it. "And then we come to something that is personal to me. It's not something I feel is worth risking our time with unless the team is in unanimous agreement."

"Who's Colonel Caldwell?" Abimbola asked.

"Guy's a legend," Dutch replied. "He's seen more action than any Marine alive. He's also the one who first assigned us to Magnus here."

"So…" Abimbola looked at Magnus. "You saying he's on Worru then."

Magnus pursed his lips and nodded. "I am. He opted to stay active and not retire by taking a station there about a year ago."

"What's this have to do with the mission?" Titus asked.

There was a moment's silence as all eyes turned back to Magnus. "I want to try and recruit him."

Another silence filled the war room before Dutch laughed. "You serious, LT? You… you wanna try and get the Colonel to join Granther Company?"

Magnus couldn't tell if the room was more unsettled by his initial statement or by Dutch's response. But he nodded at her all the same. "I do. For several reasons."

"We're listening," Valerie said, leaning in on her elbows. Unlike Dutch, Valerie didn't seem surprised in the least. Her apparent faith in Magnus gave him a sense of renewed purpose, which he was grateful for; her background as a Marine, doctor, and former senator's wife, as well as the daughter of a Luma Elder, had a way of swaying people in her direction. Not to mention she was Piper's mother. Magnus guessed everyone else took her interest as a sign of the idea's legitimacy—*so long as I can convince them*, he thought.

"First, the colonel commands all the Republic forces currently stationed on Worru. If they're called in to defend the Luma, which I'm guessing So-Elku will be sure to do, then he'll be the one to make the call."

"Garner his support and the Republic stays out of the fight," Dutch said more somberly, probably trying to earn her way back from her out-of-character outburst.

Magnus nodded. "At least for a little while. Resisting So-Elku's call for help, however, will get him court-martialed. So it's a risk he's going to have to weigh. I'd simply be giving him an alternative to being arrested."

"Seems like a gamble if you ask me," Abimbola said, flipping a poker chip and catching it. "You really think he's going to risk his career for some buckethead who is wanted by the Republic?"

Magnus took a deep breath, feeling his heavy shoulders rise and fall. "I do. That is, if we have the time to tell him what we've uncovered. *And* that I have the man who killed his son."

"What?" Dutch asked, leaning forward. "Who killed the colonel's son?"

"Nos Kil," Awen replied, her eyes staring past the table.

"The one and only." Magnus took another deep breath. "The story is not worth telling now. But the colonel will want to see our prisoner. And he'll want to know more about Moldark."

Magnus felt everyone's attention intensify.

"I'm sorry," Valerie said, looking around the table as if she'd been left out of some important information meeting. "Who did you say?"

"So this gets us to the other part—"

"Of what you've learned from Commander Longo," Awen said, knowing full well that Magnus had been speaking with the prisoner but had not shared any of his findings. Until now.

"Correct." Magnus dipped his head toward TO-96. A new image appeared on the main holo display, one of a baldheaded man with black eyes. His skin was pock-marked, and his lips were curled in a subtle but no less malevolent sneer.

"Mystics…" Sootriman said. "That is the man who killed my people and took me prisoner."

Before she could say anything more, Saasarr was on his feet and hissing toward the front of the room. "Foul wretch," he yelled, and sprung onto the table. Those seated slid back as the Reptalon advanced on all fours, teeth and talons glimmering in the projected starlight. "I will end him! I will rip his throat from—"

"Saasarr," Sootriman ordered, standing to her feet. "Stay yourself!"

As if the lizard had some sort of digital processor hardwired into his reptilian brain, Saasarr froze. Then he looked over his shoulder at Sootriman and blinked a wrinkly eyelid at her.

"Please, restrain yourself and return to your seat," she said.

"Yes, my lady," he hissed. Then he turned on the table, bringing his tail over everyone's heads in a smooth whipping motion, and returned to his chair.

Sootriman regained her composure as if nothing had happened. "Of course, we know this man under a different name."

"Kane," Valerie said. "Fleet Admiral Wendell Kane of the *Black Labyrinth* and commander of the Republic's Third Fleet."

"Correct," Magnus said.

"Then, why the name change?" Dutch asked.

"That's what everyone would like to know, including Ricio," Magnus replied.

Dutch raised an eyebrow. "Ricio?"

"Our prisoner's first name," said Magnus.

Abimbola's brow furrowed. "You are getting friendly with the prisoner… just before you kill him? That seems unusually cruel, even for you, buckethead."

"I'm not gonna kill him, Bimby. In fact, if he keeps this up, he may one day be a Gladio Umbra."

Rohoar seemed shocked by the news. "But… he's a—"

"Republic fighter pilot who killed Jujari?" Magnus pushed his lower lip up and nodded. "Absolutely. But he's also a sane, rational man who I believe genuinely wants peace in the galaxy, just like we all do. Isn't that right?" He looked at Rohoar first to make sure his point was understood. "That's what I thought.

Which brings up another important point. We're going to need to get used to this kind of thing with Ricio. If our cause is the right one, and we're all able to stay alive, we're going to attract more and more people who are tired of their current allegiances—whether that's Luma serving So-Elku, or Marines and Navy sailors serving under a nefarious leader. Copy?"

There was only a moment's hesitation before everyone said, "La-raah."

"So, Moldark?" Dutch asked, tipping her head toward the holo display.

"As far as Ricio can tell, the former admiral has undergone some sort of change."

"What kind of change?" Abimbola asked.

Magnus caught site of Awen eyeing the image. "No one's sure, but…" He stared at her. "Awen, you wanna say something?"

"It might be nothing but…" When she didn't continue on her own, Magnus prompted her to keep going. "It's just…" She looked over at Sootriman and Ezo. "You both remember back in the rotunda?" They nodded. "I saw something. Something evil. Something that, as you both well know, shook me. I… I'm used to seeing evil in the hearts of people—I doubt anyone is fully immune to hostility or narcissism. But what I saw in Kane was…" She looked back at the holo. "As if this is a physical manifestation of the presence I witnessed. I mean, not exactly, but enough for me to know it's what I saw in the Unity."

"It's dark magic voodoo," Abimbola said, drawing a strange shape in front of his chest with his thumb and forefinger. Magnus guessed it was to ward off whatever mystical spirit he supposed Awen was referencing. Magnus didn't believe any of that splick, of course, but he knew the Miblimbians were devoutly spiritual.

"I don't know what it is," Awen said. "But I know he's evil—*it's* evil."

"So you're saying Admiral Kane is now Moldark, is that it?" Valerie asked.

"I am. And it seems that both of our prisoners here have had contact with him."

"Both?" Awen looked shocked. "You went back to talk to Nos Kil again? Without me?"

"It's okay, Awen. I had it under control."

"But you know what he—"

"I said, I had it under control. Trust me."

She didn't look pleased. But she at least relented and sat back in her chair.

"Both men have confirmed—in their own way—that Kane is now Moldark. Only he's no longer a fleet admiral."

"Then what is he?" Valerie asked.

Magnus hesitated. Despite how outlandish Kane's physical change had been, this part was even more far-fetched—at least for those who had served in the military.

"What? What is it, Magnus?" Valerie prompted Magnus to speak.

"He's taken control over the Republic's entire Navy and is demanding that his subordinates refer to him as lord."

"*Lord* Moldark?" Abimbola snorted through a wide smile. "What in all the cosmos is becoming of the Galactic Republic!"

"You joke," Magnus replied, "but I can assure you our two prisoners back there are quite terrified of him."

"Terrified?" Abimbola tilted his head at the image on the holo. "He looks more like an overripe Paluvu sea pear than a warlord. And I know warlords."

"That aside, word is that he's wrested control of the armada from the Republic and is calling it the Paragon." Magnus could tell he was losing the room. This was too fantastical for them to believe. Hell, it was too fantastical for him to believe. "I had my doubts too. Until Ricio showed me this."

15

Ricio had been standing outside the conference room for about twenty minutes before the robot named TO-96 appeared.

"Hey, good looking," Ricio said.

"Hello, Commander Longo. Magnus would like you to come in now."

"And my restraints?" Ricio held his hands up. They were still bound in plasma shackles, as were his feet.

"He gave me no instructions on those."

"Which is a perfect opportunity to read between the lines."

TO-96 turned his head slightly. "I'm sorry, sir. Which lines am I supposed to be reading between?"

Ricio blinked. "Take me inside."

"Right this way, sir."

The bot led Ricio through two security doors before entering a dimly lit room surrounded by stars. A dozen people sat around a large black table, each regarding him with expressionless faces. He recognized several of them but the rest were new. Another bot stood beside Magnus at the far end of the table in front of the main holo display.

"Please, come in," Magnus said, inviting Ricio to the front. He walked around the table, careful to stay clear of the Reptalon and the Jujari especially. And the Miblimbian. And the Elonian. *Splick, pretty much everyone.*

"How's it going, people," Ricio said as he came to stand beside Magnus. Their eyes were suspicious, however, despite his attempts to soften the room. "Yeah, sucks here too." He raised his hands and smiled at them.

"Ricio," Magnus said, "these are members of my team, the ones that you tried to kill."

"Ouch. But… it's the truth."

"And team, this is one of our two prisoners, Commander Mauricio Longo of Viper Squadron."

"Guilty. Nice to meet you all." Ricio looked at Magnus. "So, you want me to show them?"

Magnus nodded.

"And our deal?"

"Wait, what deal?" The Elonian said, looking at Magnus.

"He wants a data pad to read on," Magnus said.

"Oh." The woman eased up a little.

"You have any idea how boring it gets down there?" Ricio asked her.

"Go ahead," Magnus said.

Ricio nodded and tapped the Republic Navy insignia on his flight suit's left breast. The standard issue media recorder—used to record actions and evidence on all military missions—suddenly projected a miniature scene about a meter above the black table. In it, Ricio could see Fleet Commander Brighton and Lord Moldark. The recording reproduced the entire conversation in which his commanders outlined his mission to eliminate the threats on the other side of the quantum tunnel.

Ricio noticed how everyone listening winced at the sound of Moldark's voice. "Do not fail us, commander. We are looking for you to be thorough. Execute your orders with extreme prejudice. There must be no survivors."

Ricio wasn't entirely sure what Magnus was after, but he guessed that he wanted his team to see what they were up against. Which meant this next part was extremely important. As if reading his thoughts, Magnus rolled his index finger in a circle for Ricio to let the recording keep playing.

"You are dismissed," Moldark said. But Ricio's view of his two commanders didn't change.

"What is it, Commander Longo?" Brighton asked.

"Sirs, if you will pardon my asking, what is to be your larger will in all of this?"

"Commander Longo," spat the Fleet Admiral, "remove yourself from this board room at once!"

"No," Moldark said, lifting a hand with a gold pinkie ring on it. "Let him speak."

"But, your lordship, he is just—"

"He honors me by the magnitude of his request."

Brighton looked like he'd swallowed a bug, squinting in Ricio's direction again. "Proceed."

"What I mean to ask is, if you have been given command of the entire Republic Navy, what would you have us do from here?"

Moldark stood from his chair atop the dais and moved down the stairs in a jerky motion. It was as if the man's joints and limbs were held together by elastic bands that snapped back and forth as he walked. Even rewatching this again, Ricio felt a chill go up his spine.

"I have not been given anything," Moldark said, his face filling the camera's frame. "I have taken what I want. Your Republic is weak. It has been co-opted by fools seeking their own self-interests. They do not deserve such power. So I am wresting it from them to do with it as the galaxy deserves.

"And you, Commander Ricio, no longer serve the Galactic Republic"—Moldark spat the words like an expletive—"you are pledged to the Paragon. The Paragon of Perfect Rule. Which means that when you return from your mission through the void's horizon, you will return to aid me in bringing all wayward factions into subjection to my supreme justice. And we will not stop until the offenders have been subdued and my people vindicated for the atrocities done to them."

There was a long moment before the recorded sound of Ricio's voice said, "Thank you, my lord."

Moldark sneered, before saying, "Go. Your mission awaits."

Silence replaced the holo recording as the content blinked out.

The Nimprinth leaned forward. "You actually followed that guy's orders? Damn, Ezo is not impressed with you, Longo."

But Magnus raised a hand at the man. "Let's hold off on the personal attacks, Ezo."

"Wait," Ricio said, jerking his head down the table. "So his name's Ezo?"

The Nimprinth rolled his eyes.

"Yup," said Magnus. "You get used to it."

One of the women raised her hand and addressed the room. She had blonde hair, blue eyes, and spoke like she owned the place. "I'd like to know what you have to say about this, Commander Longo. Your commanding officers say you are the highest-ranking fighter pilot in the fleet, which means you're not only dedicated to the Republic, but you're smart. You agreed to the mission, but I honestly can't believe you'd align yourself with *that* given your track record. Unless I'm misjudging you, in which case I think we jettison you out the nearest airlock."

Ricio had been nodding with her right up until the bit about the airlock. "If you think I'm so smart, what makes you think I'm not going to feed you some line just to keep you from flinging me into the void?"

"Because we have a Luma, remember?" The female Jujari

said.

"And she reads minds a lot less obtrusively than Reptalons do," the large, tan woman said.

"Okay, okay," Ricio said, pumping his palms in an attempt to slow everyone down. Having a Reptalon stab his brain with the needle at the end of its tail wasn't something he had on his life's wish list. "No, I don't particularly like Moldark. I mean, the guy's insane or possessed or something. I can assure you, I have no idea what's happening to the Republic, but that *thing*—as you say—is not a friend of mine nor the Republic's, and neither is Fleet Admiral Brighton if he's in league with Moldark, as he clearly seems to be."

"So you'll join us?" the Elonian asked.

"Lady, I still don't even know what you're all doing. I mean, aside from Magnus's talking points, but who knows if any of those are true." Ricio's assertion was met with growls by both the Jujari and the Reptalon. *Go easy, Ricio*, he reminded himself. "Granted, you all look like reasonably sane people, apart from him" He nodded toward Ezo. "And mystics know I can't think of any good reasons for such a diverse group of enemies to be working together. So my gut tells me you've got something powerful enough to hold this group together, and Magnus says you even have a plan. But if I'm going to turn on the Republic…"

"We're not asking you to turn on the Republic," Awen said. "We're asking you to help us fight Moldark and anyone in league with him."

Ricio thought about it for a second and then turned to

Magnus. "A few days ago, when you first questioned me, you said you had proof. But your AI was malfunctioning or something. What were you going to show me?"

Magnus seemed to think about it, and Ricio wondered if the man had changed his mind. "Azelon, bring up Nos Kil's confession."

The bot acknowledged the request and sent a recording to the main holo display. In it, Ricio watched Magnus and the Marine called Nos Kil bicker back and forth. Finally, when the man said something about killing Marines in the mwadim's palace, the image of Magnus lunged at the prisoner and the holo froze.

Ricio looked at Magnus for a moment and considered him. "What did he mean about the mwadim's palace and your men? Was that… is this about the ambush on Oorajee?"

"You mean the one that started this whole war?" the blonde woman added with a sarcastic tone.

Ricio looked at her and then back at Magnus. "You mean to tell me that you were on the mission that—"

"I helped *lead* the mission that got dozens of Marines killed by bombs planted by Nos Kil, who was following orders from—"

"Moldark."

Magnus nodded.

"Mystics." Ricio swallowed. "You mean to tell me he started this whole conflict just so he could take control of the Republic armada?"

"We're not entirely sure of his deeper motives, but it

certainly seems that way," Awen said.

Ricio stood in front of everyone, assembling the pieces in his head. He couldn't believe what he was hearing. But then again, it made more sense than he cared to admit. And the people before him certainly seemed to be united over the common goal of stopping the enemy. Still, he wasn't sure if he wanted to be a part of it. He had a wife and a son. And this deployment was to be his last. Instead, now he was stuck in a different damned universe, according to Magnus, and was being asked to go on another mission if he switched sides. Not to mention the fact that this particular side looked painfully outnumbered even with their fancy starship.

Then again, Moldark didn't sound like he'd be letting Ricio head back to Capriana anytime soon either. Not that this was all about turning a blind eye to ethics just so he could see his family. But then again, he'd always said that nothing meant more to him than his wife and son—and that he'd do *anything* to see them again. "Even come back from the dead," he'd whispered in his son's ear.

"I need more time," was all Ricio could think to say. He tried to summon all the sincerity he could for this next part. "And please don't take my hesitation as me questioning your integrity. It's simply that… well, I have a family. And I was hoping to see them when… when…" But the more he thought about his wife, and the more he imagined how much his son must have grown since they last held each other, the more the words caught in his throat.

"You have some time, commander," the blonde haired

woman said. "If you have family, we understand that."

"Thank you," he replied around the lump forming behind his tongue.

"But not too much time," she added. "Or else we'll get that airlock ready." Ricio studied her face and watched a small smile play at the edges of her eyes.

He smiled back. "I wouldn't expect anything else."

"You're dismissed, commander," Magnus said. "'Six, please see him back to his cell. We've got some planning to do."

"As you wish, sir," the bot replied. Ricio turned at TO-96's insistence and headed for the exit. Just before he passed through the door, Ricio looked back and said, "Thank you. Each of you. For doing what you're doing. I don't pretend to understand it all, but I do believe you're trying to do the right thing even if you're outgunned and outnumbered. You're good people." He searched their faces, waiting for someone to say something.

"Thank you, commander," Magnus said. "That will be all."

Ricio sensed a certain amount of reservation in Magnus's tone. Despite their present circumstances, Ricio far outranked the former Marine lieutenant, so that might have been part of it. But there was something else too. Ricio couldn't be sure, but he thought he saw a deep sadness behind Magnus's eyes, one that made Ricio recognize just how deeply the former Marine cared about this mission. That's when the thought struck Ricio that maybe he should be just as concerned.

16

After another day, Magnus felt confident in the plan that he and his team had come up with to raid Worru. It wasn't perfect, of course, but no plan ever was. Especially after the enemy got ahold of it and shook it to death. But that was why the Republic paid him all those creds. Or, rather, *had* paid him all those creds. Now he was a…

A Gladio Umbra, he reminded himself, still drilling the new identity into his psyche. Which, he knew, was far easier to do for himself than it was for his two brothers in arms, Michael "Flow" Deeks and Miguel "Cheeks" Chico.

His contact with them had been extremely limited over the months that he trained Granther Company back on Neith Tearness. In fact, it was mostly Valerie who checked in on them, managing their medications and monitoring their long road to recovery. Whenever Magnus had spent time with them, it was filled with lots of reminiscing and more than a few tears. And it was the tears that concerned him most.

Beneath their grief, Magnus saw the hot embers of hatred. It wasn't malevolent in and of itself—these two warriors couldn't be blamed for what they'd been through any more than someone could blame a sandcastle for being built too close to the ocean at low tide. But Magnus knew what their bitterness could turn into. He'd seen it before. Hell, he'd seen it in himself. But unlike Flow and Cheeks, Magnus had found ways to cope with it and still operate—not just as a person, but as a warrior. For his brothers, however, Magnus doubted they'd ever be able to head outside the wire again. He even doubted if they could be in the same room with Rohoar or any of his Jujari, which is why they had remained quarantined to certain sections of the ship since their rescue.

Awen said she'd need the better part of the day to close the existing quantum tunnel and open a new one outside Worru. So while she was back in Itheliana to operate the QTG, Magnus took the opportunity to brief Flow and Cheeks on their small though significant part of the coming mission, one that would keep them safely aboard the *Spire* and out of harm's way.

"You lookin' fly in those Novia threads, LT," Flow said, locking hands with Magnus and pulling him into an embrace. Magnus wore a casual flight suit made of white material with blue trim while Flow and Cheeks wore black gym shorts and white t-shirts that hugged their muscular torsos.

"I'm just not brave enough to show my legs like you," Magnus replied.

"Hell, no one is," Cheeks added, giving Magnus a similar handshake and one-armed hug. "Who's gonna compete with those thunder thighs? I know I ain't."

"Somehow I feel like you're insulting me," Flow said. "But I know you're just jealous 'cause you can't do this..." Suddenly, Flow started flexing his thigh muscles back and forth like the ping-ponging bass line of a prog dance song.

"That's so disturbing," Cheeks said, looking away.

Magnus laughed, then motioned toward the chairs in their rec room. "Can I sit?"

"What do you mean, can I sit?" Flow said, scrunching his face up. "You acting all formal on us now?"

"Maybe," Magnus said. "I have a mission for you."

"'Bout damn time," Cheeks exclaimed. "I'm so ready to be done with this starship, I tell you what. Get me planet side with a MAR30 and give me something to shoot."

"He's lying," Flow said, pulling up a glossy white chair for Magnus. "He just wants a woman. Hell, he wants five, and doesn't even care what species they are."

Magnus waved his hands. "That's already more detail than I want to know, Fearsome." The three of them chuckled as Magnus knew their thoughts turned toward the deceased member of the Fearsome Four, Allan "Mouth" Franklin.

Flow broke the grief-stricken silence by clapping his hands once and rubbing his palms together. "So, wha'dya got for us, LT?"

"Well, we're planning something big, boys."

"I knew it!" Cheeks said. "Had to be a good reason you've kept us cooped up in here. Son of a bitch."

"So what're we doing?" Flow asked. "Regrouping with battalion? Or heading out from here on something way down range?"

"Neither," Magnus said. He lowered his head and took a deep breath, knowing they'd be hanging on his every word. "I gotta fill you boys in first. And there's a lot. So if you need me to take a break at all, you just—"

"We don't need no breaks, LT," Cheeks interjected. "The last few months have made us stir crazy. Give it to us. We're ready."

With that, Magnus plunged headlong into recounting everything that had transpired after their rescue, even going over details they'd previously discussed just in case the two Marines had forgotten them. Memory loss was a common occurrence in those who'd suffered severe trauma—and Flow and Cheeks had been through some of the worst.

Their eyes went wide as Magnus covered the more recent ground about the Novia Minoosh, their connection to the Jujari, and Admiral Kane's transformation to Moldark. Magnus even offered to stop while he recounted the most recent battle in Itheliana just to let them take it all in. But to their credit, they were indeed ready to move on and absorbed the intel like they would in any other mission briefing.

"So where you want us?" Flow asked after Magnus had shared the assault plan for Worru.

Magnus took his deepest breath yet. This was going to be the hard part.

"Aw, hell," Cheeks said, throwing his hands in the air and standing up. "He's not taking us with him again."

Flow looked from Cheeks to Magnus. "Say it ain't so, LT."

"It's so," Magnus replied.

"Splick, LT!" Flow was on his feet. "You rescue us from those clawed demons only to keep us cooped up inside this starship for months, and then when we have a chance to rip some bad guys, you won't even let us out of our mysticsdamn bedrooms? What are you, our mother?"

"I need you on the bridge with the bots," Magnus said, trying to keep his voice calm.

"You hear that, Flow?" Cheeks said. "We get to babysit bots."

"Aw, hell nah," Flow replied. "Ain't no way. *Nooo way.*"

"We need orbital oversight," Magnus said, trying to keep his voice calm. "The AIs are good at resource allocation, but they still can't handle predictive modeling like Marines can. Your experience will be invaluable in helping us adjust course in the field."

Magnus knew all his rehearsed explanations were right, and he knew his logic was bulletproof. But he could already feel that he'd lost his boys. Part of their argument was true—he *had* kept them locked up. And he'd be just as stir crazy as they were, if not worse. But the more they went on, the more he realized that Flow and Cheeks were proving his worst fears to be true: they couldn't handle combat. And he'd have to show them that they couldn't despite how much it pained him to do so.

"Sit down," Magnus said.

"Is that an order, LT?" Flow asked. "'Cause it seems like that's all we've been doing for you."

"Yes, that's an order. Both of you. *Sit down*."

"I don't think so, boss," Cheeks replied. He was agitated, pacing back and forth, eyes darting around the room.

Magnus rubbed his hand over his face, then tapped his earpiece. "Come on in," he said over comms.

A door opened on the far side of the rec room. Flow and Cheeks both turned at the motion. Then they watched as two Jujari entered through the doorway.

"Those are friendlies," Magnus said calmly. "That is Rohoar and Saladin, and they helped save your lives. And if we work together, they're going to help save the galaxy." He hadn't even finished the sentence when he noticed Flow and Cheeks's bodies tense. They made fists and prepared for a fight. "I order you to sit down."

But the two men hadn't heard Magnus. Instead, they charged after the two Jujari. Flow even grabbed his chair and held it over his head, swinging it like a club. Magnus remained seated and chewed on his lip. This was more painful to watch than he expected. He stood up, then more loudly, he yelled, "Flow, Cheeks—stand down!" But neither man paid him any attention.

Flow hurled his chair at Rohoar while Cheeks lowered his

shoulder and rammed it into Saladin. But neither Jujari was struck. Instead, both men passed through Azelon's hard light projections just as she caused the Jujari to disappear. Flow and Cheeks stumbled forward, one slamming into the far wall while the other fell on his chest with a grunt.

They both turned around to look for the enemy, eyes wide and filled with terror. But when they didn't see the Jujari, their eyes met Magnus's. He fought to hold back the emotions welling in his chest. As much as he wanted his brothers in arms to join him once again on the battlefield, there was simply no way they could. Not like this.

Then Magnus saw realization dawn on Flow's face. The look was something akin to embarrassment, then shame, and then grief. "I'm so…" Flow looked down at his hands, and then to the thrown chair. "I didn't even…"

"I'm sorry, boys," Magnus said, walking toward them now. "I can't imagine what you've been through."

Realization came slower to Cheeks, who was still panting from adrenaline. "What the hell, LT? What was that?"

"It was a test," Flow said. "Stand down."

"A test?" Cheeks looked between both of them, wiping sweat from his brow with the back of his forearm. "What kind of a sick twisted test was that supposed to be?"

"One we just failed," Flow said.

"Failed? You trying to mess with us, LT?"

"No," Flow replied again, doing the hard work for Magnus. "He's trying to keep us from getting killed. And keeping us from killing our teammates."

"Again," Magnus said, "I'm sorry. But you're not fit for duty outside this starship."

"Son of a bitch," Cheeks said, turning away from Magnus.

The mood was so heavy, Magnus felt it resting on his shoulders like a physical weight. In his heart, he wanted nothing more than to hand his boys NOV1s and have them by his side as they hit the streets of Plumeria. But that was just a dream, one that would remain a fiction in his imagination.

"My previous offer still stands," Magnus said. "If you want it, that is. I'll, uh… I'll leave you two alone and check back in later to see if you've changed your minds."

Flow nodded, a frown stretched across his large lips. "You'll know where to find us."

"Take care of him," Magnus said, indicating Cheeks with a small toss of his head.

"Copy that," Flow replied. "We'll cool off and have an answer for you later."

"Sounds good." Magnus left the rec room without another word. But once the door closed behind him, he leaned against the corridor's wall and wept.

17

"How'd it go?" Magnus asked, being the first to greet her and the away team returning from the planet's surface. Awen was surprised at how nice it felt to see his face before anyone else's, then wondered if the emotion was too obvious.

"Pretty smooth actually," she replied, trying to calm her excitement. Awen stepped aside to let the rest of Bravo Platoon file out of the shuttle and filter back into the ship through the hangar. TO-96 was last out and gave them both a parting salute before heading to the bridge. Magnus hadn't even realized that the bot had gotten a fresh telecoms emulation coating on his entire chassis, including his weapons systems. This gave the bot the same chameleon mode that the rest of the gladias enjoyed.

"Operating it was easier than I imagined it might be," Awen added.

"You had help, I'm guessing?"

Awen gave him a smug look. "Are you saying I can't handle it on my own?"

Magnus blinked in surprise. "Uh, no. I just meant that—"

"Easy. I'm just playing with you. TO-96 lent me considerable help from the Novia Minoosh."

"Ah. That's... that's great."

"It is. The old tunnel is closed, and we have a new tunnel opened that will place us one hour from Worru, well clear of its gravity well."

"That's great news."

Awen smiled at him again, noting how puffy his eyes looked. "You okay there, Adonis? You seem off." He didn't answer right away. She tried to catch his eye, and gave him a wink when she finally did. "Hey, what is it?"

"I spoke with Flow and Cheeks."

Awen's smile faded. "I take it that didn't go well."

He shook his head.

"Magnus... I'm so sorry."

"So am I." He shrugged. "But it's part of being a Marine. Some missions you just never come back from. And they're still... they're..."

"Still not back from Oorajee."

He grunted in agreement. "Mm-hm. And probably never will be."

Compassion for Magnus swelled so quickly in her chest that Awen couldn't restrain herself from giving him a hug. Surprisingly, he wrapped his arms around her and buried his face in the side of her neck. It was the most affectionate she'd ever seen him—even more than the kisses they'd shared. Something about this moment made him seem so vulnerable.

When Magnus finally let her go, Awen placed a hand over his heart. "It's going to be okay."

"Thanks."

A moment passed between them as Awen let her hand linger on his chest.

Finally, he asked, "What about you?"

"Me?" Awen's mission to the QTG had gone flawlessly, and she loved the opportunity to visit the alien city again. Plus, she hadn't endured anything like what Magnus had just been through. So, by comparison, she was having a great afternoon.

But then she was reminded that she did indeed have something that was weighing on her. And given Magnus's own transparency, maybe this was the time to bring it up. In fact, Magnus was perhaps the best person to ask in all the galaxy.

"I'm not looking forward to being back in Plumeria," she said, biting her lip and looking around. Was this hangar bay to be the site of all their deep conversations?

"Too many bad memories?"

She shook her head. "No. It's more like I'm afraid of the new ones I'm going to make."

"You mean with combat?"

"I mean, I don't know how I'm going to face the Luma."

Magnus gave her a knowing nod and then looked at the hangar's floor. "I'm not gonna lie, Awen. It's not easy."

"Speaking from experience?"

"What do you think?"

For some reason, Awen had never fully thought through the encounters Magnus had on the Bull Wraith and in Itheliana as being against fellow Marines. They were just bad guys doing bad things. But all of them—right down to Nos Kil and Ricio—had been recruited from human worlds, trained by the Navy or Marine Corps, and commissioned to serve the Galactic Republic. Whatever their new allegiances with Moldark and the Paragon were, it didn't change the troopers' pedigree. *To put it in Marine-speak*, she thought, *they're all brothers*.

"I'm thinking it must've been hard to pull the trigger against the Marines on the Bull Wraith that came after Piper and her parents. And just as hard to put down the Recon team on Ithnor Ithelia."

Magnus stroked his beard. "It was. Real hard. And if I wasn't careful, those feelings would have kept me from pulling the trigger—at least long enough for someone else to pick me off."

"So you buried the feelings and fired first."

"No."

Awen raised an eyebrow at Magnus, surprised by his reply.

"If you bury those feelings," he said, "they haunt you worse than any of the others. You never dismiss the fact that you're fighting people who—given a different set of circumstances—are your family."

"Then how do you do it and not fall apart on the battlefield?"

"You choose to defend the family who needs your help the most."

Awen searched his face, her eyes darting around his rugged complexion. She was so grateful for his insights, and felt his words console her like water on a cracked patch of soil.

Before, the universe had been so black and white. But ever since the ambush at the mwadim's palace, Awen had been plunged into a world of grey. Absolutes had been traded for a bucket full of *maybe* and *sometimes* and *sort of*. Navigating those paths was harder than she cared to admit. And while she didn't always agree with his approach to every conflict, she at least held a deep respect for his motives.

Still, his statement wasn't without its problems. She swallowed and looked at him. "But couldn't you say that the family who is misguided—your rogue Marines and my seduced Luma—couldn't you say that they need the most help?"

He nodded. "I suppose so. And I marvel at your desire to do right by them—mystics know I don't know how you do it. But those people are different to me."

"How so?"

"They've already made up their minds."

"But what if we could win them back?"

"I'm not saying we couldn't. But when their finger is on a trigger and it's pointed at someone who's committed themselves to defending the weak and protecting freedom, then you can't hesitate."

Awen didn't even realize she'd been holding her breath and let out a deep sigh. "I get that, it's just—"

"Awen. Listen." He passed his hand over his hair. "Most people, they get the luxury of talking about this sort of thing in a classroom or on a news program or over dinner. They never actually have to live it out. It's all rhetorical to them, like some mythical exercise that doesn't affect anyone except the server who has to keep filling up their wine glasses while the conversation goes on and on, round and round.

"The difference for you and me, however, is that it's not theory for us. It's real. It's right now. And it's coming for us whether we want it to or not. We don't get to have opinions that keep us warm on our couches. We have decisions to make that stay with us forever—decisions that say some people will live and some people will die.

"Trust me when I say I don't like it any more than you do. You've already heard me say that—and it's more than I've ever admitted to anyone. But it doesn't change the fact that we're here, out on the edge of the conflict, and we have nowhere else to go but through the enemy. It's that, or we run away. And I'm not willing to do that. And neither are you."

Awen nodded. He'd spoken so fast and shared so much that she hardly knew what to say in reply. But he wasn't done yet.

"If there was time to figure it all out, to get everyone to lay down their arms and talk it through…" He nodded. "I'd be all for it. But war exists because that doesn't happen, at least not a lot. So if someone is going to fight, if someone is going to be responsible for taking lives and sifting through the evil that is conflict, I can tell you one thing's for damn sure."

"What's that?"

"You're the one I want pulling the trigger."

"Mystics, Magnus," she said, folding her arms. "Don't say that."

"But it's true, Awen. Maybe the Luma taught you that all war is bad. That all fighting is evil. I'm not sure what they teach in that school. But if all war is bad, then doesn't that mean it needs good people involved? Because if they're not, what are we fighting for anyway?"

Awen stood there, unsure what to say. She felt both honored and sick to her stomach at the same time. "I never asked for this, Magnus."

"Yeah, you did."

She cast him a sharp look. "No, I really—"

"The moment someone picked on the new kid in school and you stood up for them? You asked for it. When some government made some stupid-ass decision that hurt an entire section of its constituents and you got pissed off? You asked for it. You've always been asking for it. I don't think you get that, Awen."

"Get what? What don't I get?" She heard the frustration rising in her voice.

"You were *born* for this."

She blinked away the tears that flooded her eyes, but she

refused to look away from him. Hot lines parted her cheeks and she held her arms tighter to her chest. "That may be so," she said, her voice trembling. "But I'm still afraid."

The words had barely left her mouth when Magnus reached out and pulled her into his chest. He pinned her there, still with her arms crossed, while she cried. She felt his lips kiss the top of her head. The care he was showing her made her cry even harder because—perhaps for the first time—she was worried about losing him. Not because he was a valuable asset to the team or someone she'd grown accustomed to. But because she was actually falling in love with him.

"I want it to be you, Awen," he said in her ear. She thought he was referencing what he was saying before, about the trigger and killing the enemy and everything. But then she wondered if he meant something else. Something deeper.

Instead of trying to define it, of trying to put it in a black and white box, she let it be what it was. Instead, she allowed the warmth of his embrace to pull her back from the edge of fear and keep her hidden for just a little while longer.

S0MEONE CLEARED their throat from across the hangar bay. The noise startled Awen and she looked up to see Valerie and Piper standing near an entry door. Valerie wore a lab coat more appropriate for her role as a doctor than a trooper, while Piper donned a pair of black crew shorts and a white t-shirt with the Gladio Umbra's insignia emblazoned over her left breast.

Magnus let go of Awen and motioned the two over. "Whad'ya got, doc."

Valerie pulled Piper forward. Awen could have sworn the little girl was intentionally falling behind.

"Is it my lab coat that gave it away?" Valerie asked.

Magnus nodded. "I'm guessing it has to do with Flow and Cheeks."

"It does, but…" Valerie looked at Awen. "If I'm interrupting something—"

"It's fine," Awen said. "Please. Go on."

Valerie brought out a data pad and showed it to Magnus. "I've got good news and bad news."

"Let's start with the good news."

"The good news is that Flow and Cheeks have agreed to stay behind and provide orbital oversight for the mission."

Awen couldn't be sure, but she thought she saw Magnus relax a little.

"That *is* good news," he said.

"The bad news is that that little show of yours really messed with their heads." Valerie raised the data pad for Magnus to see.

"What am I looking at?"

"Brain activity," she said. "It's a scan of a normal human male in their early thirties. Then this"—Valerie swiped to another screen with a dramatically different graph on it—"is Cheeks's scan."

Awen really had no idea what she was looking at, but the plot points were much higher and far more erratic. Based on the concern in Valerie's voice alone, Awen could tell the results weren't good.

As Valerie went on to explain the severity of Cheek's PTSD, elaborating even more on his severe head trauma, Awen noted Piper looking down at the floor. In fact, Awen was pretty sure that her protege was hiding behind her mother's leg. Awen sidestepped the conversation that Magnus and Valerie were having and knelt behind Valerie.

"Hey, doma," Awen said, using the Novia word for student.

"Hi, shydoh."

"What are you doing back here?"

Piper's eyes darted around. "Back where?"

"You can't fool me," Awen said, trying to keep her tone light and happy. "You get in trouble with your mom or something?"

Piper shook her head.

"No?" Awen scratched her chin like they were playing a puzzle game. "Hmm. Forgot to pick up your dirty clothes?"

Piper smiled for a second but then shook her head. "Mmm-mm."

Suddenly, Magnus coughed and Awen watched Piper jerk away. Her little hands clutched her mother's coat. *What in all mystics is that about?* Awen wondered.

"Piper." Awen was on her knees now, leaning toward the

girl. Valerie's body blocked them from Magnus's views. "Are you certain you're okay?"

Piper nodded again. "I'm okay, shydoh."

"But… you seem anxious."

"I don't really think I know what *ackshnos* is."

"Anxious. When you're worried about something." Awen studied Piper's face carefully and contemplated slipping into the Unity. But Piper would notice that, and the last thing she wanted to do was put the girl on guard further. "Are you worried about something?"

"No, shydoh."

That was when Awen knew Piper was lying. A little girl, on the horizon between universes, caught in the middle of a galactic war, and less than a day away from going into combat on the Luma home world—*and she wasn't worried about something?*

Awen could either press the matter now or wait for a better opportunity. Given the current stress that Piper was clearly exhibiting, Awen thought it would be safer to wait. "Well, if you need to talk, you know where to find me."

"Okay, shydoh."

"Flow isn't as bad," Valerie said as Awen stood back up. "But they're both unfit for duty, as you suspected."

Magnus sighed. "Thanks for the report."

"I'm sorry, Adonis," Valerie said, putting her hand on his forearm. "I really am."

Magnus covered her hand with his own. While Awen

didn't suspect him of any false motives, she did think that Valerie's contact was unnecessary.

Valerie let go. "I'll see you both later then."

"Sounds good." Magnus looked around Valerie's hip and waved. "Bye, Piper."

But the little girl only waved back at Awen.

As the pair went back through the door, Awen stared at Magnus with a concerned look. "Something's not right."

"No kidding. That Jujari procedure must've done something that—"

"Not them." Awen crossed her arms again. "Piper."

"Oh."

"What do you think Nos Kil said to her?"

Magnus seemed to hesitate—which felt odd. "Could have been anything."

She cocked her head a little. "You know something."

"Me?" He pulled his head back a little. "I know as much as you. And, according to Azie, Piper made sure no one is ever seeing the footage of what happened in there."

Awen bit her lip. "You don't think that he… you know…"

"Mystics, no." Magnus pressed a thumb into his temple. "Don't talk like that, Awen."

"I'm just making sure."

"Valerie said there was no evidence of physical contact."

"I know. It's just that…" Awen felt like she was underwater and gasping for air. "I don't know. She seemed afraid of you."

Magnus blushed. Which seemed strange. "Afraid of me?"

"Yeah…" She squinted. "You sure you don't know something?"

Magnus raised his eyebrows. "Maybe Nos Kil got in her head or something. Maybe it made her scared of men right now. Or maybe she's just tired. Could be a lot of reasons for her behavior."

"Could be…" Still, Awen felt like there was something more. And, for whatever reason, she felt like Magnus was hiding something. She hated herself for feeling that way. But she couldn't help it. Something was off.

"Magnus," came TO-96's voice over the hangar bay's speaker system. "Please report to the bridge for the jump to protospace."

"I'll be right there, 'Six."

"Very good, sir."

Magnus glanced at Awen. "We good?"

She nodded. "Yeah. I still think something's wrong with Piper though."

"We'll figure it out. Promise."

"Okay. I just… I don't want her getting hurt."

"That makes two of us. Now, come on. We have a universe to skip out on." Magnus took her by the hand and led her out of the hangar bay. "Time to go free your friends."

18

THE *PARAGON* NAVY followed the *Black Labyrinth's* example and drove hard into the Jujari fleets, following Admiral Brighton's forceful orders. Moldark had listened to the entire transmission, noting how the admiral's voice trembled when he spoke. He could feel Brighton's disgust, quivering at the horror of his orders. But there was something visceral about the admiral's state—as if the more he spoke, the more he believed in what he was saying. Moldark knew that his celestial presence was beginning to influence Brighton. It wouldn't be long now before the man was consumed with hate for the enemy.

The whole episode was like watching a boxer step away from the first man he'd killed in a ring. The laws spared him from any charge of homicide, of course, but they could not spare him from the reality of taking another life. That would mar the fighter forever. But it also did something else—it awakened the demon. If he could kill once, he could kill again. And he would fight to kill whether he meant to or not.

Moldark heard the killer in Brighton now. He heard it so distinctly that his own soul quivered in delight. The admiral had seen what unbridled violence of force had done. And he would want it again. And again. And again. Until the only thing that would stop him would be for someone else who'd tasted the sweetness of taking life to remove Brighton from the battlefield.

Moldark watched as a disabled Sypeurlion battleship carved a hole through Oorajee's atmosphere, its belly consumed in fire. Flames cascaded up the sides, fluttering wildly as the great ship plunged to its death in the dunes of the desert planet. With any luck, the ship would impact the planet and create a debris field that blotted out even more Jujari lives.

Just behind it, a Dim-Telok battlecruiser broke apart, its two halves flipping into the atmosphere amidst a conflagration so great that black plumes of smoke raked across the planet for hundreds of kilometers. It seemed as if a hellion monster had drawn its claw across the sky in a final act to protest its death. In the end, however, even the beast's staunchest refusal to be put down could not hold off the inevitable.

"And I am inevitable," Moldark whispered. "I will come for you all."

The alert tone from an incoming call trilled in the background. This was maybe the fifth or sixth time Moldark had ignored it over the last ten minutes. But anyone who needed him had access to his private channel, so whoever this was could wait. Though Moldark's comms officers did have control over what transmissions were routed to his private quarters. So the fact that they had not prevented this one from coming in meant that it was important. *At least according to their standards,* he thought.

Moldark sighed, spun away from the windows, and sat down in his chair, looking at the arm to review the comms display. The transmission data read Forum Republica and gave no other information about the caller. Moldark tried to ignore the request again but thought better of it—he had a feeling that whoever this was wouldn't stop until they spoke to him.

As soon as Moldark pressed the Audio icon, a voice said, "Admiral Kane, I order you to put me on screen."

Moldark thought for a moment. The voice sounded like it belonged to a senator. On Capriana. Curious, Moldark leaned forward and swiped the comms transmission open. The face of a stately man appeared, grey hair groomed meticulously around his mouth and temples. Moldark went through Kane's memories and found the name. "Senator Blackman."

The moment the senator saw Moldark—the moment he heard the strangeness of his voice—Blackman reared away from the holo cam. "Mystics, Kane. What's... what's happened to you?"

Moldark felt a certain measure of pity for the old man. It wasn't the senator's fault that he'd never seen the manifestation of an Elemental before. Then again, no one had in this gods forsaken universe—at least not to their knowledge. If they had, the rumors likely flew that someone had seen a goblin, a ghoul, or a ghost. Moldark certainly felt the same disgust when he viewed humans. But watching the senator wince in revulsion gave Moldark a certain satisfaction in knowing the man would be dead soon.

Moldark ignored the senator's question. "To what do I owe the pleasure of your call, senator?"

Blackman's lips were set in an awkward sneer of disgust as he still hadn't recovered from Moldark's appearance. His eyes searched the screen as if something might explain Moldark's blistered skin, black eyes, or razor-like teeth. But there was no explanation, *at least none he'll be content with*, Moldark thought.

"We're getting reports of catastrophic enemy losses," Blackman said, finally finding his nerve.

Moldark waited for more, expecting some judgement to be rendered, but nothing came. "And you consider this a bad thing?"

"Well," Blackman huffed, "when your orders were to defend Republic interests and prevent—"

"You trained me to start wars, senator. Further, you charged me with subduing the enemy at all costs."

"Yes, but the mere presence of a fleet does the majority of that work on its own. Wouldn't you agree, admiral?"

"So your philosophy allows you to build weapons but subsequently compels you not to use them?"

Blackman scratched the top of his forehead. "Honestly, I

don't know who I'm talking to here, Kane. And I sure as hell don't know what you did to yourself. But our agreement was that you would look to obtain the device from the mwadim and deliver it to us. Instead… well…" The man's face grew red and his voice rose. "Instead we have a PR nightmare on our hands that we may not recover from for a century. I can't reach any of the other fleet admirals, and I want to know what in mystic's name you're doing out there on the edge of the quadrant! On top of it all, you completely failed to kill So-Elku like I ordered you to! Need I remind you that the Nine gave you control of Third Fleet to serve our purposes and not your own?"

Moldark let the exasperated politician catch his breath before speaking. "Are you done?"

Blackman looked left and right as if checking the room before he exploded. "What do you mean *am I done?* Is that all you have to say for yourself? Kane, you're clearly out of control out there. We're hearing that you're quite literally crushing the Jujari fleet and their coalition forces using not just your fleet, but all Republic fleets. You're breaching all rules of engagement, and I have a media hailstorm erupting outside my office as we speak."

"Senator, I—"

"No, Kane! This is not what we agreed upon. You're out of line, you're… you've… We're calling you in."

Moldark wasn't sure what the term meant. He let his mind search Kane's and found the words tucked away in an emotionally debilitating compartment reserved for only the gravest of circumstances. "Calling me in," he repeated without emotion.

"Yes," Blackman blurted out, sweat forming along his forehead.

"I see. And when would you like me to return?"

The senator looked incensed, his lips sputtering in a failed attempt to form coherent words. "Now!"

Moldark considered this and felt the timing rather amusing. He turned his enormous captain's chair around until he faced the waning space battle. While the Republic's technology was inferior to that of his people, it did serve the purpose of defeating the Jujari. That, and the archaic nature of it all had a certain charm, one that made Moldark smile. He watched as another Jujari vessel rolled out of orbit and began its death plunge toward the orange planet's surface.

"Mystics, man. Answer me!"

"Answer *you*," Moldark restated for clarity, lifting an eyebrow for emphasis. "Very well. I will come to you as soon as my affairs here are in order."

"Your affairs? Once *your* affairs are in order? Admiral, I don't think you understand what's happening here. You are being charged with treason. Treason! We have already ordered your arrest and you will either come willingly or by force."

"My arrest?" Moldark chuckled. "How quaint."

"Quaint?" Blackman seemed flabbergasted, unable to breathe. "You will surrender yourself to—"

"To who?"

"To the crew of—"

"To the crew of my ship who bow to my every whim? To the other ships in the fleet who are taking orders from me and me alone? And if not them then who, exactly, are you sending to fetch me, dear senator? It seems that the prudent course, if I were you, would be to not rush this last part. One never knows the peril they hasten when driven by fear."

The senator wrinkled his nose and leaned in to the holo cam. "Do I detect a threat from you, admiral?"

"Not at all," Moldark said like an animated parent speaking to a child. Then his voice darkened with delight. "It's an omen."

19

AZELON BROUGHT the *Spire* into Worru's orbit without any resistance from the Luma. In fact, if she was to be believed, no one on the planet even knew the ship was there, thanks to the Novia's cloaking technology.

The shuttles, however, weren't as fortunate and required that the pilots traverse to the planet's far side, make entry, and then travel below radar on approach to Plumeria. In addition to the two shuttles that carried Granther Company, two more shuttles accompanied them to ferry any Luma prisoners that Magnus and Awen found.

TO-96 and Cyril sliced several databanks to access ship logs for vessels native to Worru. They stole four identification tags and reassigned them to the shuttles, making the ships appear to have come from another city on the planet's far side. So far, the plan was working like a charm, and all four shuttles had touched down in docking bays thirty-four through thirty-seven.

"If I'm not back in sixty-minutes, you proceed to waypoint Juliet Zero Two," Magnus said to Awen.

"We head to Grand Arielina," she replied.

Magnus nodded. "And don't think twice. Just get in as fast as you can, find Willowood and the others, and get out. If the codex is within reach, get it, but it's not a main priority."

"Understood. But what about you?"

"He's either gonna arrest me or come along for the ride. You'll hear it over comms."

Awen took a deep breath. "Be careful."

"Be dangerous," he replied with a wink.

"Sure." Then she hit the ramp door button with the heel of her hand and watched a sliver of moonlight pierce through the darkened cargo bay. The ramp hadn't even come down halfway when Magnus kissed her, put his helmet on, and vaulted through the gap. She hit stop, then stared at the darkened Plumeria skyline.

"Now what?" Silk asked, standing directly behind Awen with her NOV1 laying over her shoulder.

"We let Magnus be Magnus and wait."

MAGNUS MOVED ALONE through the streets of Plumeria. His Novia armor was in chameleon mode, allowing him to operate without risk of being seen. But given how quiet everything was, he was more worried about being heard than seen.

For someone who'd developed a deep resentment of the Luma, he never imagined he'd be on their homeworld three times in less than a year—depending upon what universe one was counting time in—and certainly not to save a handful of their asses. But, like Awen, he'd been changing—*and for the better*, he noted. This first part of the mission, however, was not about the Luma. It was about the Repub, about the Marines, and about his relationship with one of the Corps' legends.

Magnus followed the vector waypoints on his HUD until he stood outside the colonel's residence. It was a two-story stone building in a nice part of the city—though Magnus guessed the "nice parts" of Plumeria outnumbered the "not so nice parts" a hundred to one.

He double checked the time to see he had forty-nine minutes left before needing to either get back to the shuttles or send them on their way.

"Azie, you seeing this lock?" Magnus asked over comms as he zoomed in on the front door.

"Affirmative," she replied. "Please stand by."

Magnus waited a moment, keeping his vision focused on the security panel, when Azelon said, "Sir, please raise your left wrist toward the security system."

"My left wrist?" No sooner did he lift his arm than a hard-light emitter on his wrist projected a replica of Azelon's robotic hand. Magnus almost winced at the apparition but managed to hold still.

"Please keep me steady, sir."

"You got it, Azie."

Magnus watched a series of lights blink along the home security device as Azelon's hand went to work, moving faster than he could track. A soft chime issued from the door, followed by a feminine voice that said, "Welcome, friend of Colonel William Caldwell. Please come in."

Magnus swore. Everything seemed louder when trying to be covert. Still, he had to remind himself that such a sound would be white noise in this neighborhood. Hopefully the colonel felt the same. The hard-light emitter faded and Azelon's hand disappeared.

"Thanks, Azie."

"My pleasure, sir."

The door slid open and Magnus stepped into a spartan hallway. An opening on either side led to a living room and an office respectively. The hallway terminated at the kitchen while the stairwell—he assumed—led to the bedrooms. The colonel had lost his wife years ago, so unless he had a mistress for a sleepover, the colonel should have been alone.

Magnus switched from night vision to HSI—high sensitivity infrared. Instantly, he saw a single warm body lying in bed on the second story.

"I have eyes on the colonel," Magnus informed Azie. "Proceeding upstairs." He powered off chameleon mode to conserve energy and switched his NOV1 to its new mode. Azelon had modified the weapon to produce a high-voltage low-amperage discharge if Magnus needed to subdue Caldwell without permanently harming him. He laid his finger on the trigger guard and moved up the stairwell. His footfalls were slow and methodical, and he kept his hips and shoulders even, resisting his body's natural tendency to bounce up the steps.

Magnus turned right at the top of the stairs and approached the master bedroom. "Azie, can you put that door on manual?"

"Affirmative," she replied. Magnus saw a small blue LED shift colors to green.

"Thanks."

He laid a hand on the door and slid it to the right. When the opening was large enough for him to slip through, Magnus stepped sideways into the room and pointed his weapon at the bed. Caldwell was still asleep. He'd taken no more than three steps across the bedroom floor when he heard the power cycle of a pistol.

"Hold right there," said a commanding voice behind him, followed by the chime of a desk lamp turning on. A small nudge just under the back of Magnus's helmet meant there was probably a weapon pointed at the base of his neck.

Magnus brought his hands up slowly. Whoever this was, his body hadn't registered on Magnus's HUD.

"I'm not here to hurt anyone," Magnus said over his external speaker.

"Looks like a mighty big gun for someone who isn't interested in shooting it."

Magnus froze. "Colonel Caldwell?"

"I should hope so. You did break into his house, after all."

"Colonel, it's me, Magnus." Magnus felt the weapon behind his head twitch.

"You're gonna need more proof than that," Caldwell said, pressing the barrel back into Magnus's neck.

"You accepted my request to move the Fearsome Four to RIS after Nos Kil killed your son in Caledonia." The words came out effortlessly despite the cruel memories they provoked.

There was a moment's hesitation before Caldwell said, "Magnus?"

Magnus raised one hand and pulled off his helmet, making a grand display of his intentions. Then Magnus turned slowly to look at the colonel. When their eyes met, Caldwell powered down his pistol.

"Holy mystics, Magnus. What in *the* hades are you doing here? And what are you wearing?"

"It's a long story, colonel. But we don't have much time."

"Time before what?"

"Time before things go sideways. You got somewhere we can talk?"

"Sure, sure, Magnus. Just let me get some damn clothes on." That was when Magnus realized the colonel wasn't wearing a thing. He looked from the dimly lit bathroom to the bed, confused.

"I don't get it?" Magnus asked as the man stood in front of a tall dresser. "IR sensors showed you we're in bed. Did you know I was coming? You spoofed my kit?"

The colonel laughed. "I guess there are some benefits to getting old."

"I don't follow."

"Heating pad, son." Caldwell chuckled, then nodded toward the bathroom. "And I was taking a cold shower. Doc says it's good for my circulation."

"Son of a bitch," Magnus said with a grin.

"Now"—Caldwell pulled a shirt over his head and walked toward the door—"let's get us some coffee and you can tell me what's going on."

"Sir, I really don't think you—"

"Have time for coffee? Son, if there isn't time for coffee, then we're already screwed, so what's the difference?"

Magnus sighed. "Lead the way."

MAGNUS SAT at the colonel's small kitchen table, talking to Caldwell as fast as his brain would allow and still be coherent. He didn't realize just how much had happened since their last meeting here on Worru and feared this was taking too much time. But sharing the details was too important to skip. The colonel needed to know everything if he was going to make an informed decision.

When Magnus had finished, Caldwell said, "That's all

well and good, but it still doesn't explain why you caught me in my bedroom with my pants down."

"To be fair to the saying, you actually caught *me* with my pants down."

"That I did," the colonel said with a smile, sipping the last of his coffee. "So? What do you want from me?"

"Well, sir, I was hoping you'd join us." Magnus searched the colonel's face for any sign of a reaction, but the man was unreadable.

Caldwell cleared his throat. Then he licked the corner of his mouth as if searching for his ever-present cigar, and rotated his coffee mug on the table when he couldn't find it. "You've got a lot of balls coming here. You know that, right?"

"I do, colonel. And you know I wouldn't have come unless it was serious."

The old man nodded. "And what, you hoping I can sling one of these fancy alien weapons and clear buildings with you? Is that it?"

"Well, sir. Actually, I was hoping you'd help—"

"Get the heat off your ass and clear your name with the brass?"

Magnus's eyes snapped up to meet his. The thought had crossed his mind, of course, but it seemed too far-fetched to be real. Given the charges of attempted murder of a senator and whatever else the Repub had cooked up about Magnus's involvement with starting the Jujari war, the only thing that seemed like it would get them to stand down was his head on a platter.

"Actually, sir, I was hoping you'd help build our team."

Caldwell stopped rotating his mug. "Then you're serious about taking everyone on then."

"Everyone?"

"Son." Caldwell leaned into the table, making it creak. "You're on Plumeria in the middle of the night about to break into the mystic-damned capital building to try and free prisoners charged with treason against the Luma *and* the Republic. So, yes—you're about to take on everyone."

"Damn, colonel, you don't need to be so enthusiastic about it."

Caldwell laughed. "And then you're hoping I'm gonna what—help recruit Marines who might be second guessing their orders to stop you?"

"The thought had crossed my mind."

"Splick, son." Caldwell took a deep breath and let his shoulders sag. "I'm getting too old for this."

Magnus raised an eyebrow. "So… is that a yes?"

"You're a damned son of a bitch, Adonis. Just like your grandfather. You know that, right?"

A wave of relief flooded Magnus's chest like… like a heating blanket on an old man's bed.

"I'll help you however I can, son. I also felt Kane craved power for the sake of power, and now that he's morphed into this *Moldark* fellow, well, he's got a pile of hurt coming. On top of all that, I already know Master So-Elku is as vile as an old whore's hanky holder, *and* in league with the senate to boot. The way I see it, the galaxy needs a push in the right direction, son. But I'm not sure you're recruiting anyone on this side of the Corps. So far, there's no reason for them to question the chain of command, not like what you've seen. And I don't think we'll have time to recruit any of my battalion stationed here on Worru. You're on a tight schedule, ain't you, son?"

"Pretty damn tight, colonel. There's just not enough time for you to speak to your commanders, not like what we're doing here. And you haven't asked me for proof like they will."

"And they'll need it too." The colonel seemed to grow solemn as his brow furrowed. "No, there's not enough time. Which means this might turn ugly faster than a witch's tits in a tornado."

Magnus suppressed a smile, knowing what the colonel *really* meant by things turning ugly. "While the fight for allegiances hasn't come to them yet, it has to others. And that's where your voice might help in the future. That's where we need you, colonel. *I* need you."

"For those inside the Paragon, as you called it."

Magnus nodded. "I don't believe all of them want to be there."

"People like your captured pilot."

"Exactly."

Caldwell scratched his chin, then gave a soft chuckle. "Desk rash is a lot worse than they say."

"So is trigger rash. But desks are a lot safer."

"Some might argue that point." Caldwell looked straight

at Magnus with one eye half closed. "You remember how I said I accepted this station to see if the Luma were on to something? On to another way of bringing peace to the galaxy?"

"I remember you alluding to something of that nature, yeah."

"Well, they aren't. Not the way I had hoped. They're just like the suits in high towers of Capriana, making people dance but with different music. Desks kill as good as blasters. It's just harder to tell who's shooting at you. So, if there's another way to figure this out, if there's another fix for the galaxy? Leave it to a Magnus to figure it out."

"You're really in then?"

"When do we leave?"

"As soon as you turn off your heating pad and put your damned dentures in."

20

Magnus and Caldwell made it back to the shuttles without incident, and with five minutes to spare.

"Cutting it a little close, aren't we, Magnus?" Awen said as he and the colonel came up the ramp and into the cargo bay congested with gladias.

"Awen, this is Colonel Caldwell," Magnus said, introducing the two of them. "Colonel, this is—"

"Awen dau Lothlinium," he said, taking her hand and kissing the top of it.

"Magnus, you never told me he was a gentleman."

The colonel waved off the comment before Magnus could answer. "Only royalty get their hands kissed, miss" he said.

"We need to get him suited up," Magnus said, pushing past them with a hint of a grin on his face. "Azie! I need a suit and an NOV1."

"Right away, sir."

"Everyone else, get ready to move out." Magnus put his helmet on and repeated the order over comms for the other shuttle to hear. When he pulled it back off again, Caldwell was walking toward Azelon and a flight case that held a new Novia suit of armor and a weapon.

"So you convinced him," Awen said. "Nice work."

"Thanks. But it wasn't that hard. The old man's a pushover for a fight."

"I wouldn't sell yourself too short, Magnus."

He looked at her, eyebrows raised. "Oh?"

"You've got yourself quite a cause now. The way I see it, he would've been an idiot not to follow you."

"Let's hope he feels that way."

"He does."

Magnus hesitated. "Wait, did you—"

"He really respects you too, Magnus," she said, lowering her voice.

"But I thought there were Luma laws about not reading people's minds without their consent."

"Luma laws, exactly. I haven't written any for the Gladio Umbra yet. Plus, you really think I'm letting a Repub Colonel on this team without making sure he's not hiding anything?"

Suddenly, a wave of panic gripped Magnus's chest. If she'd read Caldwell's mind about his allegiance, had she read his mind about his past with Argus and Nos Kil? He swore in his head. *I do not need this head game right now.*

"You okay?" Awen asked.

"Yeah, fine. You?"

Awen winced. "Yeah… Magnus I… Whatever, let's just get this over with."

"Sounds good." He looked across the bay. "Azie?"

"He's almost ready, sir."

"Damn suit is a little tight around the midsection," Caldwell said.

"Desk life's a bitch, ain't it, colonel," Dutch said, walking to help the man with the plate armor.

"Corporal Dutch?" Caldwell asked, seeming to recognize her.

"It's just Dutch now, sir. You can drop the corporal."

"I can see my assigning you to Magnus turned out to be quite the commission."

"And I can see you put on a few kilos since the last time I stood in your office."

"Watch it. I can still court-martial you."

Dutch yanked on a plate strap that squeezed the colonel's gut. "Nah, you can't."

"You remember what I told you, Piper?"

The little girl in the power suit looked back at Awen and nodded. "Stick with you, look for enemies, keep our teammates from getting hurt without killing anyone to do it."

"Good girl. And if we get separated?"

"Make my way back here to the shuttles and wait for further instructions from Azelon."

"Right." Awen patted Piper down to make sure her suit was on right. Then she double checked her helmet before handing it to her.

"Everything's going to be okay, shydoh," Piper said, taking the helmet. "I won't let you down."

"It's not you I'm worried about," Awen muttered.

"What's that?"

Awen smiled. "Nothing. Put that on and get ready. Magnus will be giving the order any second." Awen couldn't be sure, but she thought she saw Piper squint when she said Magnus's name. "You okay?"

Piper looked at Awen and then pulled the helmet on. "I'm fine," she said over external speakers.

"You'd tell me if something was bothering you, right?"

Piper's helmet rocked up and down.

"And nothing's bothering you?"

Again, Piper's helmet moved, but left and right.

Awen sighed and raised her own helmet. "Okay then. Here we go."

GRANTHER COMPANY MOVED down Plumeria's main thoroughfare, jogging in two lines. Each suit's chameleon mode kept them hidden, while the stealth soles on their boots kept street noise to a minimum. It also helped that it was 0320 hours, so the only things awake were cockroaches and alley cats—*if the city even had any*, Magnus thought.

Plumeria was so picture-perfect it made his stomach turn. Even at night the place was fit for a scene in a fairytale holo movie. The streetlamps glowed a pale yellow, while the sandstone streets stretched out beneath purple and magenta flags lining every street he looked down.

"One klick to the courtyard," Dutch said over comms.

"Copy that," Magnus replied. He double checked to see that the colonel was in the rear with Awen and Piper. Then he decided to check in with Flow and Cheeks. A small side window opened on his HUD with an image of Flow on the *Spire's* bridge. "Flow, this is Magnus. How do you read me?"

"I'm reading you Lima Charlie, LT. Just like my girlfriend on video call—hot and spicy."

"You don't have a girlfriend," Cheeks replied, stepping into the frame.

"I do now," Flow said, pulling out a printed image of Cheeks's younger sister.

"Hey, where did you get that?" Cheeks tried to snatch the image out of Flow's hand but was warded off with an elbow to his ribs. "Son of a—"

"And how's the company's signal?" Magnus asked, trying to get the conversation back on track.

"We see you marching east on Avernon Street toward the waypoint Juliet Zero Two."

"And Azelon?"

Flow looked over his shoulder at the bot. "LT wants to know how you're doing, Azie."

"That is strange. I'm not detecting any issues with his communications suite. Is he experiencing a failure in reaching me?"

Flow looked back at Magnus. "She's good to go."

Magnus grinned. "Roger that. Make sure to light any new targets for us and call 'em out."

"Will do, LT. You stay safe."

"That's the plan."

Magnus closed the channel and felt his heart thump. He felt bad leaving Flow and Cheeks behind, but he felt even worse about getting Azelon to filter all video and audio content going to the *Spire's* bridge. It had taken some time, but the two AIs had figured out a way to swap all transmissions from Rohoar and the rest of the Jujari-filled Delta Platoon with human likenesses. Magnus needed the two Marines on this op, even if just for their eyes and ears, but he couldn't have them relapsing into a fit the moment they made contact with Rohoar or the others. It was underhanded. But it was necessary.

Magnus led the unit in silence for another few minutes before they arrived at the courtyard. He gave the order to spread out and hold. Then, over a hand-selected group channel, he said, "Nolan, Rix, and Silk."

"Yes, sir," they each replied.

"I want you on me. Abimbola, you too."

The ex-Navy pilot and the three former Marauders

acknowledged the request, and Magnus watched their respective icons move toward him on his map. When Magnus turned to face them, a detailed line-drawing of their bodies appeared in Magnus's HUD, marked with name tags and stats on each gladia's vitals.

"You all okay?" Magnus asked. "And before you answer, don't say fine. We all know what happened last time we were here."

Magnus could see Nolan's head nod on the line drawing. "It hurts, sir. Hurts like hell." Then the pilot looked to his right… to the exact damn spot where Simone had fallen to her death. "I miss her." He chuckled. "Funny thing is, I hardly knew her, ya know?" Nolan looked at the other three figures, knowing they'd spent far more time with Simone than he ever had—but he'd been at the control when Simone had fallen from the shuttle's ramp. "I see her face almost every night when I fall asleep." He let out a steady breath between pursed lips. "But I'm still good to go, sir. Ready or not, here we come."

Magnus patted him on the shoulder, watching his own hand appear as a line drawing in his field of view. "Good man."

"Thank you, sir."

"And you? Rix, Silk?"

"I'm good, buckethead," Rix said.

"Me too." Silk swung her NOV1 around. "Simone would have wanted us to come back here and kick some Luma ass. Pretty sure she's with us, waiting to make sure we do it right."

"Copy that," Magnus said. He looked to Abimbola for any additional comments but the Miblimbian waved him off. Over the company channel, Magnus said, "Okay, what'da we got, people?"

"I have visual on two sentries on the main porch," Dutch said. The targets lit up as yellow circles on the company's HUD as the armor system registered them.

"And we're reading four more guards inside the structure stationed at intervals leading up to the main dome," Flow said. Four more yellow circles appeared on Magnus's topo map.

"Seems like the night shift is lighter than we thought," Magnus said. "Awen?"

"Those are temple watchmen," she said. "Trained, but not the best the Luma has. Half the time they're students just looking to gain favor with the elders."

"Copy that. How about the prisoners?"

"Nothing yet," Awen replied. "Something's definitely blocking my ability to see inside the catacombs."

That was both a good thing and a bad thing. Good because it meant the enemy had something to hide. But bad because it meant Awen wasn't able to break through a passive defense.

"Let's take that as a good sign," Magnus said, choosing to be an optimist—at least for the time being. "Alpha Platoon, break left. Bravo, break right. Charlie, Delta, Echo, you're with me holding here and proceeding down the center once the sentries are neutralized. Proceed."

Green icons ran down the chat sidebar as Magnus watched Alpha and Bravo platoons run down either side of the courtyard. They made it to the Grand Arielina's wide front steps and sent two pair of gladias after the first two sentries. In Alpha Platoon, Ezo approached the night watchman while Valerie readied two sets of flexicuffs. Ezo snuck up behind the young man undetected, fired a single stun round between his shoulder blades, and then lowered him to the ground while Valerie bound his hands and feet with the cuffs. Then they worked together to carry the body off the front landing and into some dense bushes.

The textbook takedown took less than sixty seconds. The other team, made up of Silk and Rix, had taken even less time, neutralizing their guard in under forty seconds.

"Nice work, people," Magnus said. "Everyone else, on me."

Magnus moved into the open, stepping onto the courtyard's luxurious grass. Under normal conditions, his body would have been illuminated by the full moon and stars, but his armor's status bar said it was fully concealed. Plus, without the overlaid line-drawings he couldn't make out any of his fellow gladias, so he trusted the tech was doing its job.

They jogged clear across the lawn and ascended the front steps to rejoin the other two platoons. Magnus looked up and saw the arches of the open doors greet them like a sleeping monster's yawning mouth. When everyone was accounted for, Magnus ordered them through the entry and into the hallway.

"Rohoar, send four gladias to take out the sentries. Nothing lethal yet."

"Yes, Magnus," said the Jujari, his tone conveying considerable disappointment. "Saladin, Czyz, Longchomps, Grahban—you heard the mwadim."

Mwadim? Magnus thought, then realized he should probably come up with some sort of rank structure eventually. All these different naming conventions were starting to drive him crazy. *But mwadim?* That was just over the top.

Magnus watched on his HUD as the line-drawings of the four Jujari raced between the walls and the giant columns, keeping their presence hidden in the shadows. Then, in one coordinated move, all four emerged from the darkness—two from each side of the hallway—and yanked the Luma guards off their feet. The men vanished without so much as a scream and were subdued.

So far so good, Magnus thought. If the rest of the op went this smooth, they'd be out of here in less than thirty minutes, and no worse for wear. *But since when has an op ever gone as planned, Adonis? Don't jinx yourself.*

"You're clear until Elder's Hall," Flow said from the *Spire*. "After that, I can't see anything."

"Neither can I," Awen added.

"Me neither," Piper said. "It's like there's a big soap bubble all around it. Makes me wanna pop it with my finger."

"We might need you to do that in a sec," Magnus said to the girl. "Let's see what we find first."

The girl seemed to hesitate, then said, "Okay, Magnus."

Magnus? That was a first. "All units proceed."

Magnus padded down the red carpeted hallway, catching up to the four Jujari who'd gagged and bound the knocked-out Luma guards together in pairs and left them behind two pillars. Together, all of Granther Company moved up the tall set of marble stairs that led to the dome.

Images of the last time Magnus had been here flashed through his head. He remembered the panic he felt when his body had been rendered immobile by So-Elku. It was a helpless feeling, and he desperately wanted to avoid anything like that again. And he would, he hoped, because he had Awen. And Piper. Though the little girl had certainly seemed off lately. He desperately hoped that whatever was bothering her wouldn't affect the mission.

Magnus proceeded slowly up the steps, hearing the faintest sounds of padded boots on stone as the company followed behind him. When they got to the giant sets of gilded wooden doors, Magnus gave the order to hold.

"Dutch, try it out," Magnus ordered.

"Yes, sir."

The operator moved past him and applied her gloved hand to the giant gold handle. She pushed, then pulled, but nothing happened. "It won't budge."

Magnus swore. The next step was to see if Awen could open it, but if she couldn't, they'd need to breach it. And that was going to attract some company.

"Awen, you're up."

"Right behind you, Magnus."

Awen stepped around him and squared off with the middle set of main doors. He saw her lower her head, probably in concentration, and then he waited. Almost a whole minute went by before he finally asked, "How you doing?"

"Almost there."

Magnus's curiosity was getting the best of him, however. "So? What is it?"

Awen's voice was tight. "No questions."

"Copy."

He had to wait another twenty seconds before Awen stepped away from the doors. "There," she said, taking a few deep breaths.

"That bad?" Magnus asked.

"Just some minor protection placed over the dome. Nothing I wasn't expecting. But not the easiest energy to circumvent either."

"So… no alarms or warning bells or booby traps?"

She shook her head. "Nope. And it's empty inside too."

"We can confirm that up here too," Flow said.

"Looks clear," added Cheeks.

"Thanks, boys." Magnus looked through the walls, combining his bioteknia eyes with the armor's sensors to create a hybrid readout on the HUD. Sure enough, now that Awen had disarmed the force-field-whatever-you-call-it in the Unity, he could see that the temple was empty. "Looks like everyone went home for the night."

"Copy that," Dutch said. "Alpha Platoon making entry."

"Careful now," Magnus said, watching Dutch push open

the left-side door. A soft sliver of light appeared as she went in, her silhouette followed quickly by the rest of her platoon and TO-96. Magnus watched as the icons spread out, gladias running to the far sides of the massive circular room. Bravo Platoon went in next.

"Titus," Magnus said. "Have Charlie Platoon set up a defensive perimeter here. You have a good sightline of the hallway. No one gets through these doors."

"Copy that," Titus replied.

"Rohoar, follow me in."

"Yes, mwadim."

Magnus winced. "We've got to find a better name than that."

"But it is our most honored name."

"And I respect that, just… just stay on me."

"I understand."

Magnus pressed through the door after the last member of Bravo Platoon entered. Once inside, he could see the same vaulted ceiling as before. Cushions lined the space, and the far wall was open to the lush garden, now bathed in moonlight. Candles and torches flickered at intervals around the room, casting soft shadows across the floor. Interestingly, the gladias' bodies did nothing to interfere with the intricate lighting, replicating and recasting the firelight with ease.

"Abimbola, Rohoar. I want you and Bravo and Delta Platoons staying here. Work in conjunction with Titus if we get any company. Alpha and Echo Platoons, we're headed downstairs. TO-96, I'm assigning you to Echo."

"Very good, sir. I'm happy to be of service."

"And colonel?" Magnus asked.

"What do you need, son?"

"I'm assigning you to Abimbola and Bravo Platoon. You good with that?"

"Does he like cigars?"

Abimbola nodded. "Does he like Antaran backdraw?"

The colonel chuckled. "I think we'll get along just fine."

"Good. Awen?"

"Yes Magnus."

"Any idea how to get into the catacombs?"

"There's an old stairwell. This way."

"Please wait, Awen," Saasarr said, holding his lizard-like hand toward her chest. "Let me go first."

"He knows what he's doing," Sootriman added. "Reptalons like the shadows."

"I don't doubt that," Awen replied, and then stepped out of the way to let Saasarr pass. She directed him to a small alcove to the far left. To the naked eye, it looked like any small recess in the domed room, containing anything from a shrine to a sculpture. But upon close inspection, the small nook contained a painted door that blended nearly perfectly with the surrounding wall. The only thing that gave it away was the door's thin outline that appeared as a black crack.

"I do not see a handle," Saasarr said, patting the surface with his scaly hands.

"That's because it's in the Unity." Awen lowered her head and then reached forward, grabbing at the air. Her hand closed around something invisible. But when she pulled, the door separated from the wall and slide across the marble floor with a low groan.

Saasarr hissed something in his native tongue and Dutch stepped beside him. Both of their NOV1s were pointed through the opening and into a torchlit corridor that spiraled down and out of sight.

"After you, Saasarr," Dutch said. The Reptalon flicked his tongue, his toothy snout protruding out of his half-helmet, and then ducked into the passage and down the first few steps.

Magnus held Awen's arm, indicating she should let the rest of Alpha Platoon head down first. "Still no read on what's down there?"

"No," Awen replied. "It's like someone has set up a barrier."

"To keep us out," Magnus replied.

"Or to keep them in."

Magnus remembered that Willowood had connected directly to his head when he was last here. Perhaps that's precisely what So-Elku didn't want happening again.

Gilder was the last gladia to enter. Magnus nodded at Awen and Piper. He went to give the little girl a gentle push, to let her know it was alright and that he was right behind her, when Piper moved out of reach. The strange thing was that she had her back turned toward him, yet it seemed like... *like she avoided my touch on purpose.*

Another sick feeling filled Magnus's stomach. Nos Kil must've said something. But it would have to wait. Magnus suppressed the sensation and willed himself to stay focused on the mission.

"Whad'ya got, Saasarr?" Magnus asked, picking up the rear. His feet plodded down the spiral staircase as he listened for the Reptalon's reply.

"Something," Saasarr hissed. "Saasarr smells something…"

"Something what?" Dutch asked.

"Something sweet."

"Sweet means human," Sootriman said.

"How comforting," Valerie added.

"We're at the bottom," Dutch said. "Opens into a wide hallway, about two meters high."

"Wait for us all to get there," Magnus said, wishing the line would move faster.

"Copy that, LT."

By the time Magnus got to the bottom level, Alpha and Echo Platoons lined the walls of the wide room that seemed to stretch on for at least a hundred yards. There were torches hung at intervals, and between them…

"Doors," Awen said. "I see old doors. They're sealed shut, however."

Magnus looked at her and then at the walls. He didn't see a thing but old stonework, nor was anything coming up on his HUD to indicate that there were cavities anywhere on this level. "You sure about that?"

"Positive."

"I see them too," Piper said. "But… I don't think there's

anyone in them."

"I agree," Awen said. But the sound of her voice betrayed a lack of confidence.

"You sure there's nothing in them?"

She hesitated. "I suppose that's a relative term. Legend has it that the great Luma Masters are buried down here, their crypts sealed shut for all time."

"So you mean to tell Ezo that he is walking through an underground graveyard of mystics? They did *not* put this on the guided tour's description."

"It's okay," Awen replied. "They're just bones and dust."

"Somehow, that doesn't comfort Ezo. Come to think of it, that makes it worse."

"So you can see past the defensive wall now?" Magnus asked, trying to think of a better way to describe whatever had hindered Awen's second sight before.

"As soon as we stepped off the last stair, yes." She took a few more steps forward. "And it seems to clarify further as I walk."

"So it's a proximity thing," Ezo said, walking up beside Piper. "Is it the same for you?"

"Yup. I couldn't see anything in the Unity down here until we got off the stairs."

"Interesting," Ezo said.

"It looks like we have another stairwell at the end of this hall," Saasarr said, tongue flicking out on each S-sound he pronounced.

"Lead the way," Magnus replied. "Awen, Piper, I need you

telling us the first thing you see out of the ordinary."

"We will," Awen said.

Magnus waited for Piper to agree, but she didn't. *Why? What's going on in that little head of hers? Dammit*—he was letting the situation get to him, and he couldn't afford to be distracted.

Saasarr and Dutch moved smoothly along either side of the hallway, followed by the rest of the team. Magnus came up beside TO-96 and said, "I want you hanging back."

"Hanging back, sir?"

"On this level. I want you staying here while we descend more."

"But, sir—"

"No buts, 'Six. You're the best solo option I had for heavy armament, so I need you covering this floor in case anything… you know."

"I know what, sir?"

"Anything gets crazy."

"Crazy, sir?"

"Exactly."

The bot's eyes glimmered and his head tilted sideways.

"If you see anything, call it out."

"I will endeavor to please you, sir."

"I know, 'Six."

Magnus caught up with the others as they were descending the stairwell. Like the previous one, it descended some twenty-five meters before spitting everyone out onto yet another level of long walls and torches.

"Looks the same as above," Dutch said.

"Any signs of life, Awen?" Magnus asked.

"Negative. Just more crypts."

"More crypts and Ezo's got more creeps."

"Hush, love," Sootriman chided. "Momma's here."

"Momma?" Magnus raised his eyebrows, though no one could see them.

"It's one of their things," Awen said as quietly as she could.

"Ah." Magnus sniffed. "Saasarr, looks like another stairwell ahead."

"Indeed, sir," hissed the Reptalon.

"Lead the way."

"As you wish, sir."

Just as before, the team proceeded down the wide but short hallway and entered the far stairwell, descending single file. No sooner had they set foot on the third level than Awen froze. "There's someone down here."

Magnus looked down the empty hallway and then turned to face her. "You sure?"

"Of course she's sure, Magnus," Piper replied. *There she goes with my last name again.* Something was definitely off with her, he was certain of it.

"Don't get me wrong," Magnus said to Awen, ignoring Piper's insolent tone. "But I'm not seeing any doors down here."

"That's because they've been sealed in the crypts."

21

"You're telling me someone transported them in there?" Magnus squinted at Awen even though he knew she couldn't see his face. "Someone trapped them behind the walls?"

"Well, maybe not transported them, but opened the doors and then sealed them shut again, more than likely."

"Ezo is *not* liking this."

"Easy, love." Sootriman rested a hand on Ezo's shoulder.

"He's not liking this at all."

"Okay, everyone," Magnus said, trying to maintain control in light of this rather odd predicament. "We're going to get the prisoners out and—"

"Are we sure it's even them?" Valerie wondered.

To Magnus's embarrassment, he hadn't even thought about whether or not the people that Awen sensed might be people other than Willowood and the Luma loyal to her. "Awen? Piper?"

"I'm looking. Hold on…" Awen held up a hand for everyone to be silent. "I see…"

Magnus found himself holding his breath as he waited for her verdict. If this was not Willowood and her people, then they'd just wasted precious time on a fool's errand. But then that made Magnus wonder who else might be down here in these crypts.

"It is them," Awen said at last. The platoon let out a corporate sigh of relief and Magnus passed the word over the company channel. Abimbola, Rohoar, and Titus congratulated him and insisted they get back up fast so they could get out of there.

"We'll be up shortly," Magnus replied. *Just as soon as we figure out how to free them*, he thought of adding but didn't want to make the conversation any more complicated than it needed to be. The important thing was that they'd located Willowood.

Magnus touched Awen on the shoulder. "So how do we do this?"

"I'm going to have Piper try and help me open the doors. They are between all the torches. But they've been sealed shut using some sort of powerful force within the Unity. So it might take a second or two."

"We'll be ready."

"And I don't know what kind of condition they're in," Awen added. "I can hardly make out their life signs. I'm guessing So-Elku trapped them in there. Willowood is powerful. But if she's been harmed, or if these crypts have cut off their powers in some way…"

"We'll get them out of here and get them the care they need." Magnus watched her shoulders rise and fall. "It's going to be okay. Just get them out and we'll do the rest."

"Okay." Awen took Piper by the hand and walked down the middle of the stone hallway until they reached what seemed to be the center. Then, still holding hands, the two of them lowered their heads as if in prayer. At first nothing happened. But then their suits started to glow. The light was soft, but then grew in intensity until Magnus's HUD automatically adjusted to account for the unusually bright light now filling the third level of the catacombs.

The stone floor began to tremble. Magnus felt dust and bits of stone ping off his armor. He looked up to see a steady stream of debris breaking free of the ceiling. A low rumble shook the walls, and Magnus was pretty sure that if Awen and Piper let this go on, the other platoons may be digging out more bodies than they bargained for.

He was just about to say something when, all along the hallway, several sections of stone pivoted away from the walls. The torchlight flickered as gusts of wind and soft lights spilled from the cavities. The members of Alpha Platoon, along with Saasarr, had their weapons up and trained on the openings.

Then, as if a conductor drew the orchestra to the end of the final measure, the vibrations stopped. Awen opened her eyes. "It's okay," she said over her external speakers. "You can come out now."

OPENING all the doors was harder than Awen thought it would be. Whoever had closed them was strong, and undoing their work had taken a lot of concentration and energy. She had one guess as to whose handiwork this was, and she already knew it had been assisted by research found in the codex. She knew because she felt it. She knew because the Foundation and the Nexus were a part of her skillset too.

When the doors opened and the quaking ceased, Awen returned to her natural sight and said, "It's okay. You can come out now." She reached up and removed her helmet. Piper did the same. And a beat later, Valerie walked up to join them, also removing her helmet.

The first person to emerge was a woman in her sixties, dressed in dusty red and black robes. Her grey hair was wiry and wild, and she had wrists full of bracelets, bangles, and baubles.

"Willowood," Awen yelled, then raced forward to embrace the woman. More people began to emerge from the crypts, their faces and clothes covered in dust.

"Hello, child," Willowood cried. "I wasn't sure if you'd come."

"We have. We all have."

"I can see that. Let me look at you." Willowood pushed

Awen back and looked her up and down. "Well don't you look fancy."

"It's a power suit. But there's so much to explain." Awen nearly slapped herself in the forehead. "And that's not the most important part! Willowood, your—"

"I'll take it from here," Valerie said.

Willowood turned toward Valerie and Piper, her hands slowly going to her mouth. "Oh my…"

"Hello, mother," Valerie said.

"Valerie? Is it really you?"

Valerie nodded and put her hands on the sides of her face. "It is." She and Willowood stepped forward and then wrapped their arms around one another in a forceful embrace.

"My beloved daughter, is it really you?" Willowood repeated.

Valerie sobbed through her response, which caught Awen off guard. The women had been so strong—so sure of herself—that Awen never imagined she'd hear the senator's wife cry. But cry she did, squeezing her mother tight for all she was worth.

When the two finally stepped away, neither seemed able to find the right words. Finally, Valerie said, "Piper, this is your grandmother."

"Grammie, please," Willowood said, kneeling down. "No need to be so formal around here."

"I'm Piper."

"And aren't you beautiful. You're so much taller than the last time I saw you too."

"Is it okay if I give you a hug?"

"I would like that very much."

As the two embraced, Awen found herself wiping away her own tears. The emotions had caught her off guard. She'd been so focused on finding Willowood, on keeping the fear at bay in this dark place, that she'd completely failed to imagine what this reunion might be like. She looked at Magnus, and even though he was still under his helmet, she thought her second sight showed a tear forming in the corner of his eye.

Willowood held Piper and looked up at Awen. "Thank you for coming."

"Of course." Awen sniffed and wiped her cheeks. "What else were we going to do?"

"Mother, we have so much to tell you," Valerie said. "I don't even know where to start."

"I hate to break this up," Magnus interjected, removing his helmet. "But we've gotta get you ladies outta here." He extended his hand in greeting. "Willowood, my name is Adonis Magnus."

"I know who you are, Magnus."

Magnus hesitated. "You were the one in my... in my head." He tapped a gloved finger on his temple.

Willowood released Piper, nodded, and stood to shake his hand. "That's right. And you responded very well considering how unnerving that must have been."

Magnus shrugged off the compliment. "Any idea how many people you have here, ma'am?"

Willowood turned to watch the rest of the Luma pour out of the crypts. "Last I knew, we were fifty-four."

Magnus repeated the number, sounding surprised. "And they're all politically aligned with your cause?"

"If you're asking whether or not they're loyal to the pursuit of peace in the galaxy and, therefore, worth rescuing, the answer is most certainly yes."

"Right. Okay then." He donned his helmet again and opened a channel to all of Granther Company. "Be advised, we have the prisoners. Fifty-five souls to evac."

"Copy that," Titus said. "Hallway still clear."

"Dome clear," Abimbola added.

"I, however, do have activity to report," said TO-96.

"What is it, 'Six?" Magnus asked.

"I am sensing movement from behind the walls on this level," the bot replied.

"As in rats?"

"Negative, sir. Something much larger. I advise you to ascend to Elder's Hall immediately."

"Sounds like a plan."

Magnus pushed his external speaker to 80%—not wishing to hurt anyone with the full force of Novia Minoosh audio technology—and turned to face the hallway, now bustling with gladias and Luma. "Listen up, everyone. We're here to get you topside and then off this planet. We're more than likely going to encounter some resistance. But we're prepared for that. It would go a long way, however, if those of you who are in good enough condition could join us using your… your mystical Union—"

"The Unity," Awen whispered over comms.

"Your powers in the Unity to assist us. If you're so able, I need a quick show of hands."

A little more than half the Luma's hands went up. Considering they'd been trapped down here for who knew how long without proper care, that number surprised Magnus. Granted, he hardly knew what he was asking, but figured Awen would know what to request of them. "They're all yours, Awen."

With her helmet still under her arm, she raised her voice and spoke with a sense of urgency. "Most of you know me. For those who don't, my name is Awen dau Lothlinium, and I am a former member of your sacred order, now a member of the Gladio Umbra.

"First and second year students, I want you in the rear escorting the injured. Third years and up, along with any elders, you're with Elder Willowood and myself, just behind Alpha Platoon." She paused. "I mean, the troopers here.

"Our objective is to get everyone to safety on the shuttles at docking bays thirty-four through thirty-seven. If you get lost or separated for any reason, that is the rally point. Board any one of those four shuttles that you can. And if we encounter any Luma resistance in the Unity from So-Elku and his forces, all of you are our first line of defense. Keep your second sight open and call out what you see. Understood?"

As heads moved up and down, Magnus couldn't help but feel a deep sense of pride in how Awen had just commanded the room. He wondered if these people had ever been spoken to like that before, and realized, if they survived all this, it wouldn't be the last time—not with someone like Awen around.

"Let's move," Magnus said, turning back toward the stairwell and taking the first few two in a bound.

"Sir?" asked TO-96.

"What is it?"

"I really must insist that you increase your pace."

"Trust me when I say we are coming as fast as we can. Why? What's going on?"

"The activity behind the walls is growing in scope."

"Chances are it's just the plumbing, 'Six. No need to worry."

"The plumbing, sir?"

"Mystics, yes, the plumbing. Just don't worry about it unless something starts leaking out of the walls."

"Very good, sir."

Magnus was running down the second level's hallway when TO-96 spoke again. "Given your instructions, I'm going to begin worrying now, sir."

"What? Why?"

"There is something leaking out of the walls. More specifically, the walls are opening."

Magnus was about to bark back at the bot when he noticed the walls on the second level begin to move. In the blank intervals between the torches, cracks formed and panels of stone pressed out, just like on the third level where all the prisoners were held. He double checked his HUD and even his bioteknia eyes to verify that there were no life signs coming from behind the doors. There weren't.

"Awen?" he asked, hearing the tension in his own voice.

"Uh oh," she replied.

"Uh oh?" Magnus raised his NOV1 at the nearest gap in the wall. "What's uh oh?"

"So-Elku," she murmured. "What have you done?"

22

The first decomposed humanoid corpse pushed through the gap in the nearest door, snapped its head in a Luma's direction, and lunged. Its boney hands—held together by tawny tendons and decayed flesh—drove into the woman's chest and protruded out her back. Her scream wheezed through the gaps in her body instead of her mouth.

A second Luma died when a corpse thrust its thumb and fingers into the man's mouth and eye sockets, spindly fingers pressing into brain tissue. The monster shrieked at its victim, its brittle skin all but peeled away from the eyeless skull and gaping mouth.

Magnus had no idea what to say about the things that creeped out of the crypts. All he knew was to shoot first and ask questions later. Light and sound sent shockwaves down the hallway as Magnus tore into a third creature with his NOV1.

The weapon's high-energy rapid-fire burst shredded the skull and upper chest cavity as if the thing had been made of clay and linen. But the torso and legs continued to walk toward him, so he blasted them into oblivion too.

"Holy splick," someone exclaimed over comms.

"*Holy* wouldn't be my first word choice," he replied, then aimed at another corpse and tore it apart with his rifle. Then he turned to see the rest of Alpha Platoon engaging the strange apparitions as the light from their weapons lit up the hallway in brilliant blue flashes.

"Awen," Magnus demanded, "talk to me!"

"I have no idea!" She turned on the corpse nearest her. Her suit glowed yellow in the chest, then a burst of energy shot out and struck the creature. Its arms, legs, and skull popped off the incinerated torso like someone had yanked the components off with wires.

"What do you mean you have no idea?" Magnus aimed at a third being and drilled it with a series of shots. "This is a Unity thing, right?"

"Yes, I believe so. But I don't know how it's possible. I mean, there are old stories of dark Unity users who did this kind of thing, but those are just legends. So-Elku, he's—" Another corpse took a blast from Awen, and half its body vaporized in a cloud of dust. "He's reanimated the bodies and turned them into a security system or something."

"How many are there? Can you stop it?"

"Stop it? I can't even see what he's done to them!"

He wanted to yell something back, to question what good

the Unity was if not for this, when Piper spoke over comms. "I can see it, shydoh," she said.

Awen's voice sounded surprised. "You can?"

"Could one of you please be more specific?" Magnus asked, downing a fourth creature.

"I can see So-Elku's design coming from the Nexus. He's asked the people in the crypts—"

"Can someone please tell me what she's talking about?" Magnus interrupted.

"He's reanimated the corpses using the Nexus," Awen said.

"The what?"

"The Nexus."

"Never mind. Can you stop it?"

"No," Awen replied. "I don't think so." She glanced at Piper. "Do you see a way to stop them?"

Piper shook her head. "No. They just seem sad."

Magnus furrowed his brow at Piper's comment. "Then we'll have to hold them back with conventional weapons." Over his louder speaker, now maxed to 100%, he yelled, "Everyone up the stairs! Alpha Platoon, defend the stairwell!"

Blasters screamed, drilling the oncoming crash of corpses that assailed the retreating Luma. Whatever they lacked in structural integrity, they made up for in sheer numbers. *How many mystics did they bury down here?* As if to reinforce the legitimacy of his question, the far stairwell that they'd just come from spit out more corpses.

"Keep them back," Magnus ordered. Valerie, Haney, and

Gilder defended the left side while Dutch, Sootriman, and Ezo defended the right. They walked backward toward the stairwell as more Luma filed up of the circular staircase.

"You seeing this too, 'Six?"

"If by *this* you mean an unexplained phenomenon whereby the bodily remains of deceased humanoid lifeforms have been reanimated for the purposes of dispatching intruders—namely, us—then yes, I am seeing this."

While the bot spoke, Magnus used his eyes to select TO-96's sensors suite, pulled up his optical sensors, and opened a small window in his HUD to see what the robot was looking at. TO-96 pivoted in a circular fashion, spraying a near-constant stream of fire from his XM31 Type-R wrist-mounted blaster, while his other hand released one micro-rocket after another into a grouping of the creatures further back.

"Well aren't you a one-stop munitions shop," Magnus said, smiling at the carnage the bot was dishing out.

"I disagree, sir. None of my munitions are for sale, at least insomuch as neither Ezo nor Azelon have given me that directive."

Magnus chuckled and put down two more creatures. "Dutch, VOD on this stairwell. I want it shut down."

"Copy that."

"Everyone else, head upstairs."

The gladias peeled off the formation and ducked into the stairwell while Magnus and Dutch drew together. There seemed to be no end to the reanimated corpses, and Magnus couldn't believe he was wasting so much ammo killing things that were already dead.

Dutch stowed her NOV1 and pulled out a VOD—variable output detonator. But not the old Repub version. This was the new Novia one Magnus had engineered with Azelon.

"Now or never," he said to her.

Dutch thumbed the selector pad three times and then gave Magnus a nod. "Fire in the hole." Magnus stepped aside for Dutch to retreat up the stairs behind him. Then he gave one last spray across the flooded room to keep the creatures back before darting up the circular stairwell.

Four beats later, a thunderous explosion shook the stairwell and brought chunks of stone down from the ceiling. The debris blasted off Magnus as his HUD flickered once from the fireball that licked his armor. A cloud of white dust and flames shot past him and went up and around the curve. He imagined it burst out on the next level like a dragon's burp.

His personal shield had dropped to 74% as he rounded the last corner and emerged into TO-96's level. The hallway was now full of Luma and gladias, driving a path through the undead with TO-96 in the lead. Magnus joined Dutch and started picking off assailants that tried picking at the weaker Luma.

"We could use a little help down here," Magnus said over the company channel. "Just… don't get freaked out."

"Jujari do not get *freaked out*," Rohoar said, overemphasizing the words. "We are coming."

A few seconds later, Magnus saw several Jujari appear at

the opposite end of the hallway. Rohoar's voice sounded strained. "I take it back. I think I am experiencing the sensation of *freaked out*."

"Just take out as many as you can," Magnus instructed, trying to suppress the smile forming his lips' edge. He watched as bodies started flying to the left and right, limbs and skulls popping off the corpses as they slammed into the walls. Bits of bodies pelted the ceiling as the Jujari moved through the crowded corridor. It was like watching a spotted Meglavton hedgebore burrow its way through a pack of unsuspecting flapperskrill. And Magnus revelled in it. If there was one thing those Jujari knew how to do, it was shred enemies from life and limb—or, in this case, *death* and limb.

Once Rohoar and his platoon met TO-96 in the middle, they formed a two-sided phalanx that ran the length of the hallway. The new thoroughfare allowed the Luma to make a run to the far side stairwell, which they did without any instruction. Meanwhile, Magnus and Dutch helped defend the closing end of the phalanx, relieving gladias to peel away and head toward the stairwell.

"Someone give me a SITREP," Magnus ordered.

"Exfil of the Luma is nearly complete, sir," came TO-96's voice. Magnus could see him on the topo map standing just beside the stairwell's mouth, defending it from the creatures who seemed to think his metal body would make a delicious treat. "Good. The rest of you file out of here just as fast. Dutch, I want one more VOD. Maximum damage. Take it off my hip this time." He didn't want her using more of her ordinance than she needed to. Better to share the resources than have one person go wanting when they needed it most.

Magnus and Dutch continued to backpedal as the beasties grew in number, filling in their wake as the stairwell grew closer. Magnus fired on corpse after corpse, shredding joints, eviscerating stomachs, and decapitating skulls under this NOV1's withering rate of fire.

"Ten meters," TO-96 said, coaching him and Dutch as they neared the exit. "Delta Platoon is clear. Only you, Valerie, and Haney remain."

Magnus heard a scream over comms. Out of the corner of his eye, a boney hand drove into Haney's shoulder joint. The gladia was yanked forward and pulled into the undulating sea of corpses. "Haney, no!" It was all Magnus could think to say as the former Marine medic was swept out of sight. Two seconds later, his icon blinked out on Magnus's HUD.

"Bastards," Magnus cried out as he leveled the next several creatures that tried to reach for him and Dutch.

"I'm good," Dutch exclaimed, ready to toss the VOD.

"Do it."

Dutch tossed the fruit-sized device and then ducked into the stairs to cover Magnus's retreat. He drilled one final corpse in the top of the head before stepping up and into the curved stairwell. "Move your ass, Dutch! I can still see it from here!"

Dutch replied instantly by finding an extra gear in her step, then pulling up and away from Magnus's field of view.

He'd lost track of the count in his head. Come to think of it, he hadn't even asked Dutch how much time she'd given them—which made Magnus take the steps even faster.

His servo-assist whined as he barreled up the torch-lit corridor, knowing that Elder's Hall must be less than ten meters away. The light from the domed room began to warm the top of the steps when the VOD detonated.

The blast sucked the air from the stairwell, pulling back on Magnus's body for a split second, and then sent an energy wave back through the passage. Magnus felt the blast push him forward. He meant to take the next few steps in conjunction with the assist, but the force was far greater than he expected. Instead, the shockwave flung him up and out of the stairwell like a cannon shot.

Magnus flew out of the passage and tucked into a roll. His back hit the marble floor and slid away from the opening, NOV1 trained on the collapsing passageway. When he finally came to a halt beside someone's boots, Caldwell's voice said, "Get up, son." The colonel helped Magnus stand and brushed some dust off his armor.

"You okay, buckethead?" Abimbola asked.

"I…" Magnus patted himself down and double checked his shield. The status bar read 52%. "I'm good. Thanks." Then he turned and surveyed the room.

Elder's Hall was now filled with over fifty Luma and more than half of Granther Company—the rest of the gladias were still outside on the steps.

"Is everyone okay?" Magnus asked.

"We've lost Haney," Gilder said.

Magnus felt a heart pang cinch around his throat. "I saw it."

"And we lost three Luma," Willowood said. "We are down to fifty-one"

"I'm sorry for your loss," Magnus replied.

"What *were* those things down there?" Abimbola asked.

"Not now, Bimby. We make it out of this, you can replay the footage all you want."

"I'll pass." Then Abimbola made that strange shape in front of his chest again.

"What does that mean?" Dutch asked Abimbola. "That little thing you just did?"

Magnus waved off the question. "Hey, if it helps to ward off evil spirits like the ones they just encountered down there, I'm all for the Miblimbian's mystical arts splick."

"As am I," TO-96 said, mimicking Abimbola's movement exactly. "Though I have no idea what these motions do."

"Stick to your Type-R blaster, pal," Silk replied. "It's way more effective."

"Thank you for the advice, Silk. I'm most grateful."

"Don't mention it."

"Magnus?" a voice said over comms.

"Go ahead, Titus."

"Better wrap it up in there. We've got more company."

23

Awen followed Magnus out of Elder's Hall and rushed onto the upper landing where Titus stood. Her eyes looked past the large staircase, up the red carpet, and stopped near the Grand Arielina's main entrance. Several dozen Luma stepped out of the darkness and spread out along the colonnade. Their dark blue robes sent a chill up Awen's spine.

"This isn't good," Awen said to Magnus on a private channel.

"Why not?"

"Those are the Blue Guard."

"And?"

"And what? They're assigned to protect the Master even unto death."

"We beat them last time."

"No, you didn't."

"Yes, we did."

Awen turned on him, slowing her words. "*No, you didn't.* They're only called out when the Master says the city or his own life are in grave danger. And trust me, your last showing? It didn't constitute either."

"Now that just hurts." Magnus said in a playful tone. "Guess we just need to leave a better impression this time. Can Willowood's Luma handle them?"

"I think so, but what about the codex?"

"You tell me. Any word on its whereabouts?"

Awen shook her head. "He's locked the whole city up in the Unity. It's almost impossible to get a read on anything right now. I can't even find So-Elku himself. For all I know, he's not even on the planet."

"Okay, just calm down."

Awen hadn't even realized her heart rate had gone up. She was grateful for Magnus's steadying words.

"Let's just think it through. Before, you said it was probably in So-Elku's personal quarters."

"I did."

"And where's that?"

"Two levels up."

"Well, give me the Luma and then go take a look with Piper. But be fast. I don't want to waste any more time on it than we need to."

Magnus ordered the company to spread out along the landing and take cover behind the columns going down the sides of the staircase. They had the high ground… but he seriously doubted how much of this conflict would be won by conventional weapons and strategy.

"Granther Company, prepare to engage. Watch for friendlies."

"But how will we know which Luma are friendlies?" Nubs asked.

"They won't be the ones trying to kill us, numbskull," Dozer replied.

Abimbola shut the exchange down. "Keep that off the company channel, you two."

"Sorry, boss," they replied, almost in unison.

"Willowood?" Magnus asked. "Can you hear me?"

"I can, Magnus. And your company is receiving my voice though your comms?"

"We are."

"Good. I suggest you remain where you are and let us handle the first wave. Your blasters will do only minor damage until we negate their personal force fields."

"Understood. Is there anything else we can do until then?"

Willowood let out a half laugh, like a forceful sigh through a smile. "I'm beginning to see why she likes you so much."

Magnus raised his eyebrows. "I…"

"To answer your question, yes. If any of the blue robed Luma break off and head toward you, shoot them."

"But what about their personal force fields?"

"Just pray to the mystics that you have enough magazines. Now, if you'll excuse me."

Suddenly, more than thirty Luma dressed in burgundy and black robes raced forward on either side of Magnus and then charged down the stairs. He looked further down the hallway to see the blue robed Luma begin to run as well.

"Steady, gladias," Magnus said over comms. "Let them take this wave. Fingers off the triggers."

The two groups of red and blue robes charged one another, several of them yelling as the battle lines closed. To Magnus's amazement, it was the old woman Willowood who outpaced them all.

WILLOWOOD HADN'T FELT this much adrenaline since… She couldn't even remember a time. But it felt good. The last time she'd been given a fair fight on an open field was decades before, perhaps during the Miblimbian conflict. Instead, she'd grown accustomed to the head games played in Elder's Hall and political posturing of the court. It was numbing, so much so that she often wondered why she'd remained here for so long.

But she knew why. It was her love for teaching and her love of the students. Worru, in its heyday, had been a place of learning, of true acceptance. She had thrived here, relishing the halls of academia for the freedom it afforded her. Ideas weren't tossed aside in knee-jerk reactions simply because they conflicted with partisan politics. Instead, they were examined inside and out, heralded for their virtues and critiqued with careful justice for their faults.

But now, it had come to this—a fight to the death between a wolf in sheep's clothing and the flock that had looked to him for protection. With his Blue Guard charging at her, she guessed So-Elku couldn't be far.

Willowood counted at least three dozen Luma racing at her. To call this a fair fight wasn't exactly accurate—she'd trained most of these Luma, now turned enemies. Which meant she knew their moves better than they did.

The art of Li-Loré had been entrusted only to a few, those charged with defending the Master, and those sent on dark errands that were never recorded in the Order's archives. Fortunately, both instances were scarce. That is, until recently. Ever since So-Elku's term as Master began, Willowood had noticed a shift in policies. And a shift in the Unity. She hadn't been able to connect all the dots, but when she'd seen So-Elku restrain Awen, that had been enough to tell her who the real enemy was.

The first attacker was a young man named Ouin. She'd known him since he was a boy. Now, however, he was no longer a child, but a highly disciplined warrior who'd committed himself to preserving peace in ways no one dared talk about outside these hallowed halls.

"Ouin," she yelled, hoping to catch him by surprise. But the man didn't hesitate in the least. He ran to meet her, hands swirling in a powered attack. Willowood sighed and crossed her forearms.

A ball of energy culminated in front of his chest and then leaped from his hands. Willowood deflected the blast and sidestepped Ouin's charge, bringing her hand down to touch the back of his neck. Instantly, the man crumpled to the floor. He'd survive.

The next attack came from a woman named Sonja. Willowood had been her benefactor in her final year of observances, signing the requisite documents to get her into the Blue Guard. Now Sonja pulled one hand back and pushed the other forward, attempting to overpower the old woman.

Willowood ducked under the strike and spun in a circle. Her robes and wiry hair twirled about as she came up behind Sonja and punched her in the spine. The blow would not cause any long-term damage, but it would paralyze her for a day or more.

The third combatant, one Willowood did not recognize, seemed to hesitate when he saw Ouin and Sonja's bodies on the floor.

"You don't have to join them," Willowood said, bringing her hands up in a defensive pose.

But the man sneered at her and charged. Willowood caught his right wrist in a forearm lock, flipped her body around to twist his arm in an unnatural fashion, and then fell to the ground, hurling the attacker over her head. He flew a short distance, stripped of energy, and landed unconscious on the hallway's red carpet.

Willowood paused to survey how the other Luma were doing in the opening seconds of the conflict. While a few knew Li-Loré, employing it against their various assailants with great skill, the large majority did not. Instead, they employed more general defenses—slowing physical attacks, deploying force fields, and resisting opponents in the Unity.

Most thought of Li-Loré as a physical art, but practitioners knew it was far more than that. In reality, it began—like all things—in the Unity. Learning to harness energy, to coax it into a malleable expression that manifested as a physical movement, was a years-long process reserved for only the most adept.

Despite its advantages, however, the combat forms were still subject to the laws of the Unity and could, in theory, be diffused by anyone strong enough in second sight. So Willowood noted how even the weakest Luma prisoners were at least able to resist all but the most powerful attacks delivered by the Blue Guard. Returning the attacks, however, was a different matter, as most Luma were never instructed on how to be the aggressors—only the defenders.

The fourth Luma Willowood confronted was a tall man with broad shoulders. She thought his name was Kin, but she couldn't be sure. He reached for her head, hands glowing. Had she not moved, the impact would have incapacitated her—possibly for good. Instead, Willowood ducked under his reach and landed her hand's heel against his sternum. But Kin must have anticipated the move and covered his chest with a protective field.

Willowood's hand glanced off the force field and threw her off balance. Kin caught her by the arm and hoisted her skyward. Had the man's hand been charged, Willowood might not have taken advantage of the opportunity she saw next. Despite Kin's strength—expressed in a surge to bring the old woman's body down across his raised knee—he was not quick enough to defend against the scissors kick that clasped him around the neck.

Willowood locked her knees, pulled herself up to his head, and then redirected her weight around his shoulders. The swift motion snapped Kin's head sideways and twisted his torso along with it. Again, the move didn't kill him, but he fell unconscious like a tree cut from its base and falling to the forest floor. Just as Kin's body struck the ground, Willowood moved away from him, her feet stepping deftly onto the red carpet.

For a split second, she wondered how long this might take and how many good Luma she might lose in the process. She saw Magnus and the rest of his unit waiting diligently on the steps, and she thought of Awen and Piper searching for the codex somewhere in So-Elku's private study. She prayed to the mystics that Awen found it soon… before So-Elku found her.

24

While none of their orbital sensors picked it up, So-Elku had felt Awen and the little girl arrive in system. While the two females did well to hide their presence in the Unity, they'd grown too strong to go unnoticed. Clearly, they'd made many of the same discoveries that he had in the Unity. In any other context, he would have loved to sit down with the young prodigies and share their findings together. Such was the curiosity that had accelerated So-Elku to the elevation of Master in the first place.

But this was not that hour. Instead, he'd been given access to a great gift, one that had granted him access to realms of the Unity previously unknown—to power that would allow him to bring true peace to the galaxy. His voice would be heard and listened to, just as the Circle of Nine had demonstrated. And his edicts would go unchallenged. Finally, his vision for peace—the Luma's vision for peace—would come to fruition.

That was, if these meddling fools would simply stay out of his way. He'd already taken care of Willowood and her followers, locking them within the catacombs. But he'd allowed enough transparency to remain that, should Awen and her friends show up, they might be drawn in and subdued. And thus far the plan was working perfectly. That was, of course, until they evaded the reanimated mystics.

So-Elku had watched the entire confrontation from within his study, hidden away in an ethereal shroud. Awen and her forces had freed Willowood—*the old bat*—and managed to escape the catacombs with minimal losses. He'd wished for more, for them to have been stopped completely. But it wasn't a total waste. The corpses had fulfilled their greater purposes in proving that he could reanimate the dead, and that suited him just fine.

His Blue Guard awaited Awen in the main hall, and the company of Republic's Marines stationed on Worru had already been alerted. Additionally, Awen had failed to locate the codex, a fact that relieved So-Elku. He still had so much to investigate within its pages. The manuscript was imbued with some sort of ancient power, allowing him access to more than just what the script portrayed. And once Awen and the others were stopped, he could resume his obsessive study of it.

Should all of this fail, however—though he suspected it wouldn't—So-Elku had one more plan up the long sleeve of his green robe. It had come to his attention that two of

Moldark's men had been taken captive on Awen's ship. While So-Elku wanted as little to do with the deranged Republic admiral as possible, using his men as pawns was not below him.

The Luma Master opened himself to the Unity, surged through the Foundation, and plunged into the Nexus. The codex from the Novia Minoosh had revealed these new worlds to him, giving him access to power previously unimagined by any Luma. He looked forward to each session he had with the prized tome and knew that if he could master its secrets, nothing would be able to stop him—not the Galactic Republic, not Moldark, and certainly not Awen dau Lothlinium.

Today, he would teach that arrogant young woman a lesson. He would show her that she could not escape his reach nor circumvent his well-laid plans. He was always one step ahead of her, and she would never be free of reminders of his power.

So-Elku's consciousness sped toward the alien starship in orbit over Worru. The vessel had come from the other side of the universe—from metaspace. Few souls remained onboard, most having come down to assault the Grand Arielina and free Willowood. But he found the two prisoners, both restless in their prison cells.

The first was a Navy pilot, presumably captured during a skirmish on Ithnor Ithelia. So-Elku knew the admiral was sending search parties there to look for resources. The second man was a Marine, probably arrested during the same confrontation. Whatever their reasons for capture might be, they served So-Elku's larger purposes now, whether they liked it or not. And that, perhaps, was the Luma master's favorite aspect of his new powers in the Unity. No one could see him coming.

His ethereal presence moved to the first man's cell. So-Elku eyed him, sitting on the edge of his bed, wearing black shorts and a t-shirt. Oh, what he wouldn't give to spend the rest of the day watching the havoc this pilot would cause. So-Elku reached out and seized the flow of energy forming the force field over the prison cell. Then, with the simplest thought, he ordered it to abate, causing the invisible wall to dissipate.

The pilot's head snapped toward the opening, and he studied it intently. Gone was the low hum and shimmering blue glow. Instead, there was only open air. Tentatively, the pilot stood and approached the opening. So-Elku watched him pass a hand through the space formerly occupied by the security wall. And when his hand met only air, the pilot pulled back and considered the space again. *What is he waiting for?* So-Elku wondered. The pilot passed his hand through a second time, then extended his arm. Only when that seemed successful did he step into the wider cell block.

So-Elku floated through the brig and appeared before the second man, this one a shirtless tattooed brute who paced relentlessly. When the force field fell, the Marine stepped forward and didn't even bother to test the passage before waltzing through it. So-Elku watched as a sickening smile turned the corners of the Marine's mouth into a sneer.

All that was left was to open the doors leading toward the bridge and restrict the ship's AI from stopping them. Then he'd let the former prisoners do whatever came naturally to them. So-Elku imagined they'd take great delight in playing with the starship while Awen and her forces were away.

A voice came from inside So-Elku's quarters. He'd been so caught up in the Nexus that he'd failed to monitor his own body's presence in the temporal realm. He snapped from the Nexus to the Foundation and out of the Unity, awakening within his mortal form and opening his eyes.

"We've come for the codex," Awen said again, not sure that the Luma master heard her the first time.

His eyes rolled down from inside his skull and awareness dawned on his face. "Awen. What an unexpected surprise."

So-Elku sat on a cushion near a wooden desk that looked out on an open-air veranda. Awen could see the night lights of Plumeria in the distance and wondered which of those lights were their shuttles.

"And who is this?" So-Elku asked, his lips curling into a crooked smile. "Why... I sense Willowood's blood in her. Is this—"

"I'm Piper."

"Of course you are."

"Piper, be still," Awen said over her shoulder.

"So a young lady and a child have come to wrest a book from an old man, is that what it's come to?"

"Give me the codex," Awen said, now for the third time. "I'll not ask again." She didn't want to fight So-Elku, but if he kept stalling, she'd take the tome by force.

"It's right over there," he said, pointing to a wooden lectern with a bound volume on it.

"Piper," Awen said in an even tone, "go get it."

"Sending the girl to do it? That's a bit reckless, don't you think?"

"By comparison to your activities as of late, *Master* So-Elku? I hardly think this is reckless. Taking my eyes off of you for even the briefest of moments would be far more irresponsible."

From within the Unity, Awen could see Piper lift the book from its stand and then walk back toward her. Meanwhile, So-Elku matched her gaze, heartbeat for heartbeat. Awen knew from the moment she saw him that this would end in a duel. She didn't know how it would start, but she knew who would win.

Piper came to stand beside her again, clutching the codex to her chest. "We'll be going now," Awen said.

"Just like that? No time for tea? No desire to catch me up on how your time has been living amongst the ruins of the Novia Minoosh?"

Awen hesitated. Had So-Elku seen across the void horizon and into metaspace? If so, how much had he witnessed? How much did he know? She felt the uncertainty begin to nip at her heels, and her fingers began to tingle.

"You doubt my abilities to search you out, do you?" So-Elku rose slowly from his cushion—but not under the power of his legs. Instead, he floated up to a standing position, letting his long robes unfurl before his feet touched the marble floor. "I've learned so very much. And it's a pity to think that you believe I need that dusty book anymore." He took a step toward her and Awen tensed, pushing Piper behind her. "You may have gotten away, too, had it not been for the codex. But I am far more powerful than you could even realize, Awen. So it's time that we end this."

So-Elku closed his eyes.

Within the Unity, Awen and Piper watched So-Elku materialize in his study. Here, the shapes and colors glowed in stark contrast to their muted counterparts in the natural realm. Sounds were more detailed, smells more vibrant, sensations more powerful.

Awen and Piper stood beside each other, hands clenched in fists, ready for So-Elku to make the first move.

His eyes opened and he roared, charging toward them in a blur. Awen and Piper stepped aside, letting the aggressor pass. His body slammed into the far wall, sending a shower of stone and sparks into the crystal-clear night air. Awen turned, flexed her palms, and sent a stream of yellow energy at So-Elku, whose body now flipped off the wall and sailed overhead. As soon as he landed, Awen sent a second blast. This one he caught in a green shield formed between his hands, diffusing the shot like one might put out fire with a lake of water.

So-Elku laughed. As soon as the vapors of Awen's attack dissipated, the master sent his own stream of energy at her. The glowing green spout shot from his hands, aimed right at Awen's head. But she straightened her arms to her sides and flexed her legs. A round shield snapped to life just in front of her, dispersing So-Elku's blast in a shower of sparks and a blistering buzz sound. The impact pushed Awen back slightly, but not enough that it unnerved her.

So far, the man's tactics were rudimentary—all things that she and Piper had covered during their long sessions in the Unity. If this was all the Luma master had uncovered from the codex, this fight might be shorter than she expected. But given the display of power in the catacombs, she highly doubted it. Which caused her confidence to ebb slightly. Why was So-Elku holding back? What was he waiting for?

As if in answer to her question, So-Elku said, "Shall we take this to the next level?" And then he sank into the floor and vanished from sight.

"He's gone to the Foundation, hasn't he," Piper stated.

"Yes. Are you ready?"

Piper nodded.

"Good. Let's go."

Awen and Piper left the study, rocketed through the depths of the Unity, and slammed into the Foundation much like a meteor landing on the surface of a planet. The two of them rose up from on bended knee and surveyed the forest around them. The long echoes of bird songs carried under the canopy of leaves. Sunlight filtered down in a yellow-green haze, caught by countless motes of dust swirling in the forest air. All around them, the trees stood like old sentries, shrouded in bark and limbs and leaves, standing guard for the woodland creatures in this magical place.

A whistle caught Awen's attention and she spun to her left. Piper followed the sound too, before turning again at a second whistle, this time from the opposite side. After Awen and Piper had turned several times, a low laugh bubbled up from somewhere in the woods.

"Watching you two is so quaint," So-Elku said. "It's a shame what I must do to you."

"Your threats mean nothing," Awen said. "Come out and face us."

"My threats mean everything, Awen." The voice seemed to be coming from all around them now. "For, in here… *we are gods.*"

A rush of wind from behind forced Awen to take a step forward. She spun around in time to see So-Elku drive toward her like an arrow shot from a bow. He glanced against her shoulder and sent her whirling. Piper, too, was knocked off her feet and landed in a bed of ferns.

Awen attempted to stand, but the Luma master returned, forcing her down as he whizzed overhead.

"Piper, stay down," she ordered. Then Awen looked up to see So-Elku directly overhead, diving toward them. "Look out!"

No sooner had she said the words than a shaft of granite shot up from the ground and met So-Elku in midair. The column continued to rise until it had stretched nearly out of sight.

Awen followed it until she saw So-Elku leap from the top and fall toward them again. Piper raised her hand and another column sprang from the ground, driving up toward their adversary. The Luma master disappeared as the pillar struck him. But then he leaped from its summit and continued falling toward them.

Piper commanded spire after spire to thrust from the forest floor and strike So-Elku until he outpaced her, bounding down the pillars, then landing in a crouch a hundred meters through the tall pines.

"Bravo," he said, clapping his hands. "That was marvelous. Someone has been studying hard for this test."

Awen heard Piper grunt. She looked over to see the little girl make fists and shut her eyes.

"But if you're going to—"

The pine trees bent over, their tops slamming into the top of So-Elku's head like a dozen hammers striking the head of a nail in thunderous succession. Blow after blow rained down on him, driving his body into the ground in a flurry of dirt and dust. Finally, the firs snapped straight again, released from their chore. Their needles rustled in the air as the long pines wobbled from Piper's unexpected violence.

"Piper…" Awen said in a whisper. "That was… creative."

"He's annoying me."

Awen gave her a smug smile. "Me too. But I—"

Through the trees, Awen saw the ground explode outward and So-Elku rise into the sky. He turned to face them, then swung toward them in a streak.

Awen braced herself, as did Piper. "Not this time," Awen said, gritting her teeth.

So-Elku's mad dash ended when his body slammed against an invisible wall that Awen and Piper erected around them. The blow was so forceful that the surrounding trees leaned away from the sudden release of energy. Even the shield wobbled momentarily, but Awen did her best to maintain the dome overhead.

So-Elku's body flipped away and careened into a tree, breaking the trunk in two. He rolled to a stop some twenty-five meters away, robes covered in debris from the forest floor.

"Give up, So-Elku," Awen said. "This doesn't have to end in bloodshed."

"You would kill me then?" he replied, rising to his feet and brushing off his garments. Then, as if catching the thing in a mirror, So-Elku raised a hand and touched the corner of his mouth. A red smear came away on his finger. The Luma master seemed genuinely put off by this. "Doing so would break the Luma Code. You know that."

"And you haven't done the same, *Master* So-Elku?"

"That does not change the fact that you face the same dilemma now, dear one."

Awen winced at the term. "I face no dilemma."

"Oh?"

"If killing you means preserving peace, then so be it."

"But that is not the Luma way," So-Elku replied, stepping toward her.

"You're right. It's not. But I'm no longer a Luma."

So-Elku's next step slowed. "No longer a Luma? Why, that's absurd."

"And you still call yourself one?"

"Of the highest fashion," he said as he puffed out his chest. "And you?"

Awen looked at Piper. The little girl smiled back, then said, "We're Gladio Umbra now, you bald bastard."

"Piper!" Awen couldn't believe what she'd heard. But before she could protest, Piper lowered her head and summoned long magenta-colored tendrils of electricity from the ground. They rose like thick cables, energy dancing along their surfaces, and surrounded So-Elku like bars of a cage. He attempted to leap skyward, but the tendrils closed over him, and then began to recede.

So-Elku fought against the cage, blasting it with all manner of energy. But his futile attempts dashed against the cables in dazzling displays of sparks and heat.

The bars continued to close in, contracting and descending more and more. So-Elku protested, yelling at the cage as the space grew smaller. Awen couldn't be sure, but it seemed like Piper would drag him into the ground itself, crashing him within the cage's grip.

"Piper, that's enough," she ordered. The progression ceased at once. Piper opened her eyes and looked up at Awen.

The girl wasn't so much as trembling—not a bead of perspiration was evident on her brow. "Piper, leave him there as is."

"But, shydoh, he tried to—"

"I know what he tried to do, but that doesn't mean we must do the same. Sometimes mercy means letting our enemies live with the consequences of their actions instead of letting them die from them."

Piper seemed satisfied with the explanation, though clearly not happy about it. She relinquished control of the bars with a sigh, but did not release So-Elku from his prison. He remained crouched beneath the bars' fitful sputtering and spitting, showered by miniature lightning bolts that licked at his robes.

"So long, bitch," Piper said.

"Piper! Language!"

"What? Abimbola said it."

"That does *not* mean you can say it!"

"But I was just—"

"That's enough," Awen said, feeling mortified. And yet, secretly, she smiled inside.

AWEN AND PIPER appeared back in So-Elku's study and opened their eyes. The Luma Master stood as before. But his face was contorted in frustration, eyes closed, sweat dripping down his forehead. His mortal body was contracted, hands balled into fists—and yet, he remained motionless.

"Piper, be careful," Awen said as the little girl walked over to examine him. She still clutched the book to her chest and made a full circuit around him.

"How long will he stay like this?" she asked

"You tell me," Awen replied.

"For a while then. Until we're safely away."

"I think that's more than fair."

"Fair?" Piper wrinkled her nose. "Fair means we shoulda killed him. Just like what he wanted to do to us."

Awen made to reply but found that the girl had a point. "Perhaps fair is not the best word. Releasing him once we are free is gracious of you."

"But won't he just try and kill us again later?"

Awen didn't feel up for answering these questions. At least not at the moment. They had the codex, So-Elku was temporarily bound, and now it was time to fight their way back to the shuttles. "We'll talk about this later. Right now, we've got to get everyone back to the *Spire*. Come on." And with that, the pair turned from So-Elku's study and left the man's body fighting in a fitful rage.

25

For almost three minutes, Rohoar and the other gladias had been picking off members of the Blue Guard who stepped away from the main fight. Beyond that, however, the platoons were of little use to Willowood. The fighting had become so compact—more close quarters combat than an open range scenario, as Magnus called it—that their NOV1s were a liability, not an asset. Plus, this was one round of CQB that Rohoar knew Magnus's team was not prepared for.

But perhaps Rohoar's was.

"Magnus, would it not be helpful to Willowood if we Jujari lent her our claws?" Rohoar asked. Willowood was losing several Luma to the blue-robed assailants.

"It's certainly worth asking." Magnus opened the company channel. "Willowood, would our platoon of Jujari be of any use to you right now?"

"Send them in," she replied. "But tell them to be careful."

"I can hear you, Madame Luma," Rohoar replied.

"Their attacks are powered, Rohoar. These aren't your average Luma. Stow your blasters and roll up your sleeves."

"We're on our way." But Rohoar paused and looked at Magnus. "We are not wearing sleeved garments. What does she mean?"

"She means to get ready to bash some heads, pal. Now get in there!"

"Your kind has too many worthless expressions," Rohoar growled. "Also, I do not think she knows about our own powers in the Unity."

Magnus gave Rohoar a surprised look—perhaps the man had also forgotten that the Jujari were descendants of the Novia Minoosh and the original Gladio Umbra. But he was smarter than that. Wasn't he?

Rohoar summoned all of Delta Platoon to him, maglocked his NOV1 to his back, and bounded down the stairs on all fours. His pack released long howls as they charged down the hallway. Jujari jumped to the sides of the columns and then leapt away, looking for any advantage they could as they neared the battle line. Willowood's forces were stretched widthwise, paired even with the enemy. But the blue robed fighters were thinning Willowood's ranks and threatened to punch through the line.

Rohoar's claws dug into the red carpet and his heartbeat quickened. The sound of the battle clash drew near and he looked to his sides to see the Jujari surging forward as one. On his left were Saladin, Czyz, Longchomps, and Grahban; to his right were, Arjae, Dihazen, and Redmarrow.

His tongue whipped in the wind, tasting the pheromones of his enemies as they noticed the pack of crazed predators charging at them. No matter how many times Rohoar tasted it, he never tired of swallowing his adversary's fear.

Rohoar barked an order and loosed his pack.

Several of his fighters sprang off the pillars and dove to the rear of the line, while others forced their way headlong into the fray. Jaws snapped on raised Luma arms. Claws swiped at terrified faces. Saliva and blood splashed into the air, commingling in the clash of bodies.

Rohoar came up on Willowood's right. She must have sensed his presence—that, or she noticed the look of terror in her opponent's eyes—and stepped aside to allow him through. The enemy Luma sent a blast of energy at Rohoar, but the Jujari had already pushed off the ground and was airborne, flying at the man. Rohoar's top teeth closed on the man's neck and shoulder while his bottom teeth caught under the man's opposite armpit. The Jujari clamped down hard and heard his prey scream as they struck the ground.

The pair tumbled across the floor, flipping end over end. When they stopped, Rohoar gave a final snap and felt the Luma's chest cave in. He released the body as soon as it went limp, his ears detecting the final sounds of air escaping from the puncture wounds in the cavity.

Rohoar sprang to his feet and twisted around. He was behind the enemy line now, but two Luma had noticed him. They turned toward him and moved closer, their hands in some sort of defensive fighting posture. He'd never seen the form before, but trusted Willowood's advice to stay clear of their attacks.

The two blue Luma moved closer and closer before one of them lunged at Rohaor. The second did the same, both aiming for Rohoar's chest. Just before the blows landed, Rohoar rolled to the side. He lashed out with a muscled arm and sliced through the nearest enemy's gut. Three crimsons streams of blood laced through the air as the assailant cried out. Rohoar smelled the iron on his paw as he completed his roll and then gained his feet once more.

The gut-sliced Luma was down, struggling on his knees, while the second circled Rohoar tentatively. The man lashed out several times, his fists and feet aglow with energy from the ethereal realm. Like most humans, this man didn't know that some Jujari had inherited the ways of the Unity from their Novian ancestors. So, Rohoar let the blow come.

The Luma landed a palm against the Jujari's chest. The power raced from the man's arm and impacted Rohoar like a lightning bolt. A blinding white flash lit up the hallway while a thunderclap made Rohoar's ears ring. But when the violent concussion subsided, Rohoar remained standing.

The assailant blinked in stunned amazement. Then he looked down at his hands in disbelief, clearly unable to reconcile why his deathblow hadn't slain the Jujari.

"It really is a pity when efforts don't go as planned," Rohoar said through clenched teeth. The Luma looked up at him and made to blast the Jujari again, but he never had the chance. Rohoar batted the man aside as a child might throw a doll across their bedroom. His body hit a pillar with a *thud* and then slapped against the marble floor.

Rohoar let out another howl and then charged back into the fray. More strikes from the enemy Luma struck his body, but they resulted in little more than bursts of light and sound. He absorbed the energy, storing it within a pocket in the Unity, and waited until he snuck up behind the latest adversary to challenge Willowood. Not that she needed the help—the old woman was clearly the most capable of all those rescued in the catacombs. But as the tide had turned quickly since the Jujari joined the fight, Rohoar took it as a point of personal pride to make his presence known. That, and it was fun.

The blue-robed man swiped at Willowood's head, but she leaned back and ducked under each successive blow. Her own thrusts were parried and then countered. Rohoar watched just long enough for Willowood to bend out of the way, then laid a paw on the combatant's back. It was unfair, he knew. But they'd spent enough time here, and it was still a long way back to the shuttles.

Rohoar allowed the pent-up energy to surge out of his chest, down his arm, and through his paw, punching the Luma so hard that the mystic flew over Willowood's head and sailed toward the steps leading up to Elder's Hall. When the body finally finished somersaulting and rolled to a stop at the bottom of the step, Willowood turned to face Rohoar and said, "Thank you, Master Jujari."

"My name is Rohoar."

"Well then, thank you, Master Rohoar," she said, smoothing her robes and looking around. "It seems your pack has helped us turn the tide. And rather quickly, I might add. Though I suppose I had not accounted for your powers within the Unity."

"Most never do," he said with a toothy grin.

"A point I will not soon forget." The old woman bowed, and Rohoar returned the gesture.

When the last of the Blue Guard had fallen, Willowood stuck two fingers in her mouth and whistled down the hallway. Rohoar was shocked at just how loud the action was and pulled his ears back on instinct. She waved Magnus and the others forward and then looked at Rohoar.

"Is it true you are Piper's grandmother?" Rohoar asked.

Willowood gave him a soft smile. "It is. And you know my granddaughter?"

Rohoar bared his teeth, though he suddenly remembered that most humans took the gesture to mean a threat. "I do. It is an honor to be her friend and confidant."

"Confidant?" Willowood seemed impressed by the way she eyed him. "Then you must be a very trustworthy person."

"I endeavor to be, yes."

"Well then, consider myself indebted to you for keeping

safe the heart of someone I cherish more than almost any other."

"Your daughter, perhaps? And your husband?"

"My husband has long since passed." Willowood gave Rohoar a wink. "You had it right with my daughter. Now, shall we get a move on? I'm nearly ready for some morning tea."

Magnus and the remainder of Granther Company arrived. As they did, Rohoar looked around to inspect the bodies on the floor. Many were incapacitated, but even more were slain. It looked as though the Luma had suffered maybe ten casualties, while none of Rohoar's kin had suffered serious injury.

"You good, Rohoar?" Magnus asked.

He growled. "Ready for more."

"That's what I like to hear."

"And it's a good thing too," said Magnus's teammate in the *Spire*—the one they called Flow. "Because it looks like you got some more company coming, LT."

"Talk to me, Flow," Magnus said.

"Looks like Repub Marines, entering the courtyard from three sides."

"That would be the company stationed beside the Grand Arieline," said Magnus's former commander, Colonel Caldwell. The man was old, but Rohoar suspected he still had a lot of fight in him. He also gave off a strong scent of tobacco, which meant he was probably a good tactician, at least according to what little he knew of Repub lore.

Rohoar looked at the colonel and said, "Colonel, will inhaling the smoke of one of your tobacco rolls also give me tactical supremacy over the enemy?"

"Say what now?"

"If I partake with you before we enter battle against your troopers, will it aid me in combating them?"

"Son, I don't know where in hell you get your intel from but where I come from, we save the cigars for after the fight."

"I see," said Rohoar, making a mental note. "Then you and I shall partake when the battle has subsided."

"Sounds good to me. Now, we have some Repub ass to try and dissuade."

COLONEL CALDWELL WALKED onto the top of the Grand Arielina's front steps and raised a fist. The rest of Granther Company held short just inside the front doors, staying mostly out of sight from the Marines gathering below.

"Begging your pardon, colonel," Magnus said over a private channel, "and I don't mean to question your judgement here, but you sure this is how you want to proceed?"

"First off, you're the one leading the company, son. So don't you dare ask me what I want anymore. I'm doing what I think serves you best unless you tell me otherwise. So from here on out, no more begging anyone's pardon but your own. You copy?"

"Yes sir."

"And to answer your question, yes, this is exactly how I want to proceed. So shut up and give me a second." With that, Caldwell mag-locked his NOV1 to his thigh and removed his helmet with both hands, stowing the cover under his left arm. Then he withdrew a cigar from a cavity on his chest armor and lit it with a small lighter.

Magnus felt Rohoar lean in and whisper against the side of his helmet. "He just told me he inhales tobacco smoke *after* the battle is over."

Magnus chuckled. "He does. But sometimes he finds it helpful to inhale it during the fight too."

"I have taken note. Do all your battle heroes engage in such inhalation?"

"Not all. But most of the good ones do, yeah."

"I see."

Magnus returned his attention to Caldwell. The colonel watched in placid stoicism as the courtyard began to fill with an entire company of Repub Marines. Whoever had sent them here, it wasn't Caldwell. Magnus guessed it was So-Elku's bidding, but how he'd overridden the colonel's office, he didn't know. He just hoped that the rest of the battalion stationed in Worru hadn't been alerted either, because *that* would be a fight none of them would walk away from.

The Marines marched in and lined up in assault formation against the Grand Arielina. Any other time, the colonel would be addressing them as their CO and giving them orders. But given the circumstances, it seemed as though the colonel was about to try and pull a fast one.

"Charlie Company, what is the meaning of this?" Caldwell said, his voice ringing out over the square with the trained practice of a drill instructor.

Magnus saw the entire unit swivel to look at the colonel. He couldn't see through their helmets of course, but he could only imagine the looks of confusion and comments of shared disbelief over comms at the sight of their colonel in a suit of alien armor.

"Captain Daniels," Caldwell blatted out, "what is the meaning of this?"

Dozens of heads turned and looked at a Marine with the most senior insignia on his chest and shoulder plates. The man stepped forward and removed his helmet. "Sir?"

"Don't sir me, captain. You know my damn rank by heart."

"Yes, colonel. I'm sorry."

"Quit apologizing and tell me the meaning of all this."

"Colonel, sir, we were ordered to rally to an emergency here, at the Grand Arielina."

"On whose orders?"

"Why, yours, colonel."

Magnus watched the colonel remove his cigar and blow out a long white plume of smoke. "Mine, he says."

Just then, Awen and Piper ran up and appeared beside Magnus. "Sorry we're late," Awen said from under her helmet.

"Where have you been?" Magnus looked down at Piper, who clutched an ancient looking book beneath her arms. The moment he saw her, however, the little girl turned away. "I see you retrieved the codex."

"That's it, yes," Awen replied. "We had a little trouble with So-Elku."

"So-Elku?" Magnus nearly ripped his helmet off. "You encountered him?"

"We fought him," Awen said.

"And kicked his ass," Piper added.

"Piper!" Awen whirled on the girl. "I told you not to use that kind of language."

"Sounds like a regular Marine if you ask me," Magnus said. For the briefest second, Magnus could have sworn he saw Piper's helmet poke out from around Awen to look at him.

Colonel Caldwell was addressing the Marines again, and Magnus told Awen and Piper to find cover and prepare for the worst.

"Welp," Caldwell said, toking on his cigar again. "You all passed the exercise with flying colors. No PT in the morning, and report to your stations at 1100 hours. Sweet dreams, kids. Dismissed."

Caldwell turned and gave Magnus a look that said, "Hope they bought it." As Magnus looked out over the courtyard, however, there seemed to be enough indecision in the ranks that he wasn't so sure the colonel had completed the play.

When the Marine named Captain Daniels refused to walk

back down the steps, Magnus felt a knot form in his stomach. He took a slow breath and spoke in an even tone. "Everyone prepare to engage."

"Colonel, I'm afraid I'm going to need you to confirm your insignia ident," Daniels said.

"Excuse me?" Caldwell replied, turning to face the captain. The colonel was trying to intimidate the young captain, but Magnus had a feeling this was no longer about grandstanding.

Daniels raised his MC99 at the colonel. "You told us to expect an impersonator, and that he'd be leading a small element of rogue Marines, Jujari, and Luma. From the looks of it, I'd say we found our imposter." As if to accentuate his pronouncement, the rest of the company raised their weapons and aimed them at the colonel.

Clearly, So-Elku had already gotten to the Marines, or at least one of his lackeys had. And Magnus knew as well as Caldwell did that he'd left his insignia on his Repub armor back in his home. There was no way Daniels was going to get a positive scan. Which meant he was screwed.

"Splick's about to get real, kids," Magnus said over the company channel. Green icons raced along the chat window. "Witch's tits in a tornado kind of real."

"You want my insignia ident, captain?" Caldwell asked.

"I do, sir. Very much."

Caldwell took a long drag on his cigar. "Can I give you a bit of advice, Daniels?"

"Sir?"

"When you're faced with overwhelming odds and only one way out, give your enemy hell." With that, Caldwell turned on his heel and tossed his cigar.

26

Caldwell was running toward Magnus before the cigar had hit the ground, but when the embers from the tobacco struck the marble, it seemed to trigger an explosion of blaster fire.

The colonel took two shots in the back before stumbling into the hallway. Fortunately, his personal shield had absorbed them. Magnus doubled checked his status bar and saw Caldwell's shield had been reduced to 71%. Magnus grabbed his arm and pulled him behind the center pillar while a flurry of blaster fire filled the air on either side of them.

"Put that helmet on, gladia," Magnus ordered over his loudspeakers.

Caldwell did as he was instructed, and then pulled the NOV1 from his leg. "Looks like we're back at it again, Magnus."

"And here I was thinking we'd gotten too old for this splick."

"You might be," Caldwell said, tapping the top of his helmet, "but I sure as hell ain't!" Then the colonel rolled out, firing on Daniels, and advanced to a stone half-wall.

"Covering fire," Magnus ordered. Return fire erupted from the mouth of the hallway in a hailstorm of competing flashes. Magnus's audio filters engaged, lowering the decibel level, and his visor dimmed against the explosions of color. "Alpha and Bravo Platoons, flank the courtyard. Charlie and Delta, we're holding the center. Echo, do whatever the hell you can."

As Alpha and Bravo moved out and down each side of the stairwell, Magnus stepped out to join Caldwell against the wall. Titus and Rohoar led Charlie and Delta Platoons out and sent a withering barrage of blaster fire down on the enemy. The Marines' MC99 were no match for the NOV1, but the Repub had the numbers. And until Granther Company made a dent in the enemy's force, those numbers would be a threat.

As soon as Dutch and Abimbola's forces began drawing fire with their flanking maneuver, Magnus felt a temporary respite in the volley against the building's face. "Rohoar, take your pack and exploit this."

"Right away, scrumruk graulap."

Rohoar and his Jujari tore out of the hallway and ripped down the stairs, moving so fast the first line of Marines didn't even have time to get a shot off. When the Jujari slammed into the front line, Magnus actually saw a helmet pop up into the air. The sound alone was arresting—a combination of breaking plate armor, screams, and howls.

For the moment, the company's attention had been diverted to Abimbola, Dutch, and Rohoar's efforts. This gave Magnus, Titus, and Caldwell time to fire down on the company's center in an effort to collapse their mass inward.

Magnus aimed at a cluster of three Marines in the middle of the formation and fired his NOV1 at maximum rate. The individual blaster bolts were almost indistinguishable from one another, tying together in a blistering stream of fire that chewed through Repub armor like it was made of fabric. The three Marines were driven backward, colliding with their counterparts as their bodies were ripped to shreds.

But the output had also dropped Magnus's magazine by 27%. He couldn't keep that kind of assault up for very long, not without burning through his mags faster than he wanted. He dialed back the fire rate and took aim at the Marines responding to those he had just killed. His targeting reticle locked onto a helmet, and Magnus squeezed, driving two rounds through the cap and splitting it open. He struck the next Marine in the chest and shoulder, and a third one in the abdomen.

A pang of regret grabbed him by the throat and tried to wrench his stomach from his gut. These were fellow Marines he was slaughtering, not some rogue operatives with direct connections to Moldark. Putting Nos Kil down would be one thing. But these bucketheads? They deserved better than this.

Worse, he could imagine their fear… their complete shock at all this. When they'd received their orders, they probably bought a round of shots for everyone in the watering hole that night. They were going to paradise. Drawing a duty station on Worru was akin to winning the mysticsdamn lottery. There was nothing to do here but meet cute Luma girls and try to convince them to give up their vows. Forget ever having to see combat. But now, here they were, getting drilled by some chameleon-clad unit disappearing into the night and surrounding them on three sides.

As Dutch and Abimbola laid into the Marines with withering blaster fire, Magnus saw Daniels signal their retreat. The arm wave would have been accompanied by a verbal command over TACNET.

"I got movement leading out of the courtyard, LT," Flow said.

"You got 'em on the run, baby," Cheeks yelled with a hoot.

"Granther Company, maintain pressure. But once they reach the main road, let's give them a chance to breathe."

"Sir?" Titus asked. "But they're shooting to kill!"

"And so are we, so there's no sense in putting more down if they've given up. Just wait and see."

"Yes, sir." Titus resumed his rate of fire, dialing in one target at a time using the tips Magnus had given him. He was a damn fine gladia, and Magnus was glad to have him by his side.

The Marines backed into the street, emptying the courtyard as fast as they could. Magnus looked at all the bodies left on the grass as the unit peeled away, and he saw just how lethal Granther Company had been. That, and he realized that whoever had given them the initial order had sent them into a kill box in this courtyard. Magnus would have let the feelings of pride surge through him had the enemy been anything other than Caldwell's Marines. He could only imagine the pain in the colonel's chest. But if the old man felt anything, he sure as hell didn't show it. The man was a machine, delivering one-shot, one-kill combos in numbing succession. The bastard was gunning down his own soldiers as quickly as he could…

Until Magnus realized the colonel was delivering shots to knees, thighs, and calves.

Mystics, he hadn't killed a single Marine!

Suddenly, Magnus felt like he was going to vomit. He'd been so focused on getting Granther Company to safety—on executing the mission—that he'd failed to see any other option than punching a hole in the Repub as fast as he could.

"You were right to do it, son," Caldwell said, as if listening to his thoughts. "I see you hesitating there, and I know what you're thinking. But you just keep doing your part, and I'll do mine."

Magnus almost choked on the lump in his throat. "Copy that."

The Marines were clumped together, filing into the road and seeking cover as Granther Company continued to lay down a wall of blaster fire. Magnus had supposed this was going to be a slaughter, but in the Marines' favor, not his. Instead, their weapons and armor superiority combined with their placement outside of the courtyard's kill box gave his gladias the upper hand.

As the last of the Marines exited the grounds, Magnus studied his map. "Granther Company, return to the shuttles. Flow, I want waypoints that take us around the Marines."

"On it, LT," Flow replied.

Magnus noted that he hadn't lost a single gladia in the exchange. *And yet so many Marines.* He looked at the bodies strewn across the courtyard and, again, found himself fighting to swallow. *So-Eklu arranged this.* He was sure of it.

"Yes, he did," Awen replied over comms.

Magnus double checked to make sure it was a private channel before replying. "I thought we talked about you reading my thoughts."

"When it comes to advising you, especially in battle, it's important I get the whole story. And to restate the point, yes, So-Elku arranged this."

"Mystics," Magnus said, realizing how apt it was to take the name of Luma's occupation in vain.

"He's taken care of, at least for the moment. But we need to move. You can mourn these Marines later."

"I wasn't mourning, I was just... Aw, hell, I was mourning."

"I know. And it's okay. But we've gotta save it for later."

"Okie dokie, LT," Flow said. "I've got a course marked out for you."

Magnus watched a series of waypoints and connecting lines appear on his HUD. The new route only seemed to add about five minutes onto their previous path. But if it meant keeping Repub casualties down, he'd take it.

"Thanks, Flow." Magnus accepted the new course and sent it to all units. "Granther Company, move out."

"Happy to be of service," Flow replied. "And sorry about the delay. We're having issues with the system here."

Magnus looked at Awen. "What issues?"

"Azelon seems to be preoccupied with something, so we had to do a little old-fashioned orienteering for you."

"Hold on." Magnus pinged TO-96 and instructed him to join him at the top of the steps while the rest of the gladias moved out of the courtyard. The bot headed in Magnus and Awen's direction. "'Six, Flow says there's something wrong with Azelon. You reading anything abnormal?"

"My sensors are reading all systems normal, sir. That said, I fear that I do not have sufficient connectivity with Azelon to determine whether or not she is fully operational. Though I don't see why there would be any cause for concern as we have no enemies within range of the ship."

"But we have Luma," Magnus said. He turned on Awen. "Is there any way So-Elku or the others could mess with Azie or the ship from down here?"

"Given So-Elku's recent forays into the additional dimensions of the Unity, yes."

"Splick." Magnus was really growing irritated with this Luma master punk. "Flow, Cheeks, listen. I don't know what's going on with the ship, but keep your eyes open. I want to know if you encounter anything strange. Copy?"

"You got it," Cheeks replied. "Flow says the same."

Magnus hesitated. "Wait, where's Flow now?"

"He's over trying to pull up some sort of weapons system."

"Weapons system?"

"He says you're going to need it. Our sensors are showing that the Marines are readjusting to cut you off. Seems they've figured out you're trying to head to the star port."

"Son of a bitch."

"But we got it, LT. You stay the course, and we'll try and keep them away."

"Cheeks, if you don't have to kill any of them, don't."

"I read you. Don't you worry. We'll keep the casualties low. Just trying to deter them, that's all."

"Okay, good."

"Come on, Magnus," Awen said. "Time to go."

He nodded and then started down the steps. He followed the rest of Granther Company out of the courtyard and moved into the southbound street. The fighting had started to awaken the city, evident by the lights turning on and people poking their heads out of windows and doors. Several members of his company were shouting for people to stay inside, but the sight of the strangely clad warriors only seemed to make the residents more interested.

"Go chameleon," Magnus said over the company channel. "We don't need any more eyes on us." Instantly, the icons on his map changed to white, indicating that the telecolos mode had been engaged. The only icon not yet converted was his. Magnus changed modes and looked at the horizon to his left, catching the stars between buildings. The eastern sky was starting to warm—another hour and it would be sunrise.

Granther Company tracked west, turning at Flow's first waypoint. Up ahead, however, Magnus noticed the Marines headed south along convergent streets. He was just about to call out the movement when a shaft of light streaked down from orbit and slammed into the city somewhere ahead. The resulting explosion shook the ground and sent a shockwave rippling up from the city. It wasn't nearly as bad as something like an LO9D—the type of cannon blast he'd survived on Oorjaee. Such a strike would have put countless civilians at risk. But it was enough to tear up a street and divert a pursuing enemy.

Several local klaxons blared, and Magnus could hear shouting coming down the side streets. In spite of these negative developments, however, Magnus saw the Marine movement had been stopped. The icons were doubling back.

"Nice work, Flow," Magnus said. "Keep it up."

"You got it. Incoming!"

A second streak of light screamed down from the night sky and struck the next street over. Another shockwave rocked the streets as superheated debris launched into the air.

Flow let out a whoop. "Come on, son! I should have joined the Navy."

"Don't get carried away on me," Magnus replied. "Just enough to keep our path clear."

"You got it, LT. Hey…"

"Go ahead."

"Who let you out of your cages?"

Magnus slowed. "Cages?"

"Aw, hell nah."

"What's going on?" Magnus demanded, suddenly realizing Flow was talking to someone else. "Cheeks? Someone talk to me."

"Son of a bitch," Cheeks yelled.

"Dammit, boys! What's going on?"

Awen tapped him on the shoulder. Magnus spun on her. "What?"

"We've got a problem."

"I know we do!"

"Not up there." Awen turned and pointed behind them. "There."

27

Awen felt Magnus's hand pat against her body in a wordless attempt to get her moving. When he brought his NOV1 up and fired several rounds into the Luma chasing after them, Awen scolded him. "That won't do any good!"

Magnus's volley burst against the Luma shields, dissipating into nothing more than ripples of light and yellow sparks.

"You just take care of the Marines and we'll handle this," she added.

He glanced at her. "But…"

"There's a lot, I know. If we need help, I'll let you know."

Magnus let out a frustrated grunt. "I don't like this."

"The Marines, Magnus." She pointed toward the front of their convoy. "Now get out of here."

There wasn't time to argue. And Magnus's forces would be best utilized at the head of the line—*he has to realize that*, she thought. He finally conceded the point and left her alone, but he seemed to do so begrudgingly. First there was the implication of whatever was happening on the *Spire* with Flow and Cheeks, and now this. Awen felt pretty sure that this was not how Magnus wanted their retreat to go.

"Willowood, I need you and any Luma able to fight in the back of the line," Awen said, choosing to communicate over comms instead of in the Unity as it would keep Magnus and the other platoon leaders apprised of her activity. "Rohoar, if Magnus doesn't need you, I could use Delta Platoon as well."

"Take him," Magnus said without hesitation. She could see Magnus charge along the side of the street and tap Rohoar on the shoulder as he passed. "Go. Get back there."

"Coming your way, Miss Awen," Rohoar said as he summoned the Jujari to him.

By the time Willowood and Rohoar joined her with their respective forces, the wall of Luma marching toward them had closed to a hundred and twenty meters. They were moving with purpose, heads tipped forward, hands crossed and hidden in sleeves or balled into fists down at their sides.

"Who are these ones?" Rohoar asked, licking his lips.

"The Elders," Awen said with a chuckle of disbelief. *Is this really happening?*

"And where were they a little while ago when we fought the blue ones?"

"Probably still sleeping," Willowood replied.

"So they're old and tired." Rohoar cracked the knuckles on both hands.

"No, not really," Awen said.

But Rohoar *shhh'd* her like he would a pup. "This is what helps me win. Picturing them as wrinkly old humans makes it easier."

Awen made to protest but Willowood laid a hand on her. "If it makes it easier for him…"

"Right." She smiled. "They're just wrinkly old humans."

"Exactly," Rohoar replied. "Now, let's strip them of their skins and drink their blood."

"Rohoar, I—"

"Kidding, Miss Awen. Kidding. Kind of."

Awen glanced at Rohoar with a confused smile. The look was interrupted by renewed blaster fire from the front of the line. Magnus was engaging the Marines in the absence of Flow's orbital fire. "Time to do this," she said, then looked at Piper. "You ready, doma?"

"Of course, shydoh. Let's kick some—"

"Piper!"

"*Butt.* I was going to say butt."

"Sure you were."

MAGNUS FOUND DUTCH, Abimbola, and Titus up front, leading the charge against the oncoming Marines. Caldwell's company, now under the command of Captain Daniels, had split his assault. He used the northern side streets to flank the Gladio Umbra's westward advance, while the second half of this forces had progressed far enough to double back and come at Magnus head-on. The result was significant pressure to divert them south and east—in the opposite direction of the docks.

"If we are going to make it to the shuttles, then we are going to have to drive right through them," Abimbola said, firing his rifle from behind a parked skiff. Magnus was crouched beside him, studying the map on his HUD as blaster fire filled the air overhead.

"Copy that, Bimby. The only other option is a long walk around, and something tells me they'll match us every step."

"Time to start a new collection of buckets then."

Magnus nodded. He hated that he was about to have more good Marines put down. But this was combat, and dying wasn't fair. "You and Dutch focus on anything that comes out of those side streets. Titus, you're with me on the main street. Colonel, we need any advice you can give."

"They're going to be setting sniper positions soon," the colonel said. "So keep an eye out for those, both ahead and behind."

"Dozer and I will handle that," came Silk's voice. "We'll head up top." Magnus approved, and then saw the two gladias run up and dart into a side alley opposite the oncoming enemy forces.

"The majority of the force is going to come from the center," Caldwell said, pointing a flat hand down the main street. "They'll keep us distracted and let the smaller flanking forces pick off our sides. Just don't get distracted."

"Copy that," Dutch said, nodding at Abimbola.

"Let's show them what Granther Company does under pressure. Dominate!"

"Liberate!" came the company-wide response.

"La-raah."

Again, the entire unit repeated Magnus's cue in unison.

Magnus leaned around the skiff and aimed at the closest Marine. The figure was propped against the side of a light post—*terrible cover*—shooting at something well behind Magnus's frontline position—*terrible practice*. Poor kid was probably so green that this skirmish was popping his combat cherry. But he knew what he'd signed up for. No one joined the Marines to play with toy guns. And if Magnus didn't take the kid out, the kid's MC99 would take Magnus out—*if he got lucky*. His shield's status still displayed 52%.

Magnus squeezed the trigger and his NOV1 let out a bolt in a deafening scream. The supercharged energy hit a Marine in the unprotected space under his arm and zipped crossways through his lungs. Magnus watched as the enemy locked up, unable to breathe, and pitched away from the light post, before collapsing to the ground.

Two more Marines went down under Magnus's deadly aim—one laying atop a skiff who was drilled in the top of the head, the second taking two bolts in the chest plate.

"Advance," Magnus ordered. "And watch the right flank!"

"We're on it," Dutch replied.

Taking advantage of the heavy fire streaming out from behind him, Magnus ran behind a small charging station. But even without the covering fire, chameleon mode gave him an unprecedented advantage, as it did all his gladias. Without his HUD's advanced sensors, optics showed his forces as nothing more than flickering apparitions, given away only by the muzzle flash of their blasters. To the enemy, it must have seemed as if demons appeared from the darkness, dispensed death, and then vanished in a distortion of reality.

Dutch and Abimbola's platoons worked together, one covering the side street from the opposite side of the main street while the other kept close to the mouth, throwing VODs down the lane. The exterior walls of the buildings lit up in brilliant flashes as the battle played out beneath them. Magnus noted civilians coming to look out their windows and then backing away seconds later. Others actually opened their doors to see what was going on. For highbrow Plumerians, seeing combat in their streets was probably the last thing they ever could have imagined.

"Stay inside, dammit," Magnus yelled to a woman who poked her head out. Her eyes looked around frantically until Magnus lowered the intensity of his armor. He repeated the order to get back inside and she closed the door. Magnus raised his cloak again, and then returned fire on the Marines in the center of the street.

Two Marines leapfrogged along the sidewalk toward Magnus, advancing in textbook fashion—so textbook, in fact, that Magnus had an easy time of anticipating the precise moment of transition when one Marine stopped firing and the next was about to. He placed three rounds in the first

Marine, causing him to sprawl face-first on the sidewalk. The second looked out to see what had happened, but took a blaster bolt in the helmet, straight through the visor. The combatant fell backward, his MC99 clattering behind him.

"Keep moving," Magnus said, urging his unit forward. They needed to make better time if they were going to get off this rock. "Remember to retrieve and distribute any Repub energy mags you find over 50% full." Magnus and Azelon had purposely designed the NOV1s to accept the standard issue magazines for just such an occasion.

"Son of a bitch," someone yelled. The HUD showed it was Bliss.

"You okay, Bliss?" Magnus asked.

"Damn Marine just shot me in the ass!"

Magnus double checked Bliss's position and saw that he was safe behind a skiff. The gladia's shield was still above half power. "Must've been a lucky shot."

"Must've been a big ass," Ezo replied.

Magnus repeated his order to advance and then reopened a channel to the *Spire*, hoping to get Flow or Cheeks back on the line. But neither of them responded. Worse, not even Azelon replied.

"I couldn't help but notice your attempt to hail the starship, sir," TO-96 said.

"Any idea what's going on up there?"

"Negative, sir. My apologies."

"Just let me know the moment anything changes, 'Six."

"Understood."

Magnus leaned out, pointing his weapon downrange, just as a Marine darted for cover. The man never even saw Magnus's blaster bolts coming. A staccato burst struck the assailant in the chest in a grouping no larger than Magnus's palm. The force jerked the Marine backward, flipped his legs forward in midair, and slammed his back against the ground.

Magnus paused to assess Dutch and Abimbola's progress. They'd successfully cleared one side street and were advancing on the next. But their progress was slow, and Magnus knew they needed to pick up the pace.

"Silk," Magnus said. "Any chance you can divert your attention down here?"

"Just a second."

Magnus looked up in time to see several blaster bolts streak between gaps in the buildings, headed down range.

"Okay, please repeat?"

"I said, can you divert some of your attention down here?"

"Can do, just—" Silk's voice sounded strained. "Just give us another minute. There's a small contingent of Marines trying to secure positions against you."

"Keep doing what you're doing then."

"Roger that. We'll assist you when we can."

Magnus returned his attention to the main thoroughfare and picked his next target. The sun was beginning to warm the sky. Sunup wouldn't be for another hour or so, but he'd wanted to be long gone before then. "Tough luck, Adonis. Just ain't in your cards today."

"What was that, sir?"

"Dammit, 'Six. Why are you still listening?"

"I'm always listening, sir."

Magnus gave out a sharp single-breathed laugh. "'Cause that's not creepy or anything."

"I am delighted to hear that, sir. The last thing I would want is to be frightening, eerie, or disturbing. Additionally, sinister, hair-raising, spooky, scary—"

"'Six!"

"Sir?"

"You don't need—" Magnus fired twice at a Marine who peeked around the tail-end of a skiff. "To elaborate!"

"Very good, sir. I was simply trying to establish a greater personal connection through a shared sense of mutual understanding given the intensity of the present scenario."

"You know what else you can do? Use those gauss cannons on your shoulders and take out that skiff with all the Marine's behind it."

"Will that also produce a feeling of greater connectedness between us?"

"Yes. Now shoot the damn skiff!"

"Right away, sir."

From the rear, Magnus heard the distinct report of TO-96's twin gauss cannons. The ballistic-tipped projectiles broke the air overhead and slammed into the skiff with such force that the vehicle rebounded off the street and flipped end-over-end. The blast sprayed Marines in an arc, several losing limbs in the process.

When the skiff slammed down into the street, Magnus ordered Granther Company forward. No sooner had he issued the command than several micro-missiles zipped overhead and took out no fewer than five more Marines who'd been exposed during the skiff's destruction. The explosions lit the street up, washing the buildings in yellow light.

"That was a nice touch," Magnus said to TO-96.

"Do you feel a greater sense of connection to me?"

Magnus laughed. "I sure do, 'Six."

"I am happy my missiles could bring us together then."

28

Ricio waved his hand through the space that the force field had occupied only moments before. To his amazement, the wall was gone, as if someone had simply flipped a switch and turned it off. At first, Ricio thought it was a gimmick. He envisioned himself attempting to leave his cell, only to have the person behind the controls restore the forcefield and cut his body in half. But that seemed unlikely.

He passed his hand through the space again and then waited, studying the threshold. When the wall failed to reappear, he tested it by extending his left arm out of his cell. He figured that if he was going to lose a limb, it might as well be his non-dominant hand. Still, the force field remained off. So Rico stepped out of his cell.

"Hello?" he said, turning around slowly in the cellblock. He looked at all the places that he imagined cameras might be, waving at the corners in the ceiling. "Anybody there?" But there was no reply. No one spoke over speakers, and no one rushed in to seize him.

The cellblock door was open to the corridor that ran to the control room, so Ricio moved down the hall. He was about to step into the room full of monitors when an enormous man emerged from a cellblock to his right.

"Who the hell are you?" the man demanded. His bare and bloodied chest was decorated with a lifetime of Marine tats, and he was missing an eye. Ricio thought it best not to mess with him, but he also wasn't giving up his identity to some one-eyed stranger.

"I'm someone who wants to know why we just got set free. You?"

The Marine growled. "Same."

"Seems we have a common goal then."

"For now. You Repub?"

"Eh, you could say that," Ricio said, scratching his chin. "And you're a Marine."

The big man nodded. "You the one they took from the crash site?"

Ricio eyed the man more carefully. "Were you part of the Recon team deployed on the planet's surface?" When the man grunted, Ricio raised a finger at him. "I was sent to save your dumb ass, you pathetic piece of splick."

"Watch who you're calling pathetic," the man replied, stepping toward Ricio.

"Really?" Ricio put his hands on his hips. "Of all the

insults in that sentence, you picked *pathetic* as the most objectionable?" Then to himself, he said, "No wonder they sent me to rescue him."

The man charged Ricio.

"Hey now, big fella." His hands were up and waving. "No sense in throwing our options away prematurely."

The Marine slowed. "What options?"

"You know how to pilot a starship?"

The trooper seemed to consider this more intently than Ricio gave him credit for. Maybe he wasn't a complete imbecile. "No."

"Then I'm your pilot. And do I look like I can crush a man's skull with my hands?"

"No."

"Then you're my bodyguard." Ricio extended his hand toward the Marine. "Name's Longo."

The man looked at Ricio's hand and then shook it. "Nos Kil."

"I can see that."

"Let's move, jockey."

"Copy that, buckethead."

The two of them entered the control room, and Nos Kil immediately turned toward a workstation. He swiped through several menus on the holo display before Ricio asked: "What are you looking for?"

"Comms," Nos Kil said, his eye and fingers working through the system architecture. "If we only have a minute before anyone comes to restrain us, I want to use it to get word to…" Nos Kil looked over at Ricio in a way that suggested the Marine wasn't sure he could trust the pilot.

"To Moldark," Ricio said.

"Yes." Nos Kil sneered. "You mind?"

Ricio followed the brute's eyes toward the exit. Apparently the Marine wanted to compose his transmission in private. Ricio shrugged and then stepped into the corridor just out of earshot. He wanted to chastise the tattooed war monger, arguing that they were on the same team, when he felt the words lodge themselves in his throat. *Are we on the same team?* he wondered. Given everything that Magnus had divulged about the Gladio Umbra's desire to keep evil people from doing evil things, Ricio had his doubts—enough of them that he'd already given Magnus enough intel that Moldark would have him executed if he ever found out.

"What's your name again, jockey?" Nos Kil yelled from inside the control room, snapping his fingers. "For my report."

"Longo," Ricio replied. For some reason he regretted hearing himself say his own name.

It was then that Ricio realized a startling truth. Betrayal wasn't something that happened in an instant. It wasn't a quick decision born out of an impetuous desire to *shake things up*. Instead, it was something that happened slowly, like the transformation that occurred within a chrysalis. No one knew how the worm transformed into a butterfly, but everyone could see the results when it emerged.

"Well?" Nos Kil said, poking his head out of the doorway.

"Don't just stand there. See how many enemies we're looking at. Get us some weapons and a ship."

"Right." Ricio blinked, followed Nos Kil back inside, and then stepped to another workstation. He swiped through several screens until he found one that displayed a top down map of the starship's levels. As Ricio took in the scope of the vessel, he realized it was far bigger than he imagined—nearly twice the size of a Repub battlecruiser. He couldn't be sure without studying the schematics more carefully, but he guessed the ship might even rival a battleship or dreadnaught.

"What's the holdup, jockey?"

"Nothing." Ricio shook his head and played with the map, swiping through decks and expanding one that showed life signs. "This thing is massive. But looks like there are only two souls aboard."

Nos Kil stopped finalizing his comms transmission. "Two?"

"That's what ships sensors are saying."

"But you just said the ship is big. That can't be right."

"Hell, I can pour us some coffee and we can have a meaningful conversation about it."

The Marine glared at him.

"Another time maybe." Ricio returned to his work and looked for a hangar bay. As it turned out, there were several. He chose one that harbored transport shuttles—hoping they would be outfitted with some sort of subspace drive—and then memorized the route.

"Found us some wings," Ricio said. "Ten minute walk. All we need to do is—"

"I want to take out those two pieces of splick first. Where are they?"

Ricio hesitated. "They're on the bridge. But the hangar bays—"

"Find us some weapons, jockey. If one of those is the man who did this to me"—he pointed to his eye—"then I need to return the favor before we leave."

Ricio didn't need much imagination to suspect that Magnus had inflicted Nos Kil's injury. Which posed a new dilemma. Up until now, Ricio suspected he could comply with his captors, provide them with some limited but true intel, and then wait for an opportunity to escape or be released. The information he'd given Magnus would serve their little rebellion—probably give them a small advantage, at least for a little while—but there was no way Magnus's crew stood a chance against Moldark. Then, once he was aboard the *Black Labyrinth*, Ricio would debrief with Fleet Admiral Brighton—omitting any of his minority treasonous acts—fill out the necessary documentation, and then head back to Capriana to his wife and son as a civilian.

But now Nos Kil wanted to take out Magnus. "Son of a bitch," Ricio said.

Nos Kil turned toward him. "What is it?"

"They've got the armory locked down tight." Ricio jabbed a finger at the holo, making up every word. "No way we're getting in there. Better just head for the shuttle."

"I don't need weapons." Nos Kil turned back to his own holo and brought up the ship's schematic, then he identified the bridge and examined the route. "Come on, jockey. I might need you to hold him down."

R𝚒cio found himself walking behind Nos Kil, trying to think of every excuse he could to keep the Marine from attacking Magnus, but nothing reasonable came to mind. As his bare feet slapped against the glossy white floors that led to the elevator, Ricio wondered why his escape hadn't triggered any alarms yet. Surely the bridge crew or the ship's AI watched their progress.

Then he had a sickening thought—*what if we're walking into a trap?*

But that seemed improbable. If their captors wanted them dead, they had plenty of opportunity to do it already. Plus, Ricio suspected that he'd already curried enough favor with Magnus to keep him off the execution list. And Magnus and his odd squad didn't seem pathological. In fact, Ricio felt himself siding with the unlikely crew and their mission far more than he cared to admit. He *liked* helping them. And if he was being completely honest with himself, he believed in what they were trying to do.

"So what's the plan?" Ricio asked as the lift slowed at the bridge level.

"Plan?" The dried blood and swollen eye socket on Nos

Kil's face made him look like something out of a horror holo. "How about, don't get killed. And if you survive long enough, I'll tell you what I need you to do once I assess the situation."

"And here I was hoping you'd say something like, 'You take the one on the left and I'll take the one on the right.' That's how it normally works, right?"

Nos Kil sneered at Ricio.

"Guess not."

"Just stay behind me and don't get killed, jockey."

"I can do that."

The lift doors slid apart to reveal a large command bridge. A dozen workstations ran along the walls, while several stand-alone units faced the room-wide holo display that took up the far wall. Two men sat beside one another, intent on some sort of holo targeting system that correlated with a map in the main window, while a white robot was slumped in a chair by itself.

Neither man noticed Ricio and Nos Kil enter. The two crew members wore white uniforms with blue pinstripes—casual wear, by the looks of it—and soft-soled shoes. Since their well-muscled bodies seemed to make the suits tear at the seams, Ricio guessed they were Marines like Nos Kil, one tall with black skin, the other short with a dark olive complexion.

While Ricio hesitated, taking in the scene, Nos Kil did not. The beast of a shirtless barrel-chested man took off like a racing hound on a high-stakes track. Whether at the sound of his feet or the rush of air, the shorter of the two turned just in time to see Nos Kil lunge at them. Nos Kil dropped his shoulder and caught the man in the chest, driving him out of his chair and into his partner. Together, all three men fell sideways and tumbled into the floor in a heap.

Ricio ran forward to meet them, still unsure what he should do. Nos Kil rolled to his knees and started throwing punches at the black man, drilling his face so hard Ricio thought the man's skull might implode. But the shorter man threw a powerful punch at Nos Kil's side, causing the Marine to fold.

The black man pushed the enemy off him and sat up just as the short one dove after Nos Kil. Then both crew members were exchanging punches with the former prisoner—all three men caught in a violent struggle of blows, blocks, hand holds, and rolls. The black man seemed to be growing frantic, his swings becoming more impulsive and less accurate. He shouted profanity at Nos Kil as the two grappled along the floor. Likewise, the shorter crew member seemed to be losing his mind, snarling and cursing as he delivered several wild blows. The two men acted as though Nos Kil was the last man they'd ever fight. But the passion of their hatred appeared to cloud their judgement as Nos Kil was getting the upper hand even despite being outnumbered.

Pick a side, pilot, Ricio told himself. That was when he saw a blaster pistol on the floor beside one of the crash couches. It must have fallen from one of the two crew members' hips. He reached down and grabbed the weapon, bringing it to bear on the fight scene that moved into the middle of the bridge.

"Everyone stand down," he ordered. But his command

went completely unheard. Nos Kil had his hand clenched around the smaller one's throat while he jabbed at the other man's nose, causing a fountain of blood to stain the floor.

"I said, stand down!" Ricio aimed at the ground just to the side of the men and squeezed the trigger. A blue blaster bolt—much larger than he expected the diminutive weapon to produce—leaped from the barrel with a shriek. Sparks and smokey rivulets exploded from the charred hole in the floor. All three men jerked at the sound and froze, hands going up.

"That's better." Ricio trained the weapon on the cluster of men. "I need names."

"What are you doing, jockey?" Nos Kil asked with a hiss. "Shoot these pieces of splick!"

"Can it, Marine."

Nos Kil's eye went wild, his mouth turning into a snarling maw of blood-soaked teeth. "Why I ought to—"

"I can very easily poke out your other eye if you want a matching pair." Ricio stared down the sight and glared at Nos Kil's remaining eye. "Didn't think so. Now, I'm going to ask one last time—*names*."

"I'm—I'm…" The black man stuttered, trying hard to come to his senses and waving his hands at the weapon. "I'm Michael Deeks. This—this is Miguel Chico."

"And what were you doing there?" Ricio flicked the pistol back toward their workstation.

"None of your business," Chico said. "None of your damn business!"

"Oh, but I think it is my business—that is, if you want my help."

"Your help?" Deeks asked with no effort to hide is disbelief.

"Moldark's going to annihilate you, jockey," Nos Kil said, spitting out a mouthful of blood.

"You *really* don't want that other eye, do you, Nos Kil," Ricio said, tilting his head at the man.

"You don't have the balls."

Ricio smiled. "I may not have your brawn, Marine. And I definitely don't have your stomach for pain. But I can assure you, you've never seen balls the size of a Talon pilot's. So unless you want to miss out on the view, I suggest you shut up."

"What were you doing there?" Rico asked again, dedicating his attention to Deeks.

"Orbital fire support for our unit," Deeks replied.

"Magnus?"

The two crew looked at each other, then Deeks replied with a nod. "Magnus."

"Then I suggest you get back to it, Deeks."

The black man's eyebrows raised. "I… I'm not sure I understand."

"And you, Chico. You're gonna help me put this sicko back in his doghouse. Copy?" While Ricio talked, he noticed a setting on the pistol's rear graphic display that seemed to lower the weapon's discharge amperage while increasing the voltage.

Chico glanced at Nos Kil, then back at Ricio. "I can't tell if you're joking or not."

Nos Kil spat more blood on the ground. "Oh, he's joking al—"

Nos Kil didn't finish the statement before Ricio fired at his chest. The Marine's back slammed into the deck and his body convulsed, legs thrashing, arms grasping at the invisible wound. In another second, his body went still.

"What in hell is going on here?" Deeks asked.

"That's gonna be the same question Magnus asks you if you don't get back on those controls, Deeks."

"Call me Flow," the man said, standing to his feet and wiping blood from his lip. "This here's Cheeks."

Cheeks remained on the ground and closed his eyes, taking several slow breaths. That was when Ricio realized what he was looking at. These boys had seen action—*a lot of action. Enough that that they'd probably never truly come off the battlefield. Damn.*

"And that?" Ricio pointed toward the bot in the crash couch.

"That there's Azelon," Cheeks said as Flow helped him up. "The ship's AI in bodily form."

"Ship's got a dedicated bot?" Ricio asked.

Deeks gave him a nod. "Something happened to her about ten minutes ago."

Cheeks squinted at Ricio. "Say, that wouldn't have anything to do with—"

"I don't know anything about it," Ricio said. "Something

happened to the force fields and security doors in the brig. Nos Kil wanted to clear this bridge, and I decided to go along with it until—"

"Until you saw whose side was going to win?" Cheeks asked.

"Until I found a way to stop him," Ricio replied, doing his best to distance himself from the inner argument that he'd been wrestling with until a few moments ago. As a sign of good faith, Ricio flipped the weapon around and extended the grip to Cheeks, seeing as how he was the one with the empty holster. "I'll take his feet, you take his hands. Then, when I get back, we need to have a talk."

"About what?" Cheeks asked.

"About what else this ship has to offer a guy with balls my size."

29

Awen and Rohoar ordered the Jujari and Willowood's Luma into a defensive formation at the rear of the line. Piper stood beside Awen with her hands balled into fists, and Saasarr remained by the little girl's side by order of Sootriman.

The elders had exchanged their slow march for an all-out run, racing toward Awen with terrible looks in their eyes. The sight produced several heart-thumping pangs of fear since she'd never seen their faces look so malevolent before. But battle had a way of changing people—*for the worse*, she thought. For a split second, she wondered if she looked just as vile to them as they did to her. *Mystics, I hope not*. Then she remembered that she bore a helmet.

Awen slipped into her second sight and saw the Luma Elders approach in a dazzling array of flowing color and sparkling movement. Here, the sun had already risen to full height, adding its luster to the rhythmic charge of the enemy.

The enemy. Awen still could not believe she was about to dispense harm on those she'd spent the last seven years trying to emulate. How had this happened? How had things gone so horribly wrong?

"Krufka," Rohoar yelled—the Jujari command for hold. Awen looked over to see the Jujari on all fours. Their rumps and shoulders were low, heads down, fangs exposed. They snarled at the oncoming enemy, ready to charge forward. Yet Rohoar's simple command kept their feet planted, saliva dripping onto the tops of their forepaws.

Likewise, Willowood assumed a defensive Li-Loré stance—one hand forward, palm up, the other hand balled into a fist and held behind her head. Several of the Luma beside her adopted a similar pose, while the rest of the elders lowered their heads and prepared for the clash.

"Just push them back," Awen said to Piper. "Keep them from hurting us wherever you can."

"Yes, shydoh."

Awen readied herself and summoned the energy of the Foundation and the Nexus into her body. She felt it surge into her limbs, called up from the deep. Then she blew a strand of hair off her face that had fallen down inside her helmet. "Here goes nothing."

The battle lines closed in the Unity and in the natural realm, producing blasts of heat and light in both realms. The energy washed over buildings and people like a tidal wave, shoving matter and molecules away from the epicenter.

Awen held her ground as an elder drove his hand into her personal shield. The sparks of the impact made Awen wince, but she did not yield to the immense amount of power behind the punch. Instead, she wrapped energy around the outstretched fist like a rope, yanked the aggressor's arm down with one hand, and then shoved the man away with the other. Her newfound abilities in the additional realms of the Unity had made Awen strong—far stronger than even the greatest elder. The man flew backward and collided with two other Luma. The three toppled to the ground in an eruption of color.

Willowood easily defended herself against an over-anxious attacker, while Rohoar managed to bite through another Luma's personal shield. His teeth seized the assailant's arm, then his head turned and flipped the man sideways onto the ground. Another flip back in the other direction not only tore the elder's limb from his side, but smacked his head hard enough to knock him out.

"Awen," Piper screamed. When Awen looked up, a female elder had leaped into the air and was sailing down at Awen with both hands spread, ready to strike. Awen raised her hands by instinct to block the blow, but Piper arrested the woman's movement and drove her head straight into the concrete street. Awen gasped as the woman's head and shoulders buried themselves in the fissure. Sparks struck Awen in the Unity while concrete bounced off her suit in the natural realm. The elder remained motionless, her head clearly crushed from the impact.

"Piper, I thought I told you—"

"Here comes another!"

Awen ripped her attention from Piper to see another elder charge her, this time presenting some sort of javelin in the Unity. She'd never seen a weapon fashioned before and wondered if this was something of So-Elku's doing.

The elder hurled the weapon, but Awen sidestepped it, allowing it to pass by. She'd not been thinking, however, that a gladia from Titus's platoon was standing behind her. The lance penetrated the man's back, pushing his heart clear out of his armored chest. In the natural, Awen only saw a hole open and the organ shoot from the victim, bathed in a spray of blood.

She noted that his name was Andocs and remembered the red-haired man from Magnus's training back on Neith Tearness. The gladia had been a tireless worker, always eager to learn new tactics and implement them quickly once he'd gained mastery. She was only sad that her careless dodge had cost the gladia his life.

Awen saw the elder fashion another javelin and hurl it at her. This time, Awen caught the spear, twirled it around, and released the weapon's momentum back toward the attacker. The javelin struck the man, picked him off his feet, and pinned him to a second Luma. Both men fell to the ground in a heap, dead within seconds.

Willowood had dispensed with merely trying to incapacitate her victims. Instead, her lethal force was displayed by rending one victim of his hips and legs as her arm passed through his abdomen in a lightning-fast sweep. The Luma had been caught so off guard that he froze in shock, looked down at his lower half, and then screamed as his torso fell forward.

Awen's heart thumped loudly in her head as she realized her mentor—the woman she revered more than any other in the galaxy for her teaching on non-violent resistance—had just slain a fellow Luma in battle. And violently so. She wanted to scream, to protest, to make everything stop. What she feared the most had come upon her, and not even Magnus's words could calm the fire raging in her chest. She wanted everything to stop—for it to all go away. But it wasn't. And it wouldn't. The violence unfolding before her eyes was as inevitable as gravity, pulling her recklessly toward the mass of war.

Then her eyes stopped on Piper. In Awen's observance of Willowood, another elder had lunged for the little girl. Whether to grab her by the throat or yank her behind enemy lines, Awen didn't know. But she was sure the girl's life was in danger. And Awen felt violated. Not as if her own personhood was in jeopardy, but that someone would attempt to take what she loved. To capture or kill Piper—a child.

For a fraction of a second, time stood still for Awen. It was as if the entire scene around her was frozen in a multidimensional portrait, one rendered in astounding clarity. Bodies poised in the throes of assault. Blaster bolts suspended in midair. Sparks and droplets of blood trailing from slices in throat, leg, and shoulder. Everywhere around her was carnage, the gruesome display of lives turned inward, bent on destruction of the other.

There, in that still moment, Awen chose.

She chose to be a part of it despite every cell in her body wishing otherwise. She chose to resist the evil that sought to stop her and her kinsfolk. She chose to give herself to the wave of resistance that surged up the beachhead and broke against the sandcastle of So-Elku's hate.

The scene raced back to life.

Awen had awakened.

One foot followed the next, legs sweeping through the air in a lethal dance that flipped her body upside down. Feet met bone, hands struck flesh, and her body became an instrument of war. The man who tried to reach for Piper lost both arms. He fell forward, and Awen's upswinging arms launched him skyward where his body was riddled with blaster fire. It was as if she had seen each bolt streak across the warming sky and she'd sent his armless body up to be intercepted with perfect precision.

Awen's movement was an endless flow of lethal action. Her thoughts became expressions, and her expressions became parries and thrusts, blasts and blocks. Each twisting duck and every leaping kick was interconnected, joined to her ardent resolution to stop the enemy.

She extended her palms to drive an elder back, the explosion of energy turning from yellow to brilliant magenta—the color of the Nexus. The body flew into the horde of Luma, crushing several who waited for their turn at the front lines.

Two more assailants stepped in to challenge her, both raising weapons made of pure energy. Awen pictured a bar of impenetrable metal form in her hands. As the enemies' weapons came down, Awen felt the blows crash upon the long magenta shaft she held in her outstretched hands. The instruments collided and froze, spitting sparks in brilliant cascades of yellow and red, until Awen roared and thrust the attackers away. Their bodies flew back, colliding with others in a heap.

More enemies charged her, perhaps determining that she was the greatest threat. But with each attack, Awen's strikes transitioned into one another with seamless succession. She was an unstoppable force, twirling and undulating, firing and decimating. At one point, she had called so much energy up from the Nexus that she felt as if her whole body might explode. Instead, she redirected the flow and watched as it bored a path all the way through the enemy's ranks. The beam disintegrated everything it touched, stopping only when she saw it touch a residential building in the distance.

The action had been so violent that the elders stopped their assault. For the briefest moment, Awen thought she heard them gasp. Blaster fire and explosions continued at the front of the advance, but in the rear, everyone looked at Awen in stunned silence. All, but one attacker, that is.

The man thrust at Awen with some sort of glowing pike. She only caught it out of the corner of her eye. Until it vanished. Awen was sure it had penetrated her. But the man was gone.

Instead, a new scream went out from somewhere far above her. Awen looked up and saw the man falling toward the street, directly above where he'd stood a split second before. His voice grew louder as his flailing limbs did nothing to slow his fall. Awen stepped back as the man landed in a sickening *thud* two meters away.

Blood sprayed her suit while sparks struck her body. She stared at the corpse, wondering how she'd done such a thing. But Awen knew it wasn't her abilities that had done this. Not even she knew how to transport natural matter inside the Unity.

But Piper might.

Awen spun around and used her second sight to see the little girl's face. Piper glared at the dead man's body. When she spoke, her voice was strained and cold. "He was going to kill you, shydoh."

"Piper, you—"

"He was going to *murder* you."

Awen wanted to say more, but the enemy charged again.

30

Piper hadn't planned to move the man into the sky. It just seemed like the best option given how close he'd been to Awen. He'd wanted to hurt her shydoh, Piper could see it—she could sense his hostility. And she wasn't going to let that happen. Not now, not ever. So Piper moved him, and then let him go. That was all. And when he hit the ground, she felt satisfied that he hadn't survived. He was an evil person who'd wanted to do evil things. Like hurt Awen.

"Stay with the gladias," Awen yelled at her.

Piper spun around to see that Magnus had advanced Granther Company, creating a gap between where Piper stood and the rear of the line. Not wishing to make Awen more mad than she already was, Piper ran forward until she'd caught up with Titus's platoon. Then she turned around again and looked for ways to help Awen and the others.

Mr. Rohoar was doing really good. He used his super sharp teeth and big paws to slash at the Luma warriors. Saasarr was killing people too—anyone that got too close to Piper. Sootriman had ordered him to protect her. His tail was like a long whip that knocked people over or snagged them around their necks and threw them to the ground. Piper knew that Saasarr hadn't liked the Jujari before, but now he seemed to be getting along with them really good.

The enemy, on the other hand, seemed super scared of the Jujari and Saasarr. And that was good too because Piper didn't want the big doggies or the lizard getting hurt. So, like she'd done with the man who tried to stab Awen, Piper made four of the bad guys disappear. But this time, she just put them in the street. Some of their heads and arms stuck out of the pavement. But they coughed and choked, which meant they'd be dead soon anyway.

Piper's grandmother was also doing super great, dodging enemy attacks with the grace of a dancer. She was so pretty, like an older version of Piper's mommy. Her hair was just more grey and wild. And she had more wrinkles. And lots of bracelets, which Piper thought were really fun because of the noise they made.

Piper was so happy to have a grandmother that she hardly knew what to say. But there hadn't been any time for talking, so not having the right words wasn't a problem. At least not yet. Instead, Piper's chest had filled with so much warmth that the darkness had run away—the darkness that had been sitting in her heart since she'd talked with Nos Kil.

Now that everyone was fighting, the darkness had returned. It felt heavy. And Piper wanted to get rid of it. But she knew the only way to do that was to speak with Mr. Lieutenant Magnus, and that scared her. Because what if he tried to shut her up? What if he tried to hurt her like he'd hurt the other girls? The thoughts sent a shiver down her spine.

She continued to watch Awen hold off the big group of Luma elders. But the gladias with blasters were moving forward again, which was good, because it meant everyone could get to the shuttles soon.

Just then, a giant burst of light streaked down from the sky and slammed into the ground somewhere ahead. Piper's tummy tingled as the vibrations raced up her legs. Fire shot into the sky, and the gladias moved ahead some more. Pretty soon, she heard Mr. Lieutenant Magnus give the order to run, and the next thing Piper knew, she was chasing after them and headed toward the shuttles.

In her second sight, Piper turned around to make sure Awen and the others were following them. But they were still fighting. Which was not good. They needed to get to the shuttles like everyone else. So Piper stopped running and focused on the space that separated Awen and her grandmother from all the other bad people. She pictured a big wall going up, and then waited.

A woman dressed in the fancy Luma robes raised her hand to hit Awen. And Awen was ready to block it. But the bad lady's hand bounced off the imaginary wall Piper had made with her mind.

Piper grinned, and then decided that the wall should move some. She pushed it back, making the Luma's feet slide along the street. It was funny to watch them leap backward. Several of them smushed into each other, getting all bunched up like kids in a lunch line.

"Piper, go!"

Piper blinked and then focused on Awen's face. Her shydoh was yelling at her, pointing toward the rest of Granther Company.

"Okay," Piper yelled back in the Unity. "But you gotta come too!"

Awen seemed reluctant, looking back at the Luma behind Piper's wall several times before taking steps in the direction of the shuttles. Pleased, Piper began running again too. But she decided to leave the wall up, at least as long as she could. It was hard work, and she knew she needed to focus on not falling. Running was also hard work.

The gladias of Granther Company turned down a side street, and Piper followed. When she looked at where they turned, she could see a large burning crater in the ground that was filled with rubble. She guessed Mr. Flow's cannon on the *Spire* had done that. She also saw body parts from the Marines lying everywhere. They were dead though, so they wouldn't miss them.

She followed the gladias between buildings that looked like houses. Most of them had lights on. As Piper ran by, she noticed a few small faces peering out into the night. They were kids, like her. In her second sight, she could see their pajamas. Some of them had stuffed animals clutched in their arms. She waved at them, but then realized they couldn't see her in the natural realm because her suit was using the chameleon mode that made it blend in with her surroundings.

Piper slowed, deactivated the cloak, and then waved again at two kids who looked at her through a ground floor window. The little boy waved back, smiling wide. But the little girl seemed scared and hunkered down behind her stuffed hippalotaderm. Then Piper saw the children's parents yell at them and yank them away from the window. That was probably a good thing too. She didn't want the kids getting hurt. Piper felt happy that the kids had such a good mom and dad that would try and keep their family safe and sound. War was scary, and the last thing Piper wanted was for other kids to get hurt.

"Piper, move!" Miss Awen had caught up to her now. Piper waved goodbye to the kids even though they weren't by the window anymore, and then reactivated her suit to blend in with the street. She felt Awen push her forward, and Piper began to run.

They turned left at the end of the street and continued to follow Granther Company toward the shuttles. Despite how she felt about Mr. Lieutenant Magnus, she had to admit that he was doing a super good job protecting everyone while they ran.

Another bright streak of light came down from Azelon's starship and shook the city. More fire and smoke billowed into the sky. The stars were getting less bright, and the sun seemed to want to crawl out of its bed. Piper thought she was ready for the opposite—once she got back to the *Spire*, she wanted to sleep. Well, maybe eat first and then sleep.

On and on Piper ran until she thought her legs might turn into noodles. She thought about sending herself to the shuttles, then she wouldn't have to run anymore and could just wait for everyone else to get there. But then Awen would get mad, and if Awen was mad, her mother would be mad too. *That wouldn't be good.*

When the docking bays finally came into view, Piper looked at the buildings and read the numbers. They'd parked the *Spire's* shuttles a little further down than where they were right now. But it wasn't much farther.

The old man that Mr. Lieutenant Magnus had convinced to join Granther Company spoke over the comms. "Reinforcements will be arriving from the south. I'm guessing an ETA of three minutes."

Mr. Lieutenant Magnus did not seem happy about that. But three minutes seemed like more than enough time to get everyone on board the shuttles. Piper could see the proper docking bays just up the street. In another few seconds, the front of the line turned through the big opening into the first bay. Piper followed them in and saw the tall tail fins of the four shuttles rising into the air. The ramps were down, and the gladias were arranging themselves to protect everyone as they neared the little ships.

Someone pointed at Piper and ordered her up first. But she had to wait for her grandmother and her shydoh, for

Rohoar and the funny lizard. Piper turned and waited for everyone to come around the corner. But someone shouted her name. She knew the voice—all too well.

"Piper Penelope-Anne Stone, you get your tiny little butt over here and up this ramp this instant!"

Piper winced.

"Yes, momma." But just before Piper turned toward her mother, she saw blaster fire appear behind Awen and the others who were racing toward her. One of the good Luma that had been with her grandmother was hit and fell down. Piper screamed. Then another blaster bolt struck an old man in the side of the head and he toppled over. A third good Luma was hit twice in the side and then again in the shoulder. They spun sideways like a top before slamming against the ground.

No, no, no, this is not supposed to happen, Piper thought. She could feel her heartbeat thumping in her ears.

Her mother screamed for her, but Piper had to do something. Then she saw Awen waving at her and pointing toward the shuttle. But if Piper didn't do something, more of her grandmother's good Luma might die.

Suddenly, a whole bunch of Marines appeared around the mouth of the docking bay and flooded the huge door. Blaster bolts streaked across at the first shuttle as the gladia with the big NOV1 rifles returned fire.

An arm caught Piper in the stomach and knocked the wind out of her. It was Awen. She'd picked Piper up and was hauling her toward the shuttles as blaster fire skipped off the ground, sending up motes of molten metal.

Piper tried to protest, tried to kick and punch and scream to be let go, but Awen's grip was too strong. She looked up and saw her mother standing beside Mr. Lieutenant Magnus, both of them firing back at the Marines who were flooding the docking bay. They stood just below the ramp, yelling something at Awen. Piper was sure her mother was going to be cross with her for not getting on the ship sooner.

Awen was almost to the ramp when Piper saw Magnus push her mother to the side and directly into a stream of blaster bolts. In the first instant, sparks danced off her helmet and chest, disrupting chameleon mode. But in the next, the bolts went through her mother's visor and out the rear of her helmet. Her body flipped backward and struck the ground as if all the strength had left her.

Piper screamed.

But no noise came out.

Instead, she saw red. Everything went red. And hot. She was going to burst from the pain.

31

Awen watched in muted horror as she saw Magnus push Valerie away from the incoming rocket. While Magnus took the brunt of the hit—blown back in a violent explosion—Valerie was even less fortunate, her body riddled with blaster rounds. She went flailing to the ground just as flames engulfed everything.

Suddenly, a low vibration gut-punched Awen so hard she lost her breath. She felt herself go weightless, tossed away from the explosion upside down. Or was she right side up? Her vision blurred. Then her consciousness started to fade as something tugged at the sides of her grip on reality.

The only thing that kept Awen from slipping into the darkness was pain. Pain everywhere. Pain so bad she screamed. But not even screaming alleviated it. Instead, she hung there in suspended animation, screaming, feeling, fighting.

She'd lost her grip on Piper.

Awen tried to move, tried to feel beyond the terror that consumed her. But all of it was worthless. It was as though she was caught in a long fall through forever, twisting about in a constant state of agony.

Just when she was sure that her spirit had been violently stripped from the stalk of her body, Awen felt a pulse in her neck. The sensation went down into her chest as well as up into her ears. Her head throbbed, her limbs on fire. But she'd stopped moving. And she was pretty sure she was lying on her back.

No, definitely on her back.

Then she tried opening her eyes. The effort drew a knife-like sensation inside her skull. But she needed to see. Must see. Her second sight was white while her natural sight was black.

Something... something horrible had happened.

Eyes opened, Awen blinked them into submission. Shapes formed from the blurry blotches, and lines formed from the shapes, until she could make out the familiar glow of her helmet's HUD. Her eyes darted to her suit's status bar and noted that her personal shield was at 9%. Which seemed strange. The explosion could have done that—and more. But she was sure she'd been thrown far enough and high enough to rip her power suit clean off her body. Instead, it remained intact.

She sensed feeling in her arms and legs, and used them to

sit up. The headache was easily the worst she'd ever had, threatening to make her throw up. But she managed to keep the nausea under control and looked about her.

To her shock, Awen was not more than ten or eleven meters from where she'd stood when the rocket hit Magnus. *But that's impossible.* It felt as though the blast had carried her halfway back to the Grand Arielina.

Then a new thought struck her.

Piper.

Awen looked toward the shuttle, which seemed in near-perfect condition, and noticed a small figure standing with its back toward Awen. It took only a moment more for Awen to realize it was Piper. And the body she stood over…

Awen blinked.

It was Valerie's.

The blaster fire was gone. In fact, the entire docking bay was still, save for small movements touching Awen's peripheral vision. She looked around and saw that everyone—everyone who'd been standing in the docking bay just seconds ago—was on the ground. People were sitting up slowly, like she'd done.

Awen pulled her helmet off, wincing from the pain. "Piper?" she called, unable to recognize the sound of her own voice. "Piper, are you alright?"

But the little girl remained motionless.

Awen climbed to her feet but reached for the ground several times to keep from falling over. Other people around her were attempting to do the same but with worse results.

Her equilibrium was completely off center. "Piper," she said again, not knowing if she could manage more words before throwing up.

And she did throw up, falling to her knees and covering her own hands in vomit. Still, the little girl remained frozen with her back toward Awen.

"Doma, speak to me. I…" Awen wiped her mouth on her suit's sleeve. "I need to know that you're okay."

"I am not okay," Piper said in a small voice.

"What… what happened?" Awen was on her feet now, moving slowly toward Piper. The girl held her helmet in her hand, head locked on her mother's charred suit of armor. As Awen got closer, she could see Valerie's helmet was blown apart. Gore spilled from the opening. Inside was a broken face and one eye falling from its socket. The beautiful woman Awen had once known was reduced to a gruesome corpse ravaged by war.

Awen put a hand to her mouth and looked away. But she needed to get Piper away from this. She swallowed the taste of bile and said, "Piper, come. We need to leave."

"No." Piper dropped her helmet. "I'm not going."

"Piper please—" Awen placed her hand on Piper's shoulder but a charge of electricity zapped it away. Awen winced and looked at her blackened fingertips. "Piper, you need—"

"Stop talking to me," Piper said sternly.

"But I must talk to you. Your mother is—"

"Don't." The little girl started shaking her head. Awen

caught sight of the tears glistening the girl's cheeks. The voice that came out next was not of a little girl, but of a tormented soul. "Don't you talk about my momma. Don't you *dare*."

Awen went to reach for Piper again, but this time it wasn't the threat of being shocked that stayed her hand. It was the harshness of the girl's tone. Something was broken. And it scared Awen.

"Then I won't." Awen looked around the docking bay. Everyone in the Novia armor was coming to, each climbing to their feet in the same daze that Awen had fended off. But the Marines…

The Marines were stone cold still.

"Can I ask what you did here?"

"I made it stop," Piper replied without hesitation. "I made it all stop."

"So, you did this," Awen said, just trying to be certain of what she'd heard.

"I made everyone stop fighting."

Mystics, this is… Awen was having trouble collecting her thoughts. *This is too much. Too terrible.* Again, she surveyed the scene and didn't see a single Marine reaching for their blaster or even trying to sit up.

Then Awen realized she had to know… had to know if they were still alive. She swallowed more of the bile taste in the back of her throat, took a deep breath, and then slipped into the Unity.

THE FIRST THING Magnus heard through the ringing in his ears was Awen shrieking. He forced his eyes open and tried to sit up, but instantly regretted both as his muscles spasmed and his nerve endings jolted him. The pain took his breath away. Even the tears that squeezed from the corners of his eyes seemed to burn the sides of his face as they ran toward his ears. They pooled inside his earlobes and made Awen's weeping sound muddled.

But he had to get to her. Pain or not. He had to.

Magnus groaned as he willed his body to sit up. The agony was excruciating. No sooner had he sat upright than his stomach heaved. He turned aside and vomited, suddenly aware that his helmet's visor was gone. The contents of his stomach splattered on the ground as a new wave of pain forced his muscles into convulsions.

More pain—unlike any he'd ever felt—threatened to steal him from consciousness, but the ferrous odor of burning flesh helped keep him awake. He squinted again. Suddenly, the HUD of his bioteknia eyes—which had been mostly dormant given his helmet's dominant properties—came into focus. They identified several things for him, the first being Piper's diminutive form standing thirteen meters away. She was looking down at the ground, unmoving. But sensors said she was alive and stable.

The next thing Magnus noticed was Awen, who was on her knees, sobbing. She was looking between Piper and the rest of the docking bay which was…

Full of people struggling to get off the ground. His

people. The gladias of Granther Company and Willowood's Luma. But many more still lay on the ground. Marines. Too many Marines to count.

As he rolled to his knees, trying to push himself up, Magnus saw Valerie's body. He looked back at Piper and saw that her eyes were fixed on her mother's open helmet.

"Splick." Magnus lowered his head. How had everything gone so horribly wrong? They'd come so far and were about to exfil when... *when I pushed Valerie away from the incoming weapons fire.*

Magnus looked down at his hands and saw that his gauntlets had been blown off. His fingers were bleeding. Hell, it felt like all of him was bleeding—skin raw and blistered.

He gritted his teeth and willed himself to rise. He heard himself roar in defiance to the pain—to the anger of knowing that Valerie had been killed. That Piper was now an orphan.

When he was finally upright, he started to limp toward the little girl. Then his legs froze solid.

"Don't come any closer," Piper said, holding out a hand.

Magnus looked down at his feet and then back at Piper.

"Piper, no," Awen yelled. "He's not the—"

"No more talking, shydoh."

Awen's mouth snapped shut.

"I... I don't want to go with you anymore. I don't. So I won't." Piper's lower lip trembled. But she seemed to fight it by lifting her chin. "I want to be by myself."

Magnus made to object, but before he could inhale a deep

enough breath, Piper looked back at her mother's body, and said, "Goodbye, momma. I will miss you."

Then without another word, Piper blinked out of existence.

Magnus fell forward and landed on all fours. His hands and arms and knees screamed in pain. He yelled and resisted the urge to pass out.

"Piper, nooo," Awen screamed. "Come back!"

Magnus watched the Elonian fall on one hand while the other reached to where Piper had been seconds before. Empowered by Awen's deep sorrow, Magnus regained his footing and limped toward her. She hardly seemed to recognize him as he tried getting her attention. Her eyes seemed elsewhere—frantic, darting left and right.

"Awen, it's me, Magnus." He tried catching her gaze, but she was inconsolable.

"LT? Can you hear me?" Flow's voice crackled to life in what little remained of Magnus's helmet. "Come in, dammit."

"Flow!"

"LT? Oh, thank the mystics. You're alive, you son of a bitch. What in hell's name happened to you guys down there?" Magnus didn't even know how to respond to the question. He hesitated long enough that Flow had to repeat himself.

"You tell me," Magnus replied. "Something… something hit us hard."

"From up here, we just saw everyone get laid out. Seems

like your armor took the brunt of it. But all the Marines? Splick, LT. They…"

Magnus waited for Flow to finish his sentence, but he didn't. More like he couldn't. "What is it? They what, Flow?"

"They're dead, man. All of 'em. Everyone three blocks out too."

Magnus wasn't sure he heard right. He shook his head, looking at the lines of Repub-clad bodies that stretched out of the docking bay and into the street beyond. "What do you mean everyone three blocks out?"

Flow seemed to choke on his own saliva. He coughed, then tried to clear his throat. When he spoke again, his voice was tight. "The *Spire's* sensors are showing a total loss of life for three blocks in every direction, LT. Marines, civilians, Luma. *Everyone.*"

Magnus felt his head swim. He wobbled, looking for something to hold onto. He was about to fall over when Awen grabbed his arm.

"It was her," she whispered in a raspy voice. She still seemed disoriented but present enough to keep Magnus from falling.

"What was her?"

"This." Awen threw a hand out beside her and made to turn, but caught herself, seemingly unable to look around. "It was Piper."

Magnus couldn't rationalize what had happened—what *was* happening. "You're saying Piper killed everyone?"

Awen nodded, pulling herself close to Magnus, fighting to

fit inside of his embrace. "I don't think she meant to. But she... I saw so much fear in her. So much..."

Magnus listened to Awen's breath run out. Her body shook against his. "So much what?"

"Hate." Magnus was about to say something when Awen added. "Against *you*, Magnus."

At this, Magnus felt as though his chest caved in. What had he done that had produced such raw emotions? Then he thought of Valerie's body. The injuries she'd sustained were not consistent with a rocket explosion, but with blaster fire. Had she been shot? Had he pushed her aside from the rocket only for her to be shot by blaster fire?

"Now... she's gone," Awen said.

"We'll find her."

"No." Awen shook her head. "I don't think we will."

"We'll do whatever we—"

"Magnus, you've got multiple hostiles inbound," Flow said.

Magnus blinked. He was still having trouble orienting himself and his body was starting to shake from the pain. If his suit's med features were still online, perhaps this whole scenario would make more sense. "Please repeat."

"I said, you have multiple hostiles moving on your location. You gotta get out of there unless you're ready for round two, LT."

"That would be the remainder of the battalion," Caldwell said from the other side of the shuttle's ramp. He'd removed his helmet and was moving toward Magnus and Awen. "Time we get on these shuttles and get you seated, lieutenant. Unless your little lady knocked the flight systems out too."

"All systems are normal," TO-96 said, walking toward Caldwell and Magnus. "Whatever Miss Piper did, it only affected biological infrastructure."

Magnus licked his broken lips and then spit blood. Based on a visual inspection of the docking bay alone, Magnus knew Granther Company was out of the fight. While Piper's cataclysmic act had spared the gladias and Willowood's Luma, the fallout was still not something anyone looked like they'd get over in the next few minutes. This engagement was over.

"Everyone on board," he said, trying to fill his voice with as much strength as he could, but the effort was exhausting. "Find an open seat on any of the shuttles. Azelon, you copy?"

"I am here, sir."

"I'm not sure our pilots will be able to get us home. We're… we're all…"

"Not to worry, sir. I will be able to supplement piloting for all four ships if needed so long as my resources are not placed in too high a demand elsewhere. I do expect planetary defenses to be in effect, but barring any unforeseen use of force outside of this system's known armaments, I do not anticipate this to be a problem."

"Understood. Just get us home."

"I will, sir."

"You want me to blast the last of the battalion, LT?" Flow asked. "I've got coordinates dialed in."

"Negative. Not unless absolutely necessary. There's already been enough bloodshed for one day."

"Copy that."

Magnus turned his attention to Awen. She was still trembling, probably suffering from shock. "Come on, let's get you on board."

But Awen resisted Magnus. She was looking at Valerie's body. "We're just going to leave her?"

"No, but that's not your job. The others will take care of it."

Awen seemed to crumple under the words—so much so that Magnus thought he'd have to carry her up the ramp, though he doubted he had the strength.

Suddenly, Willowood appeared from one side and touched Awen. A surge of something seemed to bring Awen back to life. She stood up straight and look around. "Willowood?"

"Yes, child," the old woman replied. "I'm here. And so is Magnus. We need to get you onto this shuttle."

"Shuttle?" Awen looked up the ramp, and then noticed Magnus. Her wide eyes looked up and down his body. "Mystics, you're hurt!"

"And you can fuss over me all you want, but you've got to get on the damn ship first."

Awen seemed to accept this and nodded at him.

"Come, child," Willowood said, touching Awen on the elbow and guiding her forward. "There is much to do, and none of it here."

"Yes," Awen nodded. "Yes, we should leave."

Willowood winked at Magnus and nodded him toward the ramp. "Lead her by example."

Magnus felt compelled to follow the instructions and began ushering Awen up the ramp as if his feet were on autopilot. The pair of them walked into the shuttle and found seats along the starboard wall. Magnus buckled her in and then attended to his own harness. Willowood sat beside him.

"Your granddaughter," Magnus said, looking into Willowood's sorrow-filled eyes. "We can't just leave her here."

"We will find her. But not today."

"But…"

"Are your responsibilities complete, Magnus?" Willowood asked.

Magnus felt the question was odd, but it forced him to go through a mental checklist. He'd given the orders for the company to board the shuttles. He'd secured pilot redundancies if Nolan and the others were unable to fly the ships. And Flow was standing by with orbital support if it was needed. Already the ramp doors were closing shut. So long as the shuttles took off, then—"Yes, I believe they are."

"Good." Her hand rested lightly on his leg. A moment later, Magnus lost consciousness.

32

"Are they scrambling fighters?" Ricio asked Flow on the *Spire's* bridge. His heart sank. "If so… that looks like three entire squadrons."

"If all those little floaty dots crossing the ocean aren't flying people, then yeah, I'd say they're scrambling fighters."

"The enemy fighters are less than twenty-five minutes to intercept," Azelon announced.

"Why?" Cheeks asked. "You suddenly change your mind and want back in with your pal's team?"

"Oh, I want in, alright. But for the good guys this time." Ricio turned to Azelon. Apparently the ship's robotic counterpart had been revived in the time it took for Ricio and Cheeks to haul Nos Kil back to his cell and reactivate the containment field. "Bot, please tell me you've got something I can use to help the shuttles get home."

"Hold up, hold up," Cheeks said, waving a hand in front of his face like something stank. "You mean to tell me that you're not only willing to turn on the Repub, but now you're willing to kill 'em all too?"

"Is that so far-fetched?" Ricio said. "What were you before, Marine? A private?"

"Very cute."

"He's got a point though, Cheeks," Flow said, nodding in Ricio's direction. "I mean, we just toasted a whole bunch of our boys down there. Magnus did too. It's kinda what we do now."

"Yeah, but that's us," Cheeks protested. "You know, the rebels. This guy is just…"

"I'm just Mauricio Longo, and I'm gonna help whether you like it or not, private."

"I was a corporal, for the record." Cheeks put his hands on his hips. "And a damn good one."

"I don't doubt it. All I'm saying is that if this whole thing is as bad as Magnus says it is, then I know where my allegiances lie, and I want to do my part in helping those shuttles to safety. Any more questions?"

Azelon stepped forward. "Commander, in using the phrase *something I can use to help the shuttles*, do you mean a highly maneuverable combat-ready gunship?"

"Sounds about right. You got anything like that?"

"Affirmative. Please follow me."

"You sure that's a good idea, Azie?" Cheeks asked as the two headed toward the exit.

"Cheeks, let it go, man," Flow said.

The bot paused and turned around to face the former Marines. "If it turns out to be a poor idea, I will detonate whatever vessel I place Commander Mauricio within. Is this acceptable?"

Cheeks cast Ricio a crooked grin. "Whad'ya say, flyboy? Work for you?"

Ricio puffed out his chest. "I can assure you that—"

Suddenly, Azelon cupped her hands together, made the sound of an explosion with her mouth, and pulled her hands apart—fingers fluttering.

Ricio ignored the disturbing gesture and tried to restate his position. "I can assure you it's not going to come to that."

"But if it does…" Cheeks pointed at Azelon. Right on cue, she cupped her hands again, made the explosion sound, and fluttered her fingers.

"Mystics, I got it," Ricio exclaimed. "Enough with the threats already."

"So my pantomime worked?" Azelon asked, studying Ricio's face.

"Splick, yes. It worked. Now can we just get to the damn starfighter?"

"Of course, commander."

Ricio followed Azelon through the bowels of the ship until they reached a hangar bay that contained a crescent-shaped red ship. It seemed to be a highly modified light freighter and it sat on a six-pointed landing gear with its loading ramp extended.

Ricio whistled and put his hands on his hips. "Well, would you look at that."

"Look at what, commander?" Azelon asked.

"Seems you've done plenty of work on her too." Ricio walked beneath the hull, eyes racing along the ship's belly. "NR220 blaster cannons, K91 torpedo bays... not exactly a stock setup on a Katana-class. Very nice. And with the additional ion-propulsion ports, I bet she really screams. What's her name?"

"Commander, the *Geronimo Nine* is not the ship I have designated for you."

"It's not?" Ricio stopped. "Listen, I can assure you, I'll be able to unload a world of hurt with this old girl."

"I don't doubt that, sir. However, I can assure *you* that you'll be able to unload additional worlds of hurt, as you say, with what I have down here. Please, this way."

Azelon led Ricio through a bulkhead door and into a much larger hangar filled with square bays. Each space was marked in Novia Minoosh lettering that Ricio couldn't read. But if the nomenclature was anything like galactic common, he figured the scripts were numerals. She gestured him toward the first bay and extended her hand. As he stepped around the corner, Ricio stared at a black vessel suspended from a yellow gantry arm. The crane crossed the room and led toward an environmental force field—the other side of which was raw void. "What in the hell is that?"

"That is the negative vacuum of space, commander."

"No, I mean *that*." Ricio pointed up at the craft hanging from the hoist.

"That is the DS4-R9-21-21-B—"

"Mystics, you lost me."

Azelon cocked her head sideways. "And yet I find you presently before me. Please help me understand your state of mind."

"No, I mean that name, Azie. You're killing me."

"I am doing no such thing, commander. Given your newfound affiliation with the Gladio Umbra, my protocols do not allow me to harm you. Additionally, your vital signs do not indicate—"

"Sweet mother of Vega's pustulant offspring, I don't mean that literally. What is wrong with you?"

"Why, sir, I do not believe I am experiencing any new system anomalies. Do you suspect I have been compromised?"

"That"—Rico pointed aloft—"is that my new fighter?"

"Yes. As I was saying, that is the DS4—"

"No, no. It's gotta have a better name than all that worthless splick. Let's call it… a Fang."

"A Fang, sir?"

"It looks like a long sharp fang, doesn't it?" The craft was shaped like an incisor, rectangular in the stern, and tapered to a blunted tip in the bow. The sides extended out to slender wing-like surfaces, giving the entire craft a concave shape, while two sets of twin vertical stabilizers protruded from the top and bottom of the fuselage. From below, Rico could barely make out the semblance of a cockpit's front-facing window.

"Damn, this thing looks badass," Ricio said, letting out a low whistle.

"Badass, sir?"

"Yes, Azie. Badass."

"Commander, I can assure you that your *Fang*, as it were, is neither poor in condition, nor does it possess a biological posterior."

"Mystics, Azie. I mean it looks great."

"Ah. I am unfamiliar with your colloquialism. Shall I add it to my lexicon?"

"It wouldn't hurt."

"Very good. Regarding your ship, I have already made all the necessary changes to the flight system to make them legible for you as well as to conform to your species' physiology."

"Azie, you shouldn't have." Rico tried looking for a port or ramp or some other means of getting onboard. "So?"

"So?"

"So, how do I get in?"

"So, there is a biometric scanner that must pair with your synaptic signature, located on the hull's belly directly underneath the cockpit."

Ricio walked toward a small module that was the closest thing he could interpret as a scanner. It looked like a red eye, tucked within two black folds of metal that acted like lids.

"So, am I just supposed to stand under it?"

"So, yes. Additionally, is there a particular reason we are starting every sentence with the sub modifier *so*?"

"No, Azie."

"I didn't think so."

"And how the hell do I get in?"

"Stand under the iris and remain motionless until you hear the chime."

Ricio walked beneath the red lens. "How long does this—"

A soft trill rang out overhead.

"Congratulations, your body's unique identifiers have been paired with this Fang."

"Congratulations?"

"Isn't that how the term congratulations is used where your kind comes from?"

"Azie, my new friends are about to get attacked down there. Can we please save the vocab lessons for later?"

"I did not realize that you felt our conversation was sidetracking you."

"Son of a bitch."

"Irrelevant. I see no correlation between my statement and the offspring of female breeding canines."

"How do I open the damn ship?"

"Opening damn ship," Azie said. An access hatch slid aside in the ship's belly and a platform descended. The majority of the lift was composed of a reclined chair that boasted a harness and what looked to be several translucent control surfaces.

"Now we're talking!" Ricio rubbed his hands together.

"Even despite your objections to our previous discourse?"

"Yes, Azie. Now, what about a flight helmet?"

"Unfortunately, sir, I have not had time to fashion one for you, and everything in the armory is tailored for the Novia Minoosh. However, all necessary ship functions that concern you can be carried out without the presence of a helmet."

"That's... good to hear. But I was more worried about keeping myself from suffering a concussion. I'm not sure how Novia physiology works, but hitting one's head against a dashboard isn't the best practice."

"You have no need to worry about that, commander."

"What, no dashboard?"

"No. My calculations predict that should your gunship suffer enough damage to cause a concussion, your body will be incinerated long before you experience the negative effects."

Ricio started to nod slowly and then made the movement larger as understanding broke on him. "Yeah. We can skip the helmet for now. No worries."

"Very good, sir. Any further objections?"

"Not yet." Ricio approached the seat and pulled the harness straps apart. Then he turned and slid back into the chair. No sooner had he secured the harness around his chest than the entire seat began to move.

"Holy splick! What's happening?"

"The cockpit's seat is conforming to your body's shape and mass." The mechanical machinations continued until the chair hugged the contours of Ricio's body better than any piece of furniture he'd ever sat in.

"This thing's more comfortable than my own damn bed!"

"I am pleased to hear that, sir. Please activate the closure button located on your right instrument panel in order to secure the cockpit."

Ricio pressed the indicated button on the translucent pane near his right hand. The platform ascended, then receded into the fuselage. As Ricio rose into the ship, the dark cockpit began to light up with holo displays, clear instrument panels, and a slender wide-view window that looked down the Fang's nose.

"Azie, just one problem. Where are the flight controls?"

Azelon paused. "Flight controls, sir?"

"Uh, yeah." Ricio gave her an irritated chuckle. "How the hell do I fly this thing?"

"I already informed you that your synaptic signature has been paired with this vessel. Were you not listening?"

"Don't you get testy with me, babe. I was just asking a genuine question."

Azelon paused again, then said, "Ah. I now see that, based upon a more thorough review of scans of your previous ship, you are used to manual flight controls. The Repub manufacturer only employed rudimentary neurological interfacing."

"Rudimentary?" Ricio was pretty sure that the Talons had the most advanced neuro-connection in the quadrant.

"Indeed, commander. Unlike your vessels, the Fang is neurologically controlled utilizing the Novia biotech interface, or NBTI. It will take several more days to fully integrate you into the Novia Defense Architecture."

"Days? Azie, I don't have days."

"I understand. You will be able to control this vessel with my help within a few minutes, though I will need to integrate you into our system over the next several days before you will assume full functionality."

"You're assuming I survive this."

"TO-96 has told me that your species enjoys optimism whenever possible."

"Perfect," Ricio said with a dry tone.

"I'm pleased you think so."

"So you're saying I fly this thing with my thoughts?"

"So, yes."

"You still don't need to respond with the word so."

"Understood. For the record, I do dislike it."

Ricio shook his head. "Just tell me how to do this."

For the next minute, Azelon gave Ricio a short tutorial on the Fang's basic handling and weapons systems using nothing more than his thoughts as inputs. She made it sound easy enough, but Ricio had a feeling it might be easier said than done. He'd have to rely on his innate skills as an ace pilot more than ever and hope the skillset transferred. Then again, if it didn't, he wouldn't be around to lament his failure.

"Are you ready to launch, sir? The enemy fighters are less than fifteen minutes from intercept."

"Let's get the party started."

"Starting up the party, sir."

Azelon initiated the engines and unlocked the docking clamp on the gantry. As soon as the Fang was dislodged, Ricio tried to imagine it hovering. Instead, however, the ship leaped up and smacked into the crane. He swore, lost focus, and felt the vessel drop out from underneath him. The whole exercise felt like riding a hoverbike for the first time as a kid.

"I have resumed control," Azelon said as the Fang narrowly missed the deck, then rose to a steady hover.

"So I launch just by thinking about moving forward?"

"That is correct, commander. Envision the ship moving where you want it, and the flight system will do the rest—with my assistance, of course."

Ricio took a deep breath and then imagined the Fang sliding forward and through the environmental field. As soon as the very first thought sparked in his brain, he felt the ship lurch forward. The sensation was so otherworldly that he felt a surge of adrenaline quicken his heart rate. Then the Fang pressed him back in his seat then shot out of the hangar and into the void.

"Splick, Azelon! This is mad."

"Again, I cannot determine your exact meaning based on your word choice, but I do believe you are responding favorably to this new experience."

"Damn straight I am!"

Ricio decided to attempt his first right turn. Even as the thought entered his mind, he felt his head naturally move to the right. At the same exact instant, the ship veered to starboard. To straighten out, Ricio thought of rolling to the left, and the Fang responded. The sensation was strange, to say the least. Never had any motion been so effortless, save that of moving the limbs and digits of his own body. Thus, the Fang felt less like a vessel he had climbed into and more like a ship he put on. It was, quite literally, an extension of himself.

Feeling more confident, Ricio attempted a barrel roll to starboard, then to port, and then to starboard again. The Fang moved flawlessly, taking his every thought and translating it into motion. He attempted a power loop, a Paraguutian Cobra maneuver, and then two Alcions in a row. With every action, he felt himself growing more accustomed to his interconnectivity with the flight system.

"I feel like I'm beginning to get the hang of this," Ricio said.

"You are doing moderately well, yes."

"Moderately?" Ricio felt put off. "Are you even seeing this right now?"

"I am fully aware of your flight maneuvers, commander. However, I am currently compensating for a mean discrepancy range of 43.25%."

"A mean discrepancy range?"

"The range is comprised of both oversteering and mental distraction."

"So you're saying I'm actually controlling only 60% of the ship's flight at the moment?"

"Approximately, yes. This will increase as your brain becomes accustomed to the operation. Additionally, you will experience a higher resolution of flight dexterity once you are fully integrated into the defense architecture via the biotech interface."

"Sounds good. What about weapons?"

"The Fang boasts four primary armament systems, which include primary and secondary blasters, missiles, and mines."

"Now we're talking."

"In addition to general shielding, the Fang also makes use of adaptive and projective shield technology."

"And since I have no idea what that means, can you handle the finer points?"

"Certainly, commander."

"How do I access the weapons?"

"Just the same as your flight controls. However, since I imagine it will be difficult for you to envision items that you have never seen before, I have taken the liberty of populating the display to your left with the ship's weapons systems. There is no need to touch the item. Instead, select it with your mind and the correlating weapon will be activated on the gunship. Discharging each weapon is likewise a product of mental initiation, for which I will compensate for timing, rate of fire, targeting, tracking, and follow through.

"Please be advised, commander, that we do not have sufficient time for a complete demonstration now as you must depart immediately if you wish to assist the shuttles."

"On it." But Ricio wasn't on it. He had no idea where to plug in coordinates, or even see a map. "Except I have no idea how to navigate this thing."

Suddenly, a cockpit wide holo display appeared in front of him. Aside from several peripheral windows outlining the ship's status, the centerpiece of the display was a topographical map of Worru's northern hemisphere.

As the view zoomed in on the main continent, narrowing on the city of Plumeria, Azelon said, "Your navigation display can be toggled to show any number of views, ranging from localized planetary maps—such as this—to multidimensional star charts. Conversely, your nav view may be minimized in place of the combat spatial display, or CSD as it is labeled in the upper right-hand corner of your holo."

"I could get used to this."

"I would hope so, sir."

"And if I want to head toward a particular destination, do I just focus on it?"

"That is correct, commander, assuming that focusing also implies a force of will to head in that direction. The more specific your thoughts, the more accurate your trajectory. In addition to the icons for your friendly shuttles, I am populating the map with targets most suited for your gunship. They include the three squadrons of FAF-28 Talons, anti-orbital defense cannons, and anti-air batteries. I have also added the sensor arrays, communication nodes, and shield generators if you feel like a cocky bastard."

Ricio raised an eyebrow. "Is that what you think I am?"

"I am merely referring to the Galactic Republic Navy personnel file I downloaded from the ships we encountered when you entered metaspace. The data has proven helpful in customizing your Fang to your personal flying style."

"Glad it helped. Though, for the record, I'm only a cocky bastard half the time."

"And yet the file says all of the time. Shall we review this discrepancy later, commander?"

"Later is fine." Ricio clapped his hands together and then rubbed them. Then he cracked his knuckles, loosened his neck, and instinctively reached for the ship's controls… which were not there.

"Sir, I feel the need to remind you that there are no physical flight controls in your Fang."

"Got it. That's gonna take some getting used to."

"Understood, sir."

"Think you can keep taking me through the ship's systems as we head to the planet's surface?"

"I would be delighted to, commander."

"Great. Let's do this." Ricio focused on the squadrons of Talons headed on an intercept course for Magnus and the shuttles. The moment his sense of will desired to head in that direction, the Fang shot forward, pinning Ricio in his seat.

33

Ricio tracked west over the planet's surface toward Plumeria, his Fang skimming less than fifty meters above the ocean. The rolling waves blended into a carpet of aquamarine blue that stretched to the coast, but the air pressure in his gunship's wake caused the water below to spray up in a long tail.

His cockpit-wide HUD displayed blue ident reticles around the four friendly shuttles headed toward him while red target reticles designated the enemy fighters and yellow reticles identified ground targets. Seeing as how the shuttles' eastbound path would take them within range of anti-ship cannon emplacements, Ricio decided it would be prudent to take out what he could before passing the shuttles, crossing Plumeria, and engaging the Talons.

The ocean gave way to wide dunes and then lush tropical

jungles. Ricio moved the Fang over the undulating topography, rising with small hills and weaving between mountain gaps. The Fang climbed as the continent's elevation increased, closing the distance to the shuttles—now less than sixty seconds away at his present speed. But the first anti-ship emplacement was fifteen seconds out.

Ricio focused on the icon and then watched the distance to target drop like his credit account on a roulette table. He glanced over at the mines icon on the small readout, and selected them with his mind. Or at least he hoped he did.

"Commander, you are attempting to select anti-ship mines for a static planet-based target."

"Do the mines go boom?" Ricio could see the top of the weapon emplacement protruding from a grove of palm trees. Its metallic dome was adorned with quad cannons, multiple sensor arrays, and a communications tower.

"If you are inferring a detonation, yes—of course."

"Then today, the mines are bombs."

"Unconventional, yet intuitive. I should warn you, however, that—"

"Mines two and three, away!" The words had hardly left Ricio's mouth when he felt the Fang rise. The gunship closed the remaining distance in less than a second and streaked passed. At first, Ricio thought the blurring foliage behind him was a visual anomaly due to his excessive speed. But as an orange flare washed over the jungle and overtook his ship, he realized it was an explosion. A damn big one.

Ricio's Fang shuddered as the shield energy was

reallocated to the aft, indicated by new lighting on the graphic representation of his ship. He also felt his body pressed further into his seat—the Fang was accelerating.

"Target eliminated," Azie said. "Shields holding. However, you are accelerating at a rate detrimental to your physiology, commander. Would you like to slow down?"

"Yes!" Ricio cried, fighting the black out that tugged on the edges of his vision. Instantly, the Fang decelerated, throwing him into his harness. Blood rushed to his head and he bit his lip. *Rookie mistake, Ricio.*

"Why didn't you warn me about those things' payload, Azie?"

"But commander, I attempted to warn you."

"Next time, attempt harder."

"Noted, sir. Those mines are meant as passive ranged attacks to be used against Battleship-class warships."

"Mystics, Azie! Don't you think that's something you should have told me sooner?"

"I did not anticipate you would use something clearly labeled as mines on an in-atmosphere target, sir."

"Yeah, well... neither did I."

"Might I suggest missiles or blaster on this next target?"

"Blasters. I want the missiles for the Talons."

"Wise strategy, commander."

Ricio focused on the icon for the next closest anti-ship emplacement and watched its range indicator start spiraling down. Then he selected primary blasters from his arsenal menu and gave his full attention to targeting.

The tower was perched on a rock precipice surrounded by standard Repub plate shielding. Ricio watched as the sunlight glinted off the quad barrels. The operators were certainly tracking something, presumably to combat whatever had taken out the emplacement to the east. "Too bad I'm too fast," Ricio said. He lined the crosshairs on the bulk of the turret just above the top edges of the plate armor and saw the reticle blink. "And they never even saw you coming."

Ricio willed the Fang to fire. The gunship vibrated as two massive spouts of blaster energy kicked from the nose, tore across the sky, and penetrated the target's shell. Two more rounds of blaster bolts followed the first, filling the tower with heat and light such that the emplacement exploded in a spray of sparks and superheated metal. Ricio pulled up, ripping through the debris field as it bounced off his shields. Feeling energized, he rolled the Fang to the left twice before leveling out.

"Cocky bastard," Azelon said.

"Hey, that was a good shot, you have to admit."

"Yet I'm still doing 43% of the work."

Ricio flattened his lips. "Whatever, bot."

"Twenty seconds to contact with shuttles," Azelon added. "I have notified the pilots of your approach and ordered the four ships to diverge into two groups."

"Acknowledged."

"Be advised that your present vector will place you directly over Plumeria when contacting the enemy fighters."

"Civilian casualties expected?"

"Not likely if their city-wide shield generators are employed, which it looks like they are preparing to engage."

"Well then, let's say we give 'em a show, Azie."

"A show, commander?"

"So they won't forget who they're dealing with in the future."

"Ah, *a show*, as in an overwhelming display of force."

"That's the one."

"Very good. Because the alternatives—one denoting a live theatrical performance, the other a pre-produced episode of holo entertainment—did not seem fitting."

"Shuttles, inbound," Ricio exclaimed, watching the four craft come up fast. He knew he'd never flown a Talon this fast in-atmo before. Yet the Fang's handling made it seem far more manageable than it ever would have been in the Repub fighter. *No doubt thanks to Azie*, he surmised. But then again, he didn't doubt that this ship was more technologically advanced even without her aid.

A breath later and Ricio's Fang split the group, racing past them with enough force that he was sure their craft were buffeted by a maelstrom of wind. "Nothing like letting 'em know they're not alone, eh old girl?"

"Old girl?" Azelon seemed to hesitate. "Are you referencing me, commander? The term seems both contradictory and misapplied."

"It's a term of endearment, trust me."

"Old girl." It seemed as if she was trying it on. "If you say so, sir."

"I do. Now, how many of these Talons did you say you can take on?"

"I didn't specify before, but I will attempt to commandeer as many as I'm able to deliver into your kill zone."

"I like the sound of that. Still, can you give me an estimate?"

"I anticipate being able to handle almost 70% of their units."

Ricio swallowed and then did some quick math in his head. With three standard squadrons comprised of fourteen Talons each, 70% was just about thirty fighters. "Which leaves me twelve or thirteen." And that thought didn't sit well with him.

For the first time since leaving the *Spire*, Ricio suddenly wondered if this was a smart plan. Given how easily Azelon had bested his squadron when he first emerged from the quantum tunnel, Ricio hoped she'd be able to take them all on, letting him pick up the pieces. But twelve Talons to one Fang? Those odds were…

"Not great."

"What's not great, commander?" Azelon asked.

"I'm flying twelve to one."

"Plus city-wide defenses."

He cursed. "Plus those." Maybe he should draw the dogfighting away from the city after all.

"Given your elevated heart rate in the moments surrounding this line of discussion, I conclude that you are suddenly worried about this confrontation."

"You could say that. I was just hoping you'd… you know—maybe have more of those Talons under your control."

"Without TO-96's additional resources, I'm afraid that is not possible. However, might I remind you that you are flying a Novia *Fang*."

"I recognize that."

"Then you are aware that, statistically speaking, you are four times the ship than those flown by the enemy, aren't you?"

"Four times the ship?"

"With regard to acceleration, speed, maneuverability, shields, armament, tactical sensors, navigation—"

"So you're saying this thing really is a badass."

"One might go so far as to say you're a cocky bastard flying a badass gunship."

"That would make a nice tattoo, Azie. You want to go in with me?"

"In, sir?"

"Never mind. Just assign me which fighters are mine."

"As you wish, commander." Suddenly, the red reticles were cut by two thirds, leaving just twelve ships.

"I took the extra one, sir."

"Thanks, old girl."

"My pleasure. Incoming transmission, commander."

"Incoming—from who?"

"From one of the outbound shuttles, sir."

Ricio cursed under his breath. The thought of trying to explain this whole situation to Magnus didn't sit well with him. There was too much to say and not enough time to say it in. Even a cursory summary would sound crazy—*hell, it is crazy*.

"Sir, if you would like to answer the transmission, simply will to accept it."

Ricio's chest tensed as he did everything he could *not* to will the communication to open. "I'm good right now, Azie. Thanks."

"As opposed to being bad? Do you fluctuate dispositions so rapidly?"

"I mean, I don't want to take the call. It will just distract me right now, and we have more important things to worry about."

"Understood, commander. I am blocking the transmission request."

"Thanks." Ricio swallowed and stretched his neck. "Crisis averted."

THE FANG ACCELERATED WELL past the attack speed of any Talon he'd ever flown. It tore through the sky so fast that Ricio was sure the wings would rip off. A small status bar on the HUD noted the percentage of Vibration Dampening that was being exerted. Ricio wondered if this helped lessen the strain on the airframe. But the thought was short lived.

"Enemy contact in five seconds," Azelon said.

Faced with more ships than he could take at once, Ricio

decided to try and focus on three. To his surprise, all three targeting reticles illuminated. For the first two, he selected missiles, hoping that his command would somehow stick despite needing to refocus on the third ship and lock blasters on it.

When he was satisfied that all three targets had been assigned, he gave the command to fire—or at least he thought it did. "Birdies two and five, away." The seconds slowed as he watched all three squadrons of Talons suddenly appear in his window. But still no weapons fired. The Talons grew from small specs to full-sized fighters in the time it took for him to yell, "Fire, dammit."

His Fang bucked as blaster fire leaped from the nose at the same time that two missiles erupted from the fuselage in a cloud of fire and smoke. He blinked. When his eyes opened, the Talons had been struck, violently exploding into three fireballs. And then it was all past him.

Ricio shot out the other side of the formation, maintaining speed and altitude, when he noticed that he was well over Plumeria. Blaster fire from the city-wide defense network launched into the sky in a weak attempt to track him. But the Fang was moving so fast that the cannons appeared to be shooting at random targets far overhead.

"Get your splick together, Ricio," he told himself. He couldn't afford to have another delayed weapons activation like that. *Nanoseconds*, he reminded himself. Nanoseconds were the difference between sprinkling the city with the ashes of your enemies or you.

"Three targets eliminated," Azelon said. "Ten enemy fighters breaking formation."

"Ten?"

"Reassigning ship allocation and prioritization."

Ricio watched as the current target reticles disappeared only to reappear over new ships, all of which were banking away from the shuttles' vectors. He decided to execute an Alcion maneuver to match but worried the speed might be too great.

Pulling back on an imaginary flight yoke, Ricio sent the Fang into a steep climb. The blood in his body rushed to his feet. Instantly, he felt the chair begin to squeeze his legs. He couldn't tell if he was just losing feeling down there or if the seat was actually trying to combat the pooling of blood in his lower extremities by clamping down on the tissue. As the Fang came up and over the apex of his climb, Ricio introduced a half roll, which presented him with a panoramic view of all the Talons headed back toward Plumeria.

The city defensive blasters were getting closer to his location, but they were nothing to worry about yet. "Can they see me?"

"Optically, no. The Fang is coated with a light-altering material that—"

"How about IR? Or something else?"

"Your ship is giving off a great deal of heat, yes. However, the signature is still so far behind you that the enemy will need to lead you well in advance of your projected vector, making all but the luckiest shot lethal, so long as you are not predictable."

"Be unpredictable. Check."

By comparison, the Talons were far slower in coming about. Ricio decided to try three more targets again, focusing on the righthand group of five Talons that were circling around. The reticles locked. Ricio thought of his primary and secondary blasters, and then willed them to fire. This time they responded almost instantaneously.

The Fang spat two distinct types of blaster bolts toward the enemy. One, like before, was fat and menacing. It made the nose of the Fang tremble as it projected away from the craft. The second emanated from the ends of the wings and came in a staccato whine that reminded Ricio of a blaster rifle on full-auto. Only this blaster rifle was putting out more energy than ten hand-held weapons.

With both weapons combined, the torrent of blaster fire tracked the enemy and met a single fighter with devastating results. The ship was torn into several pieces, and then even those pieces were riddled with blaster fire. The chunks exploded and formed a fine cloud of shrapnel that glowed white hot against the afternoon sun.

"Fighter eliminated."

"Just one?" Ricio swore and pounded a fist on the dashboard. "What about the other two?"

"My resources are currently insufficient to guide your fire, commander."

"Guide my— You're saying you've been helping me?"

"Correct. I am presently engaged with dispatching several Talons in the main contingent."

"Which means what, exactly?"

Azelon paused, then said, "Shoot better."

Ricio swung around behind the group of four fighters as they leveled out. "'Shoot better,' she says. You're completely outnumbered and the bot says, 'Shoot better.' Mystics, thanks for the helpful tip, old girl."

"It's my pleasure, commander."

Ricio gritted his teeth, focused on only one Talon this time, and willed the hand in his mind to squeeze the trigger on the flight yoke. Again, both primary and secondary blasters barked, spewing forth a cascade of alternating energy rounds. The stream caught the target in the engines. The aft exploded and sent the rest of the fuselage tumbling forward into a somersault.

"Yes, like that," Azelon said with an encouraging tone to her voice.

Ricio sneered but held his tongue. He had a job to do.

34

So-Elku cursed the bonds that held him captive. No matter how hard he tried to thwart them, the blasted bars would not budge. Worse still, he found that his ability to summon anything within the Nexus—or even within the Unity—was futile. Whatever power the child had used against him, it was startlingly comprehensive. And So-Elku had to have it.

He paced in his small cell, his feet matting the forest floor within the magenta-colored light's glow. He'd expected Awen to show up, he just never imagined she'd bring the child with her—*a turn of good fortune*, he'd mused to himself. *If only the girl had been less powerful*. And that both frustrated and inspired him.

The frustration was obvious, of course. So-Elku had no idea how long his imprisonment would last. Perhaps a long forever, stretched out over eons, in which his physical body decayed to dust while his soul lived on through eternity.

The inspiration, however, was implicit.

So-Elku marveled at Piper's power. The suspicions that Willowood's granddaughter was a true blood were understated—to say the least. She was, by all accounts, the truest blood anyone had encountered, perhaps in the Luma's entire lineage. How so much potential had been allocated to a single being baffled So-Elku… and made him sick with envy.

Piper's abilities defied imagination, and the Luma Master had witnessed it with his own eyes. Mystics, he'd been the focus of it! The fact that he'd even survived an encounter with the prodigy surprised him. Though, he guessed that had to do with Awen's influence more than anything else.

The Luma's archaic teachings of peaceful resistance and empathetic diplomacy had taken root in Awen long before she'd arrived on Worru. The Elonian's were strange that way, exhibiting much of the same values that defined the Luma—the main difference being that where the Luma sought to extend peace to others, the Elonians remained closed off, keeping their peaceful ways to themselves.

So-Elku wondered how much Awen had trained Piper, coaxing her into a place of submission that blinded the child to her true potential. But when battling them, So-Elku also noticed how the suits directed the flow of energy within the Unity. For Awen, her powers seemed amplified, giving her greater influence, specifically within the Nexus. But for Piper, the suit seemed to act as a regulator, tempering the child's abilities into manageable actions. And that piqued So-Elku's curiosity. For if what he'd seen had been merely a shadow of what was to come, he desired to see Piper unleashed upon the galaxy in the fullness of her gift. The thought sent shivers down his spine and along his arms and legs. *She would be*, he guessed, *unstoppable*.

That was when So-Elku swore an oath to himself—a promise that he would help unleash the child. That he would remove the restrictions of mind, body, and spirit. That he would set the girl's soul free and watch her tear through the cosmos uninhibited. Such would be the greatest of all his accomplishments, for the child's efforts would serve his pursuits.

"Which means she must be guided," So-Elku said from within his cage. "I will find her, and then I will mold her." A smile crept across his crooked lips.

Suddenly, a shockwave struck So-Elku in the chest and threw him back. Gone were the electrified Nexus bars as his body went tearing through the Foundation's forest like a doll's. The tall pines bent against the blast of energy, their limbs cracking in the tumult. So-Elku blasted back through one trunk after another, timber shredding into splinters. The energy propelled him like a missile, hurtling him deeper and deeper into the woods, until finally his back was buried in a hillside.

So-Elku lay there for a long while as the forest rebounded from the tidal wave of force. Trees groaned as they straightened, their aged shudders sending a chill through the air.

Then an eerie silence befell the entire Foundation. Gone were the bird songs and the buzzing of insects. Silent were the burrowing ground animals and calls of the roaming beasts. Instead, there was utter stillness.

When he finally managed to push himself out of the depression his body had made in the soft ground, So-Elku found that he was whole despite the aching head and limbs that vied for his attention. He stood slowly, fending off a wave of nausea by using his powers to shrug off the various pains that assailed him. He used those same powers to bring his attention to a single point and then hasten his return back to his physical body.

Back in his study, So-Elku strode across the room to the balcony and looked west toward the city's center. Pockets of fire formed a glowing line through the streets leading to the docking bays. He cursed and knew that the enemy had escaped him—had escaped his living dead, his elders, and his battalion of Marines. As soon as his thoughts turned to how, the revelation hit him.

Piper.

The blast of energy... it had been her. She'd done something in the Unity to keep them at bay. *And it was magnificent*, he thought in appreciation. He was about to re-enter the Unity when he spotted the four Novian shuttles rise into the night sky. Their thrust vectors changed, and suddenly the transports headed toward the Grand Arielina. So-Elku raised a shield around himself, fearing the worst. The ships shook the air, rocketing toward him. He prepared for the ground to explode out from underneath him. But the violence never came.

Instead, the four shuttles roared by, passing overhead only a few meters from the great spire's peak. Their engines shook the building, fleeing to the east in a rush to escape the city.

So-Elku searched his feelings. He sensed that the Marine colonel had abandoned the planet, and that more than half of the Marines stationed with him had been slain. So-Elku tried to remember the name of the remaining company commanders who had been stationed on the far side of the city, the ones who'd most likely survived whatever Piper had done.

"Captain Forbes," So-Elku projected to TACNET. "Do you read me?"

"I do," replied the captain, sounding out of breath. "Who is this? Your ident sig is not registering on—"

"This is Master So-Elku. Colonel Caldwell has been killed, as well as most of your men stationed at the Grand Arielina's garrison." Surely the trooper could see in his helmet what So-Elku was reporting.

"Yes, Master Luma. I can confirm that Caldwell is missing, and two companies have taken heavy casualties… too many for the system to tabulate still. We're en route to the hangars. Almost there."

"I'm sorry for your losses, captain. You've no doubt seen the departing shuttles?"

"We have. We'll detain any additional vessels from taking off. We're turning into the hangars now." It took several seconds for the captain to speak again. When he did, his voice was tight. "Mystics... they're... they're *dead*."

"Forbes?"

"Their bodies are... they're *everywhere*."

"Are you able to track the shuttles?"

"Affirmative," Forbes replied, but his voice sounded distant. "We're... we're tracking four ships with registered idents."

"Those are stolen idents, captain. I want them stopped at all costs."

"I'm sorry, Master Luma, but my orders—"

"Your colonel is missing or dead, you've lost half the troopers in your battalion, and the people responsible for it are in those shuttles." So-Elku felt exasperated but he couldn't help himself. He tried to calm his nerves. "I'm not telling you how to do your job, captain, but it seems to me that you'll want to scramble whatever Talons you have and take out those shuttles."

"Again, sir, I recognize your authority on behalf of the Luma. That said, your wishes are secondary to the Marine Corps' standard operating procedures."

So-Elku ground his teeth. This wasn't getting him anywhere, and the enemy was getting away. The master slipped into the Nexus, channeled his energy toward the captain, and willed the man to hear him—to *know* his desire. "You'll scramble the Talons immediately, captain."

Forbes hesitated. For the briefest of moments, So-Elku

wondered if the trick would work. Then the captain struggled with the words: "I'll—scramble…"

"Yes, captain?"

"I'll scramble Talons immediately."

"Very good," So-Elku said, slipping out of the Nexus and placing his fingertips together. "Thank you, Forbes."

"We are here to serve, sir. Forbes out."

SO-ELKU WATCHED the star fighters like a tired hiker watching the flames of a campfire after a long day's walk. Blaster fire and missiles streaked across the night sky like shooting stars, lighting up So-Elku's face and mellowing his mood. *Everything is as it should be*, he thought, marveling at how things were coming undone for the Republic, for Moldark, and for those who rebelled against the will of the Luma.

He could sense Willowood on one of the shuttles. She was with Awen. And the two of them had taken many of the Luma who'd been loyal to the old hag—several elders included. So-Elku cursed this development but quickly rested in the fact that the shuttles were severely outnumbered, as was the single alien fighter that attempted to take on an entire squadron by itself. *Noble*, So-Elku noted, *but futile*.

With any luck, the prisoners he'd released onboard the orbiting starship would disable the vessel shortly, and the rebels' hasty escape would be thwarted. All that was left was to find where the child had gone, for hers was the only life force he was unable to locate.

So-Elku retreated into his study and looked for the codex on the lectern, as was his hourly habit. But it was gone, just as he suspected it might be. Awen and Piper had made off with it, and that fact rankled him to no end. He would recover it, though. Somehow, he would find it and make it his own again. There was still so much to learn. And he could find Piper even without it. So-Elku had enough knowledge to search within the Nexus, and he suspected she'd hidden herself away there.

He was about to slip into his second sight when he felt a disturbance in his spirit—one that arrested him like a strongman grabbing him by the robes and spinning him around. There, not far away, was a presence. *Her* presence.

"But how can this be?" he wondered aloud, turning back toward his balcony. A cold wind suddenly blew through the curtains and pricked his skin. So-Elku moved toward the opening, toward the star fighters that twisted and shrieked above the cityscape, then closed his eyes to ignore the distractions.

The Luma master searched with his feelings and opened his senses to the space around him. He stretched out and began to probe, pushing himself forward like a blind man on the edge of a cliff, expecting his fingers to discover the place where the ground gave way at any moment.

Then, suddenly, he found her.

Piper sat in the tower above the Grand Arielina, holding her knees tight against her chest. The Republic Talons chased Ricio's starfighter like a pack of wolves after a willow hare. But Piper knew that Azelon was helping him, so he'd be okay. They'd all be okay. Everyone, that is, except her mother.

Magnus had killed her.

Which meant Nos Kil had been right after all. Magnus *had* killed women before, and Piper's mother was simply the next. Which made Magnus a monster. She wouldn't have believed it—couldn't have believed it. But she'd seen it all happen with her own eyes, and there was no denying just how horrible he was. She cursed him using every bad word she knew, and even made up some new words that she didn't know.

Suddenly, Piper remembered all the dreams she'd had of Magnus saving her life. The images were so vivid—the emotions so strong. She'd watched him climb over piles of rubble just to find her, to rescue her. He'd been her hero. He'd been the most important man in her whole world. But no more. All those dreams were nothing more than dark fairytales made up by her imagination. Magnus would not be coming to rescue her. He'd be coming to kill her next.

Then Piper silently thanked Nos Kil. She thanked him for helping her escape when she did. Without that, Piper might be in Magnus's evil clutches even now.

A shudder went through Piper that made her feel cold.

Normally, she'd run inside to get warm. But not tonight. Tonight she would sit here and watch the city burn. She would let the cold in to numb the pain in her heart. Maybe it would erase the images she saw in her mind's eye, the horrific mutation of her beautiful mother's face. Maybe the cold would freeze them like ice, and then Piper could smash them and break them into a million tiny pieces that not even she could put back together again.

Without even knowing it, tears had started flowing again. She'd cried so much since arriving in the tower that she wondered where all the water came from to feed her eyes. The wind lashed at her body, tugging on her hair. But the wind only served to make her colder, and she embraced it, welcoming it into her heart. Maybe it would help her heart stop beating. Or maybe it would just help freeze the tears and keep them from forming.

"I am so sorry for your loss, my child," said a low voice behind her. Frightened, Piper turned and blasted the intruder with a stream of magenta-colored energy. But the person exerted some sort of shield to deflect it, sending the colored light into the pillars and floor and ceiling. When the barrage subsided and the light returned to normal, Piper could see a silhouette moving toward her.

"Stay where you are," Piper ordered. "I can do worse."

"I don't doubt that," replied the person, most definitely a man, given how deep his voice was. "But I'd gladly risk my life to make sure that you're alright."

Piper was startled by the sense of care that she heard in

his words. It seemed genuine. And in light of how *another* man had just brought ultimate harm to her world, she was surprised at two conflicting feelings that appeared at the same time. One was to blast this person into oblivion, tearing his atoms apart. The other was to run to him, believing he would be different than *him*. Than *Magnus*.

"However, if you wish me to leave," the man continued, "I shall."

"No, wait." Piper held up a hand. "Who are you? Step out of the shadows."

"I fear you will not wish to see me, dear one. I am merely here to ensure your safety, then I will be gone."

"I am safe."

"Then I will be on my way."

"No…" Piper didn't know what to say next. She was grateful for the company. The truth was that despite her pain, she desperately wanted to be with her grandmother right now. And maybe even with Awen a little bit too, although Awen's love for Magnus was confusing. Piper wanted someone to hold her. To tell her that everything was going to be okay. "I don't want you to go."

"But if you are safe, then my presence here is not needed."

"But it is, whoever you are. Thank you for checking on me. But…" Piper pushed herself off the tower floor and squinted in the shadows. "How did you know I was here?"

"I could sense you… sense your grief."

"My grief?" Piper felt her throat tighten. "So you're a

Luma?" She stiffened her arms and lowered her head, preparing for another fight.

"I have no desire to fight you anymore, my child. Only to help you… to show you the ways that the others refused to."

"Others?" The man's words were curious. "Refused to?"

"Of course. That suit you wear."

"It's my power suit."

"And does it give you power? Or does it confine it?"

Piper tilted her head. She wondered if she should slip into the Unity to see who this man was, but she suspected that he might hide himself in shadow there as much as he did here. "My suit helps me."

"In what way?"

"It keeps me from hurting others."

The man's voice sounded surprised. "Hurting others? That cannot be. A child like you?"

"It's true." Piper felt the memory of her father's death come rushing back, and with it, a new thought, one that made her weep. "I'm an orphan."

"An orphan?"

"I killed my father. And now my mother is dead because of… of…"

"There, there, young one. Everything is going to be alright."

Those were the words she desperately needed to hear. She didn't even care who this man was or how he'd found her, she was just grateful for those words. They felt like a warm blanket or a hot cup of chocolate milk. They felt like Talisman.

Talisman that kept her from hurting people.

"I'm not safe," Piper said. "You need to stay away."

The man gave a soft laugh. But it wasn't directed at her, she felt. Instead, it seemed directed at her statement. "But you are safe, Piper."

"You—you know my name?"

The man ignored her question. "You may very well be the safest person in the galaxy. That suit was not meant to keep you from hurting others, it was meant to keep you from being who you were truly meant to be."

"I... I don't understand." She was getting frustrated. "Who are you? Tell me now!"

"If I promise to help you discover who you really are, if I promise to help you stop those who've hurt you, will you promise to give me a second chance?"

Piper squinted, trying so hard to see the man. "A second chance?"

"We all need second chances, don't we? If you give me one, I'll show you what Awen wouldn't. I'll set you free to explore the Nexus without limits. No rules. No discipline. Just pure freedom, the way you deserve it. Then, together, we will keep all people from getting hurt ever again."

Piper was moved by the man's words in a way she couldn't explain. Where Awen had tried to limit her, to scold her for doing wrong, to give her a suit that suppressed her powers in the Unity, Piper sensed the opposite from this stranger. There was something curious about him, something she felt she could trust. The wind played with her hair and licked at her tears while the blaster fire from the star fighters flashed against the man's green and black robes. And Piper knew that she would give him a second chance.

35

Three fighters remained in the group of Talons that swung around to the south. Ricio accelerated to match their speed, then feathered off his throttle, noting just how fast the Fang was by comparison. Azelon wasn't kidding when she said the Fang was four times the ship that the Talon was. *And then some*, he thought.

He decided to have one more go with blasters before using his missiles again. Like any pilot worth their ass pad, he knew to save the majority of the guided ordinance for shots he couldn't afford to miss. But right now, in the opening moments of the dogfight where the enemy was still getting its bearings, blasters would do just fine.

Feeling more confident, Ricio targeted the two rear-most Talons in the triangle formation. As soon as the reticles displayed a lock, he fired both blaster cannons—this time altering their delivery timing. The smaller bolts from the wings shredded shields and created a soft spot for the larger rounds, which drilled into the ships and tore straight down the fuselages. Ricio thought it was a lot like popping pieces of greedum fruit from the peels.

A second later, he flew through the debris field and targeted the third Talon. The enemy pilot must've seen his wingmen get destroyed because he pulled a textbook Paraguutian Cobra maneuver. The Talon slowed, pitched up into a quick-flip along its horizontal axis, and then—

Ricio was caught off guard. Instead of finishing the maneuver—resuming forward flight and landing well behind the pursuing enemy—this Talon's pilot decided to roll, pointing its nose straight at Ricio's Fang.

The man hadn't a clue how fast Ricio was traveling or else he wouldn't have attempted such a risky move. Blaster fire lit up Ricio's HUD, but he'd already ducked under the Talon and avoided what would have been a catastrophic collision. He watched his display to see the Talon stall out of the hasty assault and then regain an attack vector heading north…

Which was where the other five Talons were coming from. He didn't have time to get a lock, so Ricio flew down as close to the city as he dared. Seeing a wide thoroughfare ahead, he dipped down and decided to use it as cover. If he guessed right, the Repub pilots would refrain from firing into the city unless an evacuation had been instituted.

The buildings whipped by him in a blur—the air fighting him as he swept into the hand-made canyon. He watched on his HUD as the enemy ships passed overhead by two-hundred meters.

"Time to punch it!" Again, Ricio pitched up to execute an Alcion maneuver. He came over the top of the high arc inverted, then rolled out to see the five Talons with a sixth one trailing behind them—the one he'd missed before. He wouldn't miss again.

Ricio spent his full attention on the trailing fighter and sent blaster rounds from both cannons into the ship, tearing off its wings and detonating one of its torpedoes. The resulting explosion sent the ship catapulting forward and down where it impacted a building. A wave of fire wrapped around the structure, pulled it off its base, and sent up a plume of dust and smoke that blotted out the block.

Ricio wasted no time and targeted three more Talons. He selected missiles, then launched them. "Birdies one, three, and six, away." The guided munitions flared like the sun as they streaked forward. Ricio could hear the propellant from inside the cockpit. The missiles searched hungrily for their prey, dipping and weaving as the enemy fighters attempted evasive maneuvers. But there was no stopping the Novian tech. In three distinct *pops*, the targeted Talons blew apart in a dazzling light display that must've looked like fireworks from the city streets.

Ricio rolled clear of the debris field and targeted the last two Talons. Up until now, he'd hardly thought about the pilots he was killing—he'd been far too busy trying to fly an alien gunship with his mind. That said, he almost felt ashamed of how little thought he'd given to these Navy pilots. He'd been given the gift of time. Time to sit with Magnus and hear about what was happening to his beloved Republic, to the Luma, and to the prospect of true peace in the galaxy. He'd been allowed to make up his mind as to who was right and who was wrong in this fight. But these pilots? They were dying in the midst of their ignorance. And it pained Ricio's heart.

Deciding whose team he was on scared him. Fighting for Magnus's side meant he'd probably never see his wife and son again. He could desert, of course—using the opportunity to run back to Capriana. But Azelon's threat of blowing him up probably wasn't hyperbole. Nor would Moldark's threat of executing him be if he ever caught him back at home without checking in.

No, Ricio hadn't come this far simply because of the opportunity to escape. He'd come this far because he believed in Magnus's cause. Moldark needed to be stopped. And if Ricio helped Magnus and his friends, then his wife and son had a chance to be safe—to survive what was coming next. Ricio would die for that.

The target reticles glowed, the lock icons pulsing at him, willing him to fire.

Maybe, if given more time, these Repub pilots would have chosen the same as Ricio. But as it was, their mission was to take the shuttles down, and he wasn't going to let that happen. If that day did come—where he could talk to them before they ran to the flight line and went up, if he could reason with them like Magnus had done with him—Ricio would gladly take the time to speak with each of them if it meant sparing their lives. Today, however, there was no time.

"Birdy five, away." Ricio loosed his last missile on the left Talon and turned both blaster systems on the right. His cockpit flashed with light as the missile sped toward its mark and the blasters chewed into hull plating. The enemy fighters exploded a tenth of a second apart, producing a near simultaneous explosion that showered the city with fiery fighter fragments.

As Ricio flew through the falling remains, he kept the ship steady, holding off on his usual post-kill barrel roll. Instead, he grieved for the pilots who'd lost their lives without even knowing what they'd died for. Could it be said of them, perhaps, that they'd died defending the Republic? Died in honor of the pursuit of peace? He supposed part of it was true, but it made Ricio's stomach twist and did nothing to make him feel better. Instead, he could only focus on the lives in the shuttles—those he'd sworn to protect. Awen. Magnus. The Jujari, the Reptalon, and the huge Miblimbian. The Nimprinth that always spoke in third person and his mismatched Caledonian girlfriend. And the little girl with the blonde ringlets. The cosmos had brought them all together…

"And it's gonna be the cosmos that sees us through," he said aloud.

"Please rephrase your statement, commander."

"I was just talking to myself."

"As, yes. I have noticed your kind doing this regularly."

Ricio brought his Fang around in a low turn, remaining below the defense cannons' firing arcs. "How goes the fighter hunting, old girl?"

"I have successfully eliminated all remaining targets. The shuttles are free and clear."

Ricio let out a holler and pumped a fist.

"Are you alright, commander?"

"Yeah, baby. We did it."

"I concur. However, your exclamation is such that—"

"It's what we do when we're excited about something, like successfully saving those who we're trying to protect."

"Ah, I see. Well, in that case—" Azelon screamed over comms. At least that's how Ricio interpreted it. The sound was something between a shrill shriek and a mechanical cackle. He winced and placed his palms over his ears.

"What the hell was that?" Ricio asked when it finally subsided.

"I was returning your congratulatory exclamation, commander."

"We need to work on that."

"I have added it to my list of subjects to return to at a later time."

Ricio worked his jaw in an attempt to get the ringing in his ears to subside. "So, back to the *Spire* then?"

"Indeed, sir. If you would please accompany the shuttles, I will ready the hangar bays for your return."

"On it."

Ricio pushed the Fang forward, accelerating away from

Plumeria and over the tropical forest once again. He stayed low, turning beneath rock ledges and following the contours of the low hills. He passed the wreckage of the second emplacement he'd destroyed, and then began the long descent toward the ocean, feeling his stomach flutter. The aquamarine blue stretched to the horizon in all directions. Several seconds later, Ricio swept over the first turret he'd annihilated.

"Damn, old girl. You seeing the size of that crater?" Ricio asked.

"I am, sir. I am recording the data as I have never witnessed the effects of a mine used on a surface target in atmosphere before."

"That makes two of us."

As Ricio shot out across the ocean waves he could see the shuttles ahead, appearing to hover like seabirds in an updraft. He dialed down his throttle as he closed the gap, willing his Fang to come even with them. He was certain the other vessels had seen him on radar so he would need to hail them. But how, exactly, would *that* conversation go? *Hey, remember me? I'm that guy Ricio that tried to kill you a few days ago. Oh yeah, I broke out of prison too. But then I had a random change of heart and decided to turn on the Republic and everything I knew in a hasty effort to help save your sorry asses.*

Before Ricio knew it, he'd pulled even with the formation. "Azie, how do I open a channel to them?"

"You only need think it, commander, and the channel will be opened," Azelon replied.

"Yeah, cause that's how I thought it was supposed to

work."

"Well done."

"I was kidding."

Azelon paused. "I have so much to learn about your species."

Ricio did as she instructed and noticed a green comms channel icon display on his HUD. "Transport shuttle bound for the *Azelon Spire*, this is Commander Ricio Longo. Do you read me?"

There was no answer. Ricio almost asked Azelon for help but decided to try again first.

"Transport shuttle bound for the *Spire*, this is Ricio, the guy…" He bit his lip. "The pilot you had in the brig. Do you copy? Over."

"We copy, Ricio," said a man's booming voice. Ricio turned and saw a dark Miblimbian face appear in the closest shuttle's bridge window. "And just who in the hell let you out of your cell?"

"I suppose you wouldn't believe me if I said I didn't know."

"No."

"I don't blame you." He chuckled. "Listen, I just wanted to let you know that the skies are clear and I'll be at your three o'clock all the way back to the *Spire*."

"And then what? You booking it back to Moldark?"

"That's a negative, mister…" Ricio waited, willing the man to identify himself.

"Abimbola," he finally said.

"Then that's a negative, Mr. Abimbola. I'm with you for the long haul."

The big man hesitated. "We are grateful for your help. Yet you still have got a lot of explaining to do."

"Don't I know it. Everyone okay in there?"

"All things considered, yes. Several people need medical attention. But it could have been a lot worse." A short silence filled the channel. Ricio wondered if maybe the giant was warming to him. "We saw a lot of fancy flying on radar. Was that you, jockey?"

"Eh. Nothing the old girl and I couldn't handle."

Abimbola's eyebrows lifted high. "You are already calling *that* fancy starfighter old?"

Ricio laughed. "Sorry, not the fighter. Azelon."

"I've been nicknamed again," the AI said.

"Have you now," Abimbola replied, smiling.

"Yes. And according to an ancient Novian proverb, it seems I am well loved."

"Well loved?" Ricio repeated. "Okay, I'm game. What's the proverb?"

"A person with many names is much loved," Azelon replied.

Ricio shrugged. "Then it seems you are loved indeed."

"As are you, commander," Azelon said.

Ricio tilted his head. He had to admit, playing with this AI was more fun than he expected it to be. "Okay. I'll bite. What nicknames make me much loved?"

"You're the best cocky-ass bastard I know."

36

Magnus felt himself arrive at consciousness like a hover train pulling into a station after a slow crawl out of a subterranean tunnel. He opened his eyes to the dim lights of sickbay, noting that his bioteknia interface was running in standby mode. Only a small icon blinked in the lower right corner. He had no idea how long he'd been out or how he'd arrived back on the *Spire*, but a quick consult from his interface would answer several of those questions.

Magnus was a breath away from hovering his focus on the icon when a thought struck him. A dark thought. A thought so painful that his heart was already wrenching at the idea of it before the vapor had fully formed. But he couldn't stop the sentence from coming, just like he couldn't stop the sun rising.

My eyes, he thought. *They were a gift from... from* her.

On another planet at another time, one that felt so long

ago from the present, he'd awakened in a sickbay much less refined than this one. There, he stared into the eyes of an angel, one who'd given him the gift of sight. The gift had stripped him of his career, of his future. At least the one he cared about at that time. But in the process it gave him a new direction, a new future, which led him here. Only the angel wouldn't be coming around a corner to inspect his injuries.

"Valerie..."

Magnus hardly recognized his voice. It was tight and dry. But it was his nonetheless. He blinked, trying to encourage his thoughts past the sorrow that twisted his gut in a hundred different directions. But the damn little icon in the lower right reminded him of his eyes. Of *her*.

"Valerie."

This time when he said her name, tears came. She was gone. He didn't understand how. Couldn't see how. But she'd been gunned down. He saw her body, her open helmet, her broken face. He winced, squinting against the memory, forcing it into the depths where it belonged. It was a fiction, after all. Wasn't it? Just a bad dream. Valerie wasn't really dead, and Piper wasn't really gone. *It's all just a bad dream*, he thought. *And now that I'm awake, we can get back to whatever it was we were getting to, and life will work itself out.*

Only, it wasn't a dream. It had been real. All of it. And he'd lived to see it. To witness the horrific loss of a woman he cared for, and to see the pain in the face of the little girl he loved so very much. But worse than losing Valerie, Magnus realized, was losing Piper.

The way the little girl refused to look at him broke his heart. Her defiant posture burned a hole through his chest a fathom deep, and then some. It cut him, like a Jujari sword. Like a duradex blade. It cut him deeper than any pain he supposed he'd ever felt. Even more than the pain of losing his brother. And that startled him. But he supposed he knew why.

Argus had chosen his own fate. He'd known what he was doing. He'd known the end he was racing toward. Any other Marine could have caught him, but fate made sure it was Magnus.

Piper though? She was different. She hadn't chosen this. Instead, fate chose her. Something had happened to her when was with Nos Kil. Something had broken inside of her. Magnus blamed himself for it, of course, and Awen had tried to argue the failed logic of it all. But Magnus knew that somehow, he was responsible… for allowing Nos Kil on the ship. For not killing him when he had the chance. *Chances.*

The accident with Valerie was unspeakable, and he couldn't blame Piper for her anger and pain. But Magnus longed to know what else he'd done to hurt Piper. He longed to go back in time and put all the pieces together again. But try as he might, he couldn't figure it out. It was like trying to put one of those old puzzles together in the dark—hands fumbling with a thousand pieces but never arranging them well enough to fit.

Magnus heard beeping as he sat up. His head swam, so he gripped the sides of the table to keep from falling. More beeps, some corresponding with his pulse, filled the small chamber. He willed them to slow as he tried to control his breathing.

He cleared his eyes again and tried to focus on the central hexagonal room. Several other people slept peacefully in the chambers extending from the walls. All the lights were low, and Magnus wondered if it was the middle of the night. Again, the small icon pulsed in the lower right-hand corner of his vision. Just a quick focused effort would open it and tell him what time it was. But it would bring the pain of Valerie's death too, and he wasn't sure he could handle that again. Not yet. In fact, he suddenly wondered if he'd ever be able to handle it. That damn blinking button was going to be his eternal reminder of her. *Son of a bitch.*

He swung his legs over the side of the table. For the first time, he noticed fresh pink skin on his kneecaps. More on the tops of his feet. Shins. Thighs. He pulled his hands off the edge of the table and looked at his arms. They were covered in patches of pink skin, like a newborn baby's. Then he touched his face.

His beard was gone, as was the rugged feel of his weathered skin along his cheeks, nose, and mouth. His forehead was tender, as were his ears. His head had been mostly shaved, leaving him with a fuzzy crewcut like the old timers wore.

Magnus rubbed the back of his neck as the gravity of the situation dawned on him. Apparently, he'd been in too much shock to realize just how bad the rocket had damaged him. This amount of skin grafting was consistent with people who'd nearly died from third degree burns. The fact that he'd even made it this far must've been... *a damned miracle*.

He took a deep breath and muttered a small prayer of thanks for whoever had overseen his surgery. Or surgeries. How long had it taken? And just how long had he been out? The questions finally got the better of him and, against the protest of his emotions, he decided to check the time. He looked at the pulsing icon and powered on his eyes.

The hexagonal lattice grew from the center of his vision like a spider web built at high speed. Then it faded into the background while several status bars illuminated in the corners. He instinctively looked at the date and time stamp, and his heart sank.

"Four days?" He rubbed the back of his neck again, then rolled his head. "Splick."

Suddenly, he noticed another icon blinking in the upper left—it was a notification for one new message. "Just one?" he asked himself, knowing the humor would be lost on anyone else. *Since when does someone in charge only get one message after four days?*

Magnus hovered his attention over the message icon, and a window appeared in the foreground. He knew it didn't matter how his head was orientated, but he still felt compelled to raise it level when watching these.

"Hello, sir," said an image of a familiar bot standing just inside sickbay. "This is TO-96, in case you need a reminder. In the instance where you awaken while the rest of the crew is sleeping, this message will serve to orient you in the interim.

As such, let me be the first to welcome you back to the *Spire* and bid you a very early good morning.

"As you've probably already noticed, you've undergone substantial skin grafting due to the burns you suffered in the rocket attack. While your adrenaline maintained your primary bodily functions following the blast, Willowood eventually placed you in a controlled stasis upon your departure in the shuttle.

"Also, you will be pleased to know that the surgery was a violently concussive success."

Magnus raised an eyebrow. "You mean *smashing*, 'Six."

The recording pressed on. "Azelon and I conducted the skin grafts while Willowood attended to your soul."

"My soul?" Magnus asked, putting a hand to his chest. The thought of some squirrely old lady tinkering with his insides made him uneasy.

"Your new skin will take some time to acclimate, but it should blend rather well with your existing architecture, far exceeding that of current Repub standards. Azelon noted that the procedure went far more quickly than had you been a Novian patient—given all their hair. She assured me that your beard will grow back relatively soon.

"As for the rest of the crew, everyone seems to be recovering rather well from minor injuries. Unfortunately, our three losses include Andocs, Haney, and Stone."

Just hearing 'Six mention Valerie's last name made Magnus's heart ache.

"Additionally, Piper's whereabouts are currently unknown,

though both Willowood and Awen, along with a small contingent of the Luma, have given themselves to searching for her within the Unity.

"As for us, we have temporarily retreated to metaspace and are monitoring the area around the quantum tunnel. So far, our retreat has gone undetected and there has been no sign of activity on either side of the void horizon. Additionally, Azelon's systems have been restored, so there is no need to worry about any more security breaches. It seems that Miss Piper's earlier tampering did more to the *Spire's* infrastructure than we'd previously noted, resulting in secondary malfunctions of the brig's security features. But, as I said, everything has been restored.

"Before I sign off, it is worth noting that Commander Mauricio Longo helped ensure our escape from Worru via his use of a Novian starfighter—with Azelon's supervision, of course."

"Ricio?" Magnus said in surprise to the recording. Maybe his hard work at trying to persuade the pilot to join them had paid off. *But who the hell let him out of the brig?*

TO-96's message moved ahead before Magnus could give it more thought. "It seems that he and Nos Kil escaped from their cells, which is a conversation you will no doubt want to have with Azelon and Ricio at a later point. The interruption of orbital fire support that you overheard with Flow and Cheeks was due to a skirmish between them and Nos Kil. Again, Ricio helped your men subdue the prisoner and return him to his cell. One might say that the Repub pilot helped saved the day *twice*... in one day. Now that I think about it, that sentence needs work. In any case, I would be remiss if I did not encourage you to praise him upon your next meeting.

"Your crew and your ship await you, sir. We are grateful for your presence, your health, and your leadership as you guide us toward the next objectives—whatever those may be. TO-96 signing off. End recording."

The window blipped out of existence.

Magnus was left staring at his chamber's sidewall with his legs still dangling off the side of the bed. He felt slightly unnerved that so much had happened without him. But he was grateful that everyone and the ship were at least safe for the time being. Stowing away in metaspace to regroup was definitely the right move, and he made a mental note to thank whoever came up with that course of action. Not only would they be safe, but the time dilation would give them an opportunity to come up with their next steps.

Magnus decided to try his legs and slipped off the table. His nerve endings shuddered for a moment, sending sparks of minor discomfort to his brain from various parts of his body. But it wasn't painful. In fact, it felt good—like stretching out the soreness of muscles too long in one position. He moved his back and arms, but suddenly noted that his new skin still seemed tight. Certain motions made the patches stretch, and —based on the shooting pain it caused—he decided not to make those movements again, at least for another day or two.

As Magnus's began deciding what he wanted to do next, a thought came to mind. Something in TO-96's message stood out to him. Something that piqued his curiosity. It was the item about Azelon's system being *restored*.

"Azelon, are you there?"

"Of course, Magnus. It's nice to see you are awake and feeling better."

"No small thanks to you."

"It's an honor to serve you, sir. And I see you viewed TO-96's recorded message."

"I did. Though… how do you know that?" But Magnus wasn't quite ready for what he was sure would be a tedious explanation. "You know what? Never mind."

"As you wish, sir."

"Azie, I've got a question for you."

"Blaster bolt."

Magnus paused. "Ah… what?"

"Is that not the correct colloquialism? *Blaster bolt*?"

"I'm not following."

"TO-96's lexicon recommends using a reference to a fired rifle when positively responding to a request for more information."

Suddenly, the right word dawned on Magnus and he couldn't help but laugh. "You mean *shoot*."

Azelon was slow in replying; Magnus wondered just what was going on in that big, beautiful brain of hers. "I have successfully updated my file on this for all future instances. Please shoot."

Magnus grinned. "'Six mentioned that your brig systems had been restored. Is that accurate?"

"It is, sir. I have regained control of all security doors and sensors."

"Would that happen to include any recorded data from those sensors? Say, video and audio?"

"Yes, Magnus. All sensory data is stored locally with or without my presence, though I am the only one with root access to it."

"So… do you have full records of Nos Kil's cell in the brig?"

"I have complete file set of his cell's cameras."

"Which includes the conversation he had with Piper?"

"As I said, sir, I have access to a complete file set of—"

"Can you bring up that conversation, Azie?"

"Processing request. Please stand by."

Magnus waited, suddenly aware that his heart rate had increased and he could feel the blood rush to his face. His battlefield experience had taught him how to subdue an adrenaline rush, but he could already feel his fight or flight instincts going into overdrive. To think that he was about to hear Piper and Nos Kil's conversation and to see what had happened… He shut his eyes against whatever foul images his imagination tried to play on him. *No, Nos Kil never touched her*, he reminded himself. At least that is what Valerie's analysis had told them. But maybe Azie's footage would contradict that? *Mystics, I hope not.*

"How would you like to review the requested data?"

Magnus blinked himself out of his thoughts. "What's that?"

"The data, sir. Of Nos Kil and Piper's conversation. How would you like to review it?"

"Can you send it to my eyes? Maybe feed me the audio through the overhead speakers?"

"Your bioteknia eyes have transducers that are applied directly to the bone of your eye sockets specifically for the purpose of two-way audio transmission. Were you not aware of this?"

"No." Magnus thought he should ask Valerie about this. Then a rush of heat flooded his neck and surged into his face. "I wasn't made aware. Proceed."

"Sending data to your eyes. Please stand by."

Magnus paced the floor when a security camera feed filled his vision. It was as if he was perched in the upper corner of Nos Kil's cell, looking down at the man with Piper on the other side of the forcefield. Magnus knew better than to try and watch this standing up, so he reached out and found his medical bed to sit down.

"Psst, little girl," Nos Kil said from on his bed. Magnus felt his skin crawl as the shirtless man spoke. His bloodstained skin was in stark contrast to Piper's sweet face and blonde ringlets.

"You're a bad guy."

"Why would you say that?" Nos Kil replied.

"Because you tried to kill my friends."

"Tried to kill—? Listen, I was defending my men. Your *friends* attacked *us*."

"But Magnus said you were—"

"The bad guys?" Nos Kil shook his head in disgust. "First I'm the bad guy, and then I'm an unarmed prisoner and Magnus does *this* to me."

"Magnus hurt you?" Piper asked. Magnus hated where this conversation was going. "Maybe there's something I can do to help you."

"Piper no," Magnus said, instinctively willing her to stay away. But he knew the effort was pointless.

"Like what?" Nos Kil asked as he sat up.

"When I'm sad or hurt, sometimes I just need someone to talk to," Piper said.

"Well, I could use a friend right now."

"Then I can do that, I suppose."

Magnus felt his stomach turn as Piper walked into the cellblock.

"Do you know what it's like to feel different from everybody else?" Nos Kil asked.

Piper didn't respond at first, but eventually gave Nos Kil a slight nod.

"Yeah. That's how I feel… how I've always felt. Like I don't fit in with everyone else. And that's not a lot of fun, you know what I mean?"

Again, Piper nodded and took another step forward.

"Sometimes, I feel like I have all this stuff rolling around inside of me, and that if I let it out, people will just push me away. Because they don't understand me. But then I think it's more than that. That maybe they'll push me away because they're…"

Piper took yet another step forward. Her face seemed so curious. The entire conversation felt wrong, and Magnus couldn't believe he'd allowed it to happen on his watch.

"Because they're afraid," Piper said.

Nos Kil snapped his fingers and Piper jerked upright—eyes wide. "Because they're afraid." He waved a finger at Piper. "That's exactly right."

"People are afraid of what they don't understand."

Nos Kil sat up straight. "You know, you're absolutely right. What's your name?"

"My name? I'm… I'm not allowed to talk to strangers."

Again, Nos Kil waved a finger at her. "You're a very smart young lady."

"What's your name?"

"Ah, ah, ah—I'm not allowed to talk to strangers either."

Piper lowered her forehead and gave him a bashful smile. "You're covered in blood. Why?"

"Because they're afraid of me."

"Why are they afraid of you? You're locked in there, and we're all out here."

"That's a very good point. Personally? I think it's because I know something that Magnus doesn't want anyone else to know."

Magnus felt his chest tighten. *Mystics, is this it then? Is he going to tell this child about the night on Caledonia?* He wanted nothing more than to leap down into the brig and strangle Nos Kil.

"You said you had a secret. When we took you prisoner in

the city. You said you had something that Magnus didn't want the others to know."

"I did, yes. That's true."

"So that's what they're afraid of? Your secret?"

"Oh, it's not my secret." Nos Kil placed a hand on his chest, sitting up a little straighter. "But it does belong to…"

The long silence pulled Piper along to fill it. "To who?"

Again, Nos Kil shrugged.

"To Magnus? It's Magnus's secret, isn't it. He's afraid that you'll tattle on him."

Magnus couldn't see Nos Kil's entire face, but he imagined the man was giving Piper some sort of forlorn look. "Azelon, do you have a view of Nos Kil's face?"

"Affirmative." The camera view suddenly showed Nos Kil's face over Piper's shoulder. The blood had yet to dry under his eye. He looked like a monster. Magnus couldn't believe that Piper even had the stomach to approach him.

"Is that why he beat you up?"

Nos Kil pointed to his eye. "You mean this?"

Piper nodded.

"Yeah, he's pretty afraid of me. But, we'd probably better not talk about it anymore. I wouldn't want him getting upset with you too."

"No," Piper said, stepping to within a meter of the shield.

"Dammit Piper," Magnus said, slamming his palm with his opposite fist.

"He doesn't have to know. Plus, if you don't tell me, I can just find out for myself."

"Can you?" The prisoner raised his eyebrows and pushed his broken lips up in appreciation. "So you're one of those Luma then, aren't you."

"Not a Luma. A gladia. With the Gladio Umbra."

Again, Nos Kil nodded in appreciation. "Well then, I guess there's no point in keeping secrets from someone like you. And I can see why they'd be afraid of you too."

"You can?"

"Sure. You can probably read people's minds if you want? Probably do other really amazing things too, I'm guessing. Like, I don't know… what's the most amazing thing you think you can do?"

Piper let out a small laugh. "I just learned to do something new."

"Really?"

"I can move things through the Unity."

"Mystics, Piper!" Magnus could feel the new skin on the backs of his hands straining. "What are you doing?"

"Move things?" Nos Kil said. "That sounds like a neat trick."

"It is. I can take things from anywhere around me and move them through the Unity to anyplace else far away. But…"

In the pause, Nos Kil studied Piper's face in a way that made Magnus want to reach out and push out his other eye. "But you'd get in trouble if they found out?"

"Yes, sir."

"I guess that makes us friends then." The prisoner took a

breath, looked around his cell, and then placed a hand on his chest. "My name is Volf. Volf Nos Kil, from Haradia."

"I'm Piper. Piper Stone, from Capriana."

Magnus shook his head in irritation. If he could have closed his eyes to make the image go away for a moment, he would have. But he couldn't. This was happening—no, this *had* happened. And there was nothing he could do to change it.

Nos Kil repeated her name in a smile. "That's a pretty name, little one. But, now that I think of it, you're not so little, are you. And maybe that's what makes them afraid of you, just like they're afraid of me. On the outside, we look like people that they can take advantage of. But on the inside, where they can't see, we're really big. We're…"

"Invincible."

Nos Kil turned his head and gave her a look that betrayed nothing short of marvel. He repeated the word and smiled. "I like that. Yes."

"Well, you've told me your secret. Would you like if I told you mine?" He hesitated, then turned away from her. "No, I can't."

"No," Piper said, stepping right up to the forcefield.

"Piper!" Magnus gnashed his teeth. "For the love of all the mystics, what are you doing?"

"Please, you can tell me," Piper said, her voice pleading with him. "It's okay. I won't tell."

"But I don't want you to get in trouble with them."

"I won't."

"But how can you be sure?" Nos Kil turned off his bed and sank to his knees. *His knees, dammit.* He bunched his bloodied knuckles into fists and held them against his tattooed chest.

"Because I won't tell."

The prisoner slowly let his hand fall and then lowered his head. "Okay then. But only if you're sure."

"I'm sure," she said. Piper sat down and crossed her legs.

To Magnus's horror, Nos Kil began to tell Piper the events that unfolded in the hotel basement on T'io Mi'on, but with one difference…

Magnus was the one who'd raped the island women, and Argus, Caldwell, and Nos Kil were the ones who'd broken in to stop *him*.

All the blood rushed to Magnus's head as he made Azelon switch views so he could see Piper's face. Tears streamed from her eyes—her face tormented and terrified. She pleaded with Nos Kil, telling him that his account wasn't true—*couldn't be true.* But Nos Kil assured her, as only the most skilled abusers can, that it was true, that he'd rather die than lie, that she could even check with Magnus… *if* she was willing to get in really big trouble.

Nos Kil went on to tell how Magnus shot the young Marine named Caldwell, and then—faced with the consequences of his actions—he gunned down his own brother in cold blood. Magnus had always been jealous of Argus's success, threatened by his reputation in the Marines, and decided this was his moment to get rid of Argus once and for all.

Piper sobbed, her small shoulders heaving up and down. Magnus wasn't sure what was worse, that Nos Kil would dare to tell such lies to a child or that Piper seemed to accept it. Then again, Nos Kil had manipulated her masterfully, which made Magnus sick to his stomach.

"The only reason I lived was because reinforcements barged in the room. But because he outranked me, they believed his side of the story, not mine."

"No," she said, shaking her head. "No, this can't be right."

"And it's not right, Piper. They took me and locked me away while Magnus went free. And here I am, still locked up, unable to defend myself, unable to argue my case."

"No, no, no." Piper's hands were on her head now as she fought sobs of anguish. As she sank to her knees and lowered her head to the ground, Magnus saw Nos Kil's broken lips curl into a smile.

"Surely you've seen how he looks at women, how he barks orders at his men. How aggressive he is in battle. You've seen that, haven't you?"

Piper nodded, hands still clutching her head.

Nos Kil sighed. "I suppose it's only a matter of time before he acts again against someone you love. Maybe even against you."

Piper let out a shriek. It startled Magnus, just like it startled him the first time he heard the sound ricocheting through the brig and into Ricio's cell block.

"Beware of Magnus, Piper." Nos Kil's voice was barely audible above Piper's weeping. "Beware of the evil inside him."

"Kill the feed, Azelon," Magnus demanded. The recording blipped out of existence, and Magnus turned toward the exit.

37

Magnus tore down the hallway toward the brig, anger surging through every blood vessel in his body like liquid fire. But it was more than anger—there was grief, too. A righteous indignation that carved trenches in his soul for the liquid fire to course down.

He stopped at the security door. "Open it."

"Sir, may I inquire the nature of your—"

"Open the damn door, Azie."

"Access granted."

The door slid open and Magnus marched into the control room. As he crossed in front of the monitors, he saw Nos Kil out of the corner of his eye. The man was apparently asleep on his bed, arms folded behind his head.

Magnus stopped at the next door. "Azie?"

"Again, sir, I feel it is my duty to—"

"It's your duty to open the door."

"Given your elevated—"

"*Open the door.*"

There was a momentary pause, and then the security door into the cell block corridors opened. Magnus didn't hear his grinding teeth. He only heard the sound of his bare footfalls against the glossy black floor. He spun left into the first cell-block and saw Nos Kil lying on his bed.

"Force field down," Magnus said. This time, Azelon did not contest the order. Instead, the shimmering blue field vanished and the only thing between Magnus and the sleeping prisoner was open air. The room stank of body odor from a man who refused to bathe.

Magnus stood over Nos Kil when the prisoner opened his one eye. He'd barely gotten a word out of his mouth when Magnus grabbed his leg and yanked him off his bed. Nos Kil's body landed on the floor with a thud and the man let out a grunt. The prisoner momentarily halted Magnus's momentum as he latched a hand onto the corner of the bed, but Magnus jerked hard and Nos Kil lost his hold. The prisoner's shirtless body squeaked along the floor, his palms trying to gain traction.

In one motion, Magnus threw Nos Kil's leg aside and then thrust himself backward. His left elbow dropped on Nos Kil's face, breaking the cartilage in his nose with a sickening crack. The prisoner grabbed his face and roared, twisting out from under Magnus's weight.

With the man on his left side, Magnus sat up and drove

three consecutive punches into Nos Kil's right kidney. Nos Kil's convulsed, recoiling from the blows like a thrashing snake. He rolled once more to stare up at Magnus with a wild look in his eye.

"She leave you, Magnus?"

But Magnus wasn't interested in talking. He drove his fist across Nos Kil's face, snapping something in the man's jaw. He pulled back for a second blow when the prisoner punched Magnus in his belly. The blow was hard enough to knock the wind out of him. Magnus gasped, but returned the strike, pummeling the man's gut with a left hook, then a right. He knew he'd broken ribs as his knuckles went deeper into Nos Kil's sides than they should have.

The prisoner pulled himself into a fetal position, trying to ward off the attack to his rib cage. Seizing the opportunity, Magnus went to deliver a third devastating blow when a fist came up from the fetal form and struck his mouth. The blow sent a shock through Magnus's skull and rattled his head. His eyes blinked out for half a second before returning to normal. Something had broken free in his mouth, and he tasted iron.

Nos Kil took advantage of his opponent's hesitation, rolled to the left, and swung his fist for the other side of Magnus's jaw. Magnus deflected the blow with his forearm but used the momentum to flip Nos Kil over and onto his belly. In a flash, Magnus was on the man's back, one hand grabbing what little hair there was and yanking his head back. With his other hand, he delivered blow after blow after blow to the Nos Kil's right flank, each hit forcing the air from the prisoner's lungs.

Magnus was midway through another punch to the man's side when Nos Kil spread his legs—giving him optimal leverage against the floor—and spun his hips and torso so violently that it flipped Magnus onto the floor. He landed on his shoulder with a grunt and watched as Nos Kil pushed himself off the ground and stood up.

Nos Kil wiped blood from his chin with his thumb. "Or maybe she's dead. Shame."

Magnus rolled to his feet and brought his hands up. He circled Nos Kil in the cell block, his bioteknia eyes scanning the prisoner's body. The display suggested Nos Kil suffered from internal bleeding and that a vital organ had been ruptured. Based on the way Nos Kil was hunched and limping, Magnus guessed the scans were right.

"It won't be long now," Magnus said as he panted for breath, then nodded at Nos Kil's side.

His opponent stole a quick glance at his torso and looked back into Magnus's bioteknia eyes. "Better get this over with then." Nos Kil clicked his tongue and threw a left hook at Magnus's side. Magnus blocked it and countered with a left hook to Nos Kil's head. The prisoner leaned away and followed through with a right uppercut to Magnus's rib cage. He felt the jolt go straight to the top of his head—*this bastard is still strong*. Then Magnus blocked with both arms close to his head as another left hook came barreling toward his face.

No sooner had the blow been absorbed then Magnus

brought his knee up and into Nos Kil's wounded side. The blow would have been enough to drop any other opponent cold, but not Nos Kil. Instead, the man let out a grunt, grabbed Magnus's leg, and thrust upward. Magnus fell backward and slammed into the floor. But Nos Kil still held his leg. The assailant stepped around it and placed a knee on Magnus's gut, raising his right fist to drive a blow down on his face.

Magnus wrenched his leg to the side and threw Nos Kil off balance. His opponent fell but caught himself, giving Magnus just enough time to roll and regain his feet. This time, he threw his right leg in a roundhouse kick toward Nos Kil's kneeling position. The kick was deflected. Magnus threw a left hook and it too was batted aside. He threw a right jab. Nos Kil must have known it was coming and blocked it. But Magnus had only feinted the punch—instead, his left hook went under Nos Kil's arms and sent a blast of anger-filled energy ripping through the man's side.

Nos Kil doubled over. Magnus wondered if this was it—if that had done the man in. But he knew better than to underestimate an opponent. He reached down, grabbed the man's hair again, and yanked his face up. A spray of blood arced across the cellblock. Before the liquid even landed, Nos Kil grabbed Magnus's arm and pulled. But as Magnus jerked away, he inadvertently helped Nos Kil stand.

Magnus blocked a right jab, a left hook, and a right uppercut, all fueled by a fresh wave of energy in his opponent. He backpedaled along the cellblock floor, defending against two more forceful punches to his head and stomach. As Nos Kil sent another full-force jab, Magnus moved out of the way, grabbed the man's arm, and thrust him across the room in line with his punch.

Nos Kil stumbled forward and turned around. The man was winded and weakening. *Finally*, Magnus thought. But it didn't matter. He would fight Nos Kil as long as it took. Because this wasn't for him. It wasn't for the Repub, or even for the galaxy. It was for Piper.

Nos Kil roared and Magnus charged. The two met in the middle as Magnus threw his right fist at Nos Kil's bloodied face. The prisoner made to deflect it, but Magnus's punch had been thrown with so much speed, the failed attempt did little to divert the blow. Instead, Nos Kil's head snapped back. Magnus followed the punch with a second one, landing only slightly less hard. Again, Nos Kil's head went back.

The third punch, however, was blocked, and Nos Kil retaliated with a left hook into Magnus's side. Magnus tried to step away but only managed to lessen the impact marginally. He felt something give and suspected a rib cracked. In any other situation, the pain would have been overwhelming. But here, something drove him that was beyond anything he'd ever felt. He'd never had a daughter, of course. But if he'd had one, he'd want her to be just like Piper. Now the little girl was fatherless *and* motherless. And both had died on Magnus's watch. That someone like Nos Kil would try to take advantage of a small innocent child—*and for what? Their own vendetta against the Republic?* All those thoughts fueled Magnus as he glared into Nos Kil's eyes.

Magnus brought his left leg around and kicked Nos Kil. The blow was deflected. Magnus jabbed twice, air shooting out between his gritted teeth. Again, Nos Kil blocked. But Magnus could sense the man's parries were weakening. He threw another left hook, left hook, right uppercut combination and felt his fists connect against Nos Kil despite his opponent's attempts to ward them off.

Nos Kil retaliated with a less-than-powerful left hook, which Magnus deflected. It was followed by a right jab that Magnus batted out of the way. Nos Kil was wheezing now, blood and saliva streaming from his mouth. But still he fought on, kicking up at Magnus's head. The attempt was strong but poorly aimed, and Magnus ducked beneath it, then pushed the leg aside, giving added momentum to Nos Kil's kick.

The act made Magnus's opponent wobble, and Magnus used it to jab twice at Nos Kil's exposed face. Both strikes snapped the enemy's head back, dazed eyes returning to look at Magnus.

"You should have killed me on Caledonia when you had the chance, Magnus," Nos Kil said in garbled speech. He could hardly keep his hands up to fight.

"A mistake I'll never make again, you son of a bitch." Magnus took two steps back, raced forward, and leaped into the air. Then he threw himself into a somersault with his right leg extended and brought his heel down atop Nos Kil's head.

Magnus landed on his left leg, managed to stay upright, and watched as Nos Kil's body dropped to the ground.

Magnus stood strong, chest heaving, body aching, nose and mouth bleeding. He looked over his downed enemy, filled with emotions that were hard to identify. He saw his brother's face, saw Caldwell's son, saw the young women who'd been victimized. And then he saw Piper, tender and innocent. He saw the tears streaming from her pleading blue eyes, the heaving of her slender shoulders. And then he focused on Nos Kil, knowing this beast would never hurt anyone again.

Nos Kil's eye fluttered open. "You did it," he said in a soft wheeze. By the looks of it, the rest of Nos Kil's body had been paralyzed. "You stopped me. But you will never stop Moldark."

"Watch me," Magnus replied.

He was about to raise a foot and end Nos Kil's life when the enemy's bloodshot eye widened, staring at something in the near distance. Startled, Magnus turned to see a blaster bolt travel the short distance from barrel to head and fill the room with a flash of light and a concussive screech. Nos Kil's head bounced once and then rolled to the side. A black hole above his lone eye—permanently staring in an unnatural direction—sizzled with superheated gore.

Magnus turned to see Caldwell holster his weapon and spit once on the body. The emotions the colonel had harbored toward Nos Kil all these years must have been fierce. Furthermore, few men of war ever got the chance to settle scores themselves. Most of them were paid back in distant lands at the hands of others—a blaster bolt from someone else's rifle, a missile strike from an unseen orbital ship. But right here—right now—the colonel had the chance to settle this score for himself.

"You look like splick, son," Caldwell said to Magnus.

"I feel like it too."

"I can imagine. Can you walk on your own?"

Magnus shrugged his shoulders. "Unless you're offering a piggyback ride."

"Hell no. Let's get you back to sickbay." The two men walked from the cellblock and let Azelon close the security doors behind them.

MAGNUS PASSED another day in sickbay before Doc Campbell, Azelon, and TO-96 released him from their care. But they did so reluctantly—Doc especially so.

"You need another few days at least," Doc said. "You just gave your body one hell of a beating after another."

"Has anyone found Piper yet, Doc? Is Moldark dead?"

The man shook his head.

"Then we don't have another few days, do we."

"Listen, I'm not here to argue the safety of the crew or the ship. As far as I'm concerned, that's your department. I'm just telling you as a medical professional, your body isn't ready for anything else."

"And I take your words under advisement. But I stopped

doing what was best for myself a long time ago. No sense starting now."

Doc made to object but Magnus raised a hand. "Fine. Just... do me favor. When you get a break, come back and let me treat you some more?"

"*If* I get a break, you mean."

Doc sighed and stepped aside. "Go meet with your crew. Azelon says they're waiting for you on the bridge."

"You're a good man, Doc." Magnus patted him on the shoulder and limped by. "When I die, I'll have 'em engrave something nice for you on my tombstone."

"Like what?"

"Like, *Here lies Adonis Olin Magnus. Doc told him not to, but he did it anyway.*"

Doc chuckled. "You're a stubborn son of a bitch, you know."

"So I've been told."

MAGNUS WALKED onto the bridge as his five platoon leaders stood up straight. Dutch, Abimbola, Titus, Rohoar, and Awen greeted him as he stepped toward the captain's chair. Each leader had several members of their respective platoons with them, all notable in their own rights. Sootriman and Ezo stood arm in arm, while Saasarr stood behind them. Berouth and Caldwell were on either side of Abimbola. Titus was accompanied by Zoll and Bliss; Rohoar by Saladin and Czyz.

Awen and Willowood also stood arm in arm, their eyes bloodshot and tender. The newest face, of course, was Ricio's. The man had helped save their lives, and he deserved to be here. The only people not present who Magnus felt should have been were Flow and Cheeks. But they still couldn't be in the same room as any Jujari, so Magnus would debrief them himself.

Azelon and TO-96 stood on either side of the captain's chair and welcomed Magnus. He sat down with a grunt, noting just how much his body ached. He was about to scold them for their projected misery. "Feels like a damned funeral in here," he almost said, and then realized just how fitting the words would have been. *Damn.* "It's good to see you all again," he said instead. "I appreciate your patience while I… while the bots did their…"

"It is good to have you back, buckethead," Abimbola said, breaking the awkward silence.

Magnus smiled. "Thanks, Bimby." Then he lowered his head and took a deep breath, knowing the next words would be the hardest. "We lost good people on Worru. Andocs, Haney, and Val—" He caught himself, cleared his throat, then resumed. "Valerie. And we're missing Piper.

"Any one of these losses on their own is significant, and I won't try to minimize the grief we're all feeling right now, myself included. Mystics know how hard this is. For everyone. I encourage all of you to mourn as you need to. It's okay to cry, and you're going to need to talk about it if you haven't already—same as me. There's no shame in that. The deep feelings we have for people… they serve to tell us just how important those lives really were."

Magnus looked everyone in the face. He sensed they were trying to be stoic behind eyes moist with sadness. He nodded, more to himself than anyone else, and ran a hand over his face. "And at the same time, we have a job to do. We're at war, and none of you are strangers to the costs involved. You all knew what you were getting involved with when you signed up, and the only guarantee we were assured was an equal shot at death. The galaxy's going to splick and we're the ones tasked with stopping it. So, until this thing is over, we all face it the same way—together and with courage."

EPILOGUE

Ambassador Bosworth's back ached from the interminably long shuttle ride to Elonia's surface. He cursed Lord Moldark for not providing something faster for him, just as he cursed the wretched man for not giving him a larger starship. The journey to this revoltingly elitist star system had been gruelingly tiresome as it was. Added to it was the embarrassment of arriving at the Chancellor's tower in a subpar vehicle. If Bosworth's required skillset included impressing foreign dignitaries, then he was failing from moment one.

"Can't this damned skiff go any faster?" Bosworth said, kicking the pilot's crash couch from behind. His knee impacted the hard back and he swore through his bloated lips, spraying the pilot's neck with dribble.

"I can assure you, sir, that I am flying your *shuttle* as fast as it will go," the pilot said, placing special emphasis on the vehicle type in an apparent effort to correct the ambassador.

"Well it's not fast enough, *pilot*. Make it go faster. The sooner I get off this blasted heap of mystics-forsaken metal, the better."

The pilot did not reply but stayed focused on the course.

Satisfied that he had put the belligerent pilot in his place, Bosworth turned his considerable girth toward the shuttle's aft, which was little more than an extended room behind the two pilot's chairs, and found his bench seat once again. He plopped down, hoping the new position might alleviate some of his back strain. But it didn't. Instead, he found himself cursing that his hemorrhoids had somehow gotten worse in the last few minutes—*as if that was even possible*, he sputtered to himself.

Suddenly, the ship dropped ten meters if not more. Bosworth felt his stomach push against the bottom of his gullet, and then slam into his pelvis when the ship righted again. "Holy hell, man," Bosworth cried.

"Turbulence, sir. My apologies."

"Apologies my *ass*," Bosworth spat, muttering to himself. "Probably did it on purpose, the little cod-faced twit. You hear me?" Bosworth raised his voice. "You did that on purpose!"

Neither the pilot nor copilot responded.

Irritated that the two men had tuned him out, Bosworth went back to mumbling to himself. "I give him one grand idea. One that could gain him unimaginable leverage, secure him a blow against our adversaries." Bosworth projected his voice toward the front. "And what does he give me? An incompetent flight crew, that's what. Pieces of splick from a hornsperion buttlebuck's anus. And two tin cans not worth their weight when melted down on Ki Nav Four!"

"Greetings, Ambassador Bosworth," said the elderly Eloninan man, extending his flat hand toward Bosworth, palm down.

Bosworth returned the greeting by placing his upturned palm beneath the offered hand. "It is good to see you again, Chancellor dau Aminrain. Time has treated you well."

"No better than it does all Elonians," the chancellor replied.

"If only the rest of us were so fortunate."

The chancellor seemed pleased by this nod to the Elonian's naturally youthful bearing and gestured toward the grand salon in his top-level suite. As Bosworth walked into the spacious living room, he watched dau Aminrain wave over three young attendees.

"Would you care for some refreshment, ambassador? You must be parched after such a long journey."

Bosworth hesitated. Had the chancellor just made a reference to the shuttle and starship he'd arrived on? As if to suggest that neither were capable of providing adequate food or drink for the ambassador? Bosworth wasn't sure if he should refuse—which would only serve to affirm the chancellor's implicit slight—or accept—which would confirm that Bosworth was, in fact, parched, due either to a lack of attending to himself or to his subpar transportation. *Blast this politicking!*

"Out of deference to my host, I am pleased to partake of whatever your chancellorship is inclined to drink."

Again, dau Aminrain seemed pleased and ordered something in their native tongue. Bosworth ignored the transaction and moved to the floor-to-ceiling windows that bordered the far wall. "What a beautiful view of the city you have here," Bosworth said. "The sunset is particularly lovely."

"Isn't it though?" The chancellor strode up beside Bosworth and pushed his robes back to place his hands on his slender hips. Dau Aminrain was one kilo to every four of Bosworth's, and it annoyed the ambassador to no end. The Elonian's pointed ears, sharp eyes, and youthful face were echoed in the rest of his physique—lean, agile, and strong, even at his advanced age. The only thing that betrayed even a hint of the long passage of time were streaks of grey that snuck into his braided hair beginning at the temples. And it made Bosworth sick. Still, he had to keep up appearances, especially if he was going to skate by the chancellor's investigative eye to accomplish his intended purpose here.

"Do you ever get tired of such things?" Bosworth asked.

"I should think not. If one does—failing to marvel at that which one serves—is one truly fit to lead?"

Bosworth found himself silently mocking the chancellor's archaic speech, wanting to spit it back at him in a snarky tone.

But that would not do. "I must concur. With such beauty, I would think it hard to forget one's station or one's obligations."

Dau Aminrain nodded as if in appreciation of Bosworth's verdict. "Well said."

The attendees returned and handed Bosworth a steaming towel that smelled of lelandria. He accepted it, washed his face and hands as per custom, and then returned the used towel to the attendant. Then he accepted a slender glass of amber liquid. The chancellor had turned to meet Bosworth with his own tall glass and inclined his head, staring Bosworth directly in the eyes.

"To your long health, good fortune, and honorable fate," dau Aminrain said.

"And to you," he replied, touching the glasses together while holding the Elonian's gaze. Only when Bosworth had taken a sip of the strong drink did the chancellor sip from his own glass. "Your falathriel is as good as I've ever had."

"Thank you, ambassador. You're very kind."

Bosworth smiled and pulled the glass away to study the liquid. "Distilled honey from the ebony bee mixed with valerian nectar. Delicate, and yet not without its own sting."

"You seem to know your Elonian drinks."

"I like to know what I'm drinking and who I'm drinking with," Bosworth replied, wiping his lips with his thumb and index finger.

"As do I," replied the chancellor. "And yet you still have not told me of your purpose here."

"No, I have not." Bosworth let the statement hang in the air, quite pleased with the fact that the chancellor moved first. Therefore, he would suspend the man's uncertainty for as long as he could. Bosworth raised the glass to his mouth and took another drink, savoring the alcoholic beverage by swishing it around before swallowing. "I have decided to stay for a while."

Dau Aminrain cocked his head ever so slightly. "I fear I must implore you to explain, ambassador."

It wasn't unusual for an ambassador to remain in their state appointed residence for extended periods of time, but such things usually correlated with special events, like treaty renewals, formal dinners, or trade deals. For Bosworth to show up unannounced and without an obvious reason for being there, it was something of an oddity.

"Well, I have recently gone through a difficult time, as you've no doubt heard. On Oorajee?"

The chancellor gave the faintest hint of a nod.

Bosworth knew that news of his death, followed by his miraculous rescue, had reached Elonia already, just as it had to all systems within the Republic. "It seems my doctors have recommended a period of rest and relaxation to recover. They fear for my heart, you see, and have said that I required a stress-free stay somewhere."

Bosworth couldn't be sure, but he thought he heard the chancellor mumble "that's not all they prescribed" as his eyes looked the man up and down.

"What was that, chancellor?"

"Oh, nothing," replied dau Aminrain, swallowing the words with another sip of his drink.

"I'm sure. Be that as it may, I have decided there is no more tranquil place in all of the quadrant than my apartment here on Elonia. Wouldn't you agree?"

The chancellor nodded once then waved to the view of the city. "As you know, your diplomatic residence is ever at your disposal, of course. Still, I would have liked to be made aware of this endeavor beforehand. Only then could we prepare a reception fit for the magnitude of your arrival."

Bosworth drew the corners of his lips back in a tight smile. He wanted to return the slight with a barb of his own. But doing so, he knew, would only draw the ire of the chancellor, and he needed this meeting to be as benign as possible so as not to raise suspicions about his true reason for being on the planet. "And yet you still managed to make time for me, my old friend. And for that, I am grateful."

"Might there be an estimated duration for your stay here?"

"My doctors have said three months, though it could be more. You will see me come and go, I imagine. But there is no obligation on your end to entertain me. Though, if I might presume upon you, a dinner once in a while wouldn't be objectionable."

"No, it wouldn't. My office will make the necessary arrangements."

"Marvelous." Bosworth tipped his glass back and finished the remainder of his drink in one gulp. "I won't hold you up any longer then." Bosworth looked to one of the attendants and shook his empty glass at her, then set it down on a nearby table. "I'll be by for dinner at your earliest convenience."

"I'm sure you will." Dau Aminrain extended his hand, palm up. Bosworth placed his palm on top, then bowed his head. Several massive folds of skin appeared beneath his chin, and Bosworth could practically feel the chancellor laughing at him in disgust. He resisted the urge to lash out at the arrogant Elonian bastard, to dress him down as the ungrateful son of fortune and privilege that he was. But, again, that did not serve the ambassador's purpose despite how much his flesh wanted to enjoy watching the man recoil under his withering verbal assault. Instead, he held the pose for the customary two breaths, and then looked back into the chancellor's eyes. "Take care, chancellor."

BOSWORTH HAD SETTLED himself in his apartment and then headed for the bathroom. His strained muscles relaxed as he lowered his enormous body into the hot bath that he'd drawn. He savored the caress of the water against his skin and tried to let his thoughts drift in time with the water that filled the marble tub.

His survival of the bomb blasts that rocked the mwadim's palace had been expected. But his capture and subsequent torture by the Selskrit had not. Nor had his failure to retrieve the stardrive. Kane had not been pleased. Moldark even less so.

But the new Paragon lord was something of an enigma to Bosworth. While Moldark seemed opposed to the Republic—the governing body to which Bosworth had committed his entire life—he also seemed in favor of the one thing that Bosworth loved more than the Republic.

Power.

And if there was anyone who was going to give Bosworth more power in the new regime, it was Moldark.

The Republic was, after all, merely a means to an end, at least in Bosworth's mind. The positions afforded to those within its governmental structures were not representative despite how often the concept was lauded among the masses. Once elected or appointed, senators, ambassadors, and chancellors did what they damned well pleased. Successful campaigning was simply the right of passage—the thing that proved you could effectively seduce constituents into believing you despite your abject abhorrence of their trivial political planks.

But Bosworth had spent enough years within the stuffy halls of Capriana that he knew the Republic's time was drawing to a close. As every civilization before it, this one would fall too. But it would have survivors. And if Bosworth had ever doubted his ability to survive, his time held hostage on Oorajee had dispelled those anxieties. He could, he dared believe, endure anything. *Would* endure anything. *The Republic may fall*, he mused to himself, *but I will remain*.

Bosworth figured that, to remain, one needed to worry far less about notoriety and far more about association. Those in the limelight spent fortunes on staying popular. They preened on holo displays, kissed ass whenever they could, and took every opportunity to distance themselves from the faults of their parties in order to present themselves as the purest of patrons.

But association was a more subtle craft, one well understood by diplomats. Since there was no election for their position, ambassadors only needed to concern themselves with how well they portrayed the power that they represented. Ambassadors themselves were forgotten as quickly as they were introduced, but their governments were not. This nuance afforded them a unique ability to either surf atop the wave of power when things were going well, or slide beneath the fallout when things were not—undetected by the watchful eyes of the populace that was more concerned with those they'd elected than those who'd been appointed.

Bosworth knew his name would never be remembered. And that was fine with him. So long as he was still standing with a hand on the controls when all the blaster fire had subsided. Moldark, he'd decided, was a means to an end, just as the Republic had been. If the Paragon's leader was successful, Bosworth would run beside him. Until Moldark's luck ran out—then he'd move on to whatever power overtook the dark lord. *Stand in the shadows but speak to the light.* The saying had become his mantra. *For no one can discard what they cannot see, but neither can they resist what they always hear.*

Bosworth felt himself slide deeper into the bath until nothing but the outline of his face protruded above the surface. The waters hid his naked form, much like the shadows. In the darkness he would be safe. They'd never suspect his meddling. They'd just blame it on everyone else.

Bosworth almost decided to drive the skiff himself. He missed the freedom and the endless horizons. But arriving at his destination without a driver would have raised suspicions. Of course, the driver would have to be dealt with, and Bosworth hated the hassle of killing people. But it was part of the job. Plus, unlike the false timeline he'd given the chancellor, he would not be on the planet long enough for anyone to discover the body.

The backseat of the luxury skiff was deep and spacious, allowing him ample room to spread out. He gazed out the window as the cityscape slowly gave way to rolling hills of green. The undulating countryside was dotted with grazing animals and simple farms that harkened to a bygone era. He tried to look over the steep mountains high above, but his eyes only caught glimpses of the stars in the fading evening sky before his neck strained from the effort.

The skiff's gentle hum ushered Bosworth toward sleep more than once, but he fought it off with sudden jerks back to reality. He had to stay focused. "How much longer?" he yelled to the driver.

"Six more minutes, ambassador."

"Very well."

Bosworth sat up as much as he could, smoothing his coat and slacks with pudgy fingers. He settled his mind and reviewed his presentation, willing himself to believe every word of it. The key to lying was not mastering how to lie, it was believing the lie until it was true. Of course, one had to be intentional about parsing what things were truths because of belief and what things were believed because they were true. Failing to do so could get you in trouble with the wrong people. So developing a robust memory had been a pastime of the ambassador's for as long as he could remember. Of course, his memory had been tested as of late. His torture on Oorajee had seen to that, as had his vile treatment at the hands of that damned Marine and his lady doctor.

When the skiff finally slowed to a stop and the driver opened Bosworth's door, the stars were in full array, displayed in the small patch of black sky that stretched between mountain ridges. The country air was fresh and cool, pricking the ambassador's skin and dispelling any lingering desire to nap.

"Shall I ring the residence for you, sir?"

Bosworth waved off the driver. "That won't be necessary."

"As you wish. I will remain here in wait."

Bosworth *humphed* and then started up the stone path. The house before him was modern and pristine, boasting sleek lines and glass walls. Waterfalls cascaded from cantilevered escarpments on the second and third levels and gathered in small pools that fed various streams around the night-lit grounds. And wherever the water flowed, fragrant bushes let off their evening aromas held close to the ground by looming trees. It was, Bosworth decided, the small country palace of a well-to-do family.

He approached the security door and wondered if the thing was even locked. So far away from nothing, there seemed to be little cause for concern. Then he smiled to himself, noting the irony of his own presence here this night. He touched the security pad.

"Please state your name," said a recorded male voice in a formal air.

"Galactic Republic Ambassador Gerald Bosworth," he replied.

"Hello, Galactic Bosworth," the low-level AI replied, repeating the annoying error that he commonly encountered. "Please wait to be seen."

Within a few moments, the door slid open and revealed a fair looking Elonian man. He stood a head shorter than the ambassador and wore informal evening wear.

A voice further back said, "Who is it, dear?"

"Just a moment, Giyel," the man said over his shoulder, then brought his eye up to meet Bosworth's. "I'm afraid I don't know you, Galactic Bosworth."

The ambassador winced. "It's *Gerald* Bosworth, Ambassador of the Galactic Republic."

The man's eyes lit up. "My apologies, ambassador. Sometimes the AI's have trouble with titles."

"As I'm aware."

The man turned and summoned his wife. She appeared from the kitchen, wringing her hands in a towel.

"We have an ambassador at our door," the husband said.

"An ambassador? At this hour? Here?"

"Indeed, ma'am," Bosworth replied.

The woman took her husband's arm and smiled warmly. "Pleased to meet you, sir…"

"Bosworth. Gerald Bosworth. And you are Balin and Giyel dau Lothlinium?"

"We are," Balin replied. "Won't you come in, ambassador?"

MAGNUS and AWEN return in BLACK LABYRINTH available on Amazon now.

For more updates on this series, be sure to join the Facebook Group, "J.N. Chaney's Renegade Readers."

CHARACTER REFERENCE

PLATOON ROSTER, GRANTHER COMPANY, GLADIO UMBRA

Company Commander

- Magnus

Alpha Platoon (Marines and Navy)

- Dutch
- Sootriman
- Ezo

- Valerie
- Nolan
- Gilder
- Haney

Bravo Platoon (Original Marauders)

- Abimbola
- Berouth
- Silk
- Rix
- Cyril
- Nubs
- Dozer

Charlie Platoon (New Marauders)

- Titus
- Zoll
- Bliss
- Robillard
- Jaffrey
- Ricky
- Handley
- "Doc" Campbell
- Reimer
- Ford

- Andocs
- Bettger

Delta Platoon (Jujari)

- Rohoar
- Saladin
- Czyz
- Longchomps
- Grahban, son of Helnooth
- Arjae
- Dihazen
- Redmarrow

Echo Platoon (Special Unit)

- Awen
- Piper
- Saasarr
- TO-96

Azelon Spire (Orbital Defense)

- Flow
- Cheeks

Character Reference

LIST OF MAIN CHARACTERS

Abimbola: Miblimbian. Age: 41. Planet of origin: Limbia Centrella. Commander of Bravo Platoon, Granther Company. Former warlord of the Dregs, outskirts of Oosafar, Oorajee. Bright-blue eyes, black skin, tribal tattoos, scar running from neck to temple.

Adonis Olin Magnus: Human. Age: 34. Planet of origin: Capriana Prime. Gladio Umbra, Granther Company commander. Former lieutenant, Charlie Platoon, 79th Reconnaissance Battalion, "Midnight Hunters," Galactic Republic Space Marines. Baby face, beard, green eyes.

Aubrey Dutch: Human. Age: 25. Planet of origin: Deltaurus Three. Commander of Alpha Platoon, Granther Company. Former corporal, weapons specialist, Galactic Republic Space Marines. Small in stature, close-cut dark hair, intelligent brown eyes. Loves her firearms.

Awen dau Lothlinium: Elonian. Age: 26. Planet of origin: Elonia. Commander of Echo Platoon, Granther Company. Form Special Emissary to the Jujari, Order of the Luma. Pointed ears, purple eyes.

Azelon: AI and robot. Age: unknown. Planet of origin: Ithnor Ithelia. Artificial intelligence of the Novia Minoosh ship *Azelon Spire*.

Character Reference

Cyril: Human. Age: 24. Planet of origin: Ki Nar Four. Assigned to Bravo Platoon, Granther Company. Former Marauder. Code slicer, bomb technician. Twitchy; sounds like a Quinzellian miter squirrel if it could talk.

Daniel Forbes: Human. Age: 32. Planet of origin: Capriana. Captain, Alpha Company, 83rd Marine Battalion, Galactic Republic Space Marines; on special assignment to Worru. Close-cropped black hair, tall.

Dozer: Human. Age: Unknown. Planet of origin: Verv Ko. Assigned to Bravo Platoon, Granther Company. Former Marauder, infantry. A veritable human earth-mover.

Gerald Bosworth III: Human. Age: 54. Planet of origin: Capriana Prime. Republic Ambassador, special envoy to the Jujari. Fat jowls, bushy monobrow. Massively obese and obscenely repugnant.

Hal Brighton: Human. Age: 41. Planet of origin: Capriana Prime. Fleet Admiral, First Fleet, the Paragon; former executive officer, Republic Navy.

Idris Ezo: Nimprith. Age: 30. Planet of origin: Caledonia. Assigned to Alpha Platoon, Granther Company. Former bounty hunter, trader, suspected fence and smuggler; captain of *Geronimo Nine*.

Character Reference

Michael "Flow" Deeks: Human. Age: 31. Planet of origin: Vega. Assigned to the *Azelon Spire*. Former sergeant, sniper, Charlie Platoon, 79th Reconnaissance Battalion, "Midnight Hunters," Galactic Republic Space Marines. One of the "Fearsome Four."

Miguel "Cheeks" Chico: Human. Age 30. Planet of origin: Trida Minor. Assigned to the *Azelon Spire*. Former corporal, breacher, Charlie Platoon, 79th Reconnaissance Battalion, "Midnight Hunters," Galactic Republic Space Marines. One of the "Fearsome Four."

Moldark (formerly Wendell Kane): Human. Age: 52. Planet of origin: Capriana Prime. Dark Lord of the Paragon, a rogue black-operations special Marine unit. Former fleet admiral of the Galactic Republic's Third Fleet; captain of the *Black Labyrinth*. Bald, with heavily scared skin; black eyes.

Mauricio "Ricio" Longo: Human. Age: 29. Planet of origin: Capriana Prime. Republic Navy, squadron commander of Viper Squadron, assigned to the *Black Labyrinth*.

Nubs: Human. Age: Unknown. Planet of origin: Verv Ko. Assigned to Bravo Platoon, Granther Company. Former Marauder, infantry. Has several missing fingers.

Character Reference

Piper Stone: Human. Age: 9. Planet of origin: Capriana Prime. Assigned to Echo Platoon, Granther Company. Daughter of Senator Darin and Valerie Stone. Wispy blond hair, freckle-faced.

"Rix" Galliogernomarix: Human. Age: Unknown. Planet of origin: Undoria. Assigned to Bravo Company, Granther Company. Wanted in three systems, sleeve tattoos, a monster on the battlefield.

Robert Malcom Blackman: Human. Age: 54. Planet of origin: Capriana Prime. Senator in the Galactic Republic, leader of the clandestine Circle of Nine. A stocky man with thick shoulders and well-groomed gray hair.

Rohoar: Tawnhack, Jujari. Age: Unknown. Planet of origin: Oorajee. Commander of Delta Platoon, Granther Company. Former Jujari Mwadim.

Saasarr: Reptalon. Age: unknown. Planet of origin: Gangil. Assigned to Echo Platoon, Granther Company. Former general of Sootriman's Reptalon guard. Lizard humanoid.

Shane Nolan: Human. Age: 25. Planet of origin: Sol Sella. Assigned to Alpha Platoon, Granther Company. Pilot, former chief warrant officer, Republic Navy. Auburn hair, pale skin.

Character Reference

Silk: Human. Age: 30. Planet of origin: Salmenka. Assigned to Bravo Platoon, Granther Company. Former Marauder, infantry. Slender, bald, tats covering her face and head.

So-Elku: Human. Age: 51. Planet of origin: Worru. Luma Master, Order of the Luma. Baldpate, thin beard, dark penetrating eyes. Wears green-and-black robes.

Sootriman: Caledonian. Age: 33. Planet of origin: Caledonia. Assigned to Alpha Platoon, Granther Company. Warlord of Ki Nar Four, "Tamer of the Four Tempests," wife of Idris Ezo. Tall, with dark almond eyes, tanned olive skin, dark-brown hair.

Titus: Human. Age: 34. Planet of origin: unknown. Commander of Charlie Platoon, Granther Company. Former Marauder, rescued by Magnus. Known for being cool under pressure and a good leader.

TO-96: Robot; navigation class, heavily modified. Manufacturer: Advanced Galactic Solutions (AGS), Capriana Prime. Suspected modifier: Idris Ezo. Assigned to Echo Platoon, Granther Company. Round head and oversized eyes, transparent blaster visor, matte dark-gray armor plating, and exposed metallic articulated joints. Forearm micro-rocket pod, forearm XM31 Type-R blaster, dual shoulder-mounted gauss cannons.

Character Reference

Tony Haney: Human. Age: 24. Planet of origin: Fitfi Isole. Assigned to Alpha Platoon, Granther Company. Former private first class, medic, Galactic Republic Space Marines.

Valerie Stone: Human. Age: 31. Planet of origin: Worru. Assigned to Alpha Platoon, Granther Company. Widow of Senator Darin Stone, mother of Piper. Blond hair, light-blue eyes.

Volf Nos Kil: Human. Age: 32. Planet of origin: Haradia. Captain, the Paragon. Personal guard and chief enforcer for Moldark.

Waldorph Gilder: Human. Age: 23. Planet of origin: Haradia. Assigned to Alpha Platoon, Granther Company. Former private first class, flight engineer, Galactic Republic Space Marines. Barrel-chested. Can fix anything.

William Samuel Caldwell: Human. Age 60. Planet of origin: Capriana Prime. Colonel, 83rd Marine Battalion, Galactic Republic Space Marines; special assignment to Repub garrisons on Worru. Cigar eternally wedged in the corner of his mouth. Gray hair cut high and tight.

Willowood: Human. Age: 61. Planet of origin: Kindarah. Luma Elder, Order of the Luma. Wears dozens of bangles and necklaces. Aging but radiant blue eyes and a mass of wiry gray hair. Mother of Valerie, grandmother of Piper, mentor to Awen.

ACKNOWLEDGMENTS

Christopher wishes to thank:

I am indebted to Matthew Titus, Mauricio Longo, and Jon Bliss for their love for all things Ruins. Thank you for helping the metanarrative maintain its integrity. You make these books tell better stories.

Additionally, I am grateful for the keen insights and professionalism of Walt Robillard, Kevin Zoll, Shane Marolf, Matthew Dippel, Joseph Wessner, David Seaman, Ollie Longchamps, and Aaron Seaman. The galaxy thanks you for your service.

To Jeff Chaney, Jennifer Sell, Molly Lerma, and Kayla Curry—you're all geniuses, and I can't believe I get to work with you. Thank you.

And to my wife for co-laboring with me in the craft of making beautiful things for the world to enjoy. I couldn't do this without you.

STAY UP TO DATE

Don't miss out on these exclusive perks:

- Instant access to free short stories from series like *The Messenger*, *Starcaster*, and more.
- Receive email updates for new releases and other news.
- Get notified when we run special deals on books and audiobooks.

So, what are you waiting for? Enter your email address at the link below to stay in the loop.

https://www.jnchaney.com/ruins-of-the-galaxy-subscribe

JOIN THE CONVERSATION

Join the conversation and get updates on new and upcoming releases in the awesomely active **Facebook group**, "JN Chaney's Renegade Readers."

This is a hotspot where readers come together and share their lives and interests, discuss the series, and speak directly to J.N. Chaney and his co-authors.

facebook.com/groups/jnchaneyreaders

ABOUT THE AUTHORS

J. N. Chaney is a USA Today Bestselling author and has a Master's of Fine Arts in Creative Writing. He fancies himself quite the Super Mario Bros. fan. When he isn't writing or gaming, you can find him online at **www.jnchaney.com**.

He migrates often, but was last seen in Las Vegas, NV. Any sightings should be reported, as they are rare.

Christopher Hopper's other series include Resonant Son, Sky Riders, The Berinfell Prophecies, and the White Lion Chronicles. He blogs at **christopherhopper.com** and loves flying RC planes and FPV race wings. He resides in the 1000 Islands of northern New York with his musical wife and four ridiculously good-looking clones.

Printed in Poland
by Amazon Fulfillment
Poland Sp. z o.o., Wrocław